Take It Away, Tommy!

OTHER BOOKS IN THE SERIES:

Breaking Cat News

Lupin Leaps In

Take It Away, Tommy!

GEORGIA DUNN

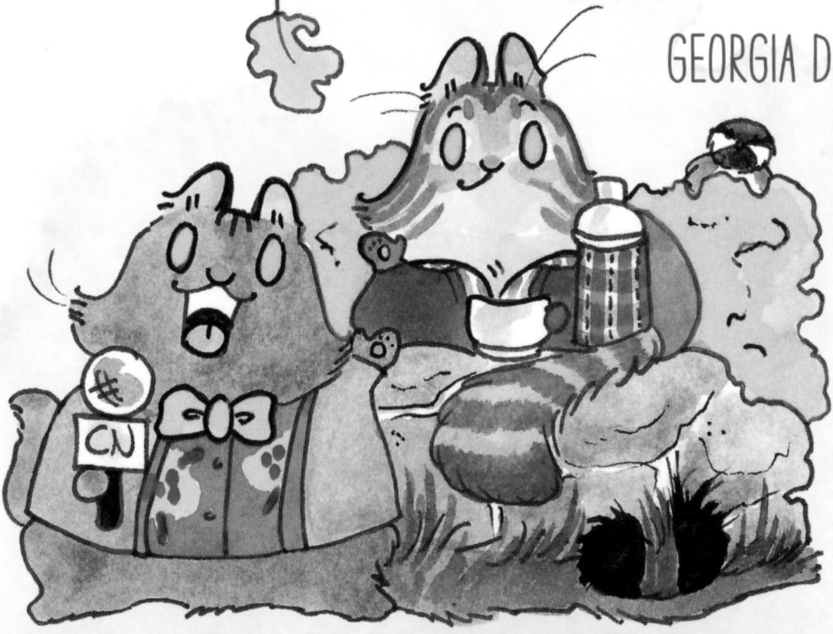

CN

A **BREAKING CAT NEWS** ADVENTURE

Andrews McMeel
PUBLISHING®

FOR MY OPA, CAPTAIN CHARLES S. QUINN JR.,

WHO SHARED HIS LOVE OF STORYTELLING

(AND ALWAYS HAD TIME TO LISTEN TO OUR STORIES TOO).

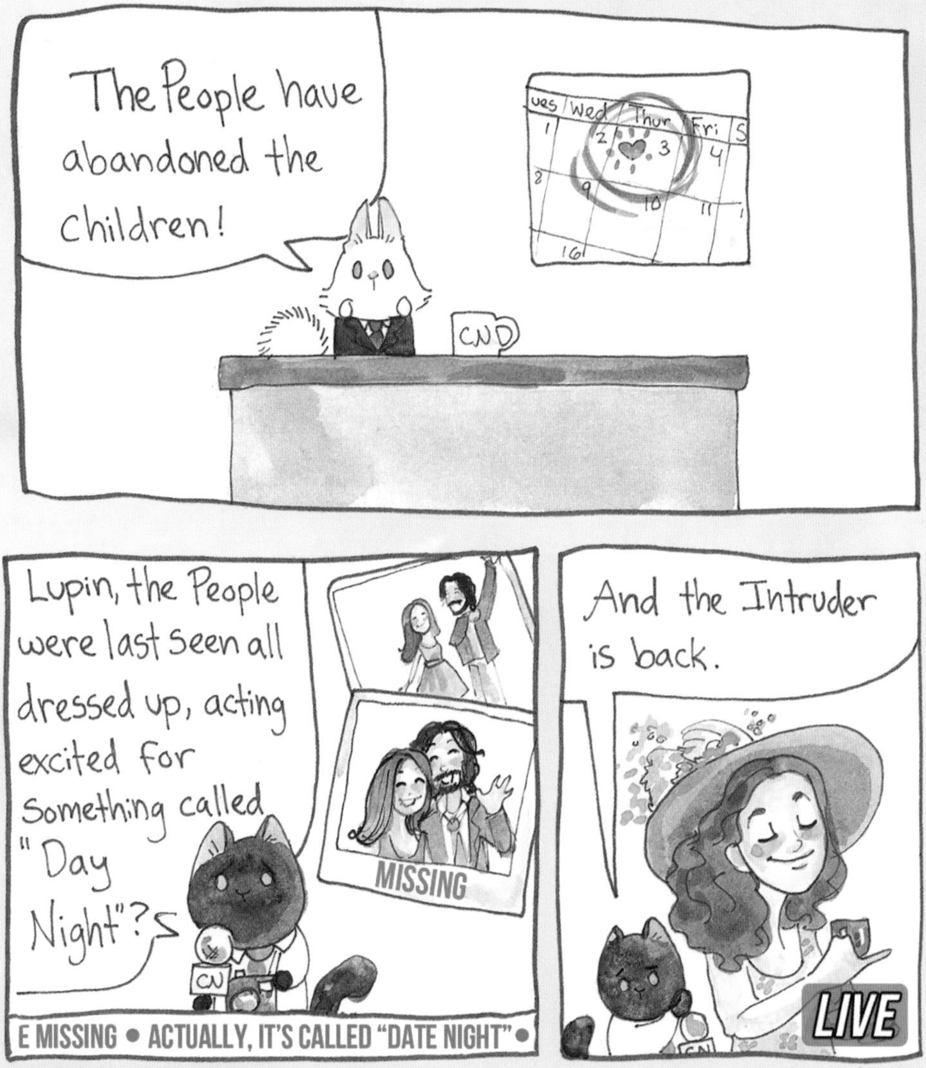

The People have abandoned the Children!
CND
Lupin, the People were last seen all dressed up, acting excited for Something called "Day Night"?
MISSING
CN
E MISSING • ACTUALLY, IT'S CALLED "DATE NIGHT" •
And the Intruder is back.
LIVE

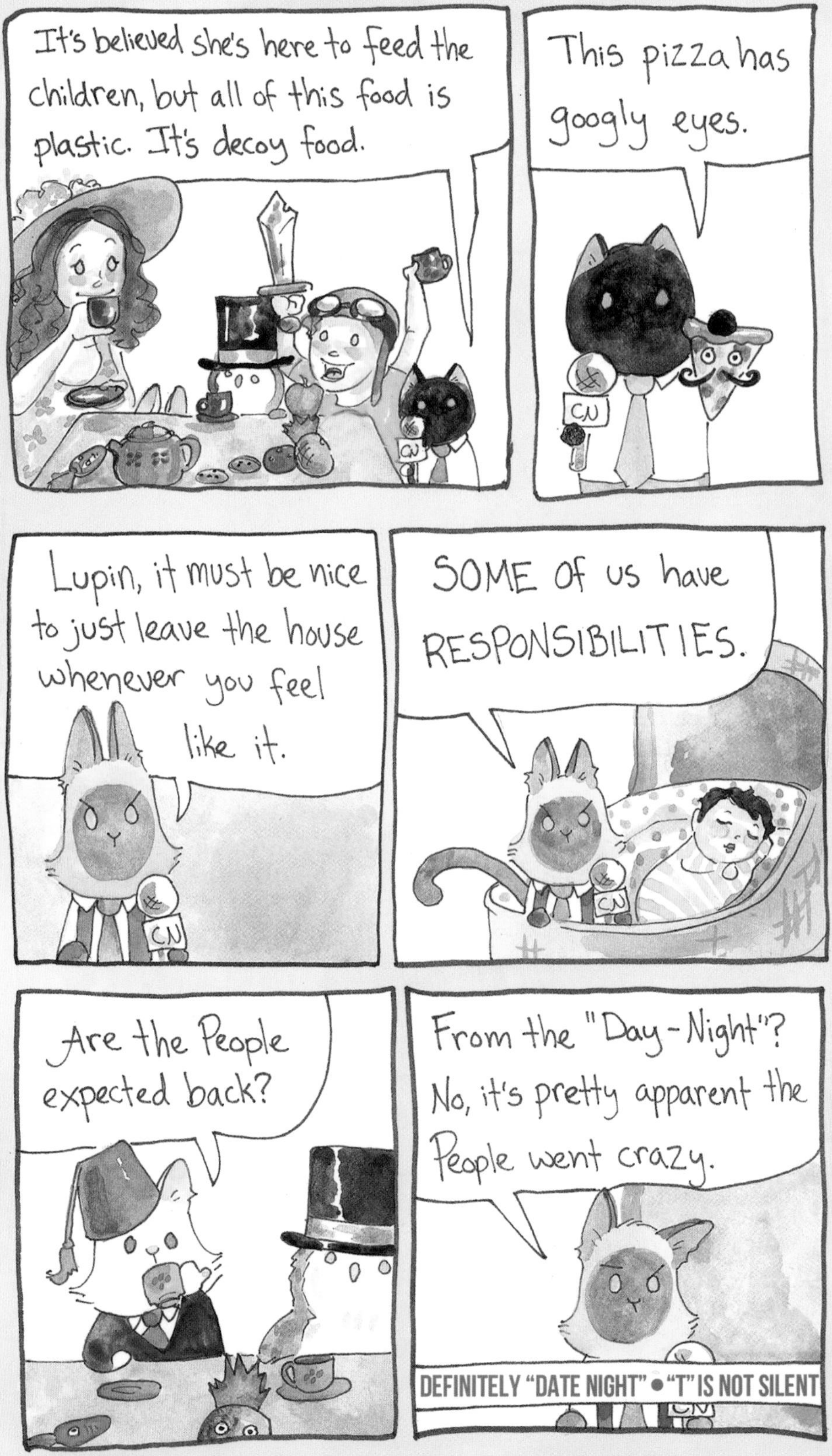
It's believed she's here to feed the children, but all of this food is plastic. It's decoy food.
This pizza has googly eyes.
Lupin, it must be nice to just leave the house whenever you feel like it.
SOME OF us have RESPONSIBILITIES.
Are the People expected back?
From the "Day-Night"? No, it's pretty apparent the People went crazy.
DEFINITELY "DATE NIGHT" • "T" IS NOT SILENT

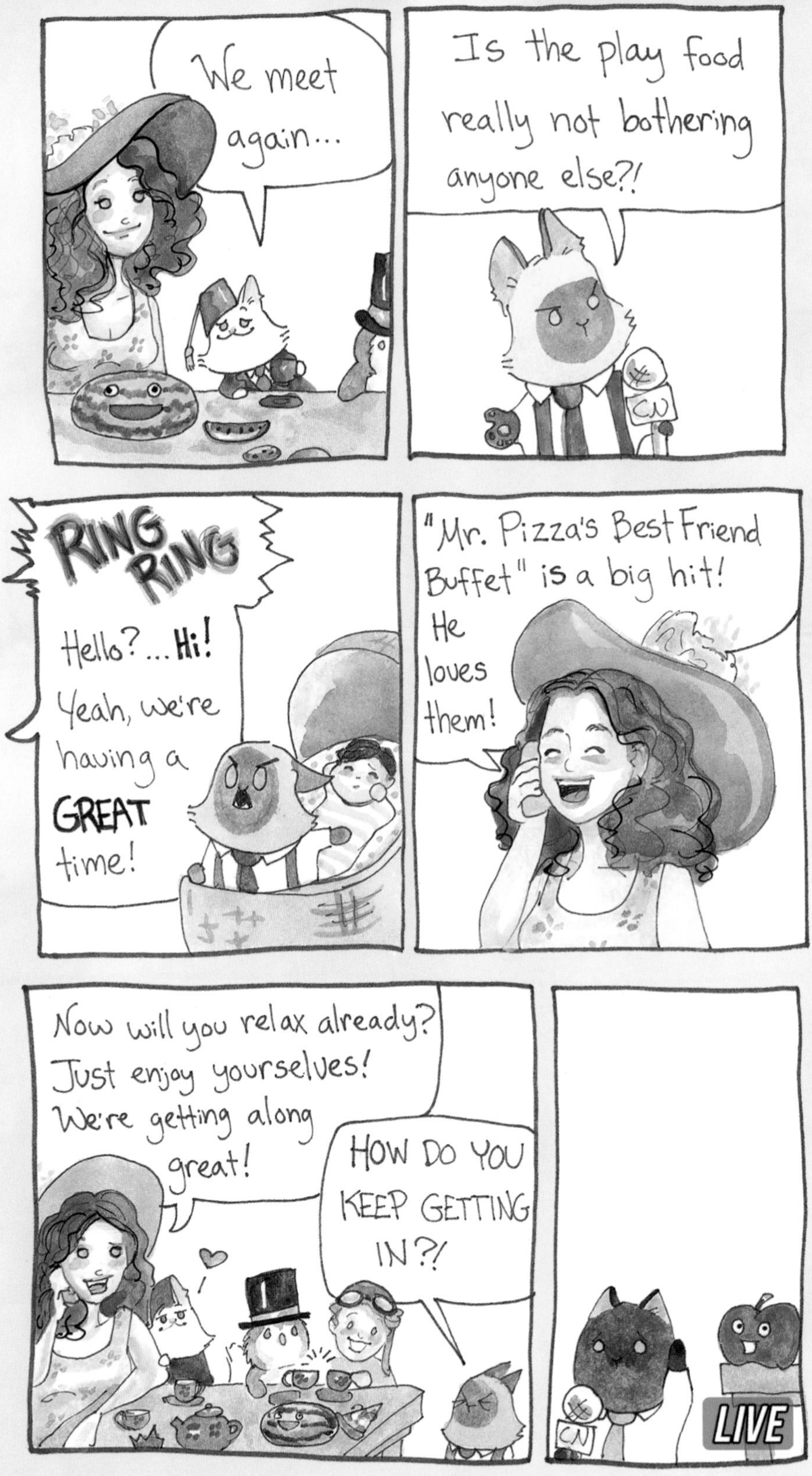
We meet again...
Is the play food really not bothering anyone else?!
CN
RING RING
Hello?... Hi! Yeah, we're having a GREAT time!
"Mr. Pizza's Best Friend Buffet" is a big hit! He loves them!
Now will you relax already? Just enjoy yourselves! We're getting along great!
HOW DO YOU KEEP GETTING IN?!
CN
LIVE

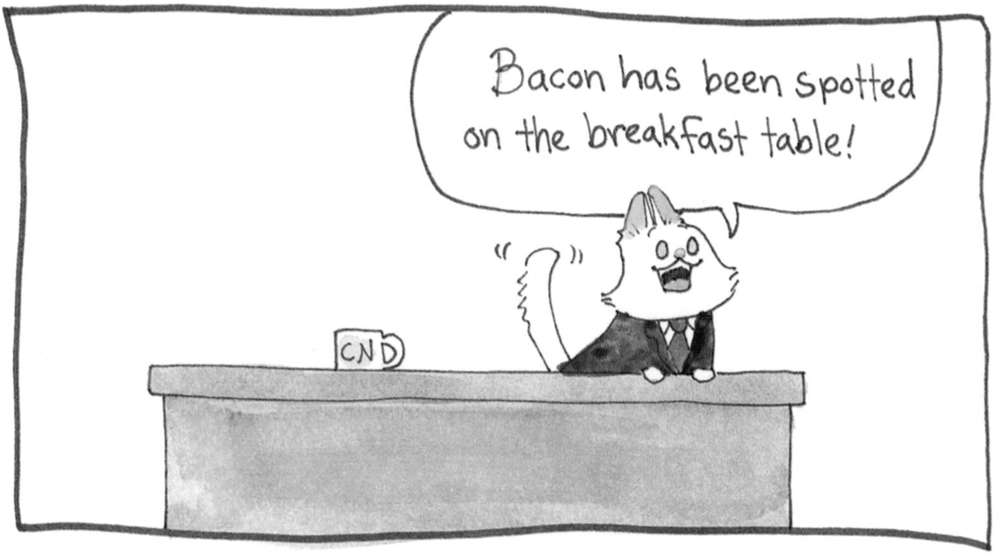
Bacon has been spotted on the breakfast table!
CND

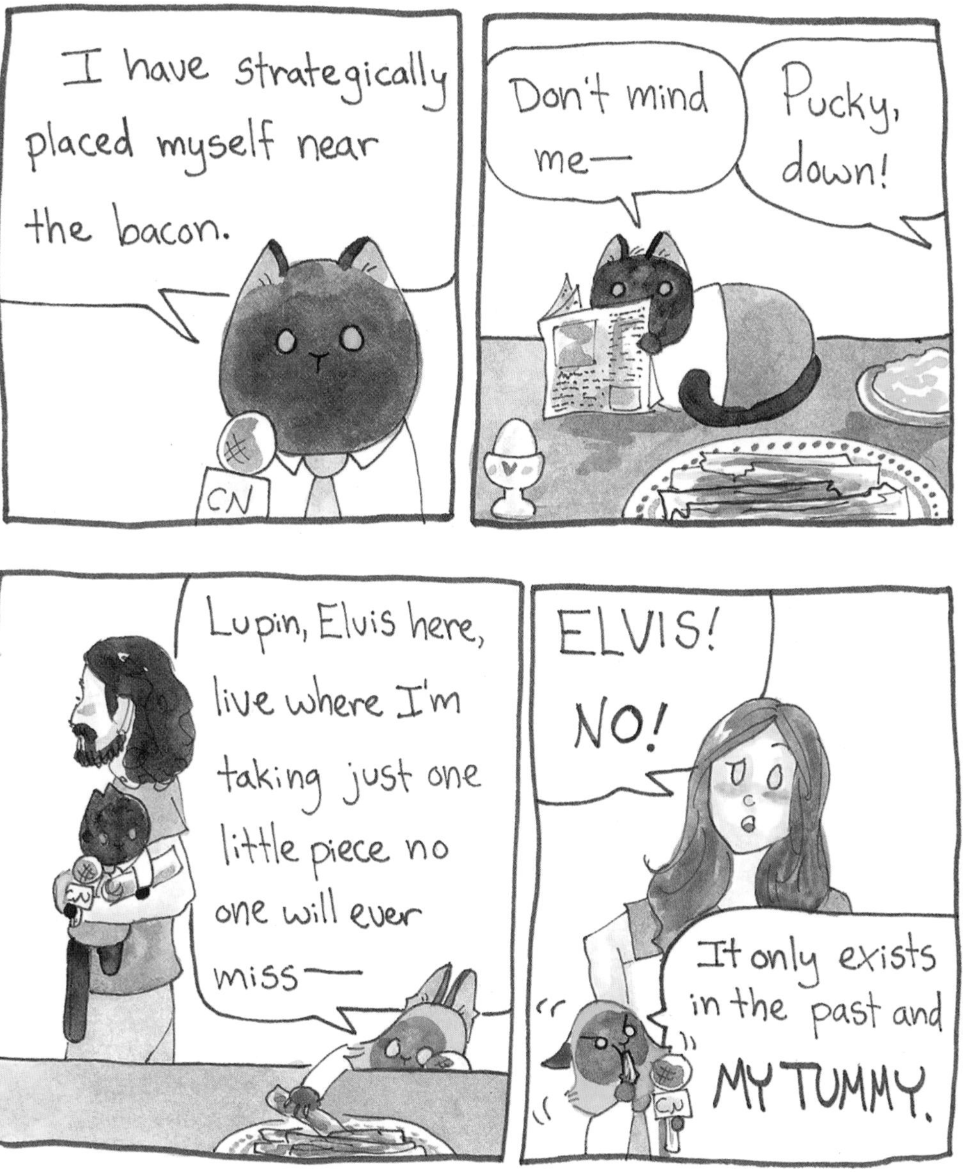
I have strategically placed myself near the bacon.
CN
Don't mind me—
Pucky, down!
Lupin, Elvis here, live where I'm taking just one little piece no one will ever miss—
CN
ELVIS! NO!
It only exists in the past and MY TUMMY.
CN

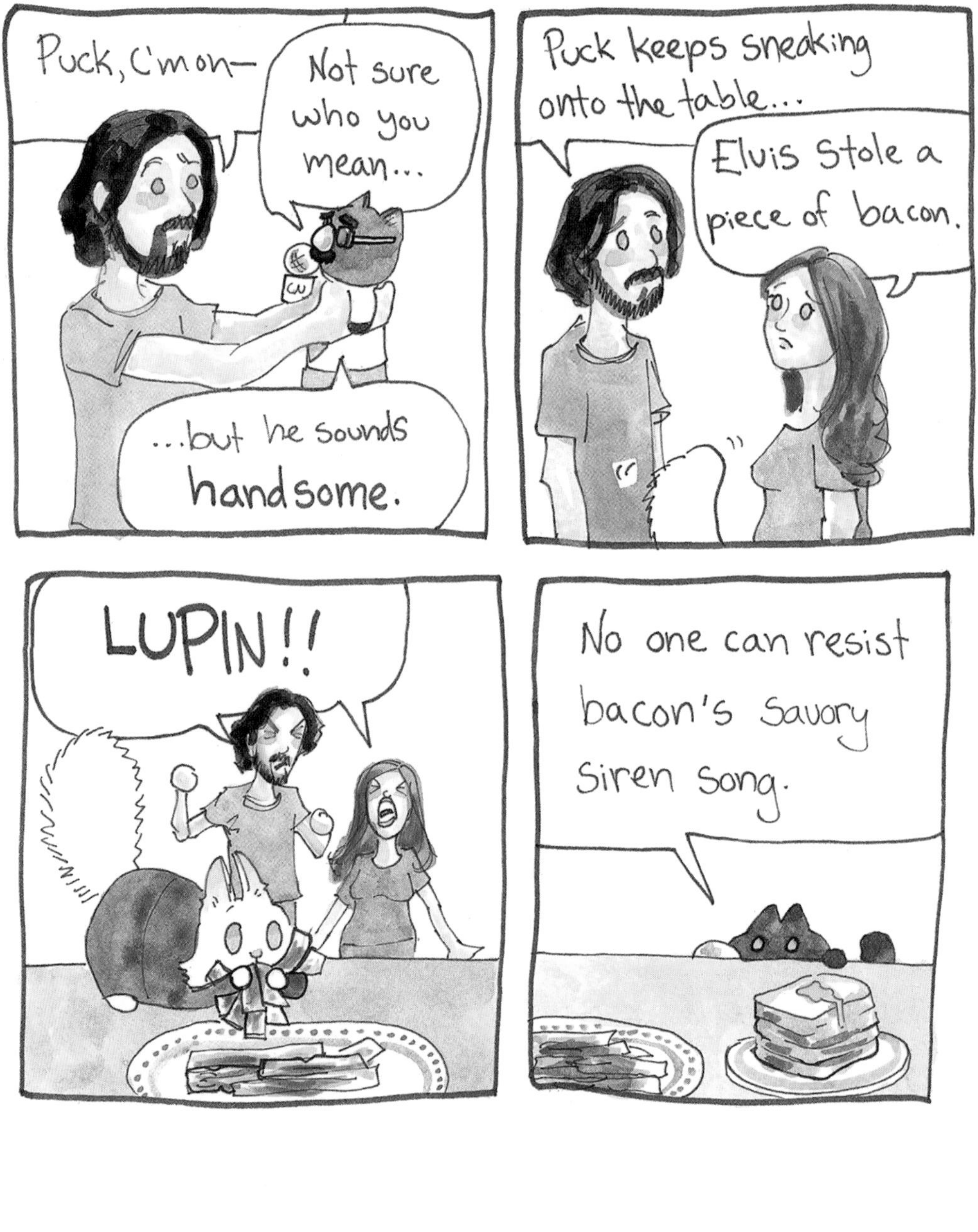
Puck, C'mon—
Not sure who you mean...
...but he sounds handsome.
Puck keeps sneaking onto the table...
Elvis Stole a piece of bacon.
LUPIN!!
No one can resist bacon's savory siren song.

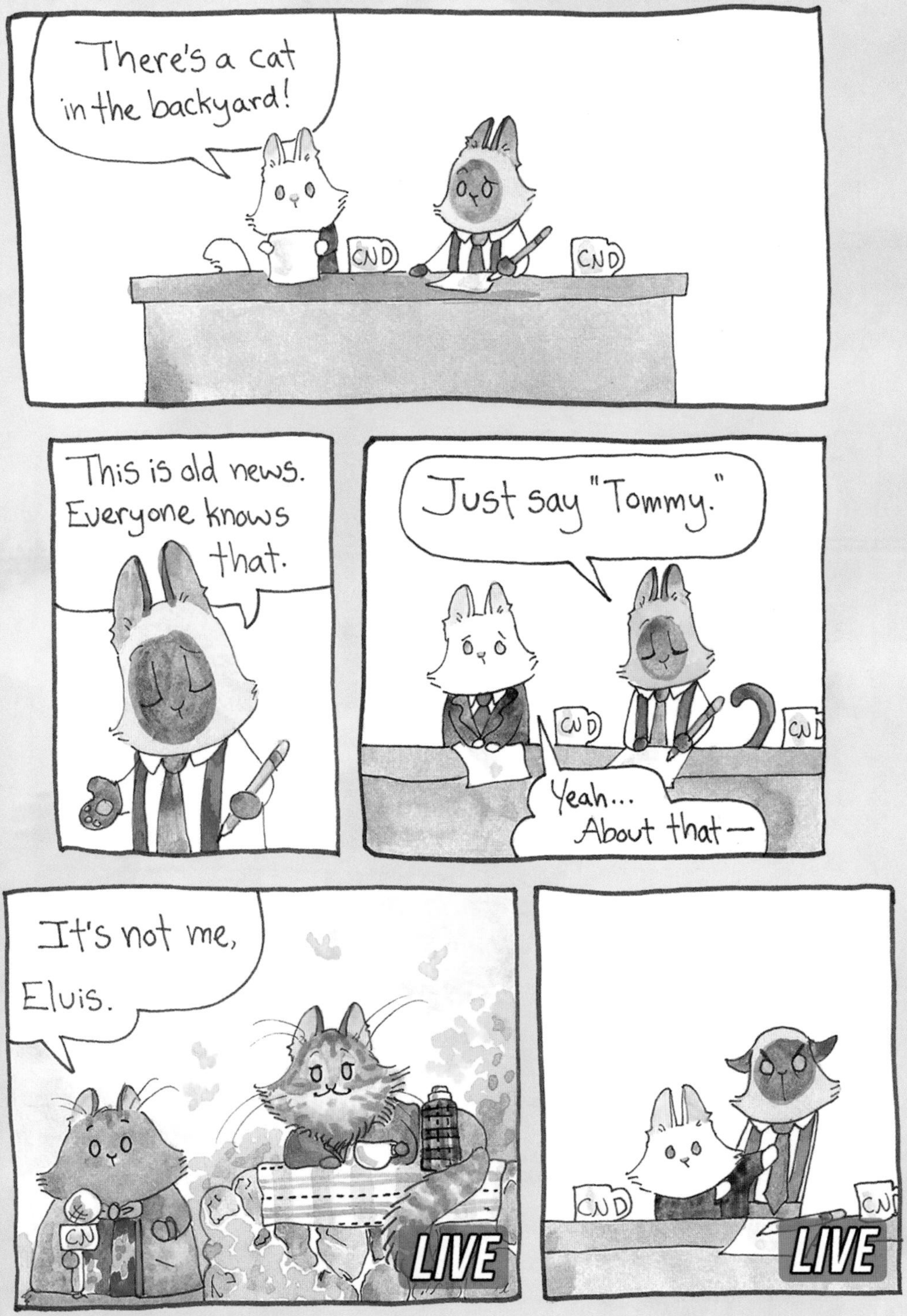
There's a cat in the backyard!
CND
CND
This is old news. Everyone knows that.
Just say "Tommy."
Yeah... About that—
It's not me, Elvis.
CN
LIVE
CND
LIVE

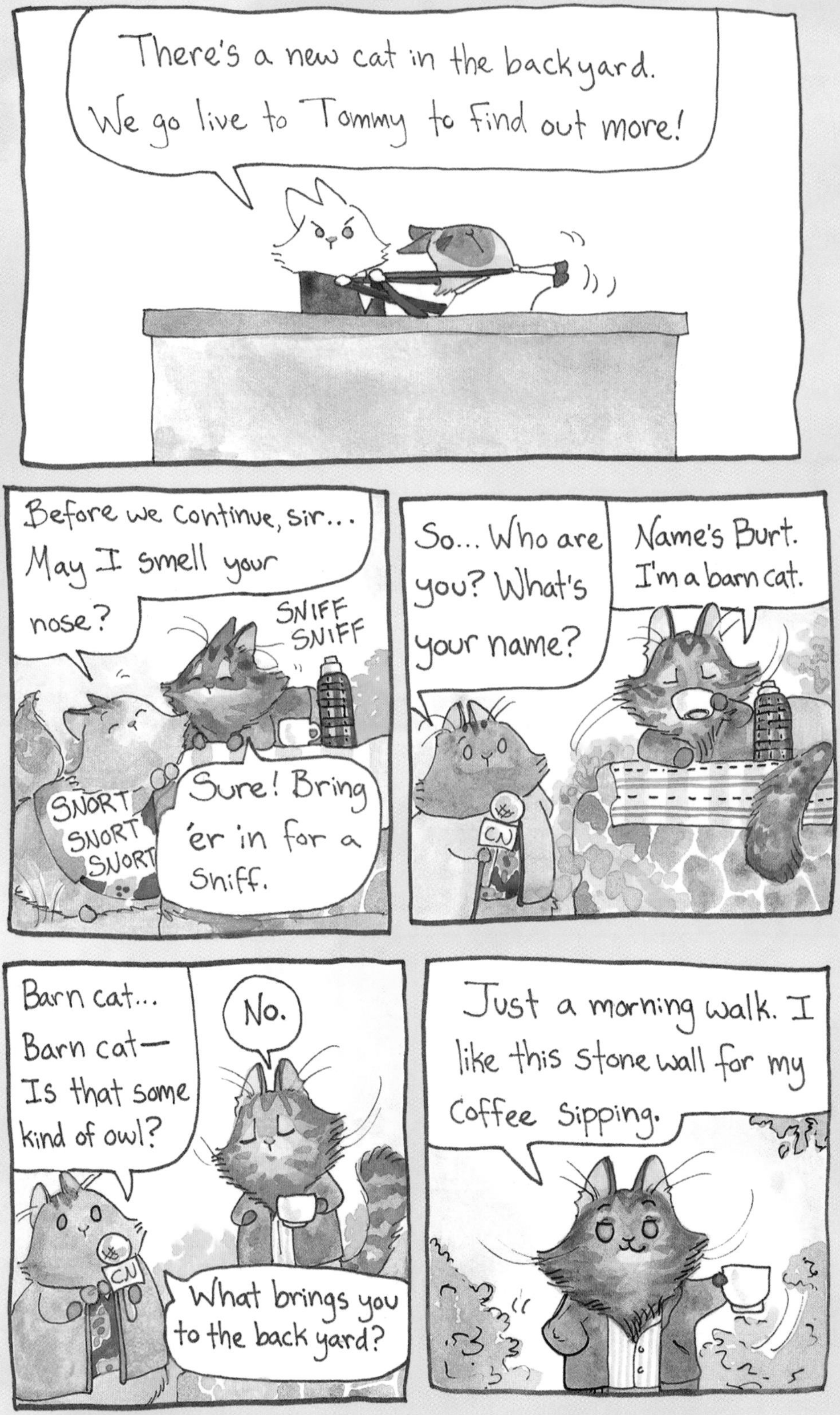
There's a new cat in the backyard. We go live to Tommy to find out more!
Before we continue, sir... May I smell your nose?
SNIFF SNIFF
SNORT SNORT SNORT
Sure! Bring 'er in for a sniff.
So... Who are you? What's your name?
Name's Burt. I'm a barn cat.
CN
Barn cat... Barn cat— Is that some kind of owl?
No.
CN
What brings you to the back yard?
Just a morning walk. I like this stone wall for my coffee sipping.

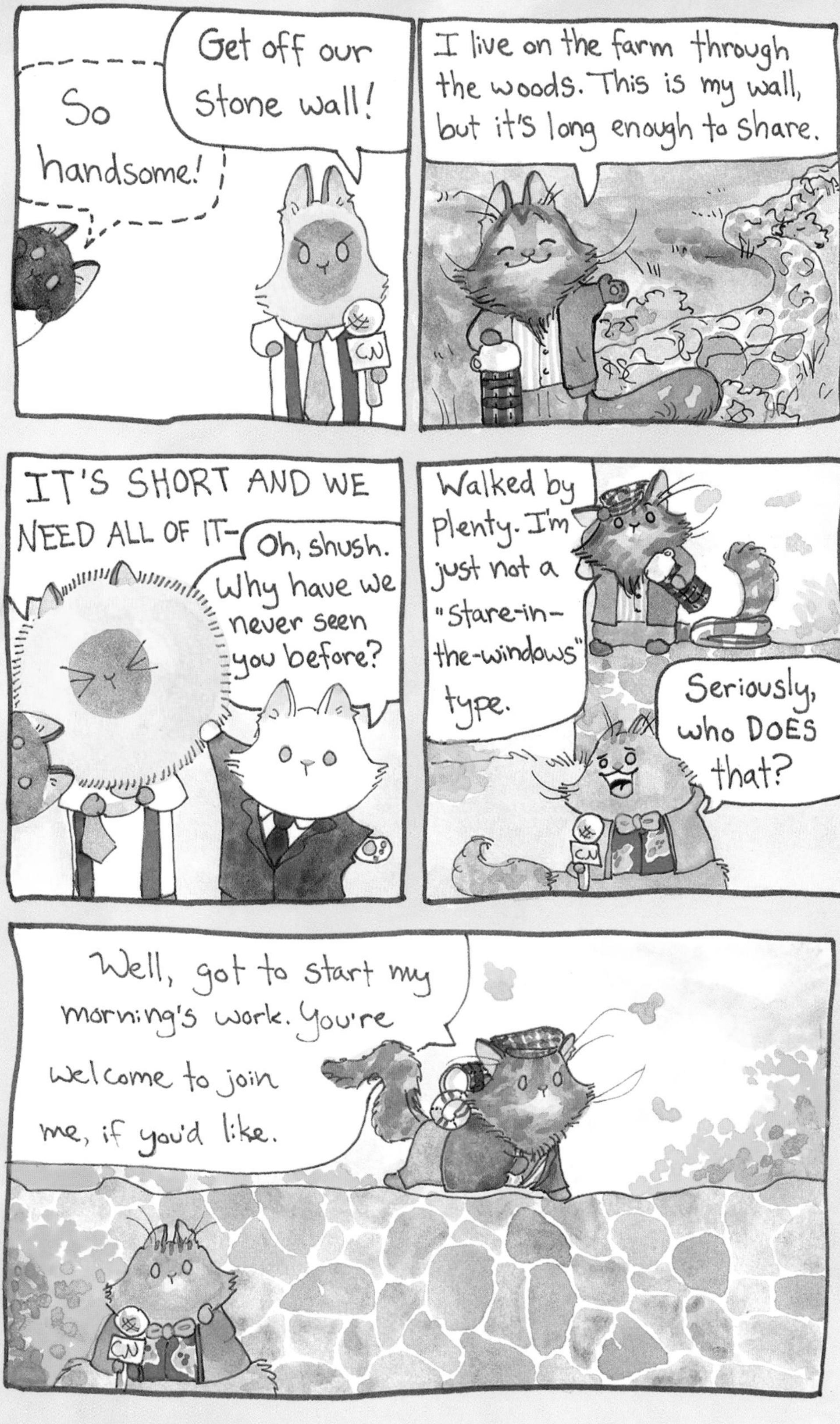
So handsome!
Get off our stone wall!
I live on the farm through the woods. This is my wall, but it's long enough to share.
IT'S SHORT AND WE NEED ALL OF IT—
Oh, shush. Why have we never seen you before?
Walked by plenty. I'm just not a "stare-in-the-windows" type.
Seriously, who DOES that?
Well, got to start my morning's work. You're welcome to join me, if you'd like.

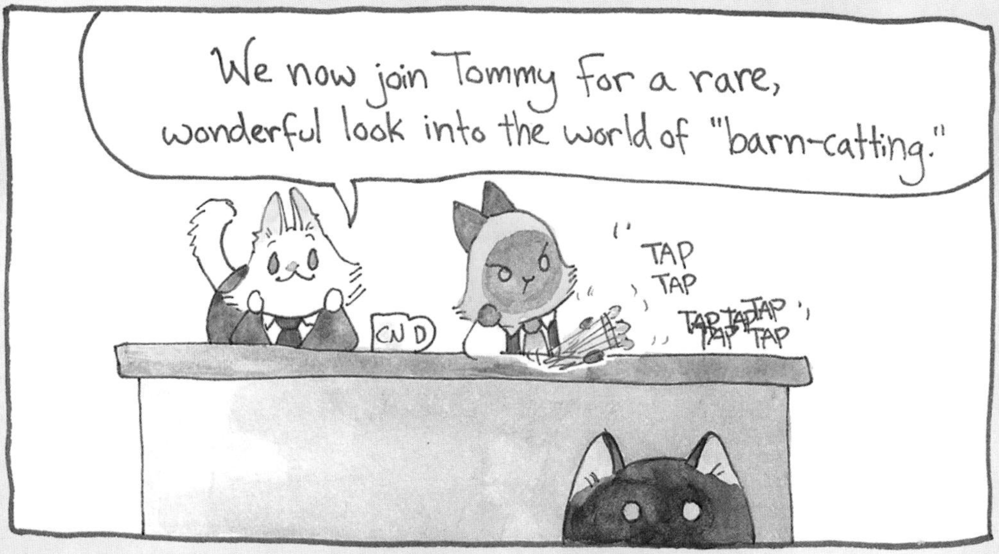
We now join Tommy for a rare, wonderful look into the world of "barn-catting."
CN D
TAP
TAP
TAP TAP TAP
TAP TAP

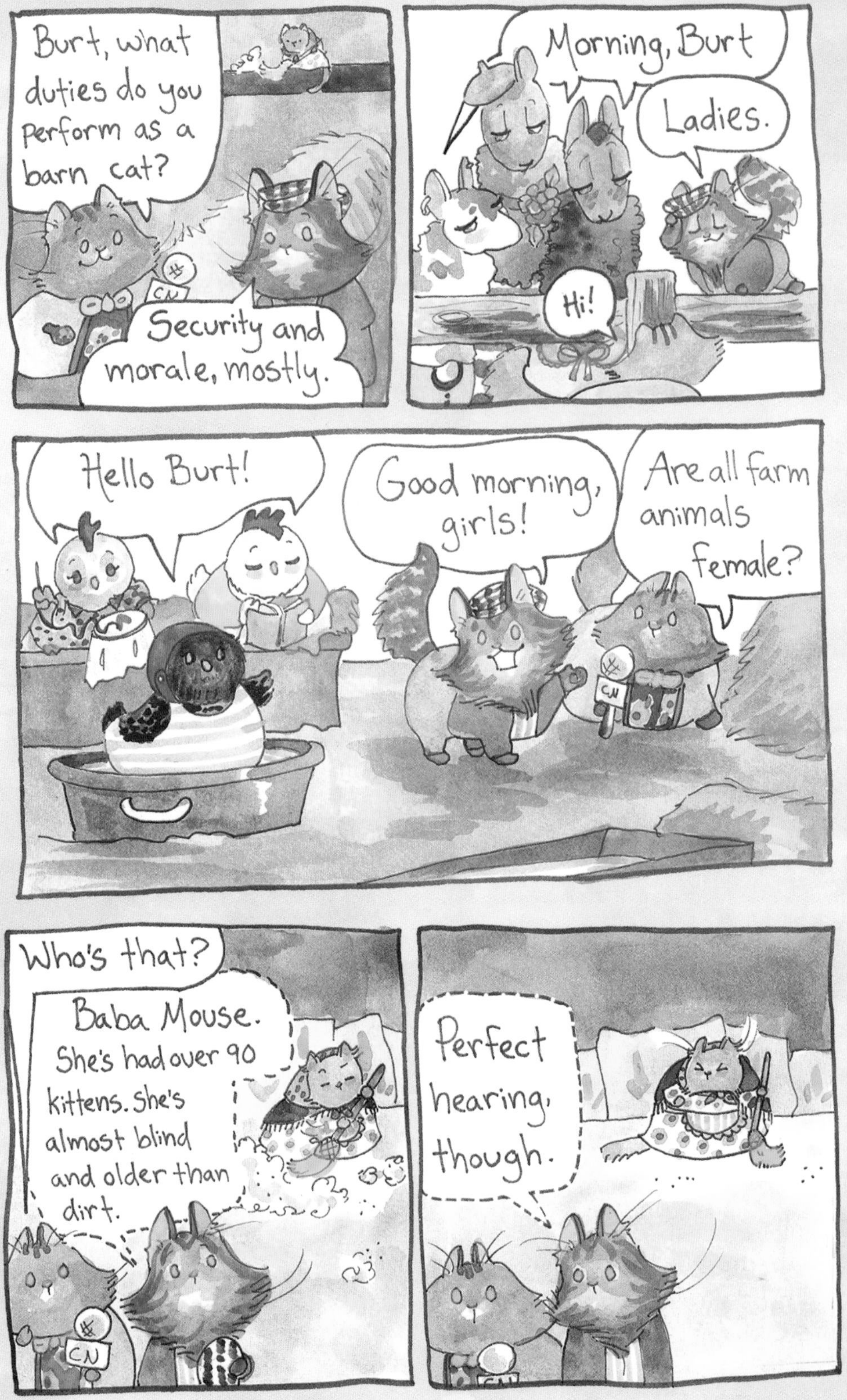
Burt, what duties do you perform as a barn cat?
Security and morale, mostly.
Morning, Burt
Ladies.
Hi!
Hello Burt!
Good morning, girls!
Are all farm animals female?
Who's that?
Baba Mouse. She's had over 90 kittens. She's almost blind and older than dirt.
Perfect hearing, though.

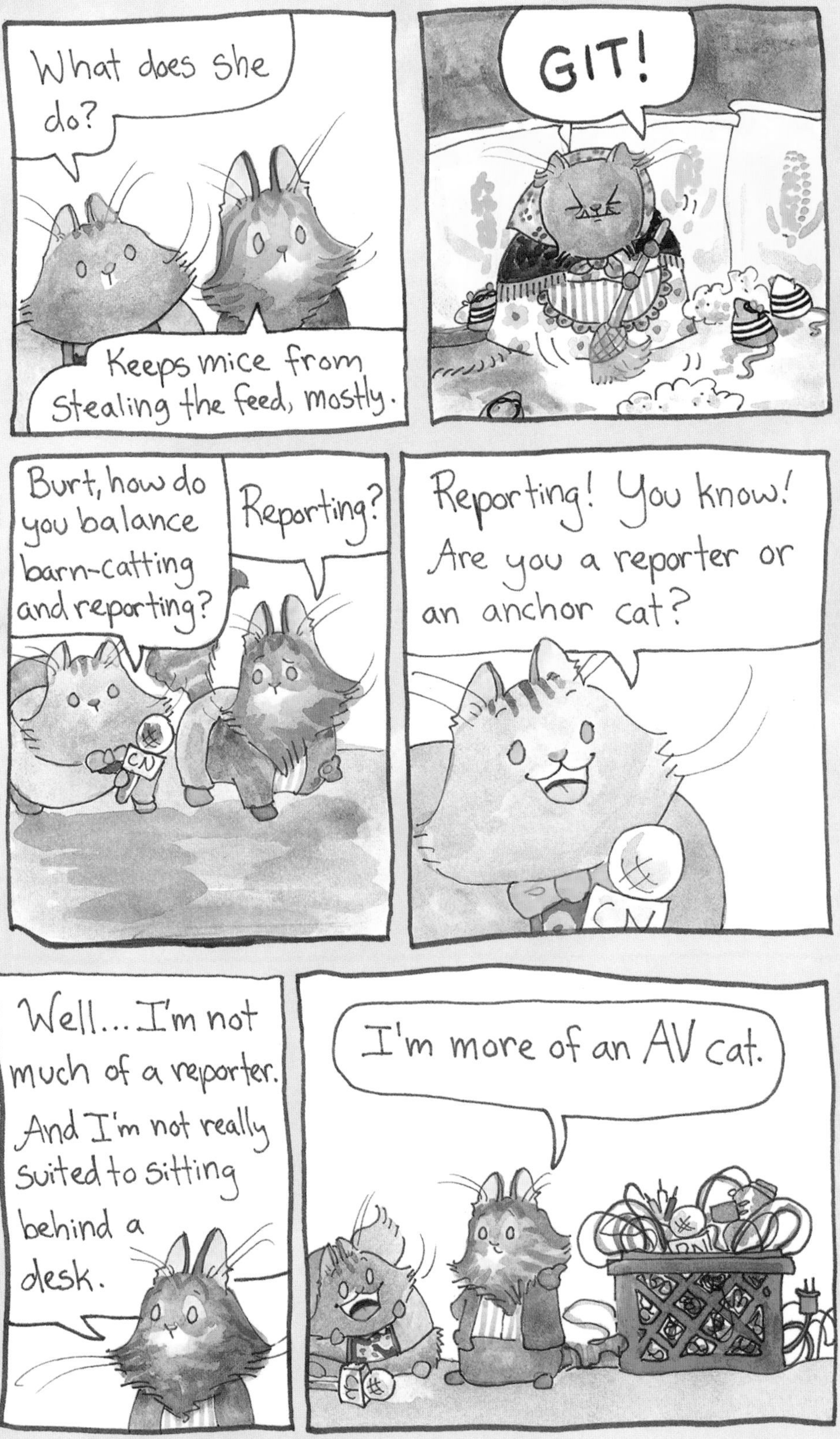

What does she do?
Keeps mice from stealing the feed, mostly.
GIT!
Burt, how do you balance barn-catting and reporting?
Reporting?
Reporting! You know! Are you a reporter or an anchor cat?
Well... I'm not much of a reporter. And I'm not really suited to sitting behind a desk.
I'm more of an AV cat.

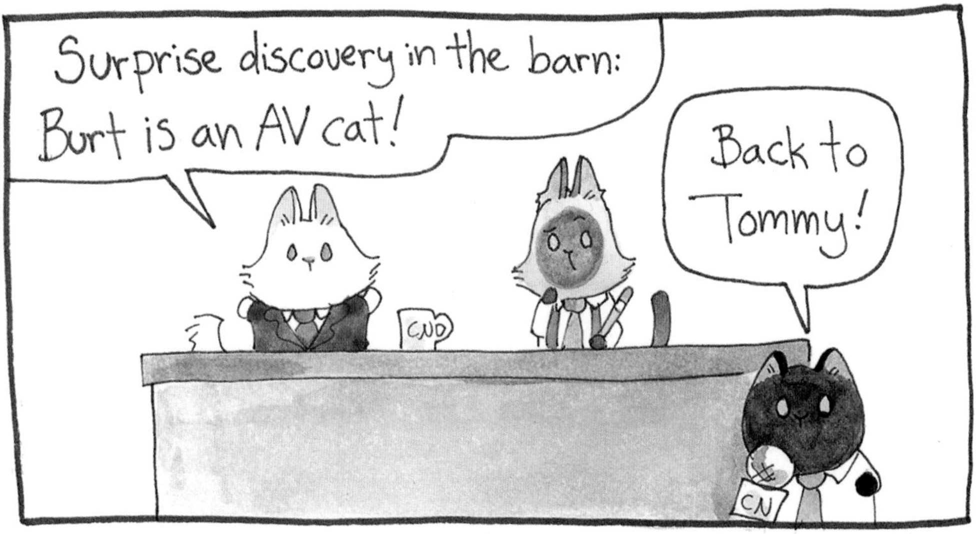
Surprise discovery in the barn: Burt is an AV cat!
CNO
Back to Tommy!
CN

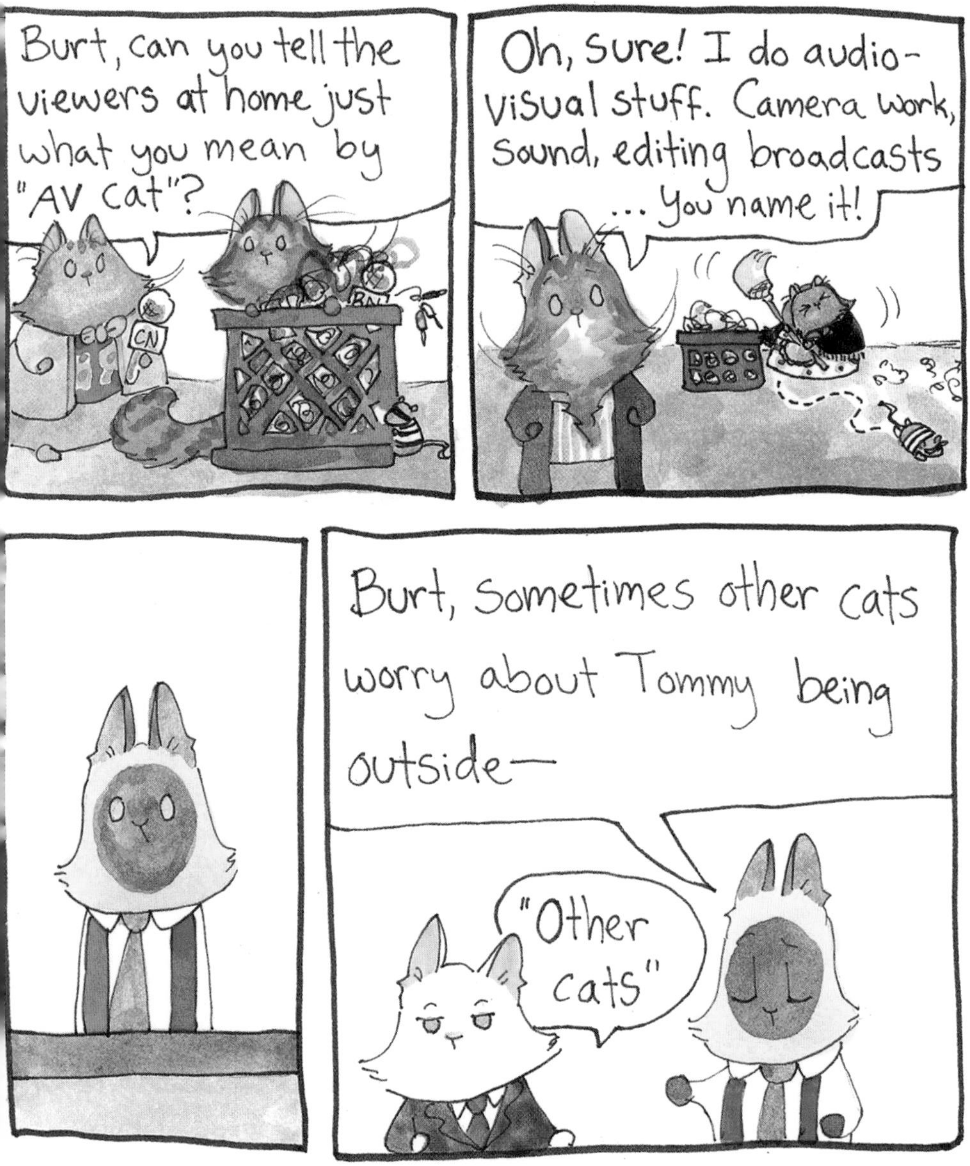
Burt, can you tell the viewers at home just what you mean by "AV cat"?
Oh, sure! I do audio-visual stuff. Camera work, sound, editing broadcasts ... You name it!
Burt, Sometimes other cats worry about Tommy being outside—
"Other cats"

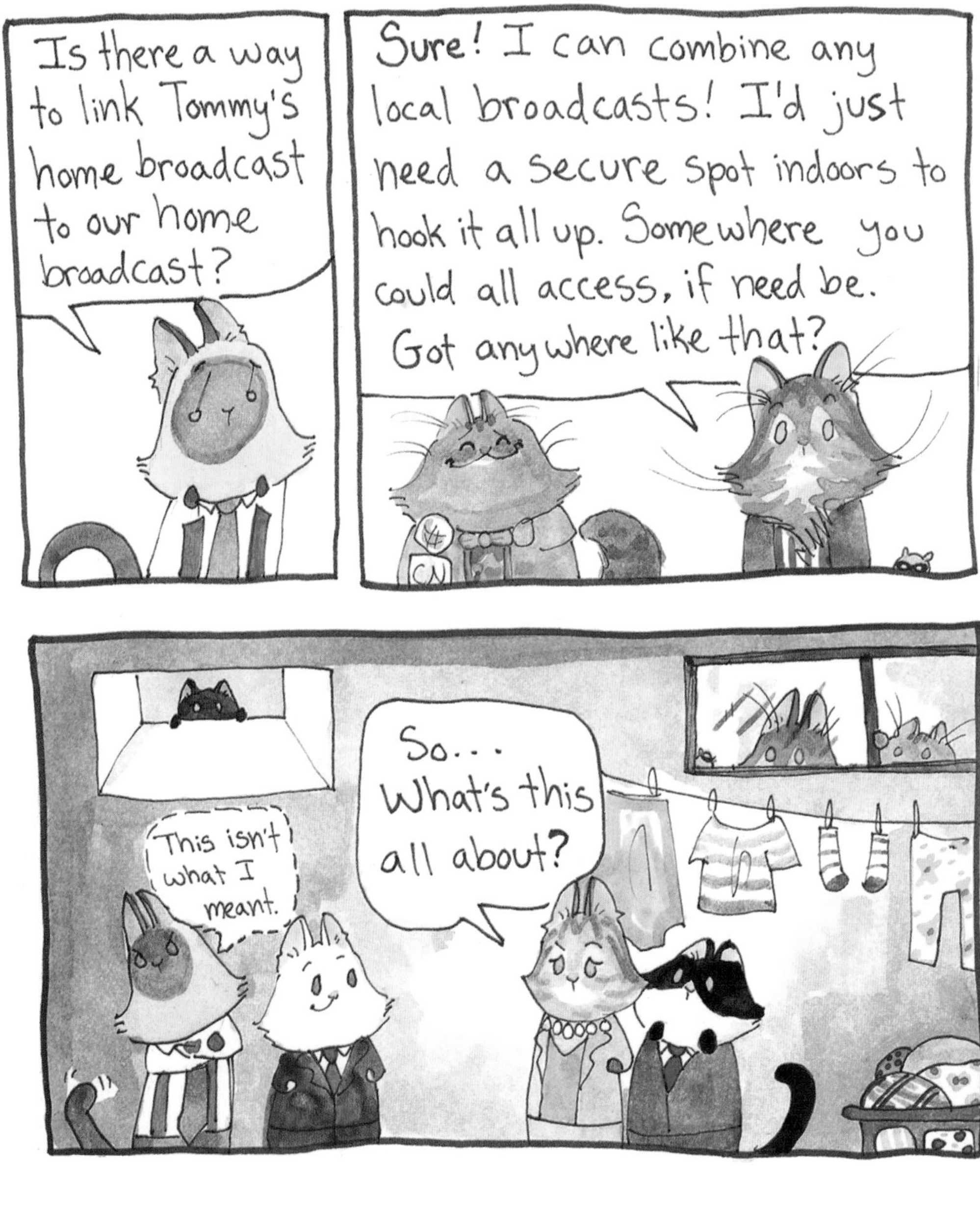
Is there a way to link Tommy's home broadcast to our home broadcast?
Sure! I can combine any local broadcasts! I'd just need a secure spot indoors to hook it all up. Somewhere you could all access, if need be. Got anywhere like that?
CN
So... What's this all about?
This isn't what I meant.

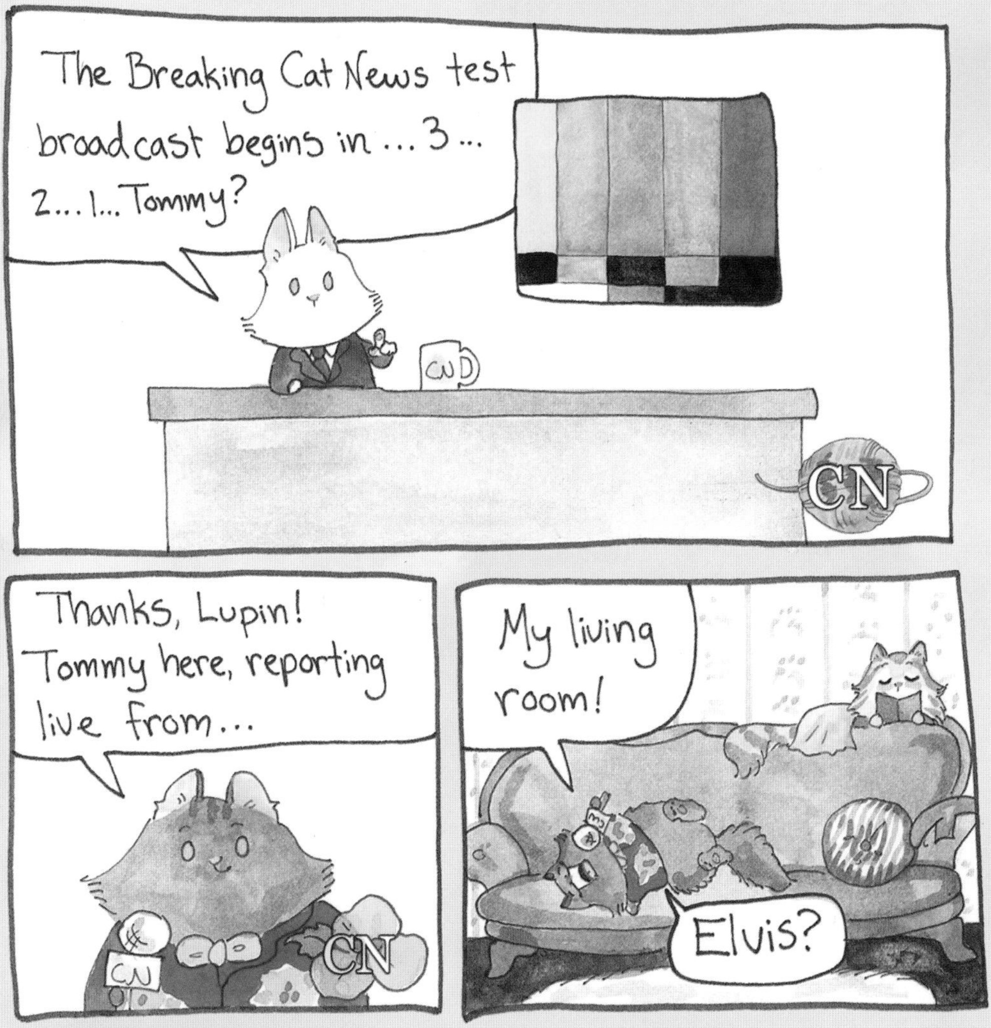
The Breaking Cat News test broadcast begins in ... 3 ... 2... 1... Tommy?
CN
Thanks, Lupin! Tommy here, reporting live from...
My living room!
Elvis?

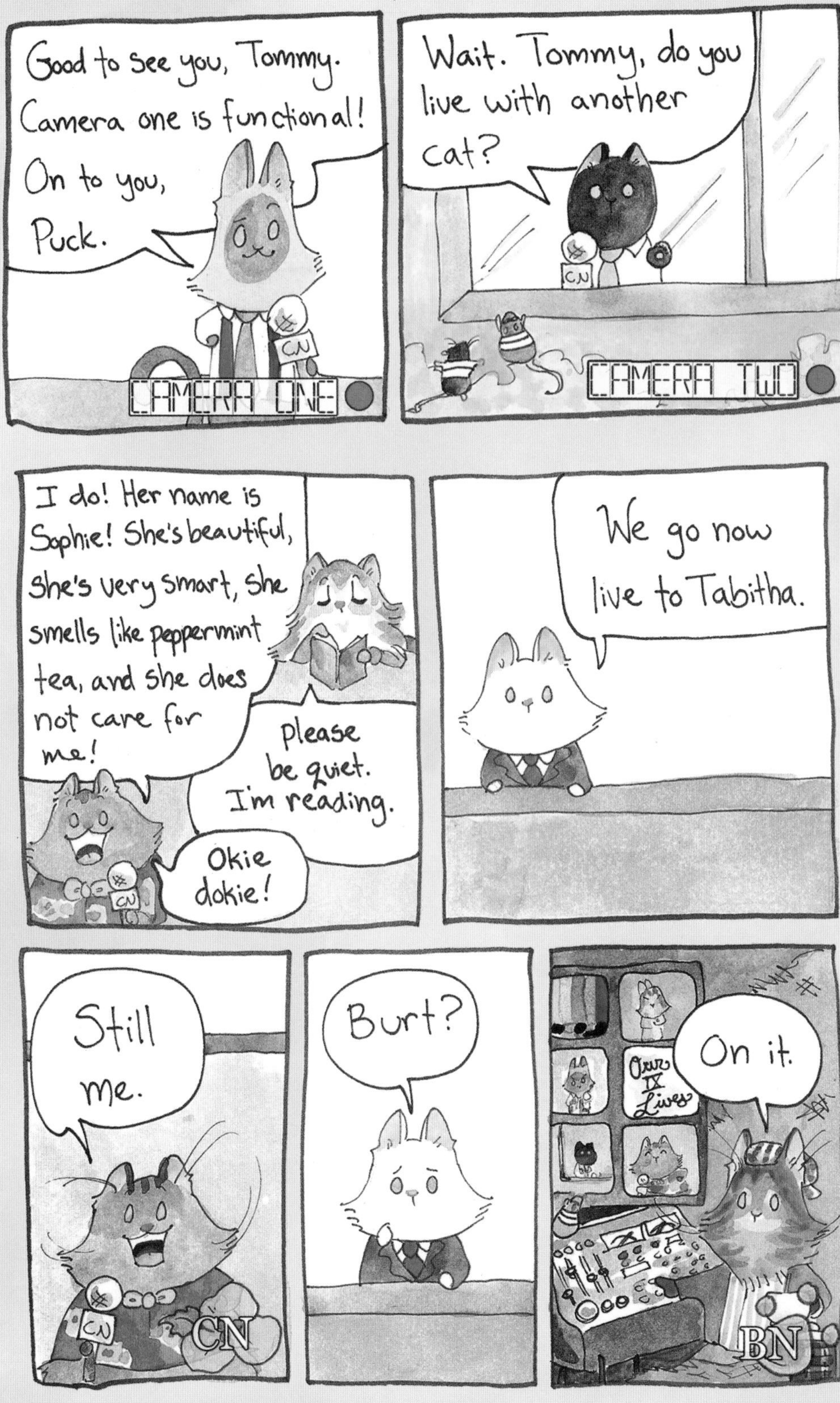
Good to see you, Tommy. Camera one is functional! On to you, Puck.
CN
CAMERA ONE
Wait. Tommy, do you live with another cat?
CN
CAMERA TWO
I do! Her name is Sophie! She's beautiful, she's very smart, she smells like peppermint tea, and she does not care for me!
please be quiet. I'm reading.
Okie dokie!
CN
We go now live to Tabitha.
Still me.
CN
CN
Burt?
On it.
Our IX Lives
BN

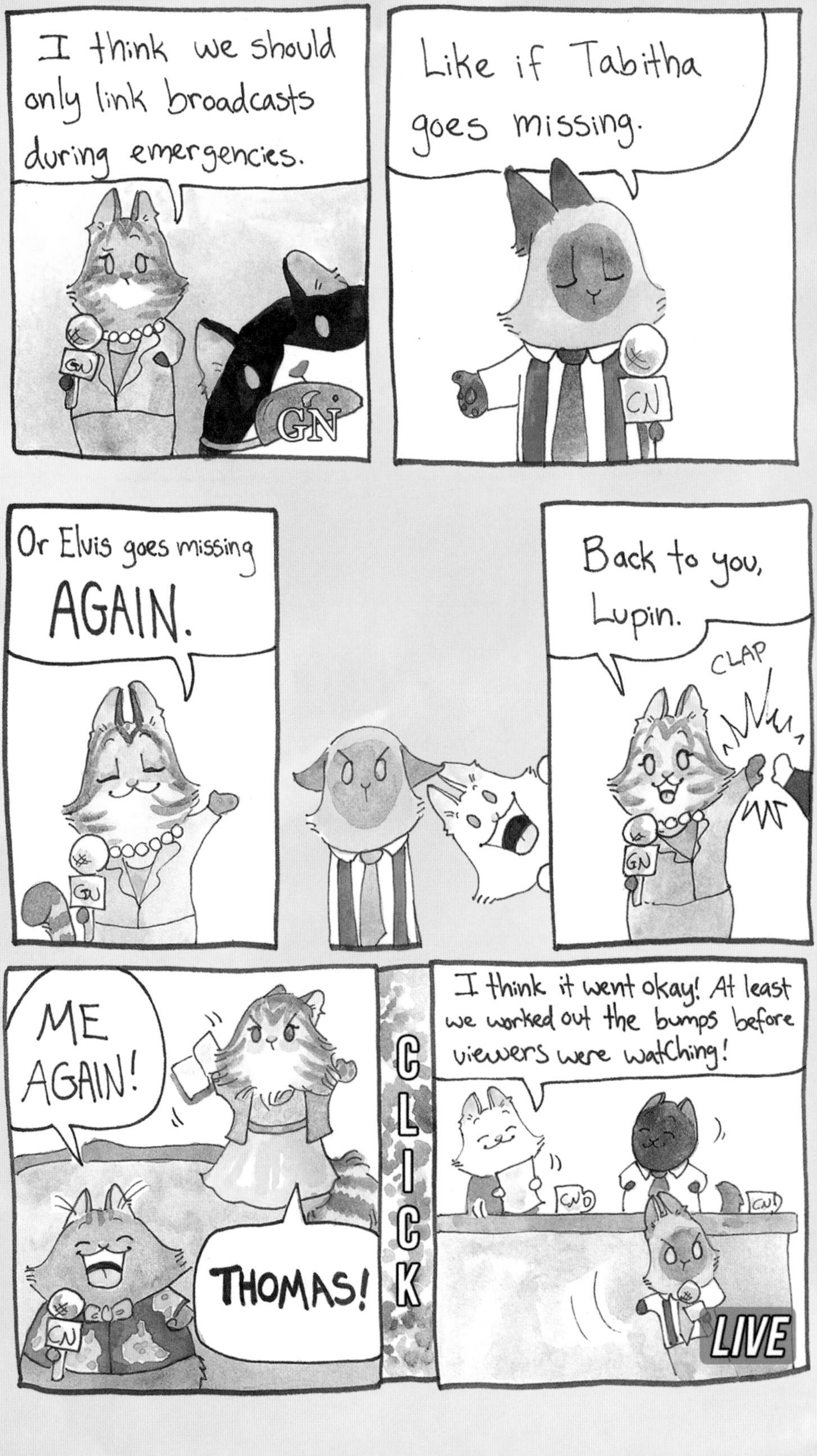
I think we should only link broadcasts during emergencies.
GN
Like if Tabitha goes missing.
CN
Or Elvis goes missing AGAIN.
GN
Back to you, Lupin.
CLAP
GN
ME AGAIN!
THOMAS!
CN
CLICK
I think it went okay! At least we worked out the bumps before viewers were watching!
LIVE

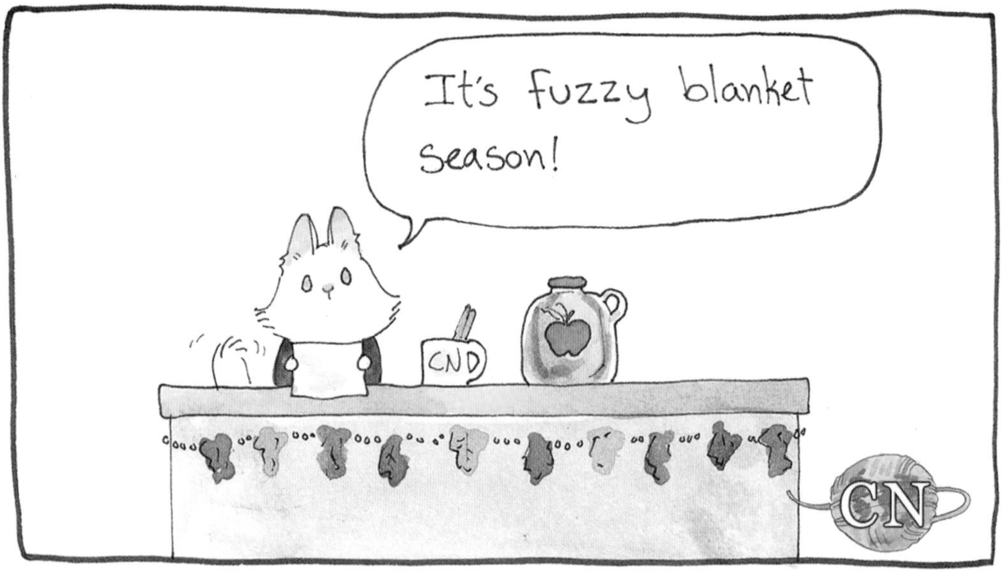
It's fuzzy blanket season!
CND
CN

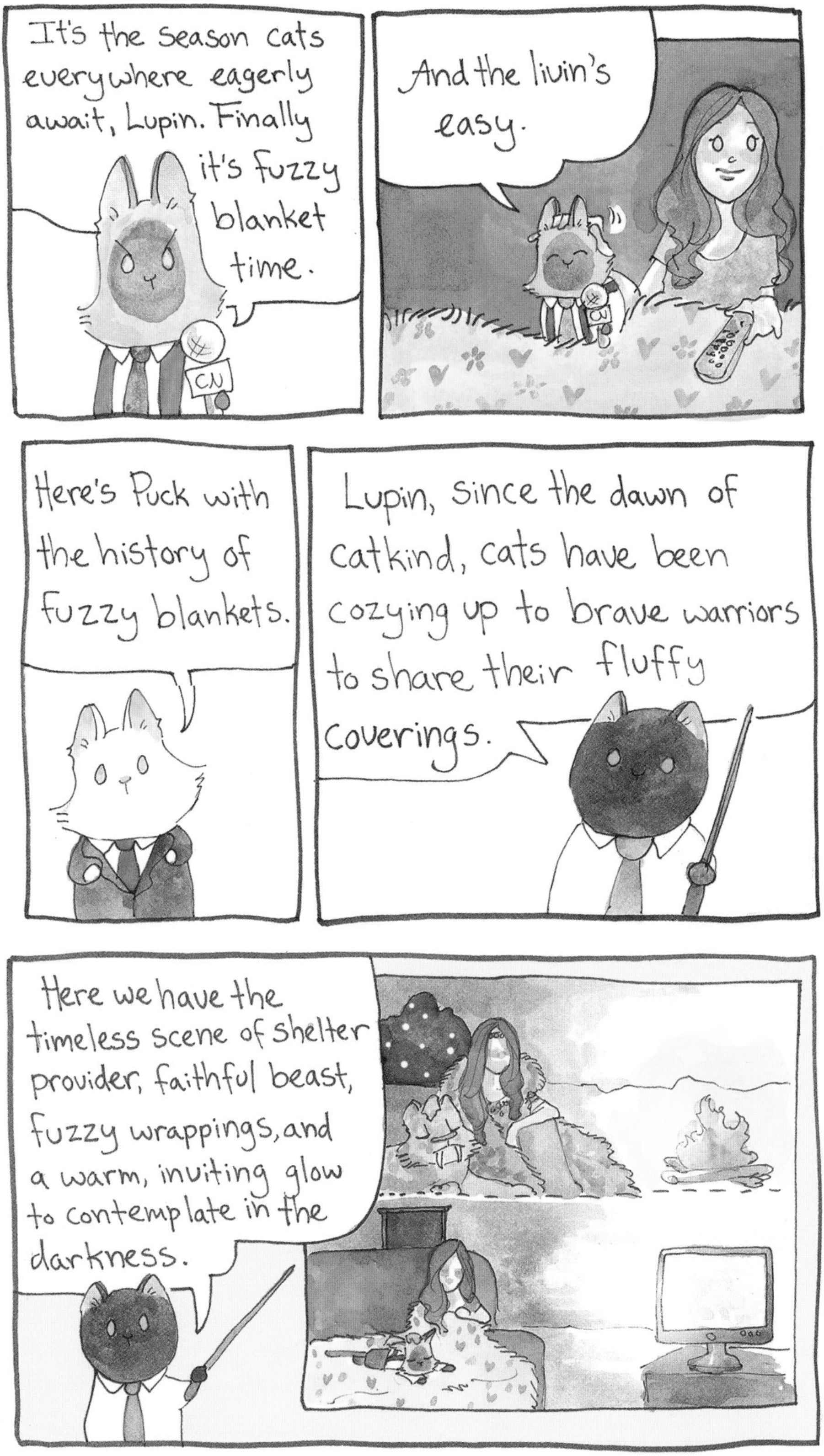
It's the season cats everywhere eagerly await, Lupin. Finally it's fuzzy blanket time.
CN
And the livin's easy.
Here's Puck with the history of fuzzy blankets.
Lupin, since the dawn of catkind, cats have been cozying up to brave warriors to share their fluffy coverings.
Here we have the timeless scene of shelter provider, faithful beast, fuzzy wrappings, and a warm, inviting glow to contemplate in the darkness.

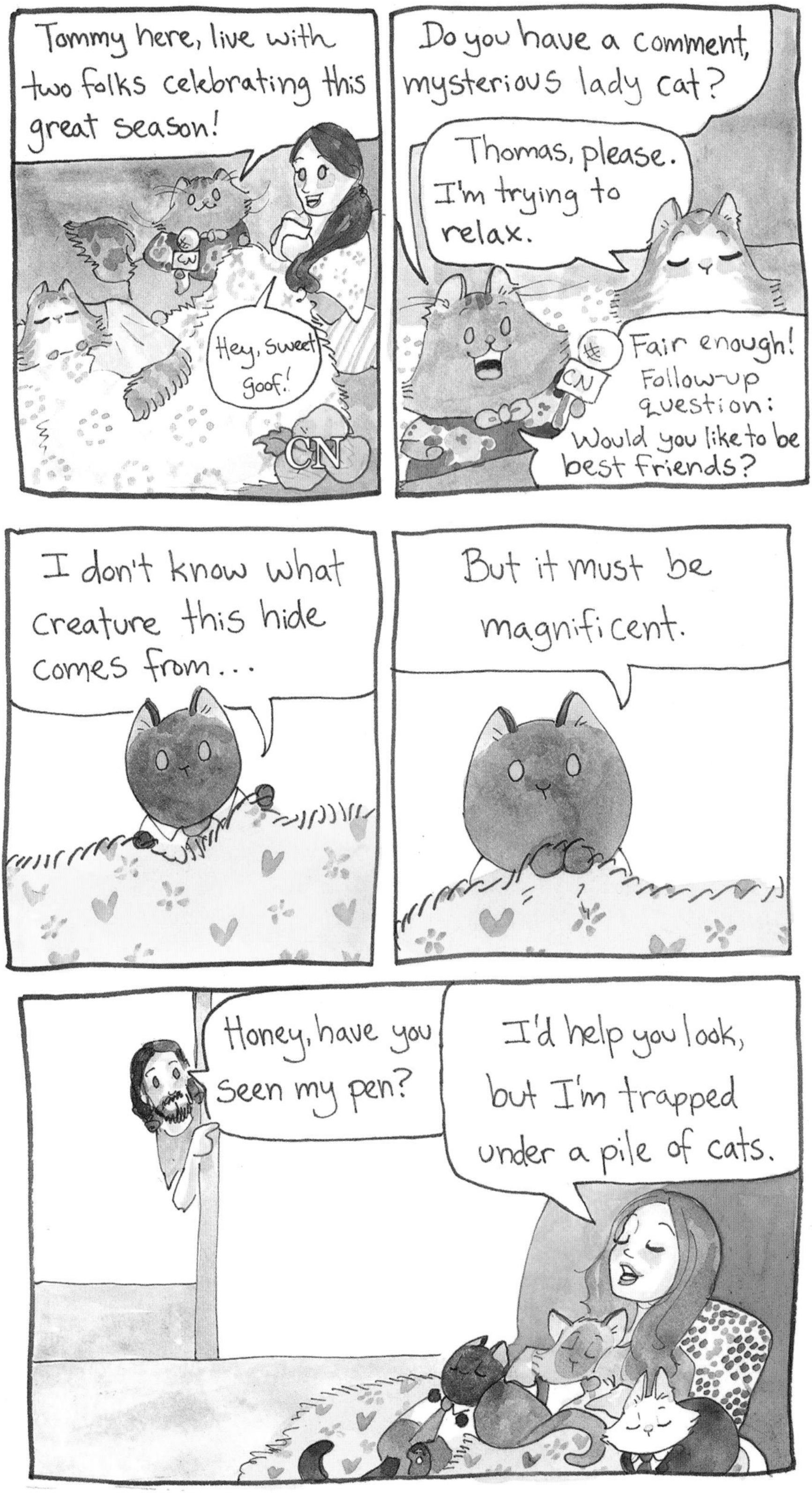

Tommy here, live with two folks celebrating this great season!
Hey, Sweet Goof!
CN
Do you have a comment, mysterious lady cat?
Thomas, please. I'm trying to relax.
Fair enough! Follow-up question: Would you like to be best friends?
I don't know what creature this hide comes from...
But it must be magnificent.
Honey, have you seen my pen?
I'd help you look, but I'm trapped under a pile of cats.

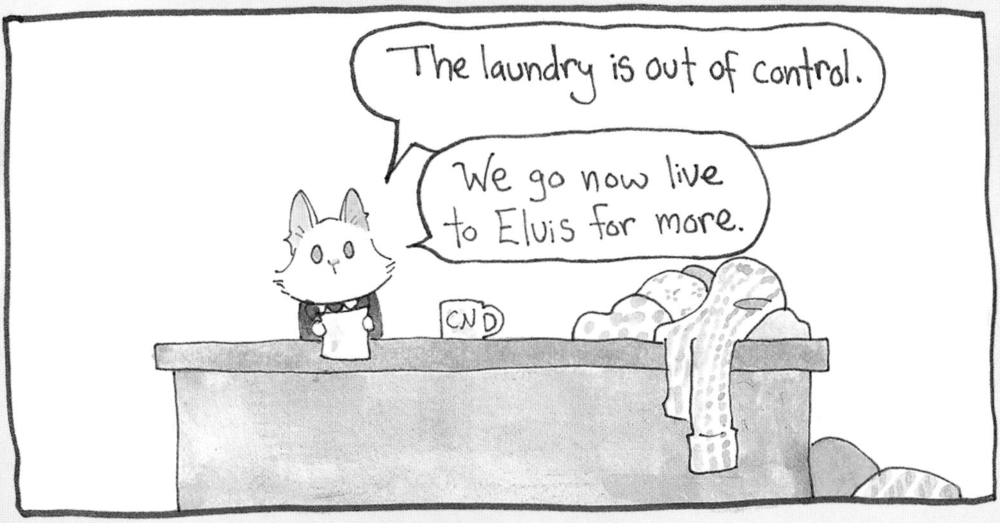
The laundry is out of control.
We go now live to Elvis for more.
CND

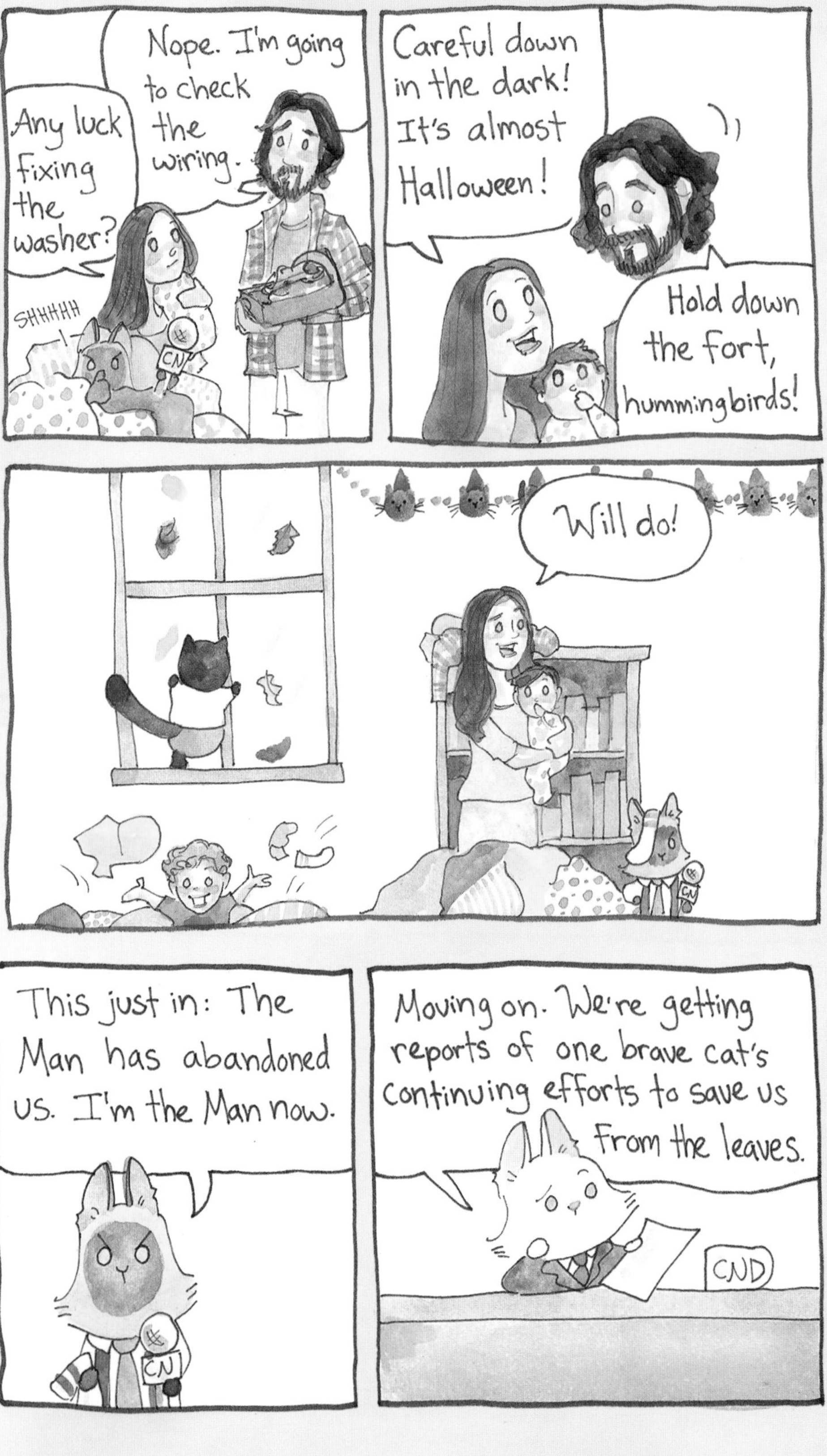
Any luck fixing the washer?
Nope. I'm going to check the wiring...
SHHHHH
CN
Careful down in the dark! It's almost Halloween!
Hold down the fort, hummingbirds!
Will do!
CN
This just in: The Man has abandoned us. I'm the Man now.
CN
Moving on. We're getting reports of one brave cat's continuing efforts to save us from the leaves.
CND

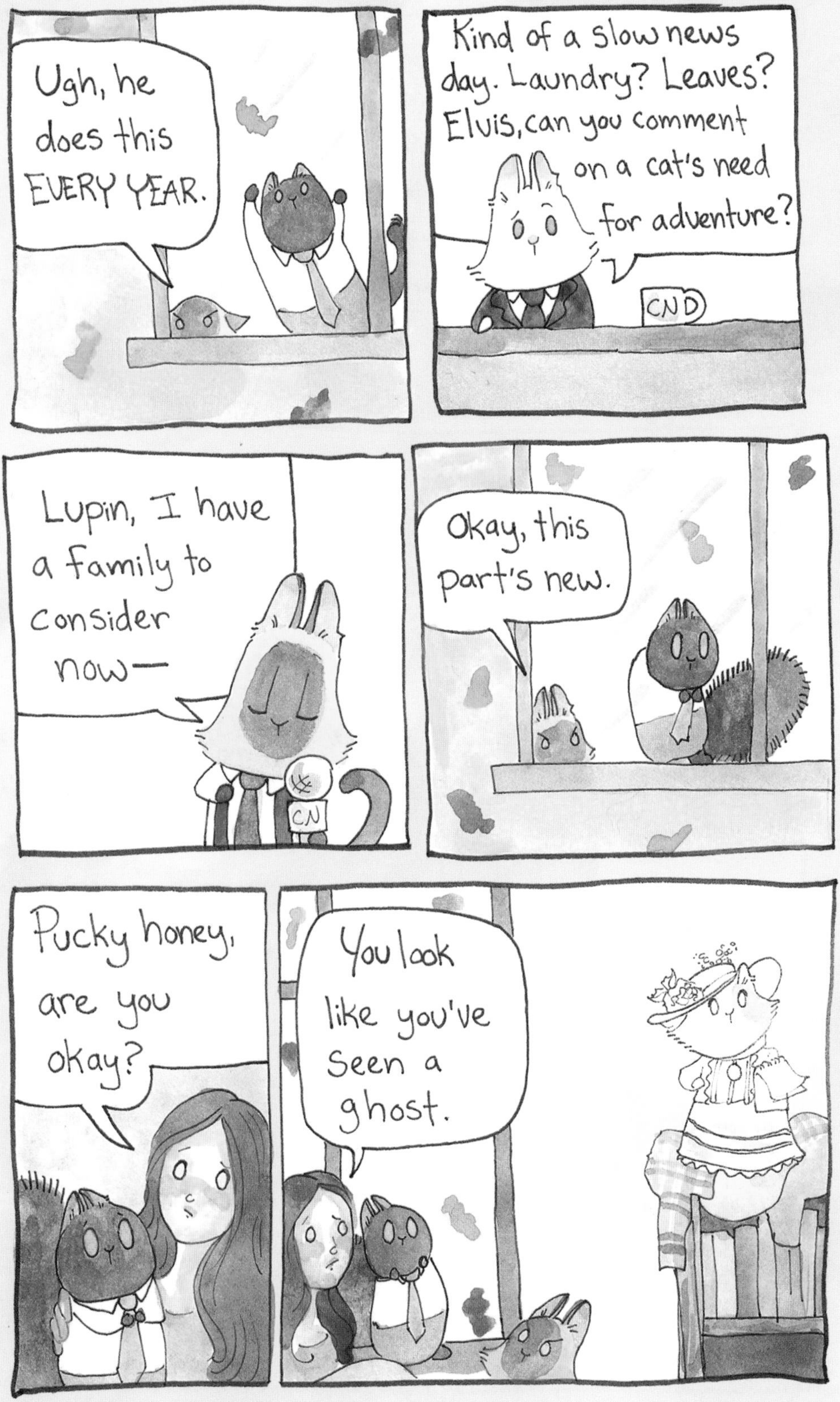
Ugh, he does this EVERY YEAR.
Kind of a slow news day. Laundry? Leaves? Elvis, can you comment on a cat's need for adventure?
CND
Lupin, I have a family to consider now—
CN
Okay, this part's new.
Pucky honey, are you okay?
You look like you've seen a ghost.

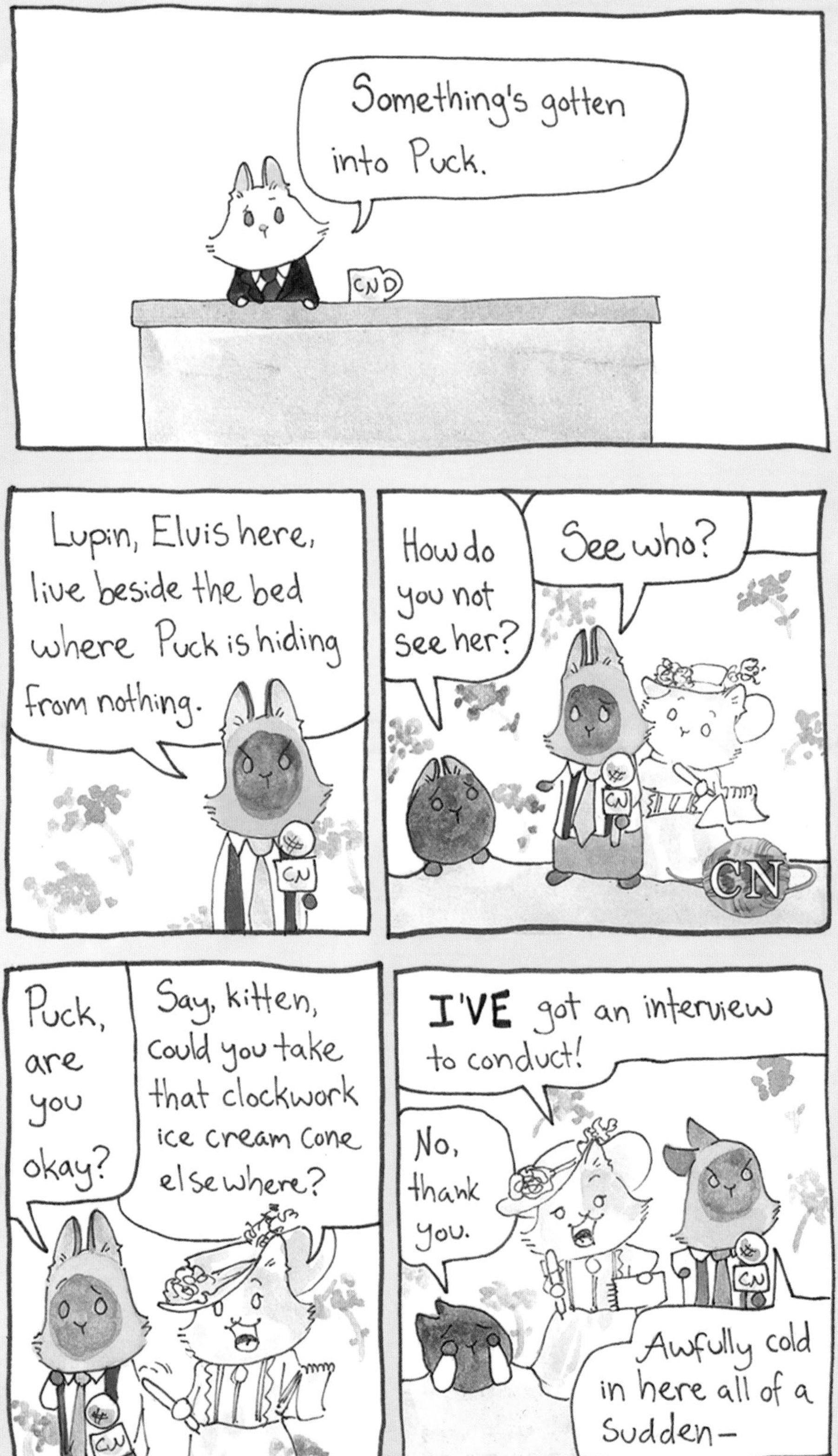
Something's gotten into Puck.
CND
Lupin, Elvis here, live beside the bed where Puck is hiding from nothing.
CN
How do you not see her?
See who?
CN
CN
Puck, are you okay?
Say, kitten, could you take that clockwork ice cream cone elsewhere?
CN
I'VE got an interview to conduct!
No, thank you.
CN
Awfully cold in here all of a sudden—

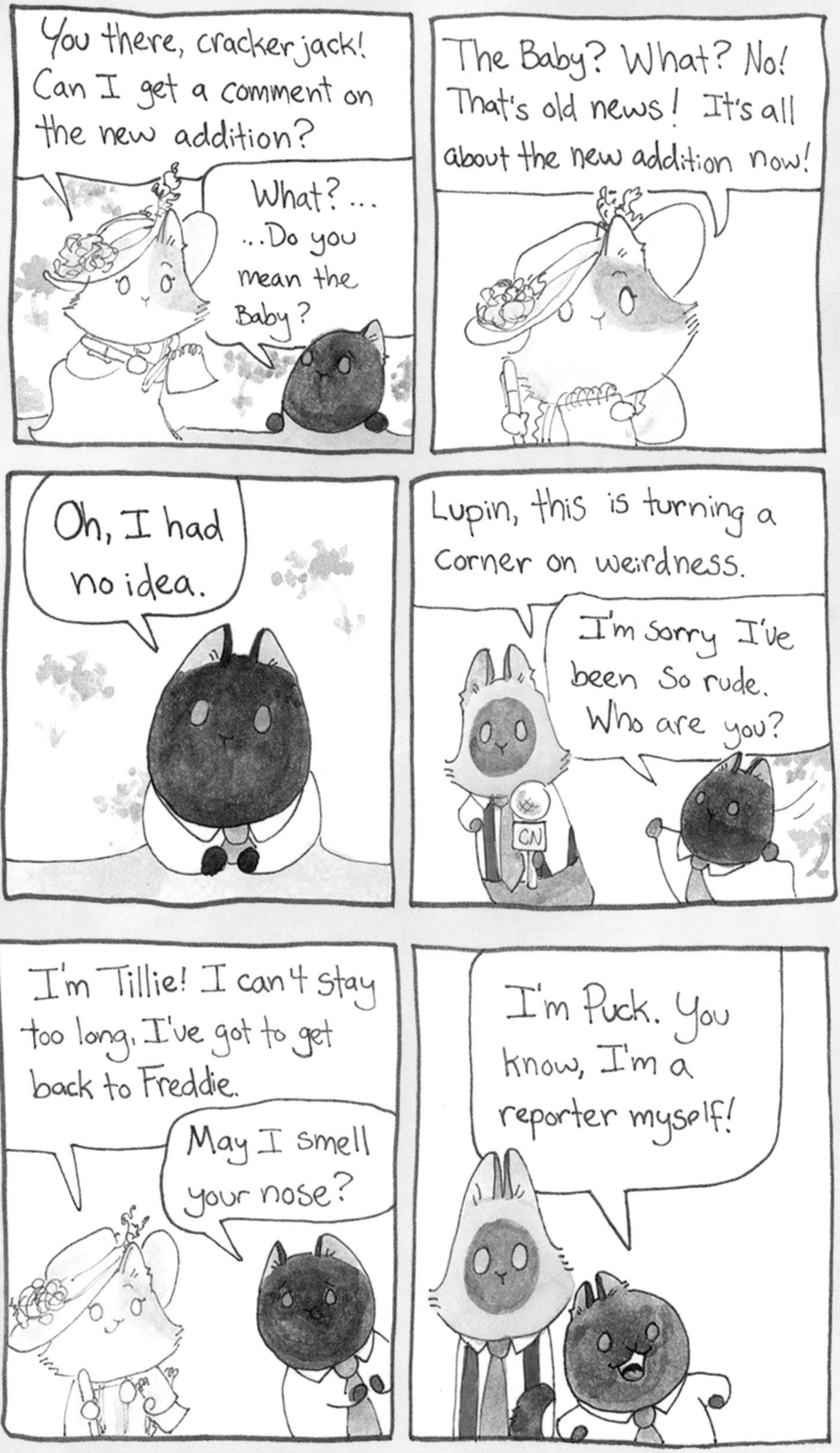

You there, crackerjack! Can I get a comment on the new addition?
What? ... ...Do you mean the Baby?
The Baby? What? No! That's old news! It's all about the new addition now!
Oh, I had no idea.
Lupin, this is turning a corner on weirdness.
I'm sorry I've been so rude. Who are you?
CN
I'm Tillie! I can't stay too long. I've got to get back to Freddie.
May I smell your nose?
I'm Puck. You know, I'm a reporter myself!

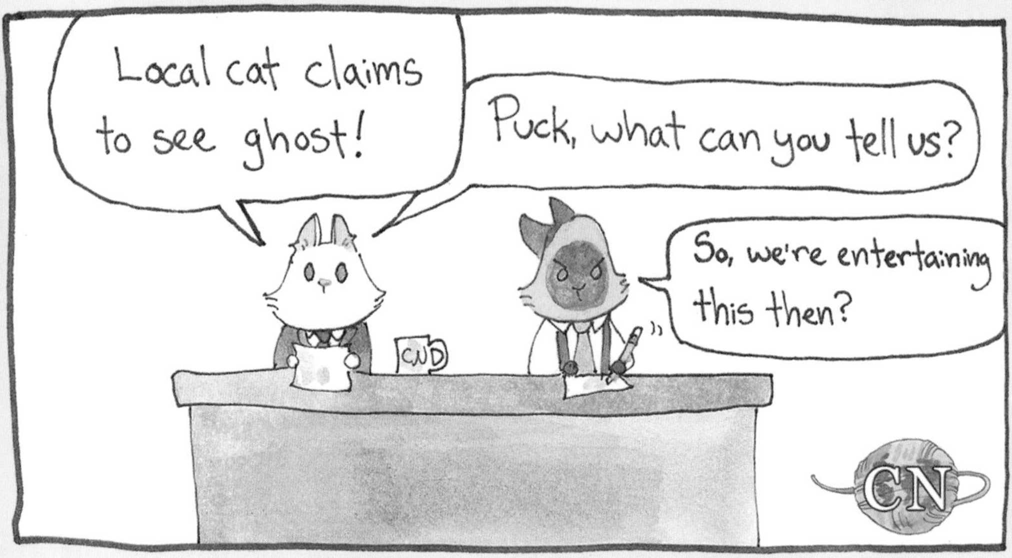
Local cat claims to see ghost!
Puck, what can you tell us?
So, we're entertaining this then?
CWD
CN

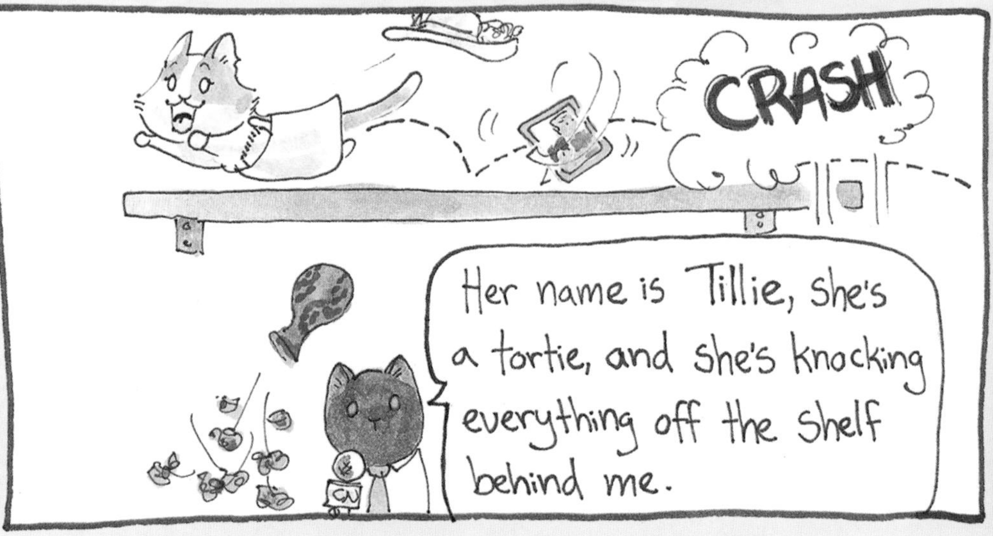
CRASH
Her name is Tillie, she's a tortie, and she's knocking everything off the shelf behind me.
CN

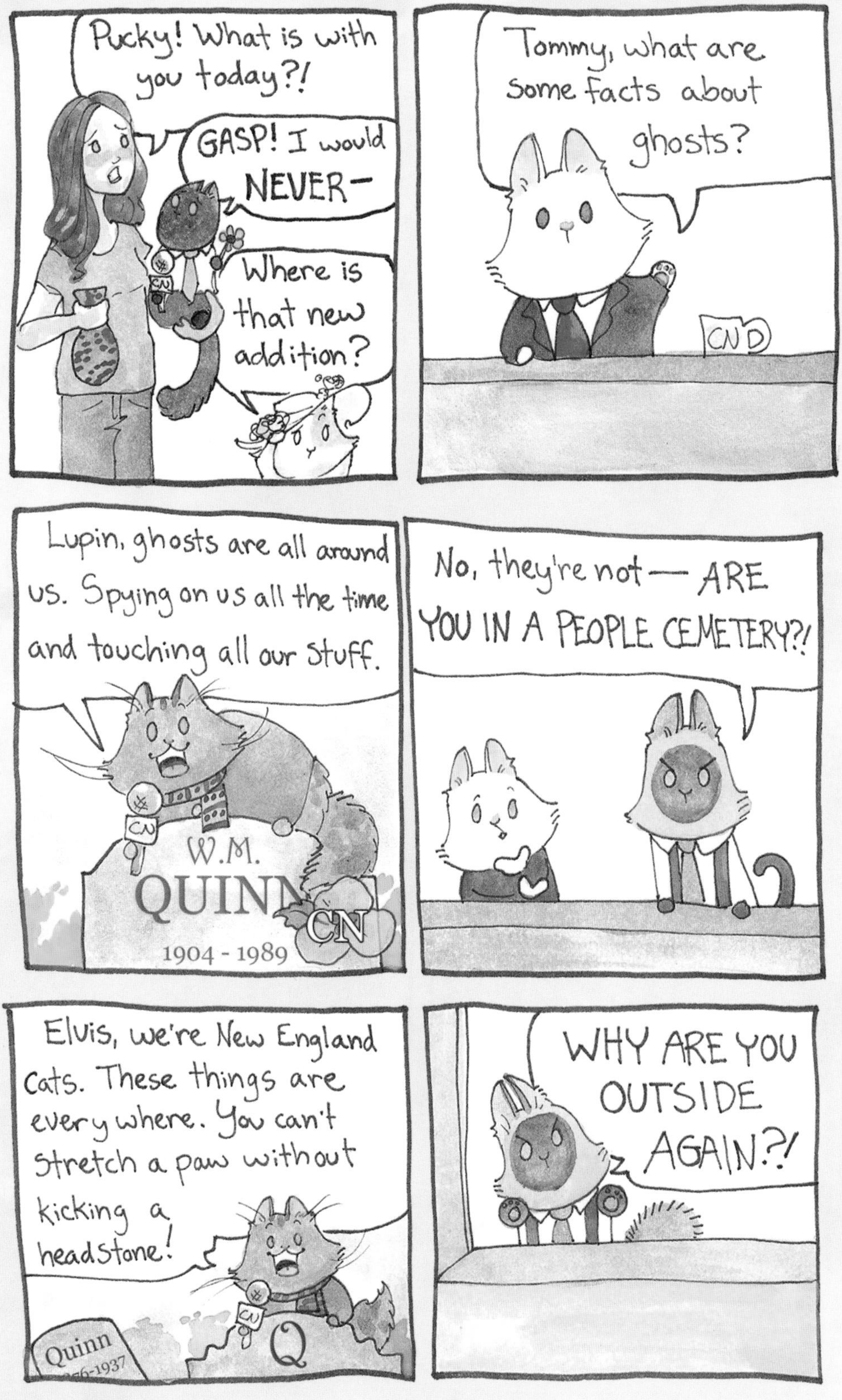
Pucky! What is with you today?!
GASP! I would NEVER—
Where is that new addition?
Tommy, what are some facts about ghosts?
Lupin, ghosts are all around us. Spying on us all the time and touching all our stuff.
W.M. QUINN 1904 - 1989
No, they're not— ARE YOU IN A PEOPLE CEMETERY?!
Elvis, we're New England cats. These things are everywhere. You can't stretch a paw without kicking a headstone!
WHY ARE YOU OUTSIDE AGAIN?!

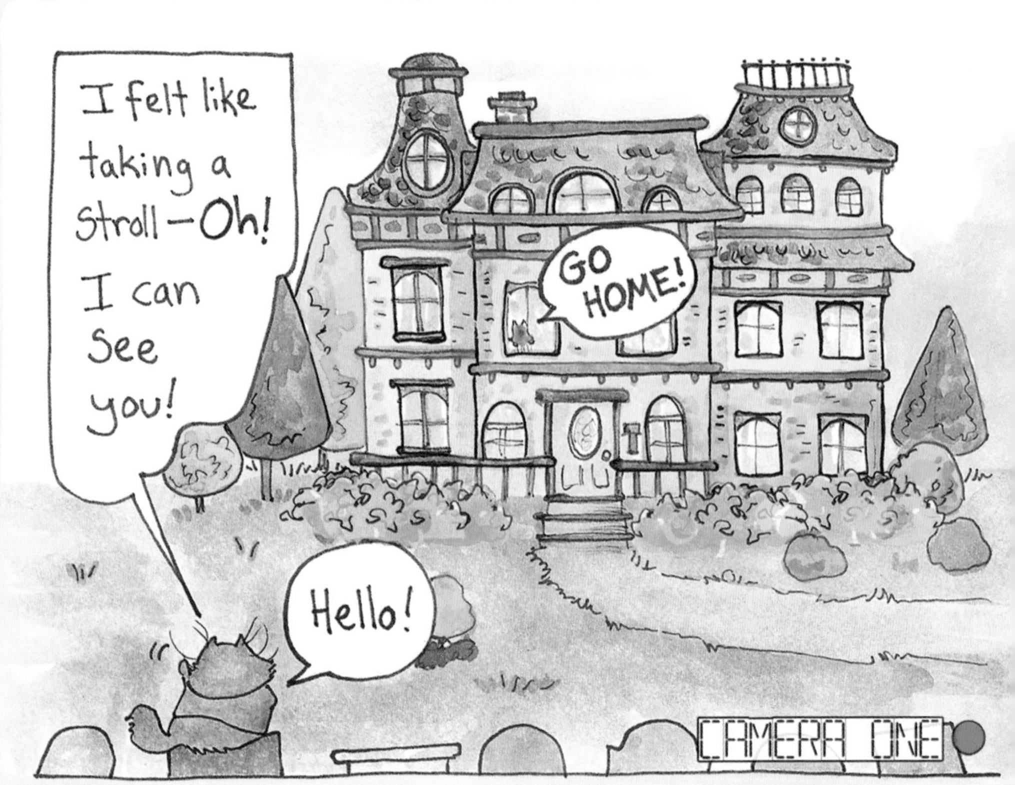
I felt like taking a Stroll—Oh! I can See you!
GO HOME!
Hello!
CAMERA ONE

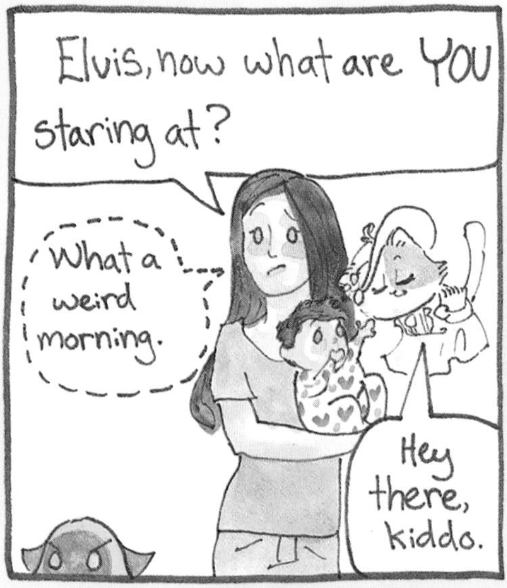
Elvis, now what are YOU staring at?
What a weird morning.
Hey there, kiddo.

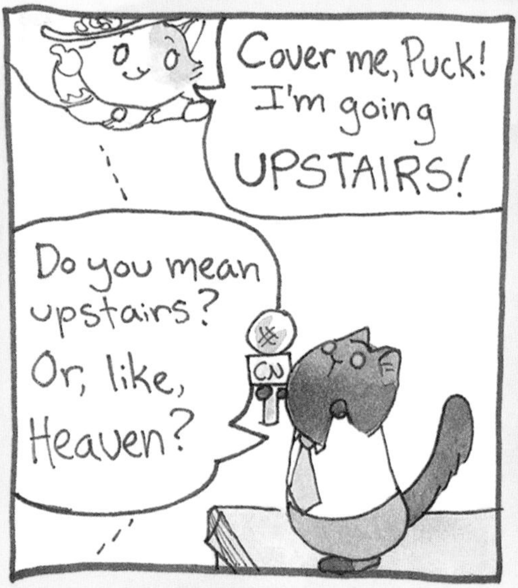
Cover me, Puck! I'm going UPSTAIRS!
Do you mean upstairs? Or, like, Heaven?
CN

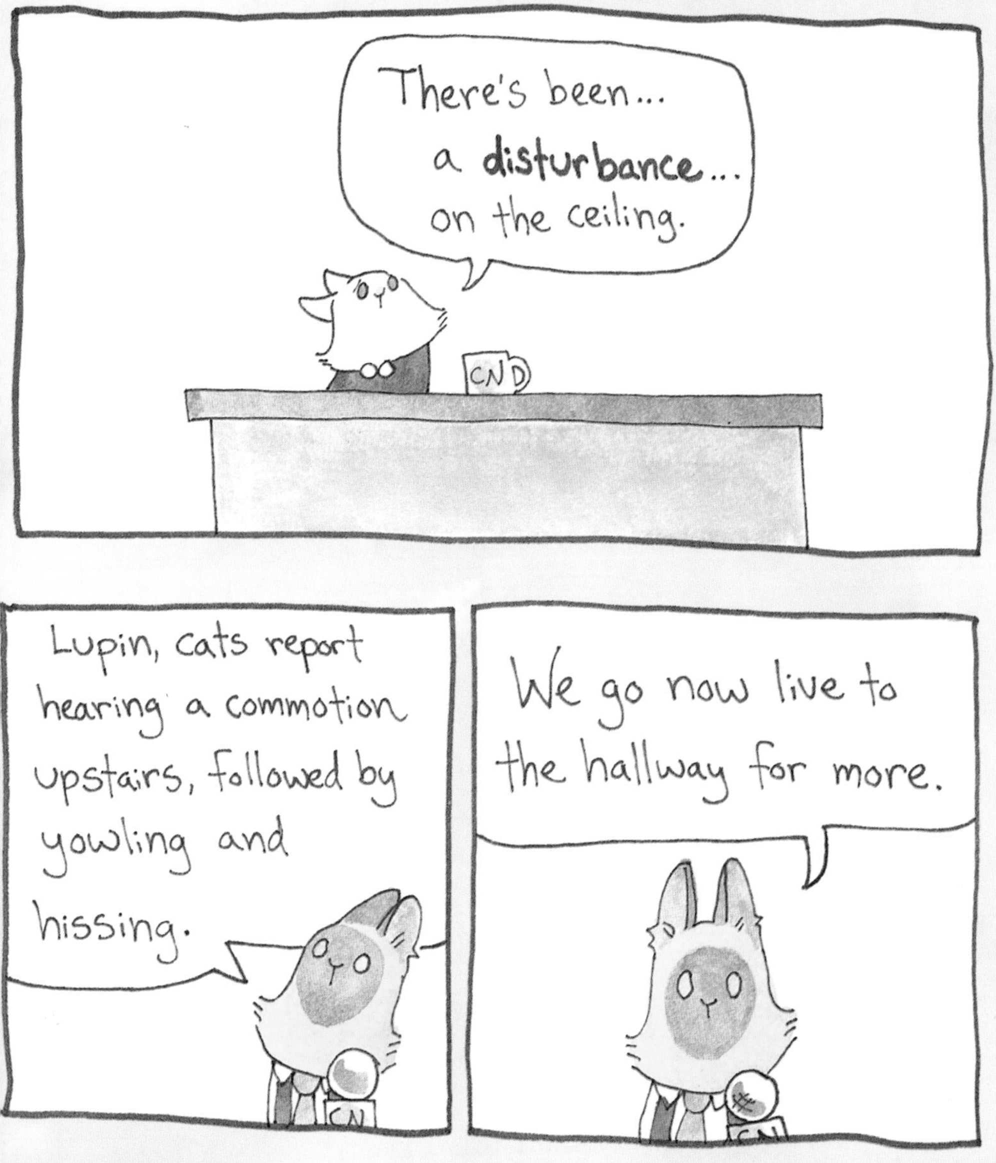
There's been... a **disturbance**... on the ceiling.
CND
Lupin, cats report hearing a commotion upstairs, followed by yowling and hissing.
We go now live to the hallway for more.

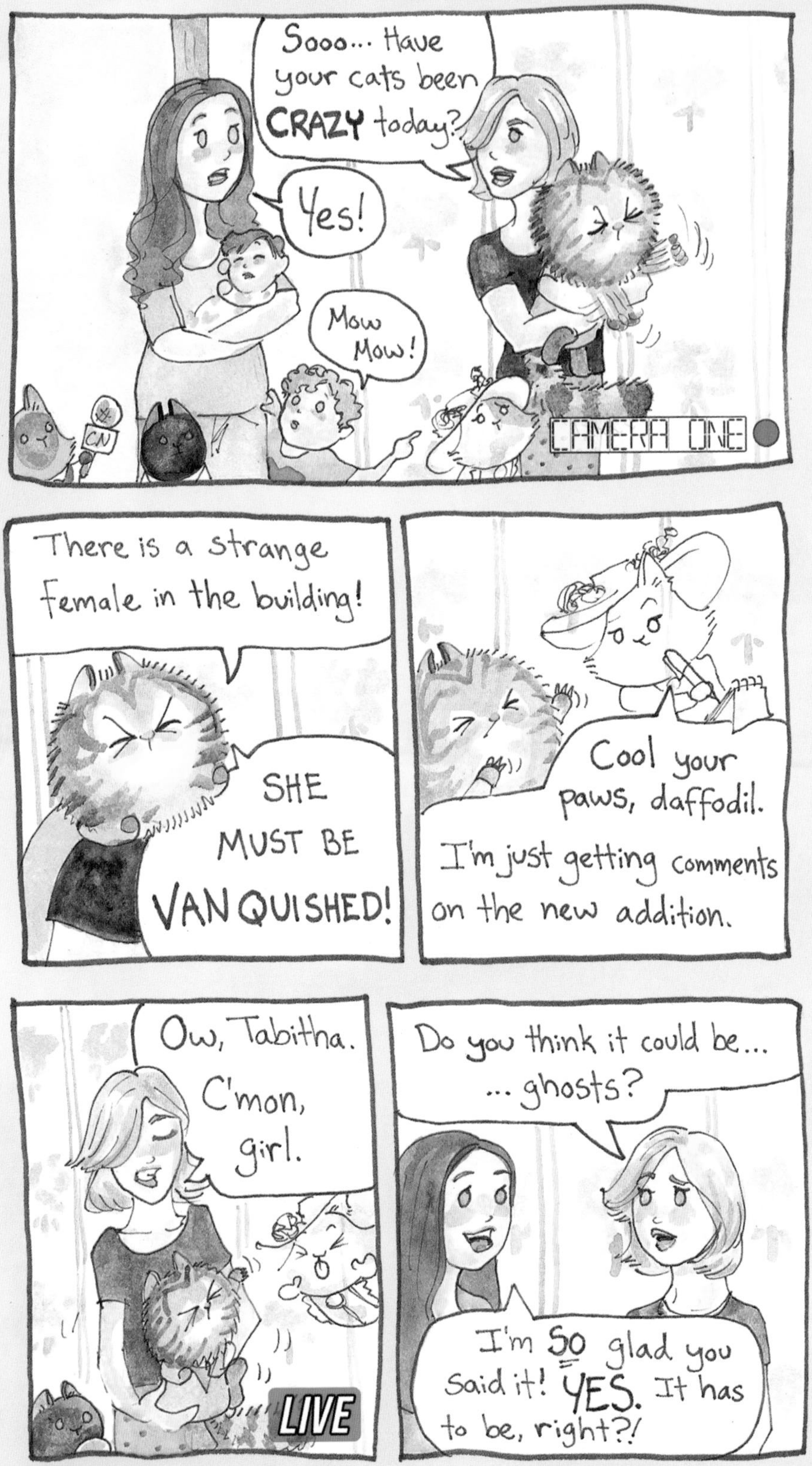
Sooo... Have your cats been CRAZY today?
Yes!
Mow Mow!
CN
CAMERA ONE
There is a strange female in the building!
SHE MUST BE VANQUISHED!
Cool your paws, daffodil.
I'm just getting comments on the new addition.
Ow, Tabitha. C'mon, girl.
LIVE
Do you think it could be... ...ghosts?
I'm SO glad you said it! YES. It has to be, right?!

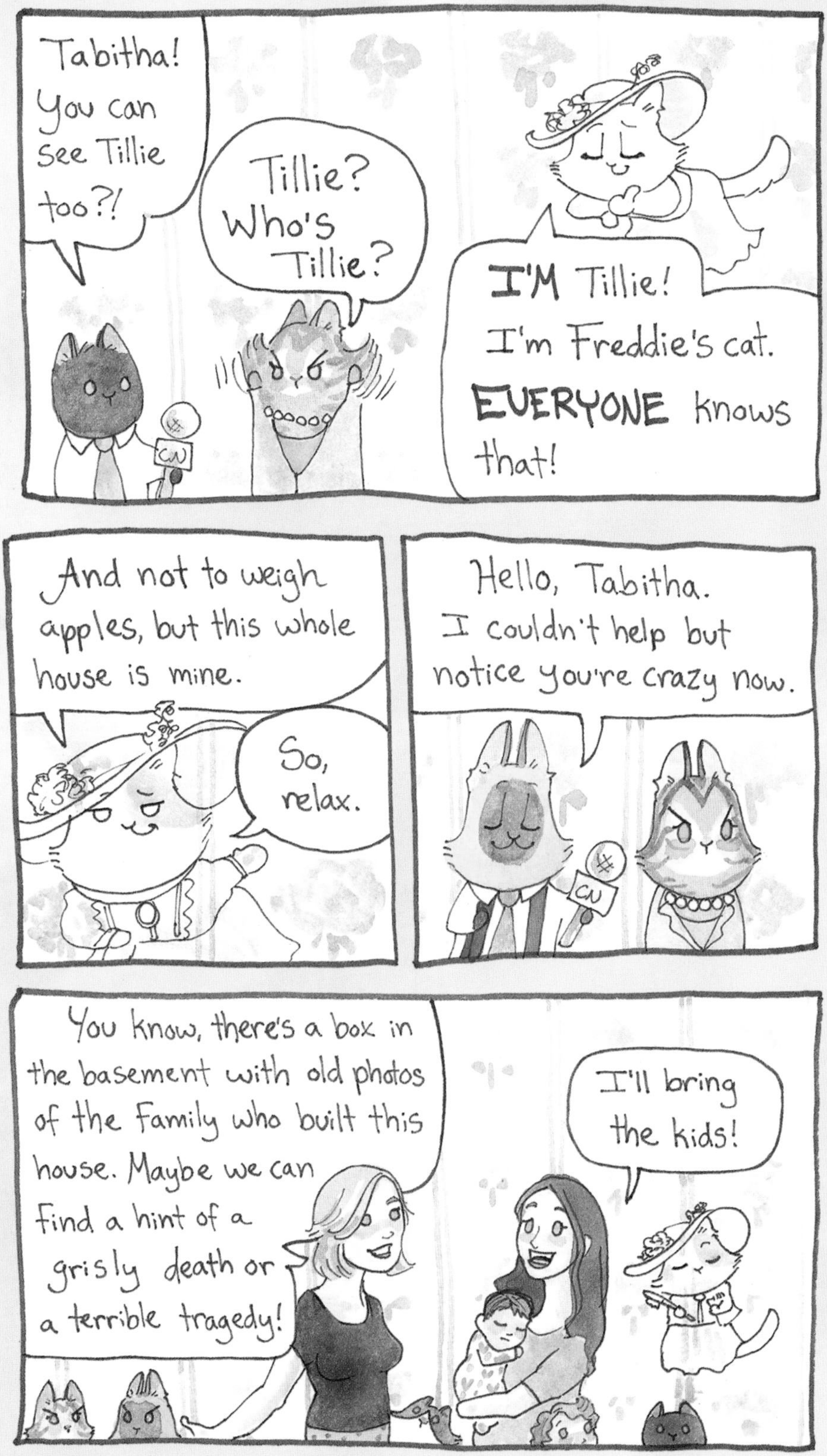
Tabitha! You can see Tillie too?!
Tillie? Who's Tillie?
I'M Tillie! I'm Freddie's cat. EVERYONE knows that!
And not to weigh apples, but this whole house is mine.
So, relax.
Hello, Tabitha. I couldn't help but notice you're crazy now.
CN
CN
You know, there's a box in the basement with old photos of the family who built this house. Maybe we can find a hint of a grisly death or a terrible tragedy!
I'll bring the kids!

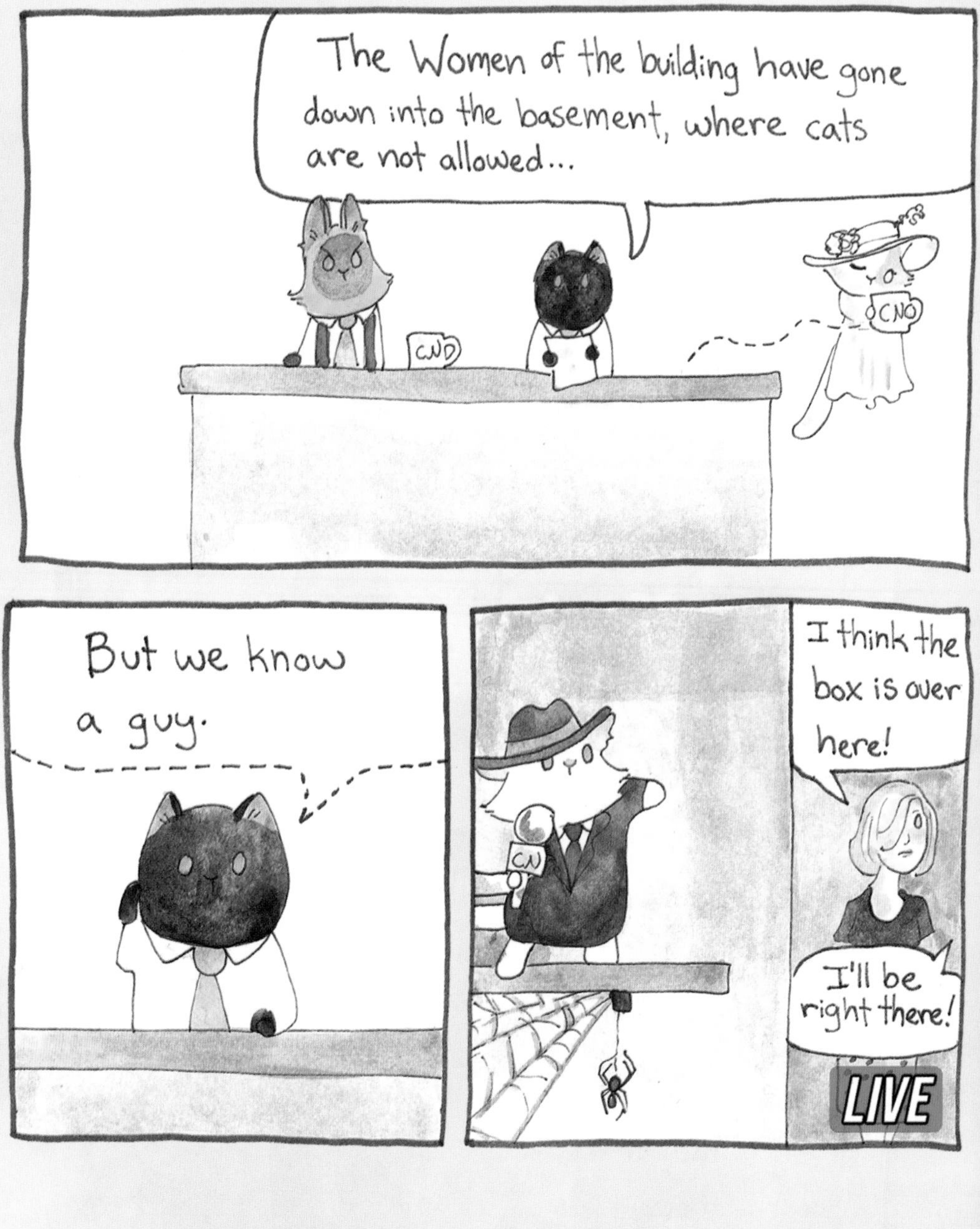
The Women of the building have gone down into the basement, where cats are not allowed...
But we know a guy.
I think the box is over here!
I'll be right there!
LIVE

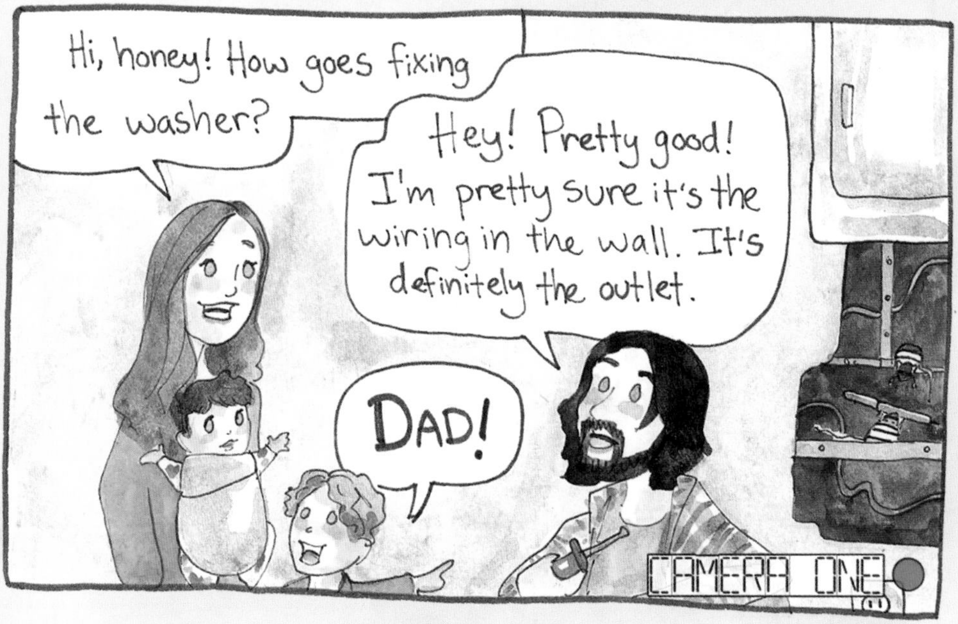
Hi, honey! How goes fixing the washer?
Hey! Pretty good! I'm pretty sure it's the wiring in the wall. It's definitely the outlet.
DAD!
CAMERA ONE

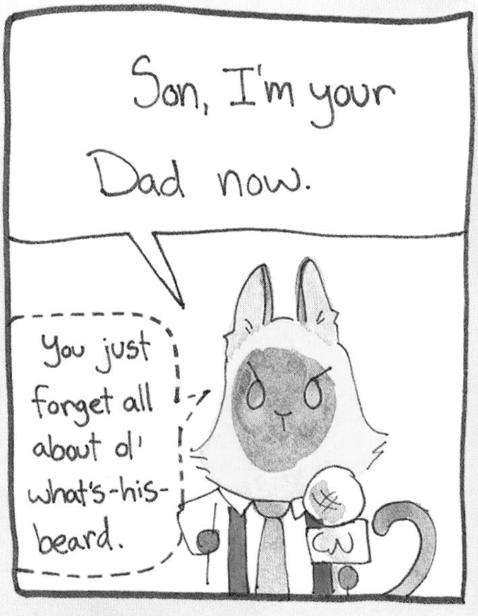
Son, I'm your Dad now.
You just forget all about ol' what's-his-beard.
CN

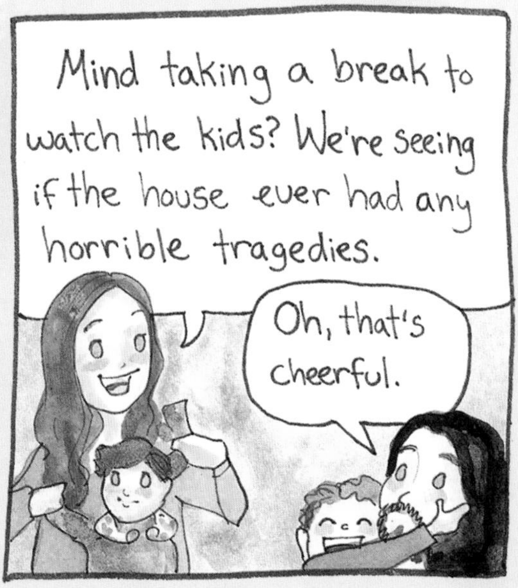
Mind taking a break to watch the kids? We're seeing if the house ever had any horrible tragedies.
Oh, that's cheerful.

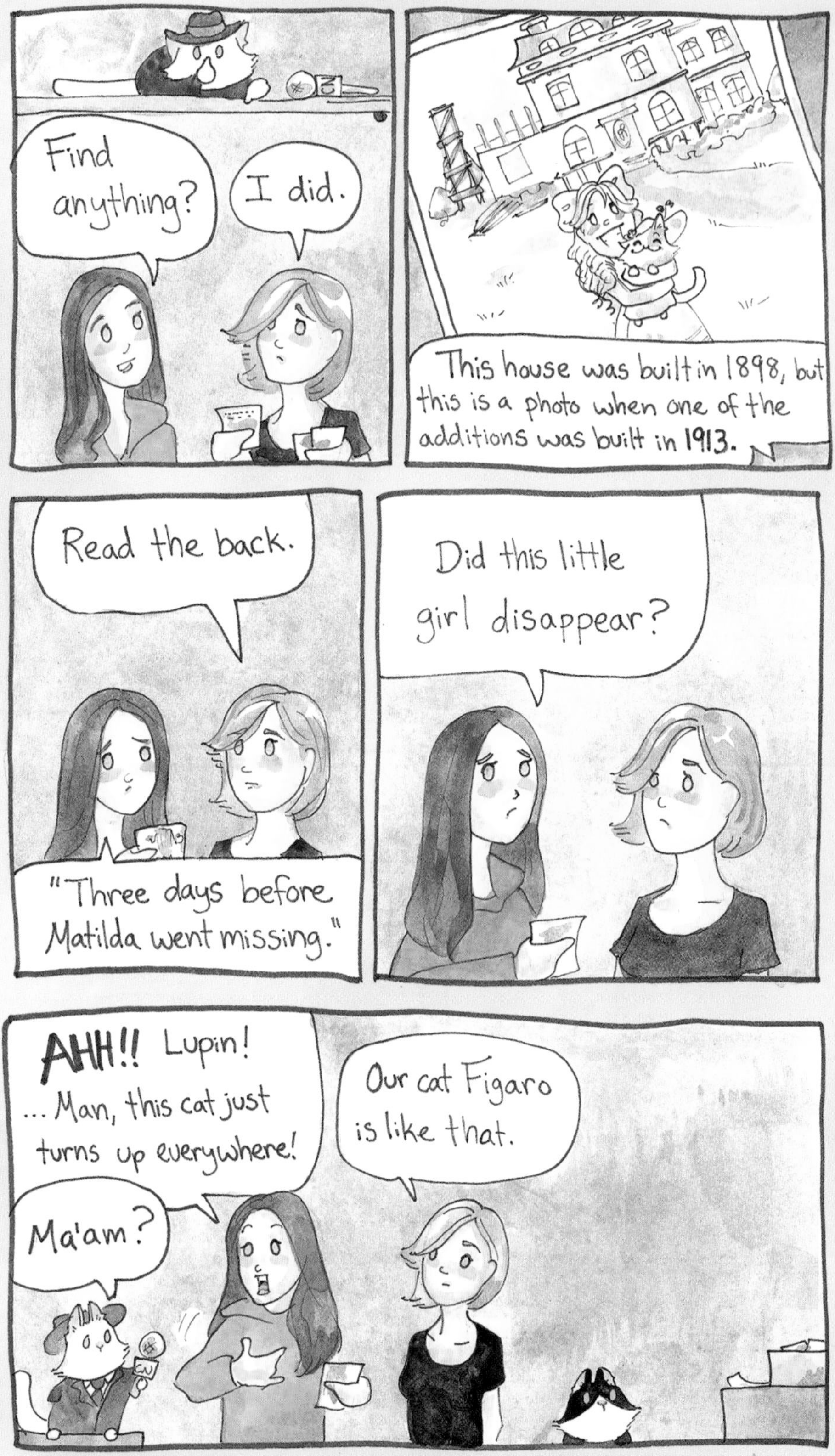
Find anything?
I did.
This house was built in 1898, but this is a photo when one of the additions was built in 1913.
Read the back.
"Three days before Matilda went missing."
Did this little girl disappear?
AHH!! Lupin! ... Man, this cat just turns up everywhere!
Ma'am?
Our cat Figaro is like that.

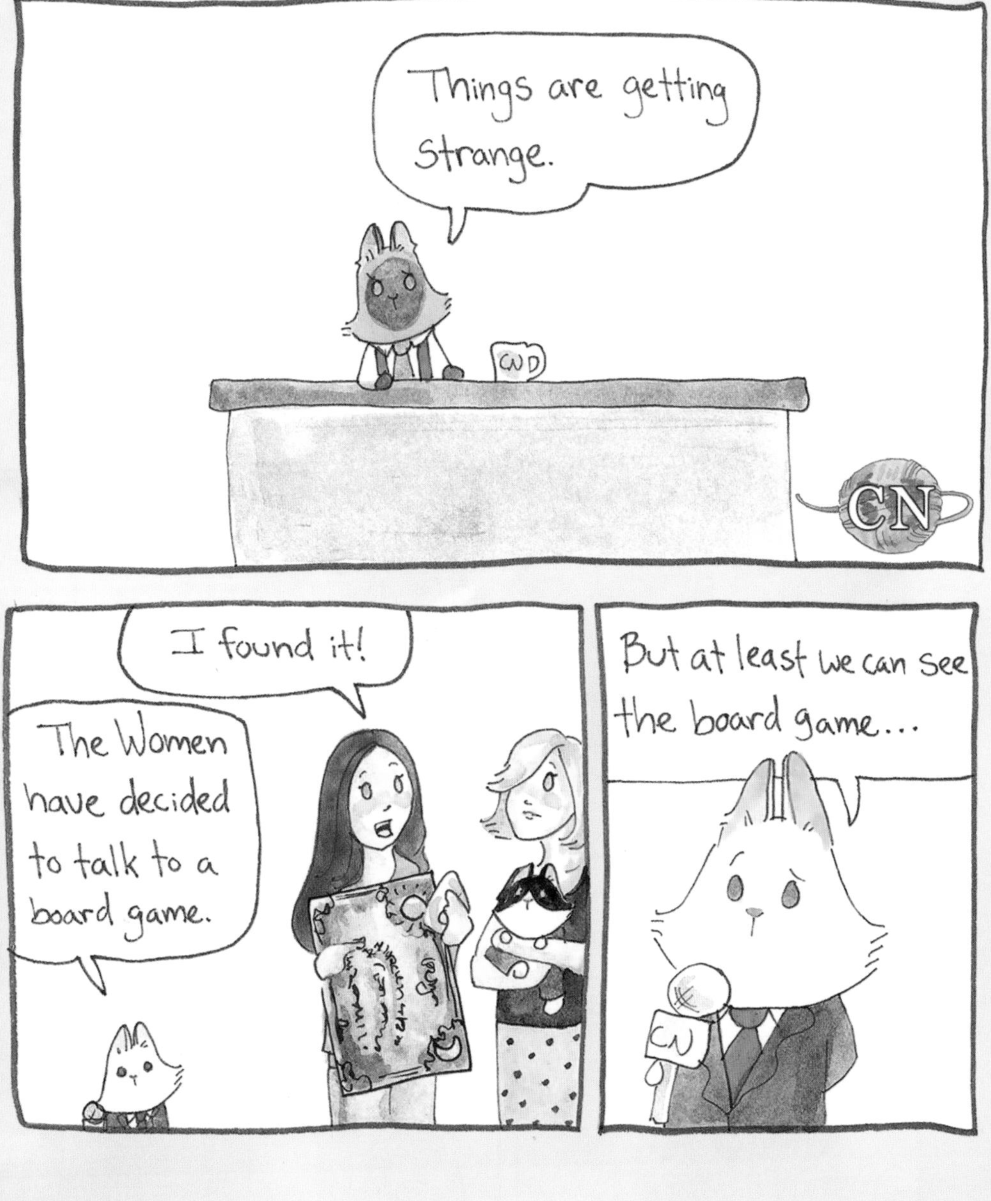
Things are getting strange.
CWD
CN
I found it!
The Women have decided to talk to a board game.
But at least we can see the board game...
CN

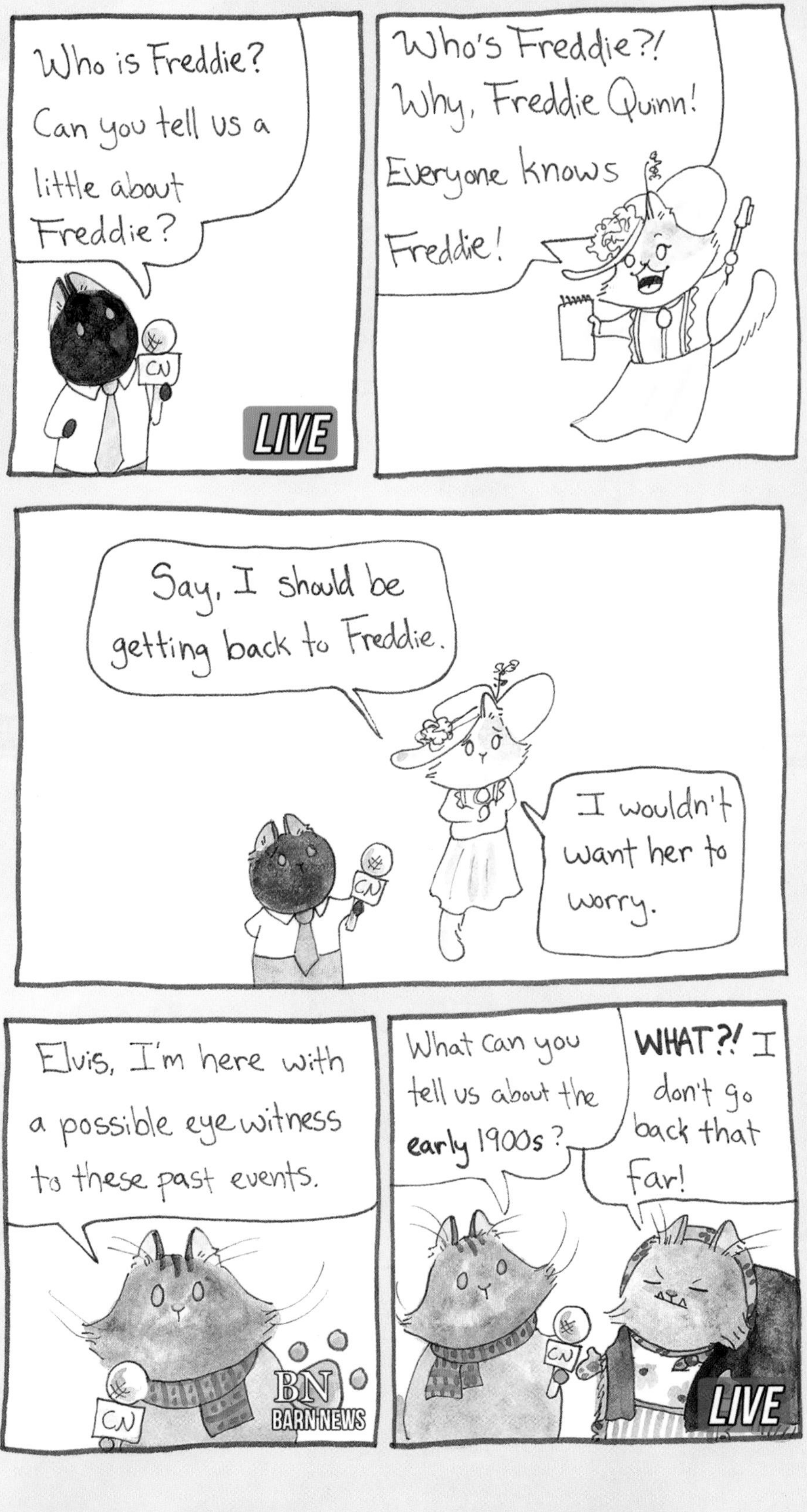
Who is Freddie? Can you tell us a little about Freddie?
LIVE
Who's Freddie?! Why, Freddie Quinn! Everyone knows Freddie!
Say, I should be getting back to Freddie.
I wouldn't want her to worry.
Elvis, I'm here with a possible eye witness to these past events.
BN
BARN NEWS
What can you tell us about the **early** 1900s?
WHAT?! I don't go back that far!
LIVE

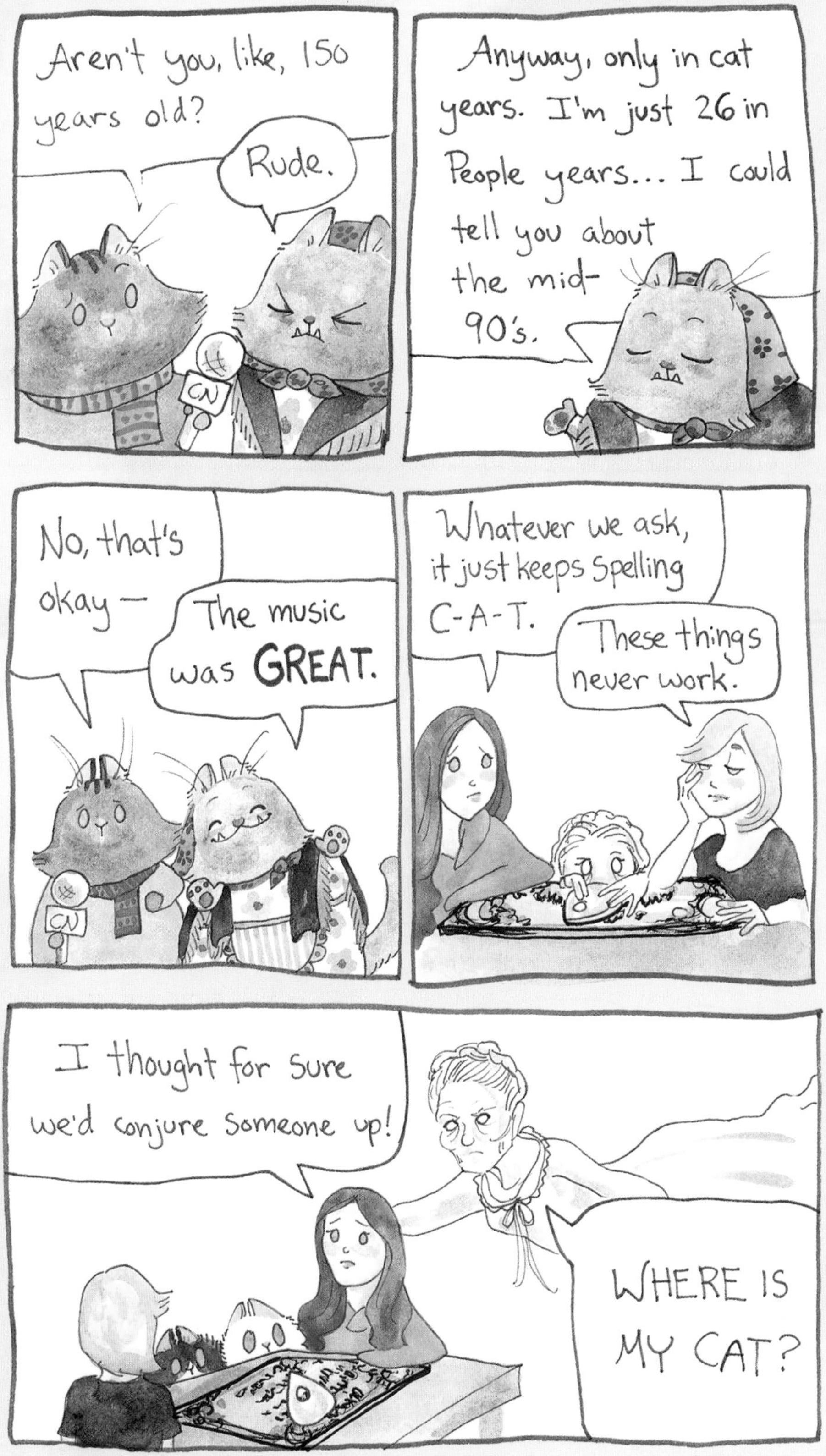
Aren't you, like, 150 years old?
Rude.
Anyway, only in cat years. I'm just 26 in People years... I could tell you about the mid-90's.
CN
No, that's okay —
The music was GREAT.
CN
Whatever we ask, it just keeps Spelling C-A-T.
These things never work.
I thought for sure we'd conjure someone up!
WHERE IS MY CAT?

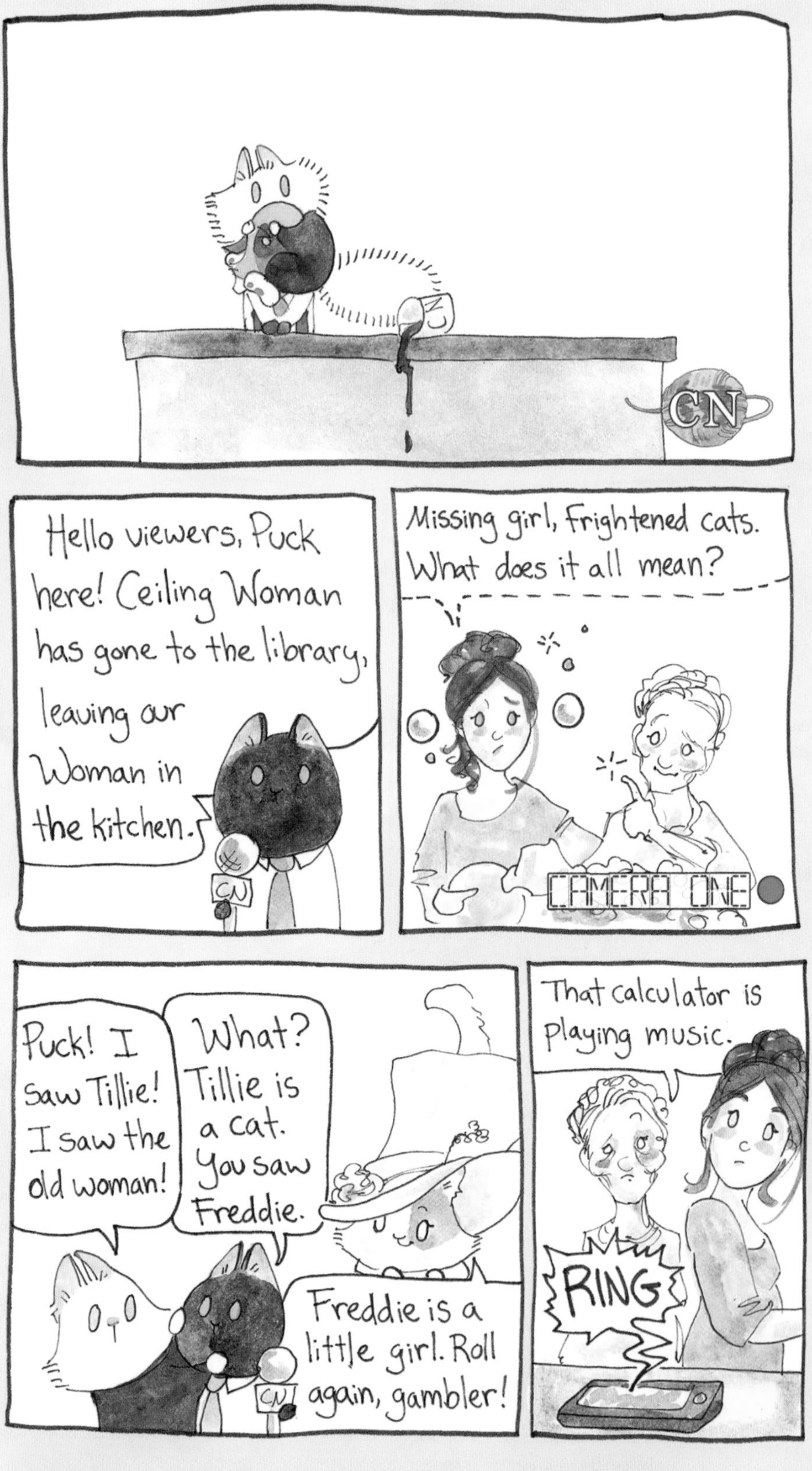
CN
Hello viewers, Puck here! Ceiling Woman has gone to the library, leaving our Woman in the kitchen.
CN
Missing girl, Frightened cats. What does it all mean?
CAMERA ONE
Puck! I saw Tillie! I saw the old woman!
What? Tillie is a cat. You saw Freddie.
Freddie is a little girl. Roll again, gambler!
CN
That calculator is playing music.
RING

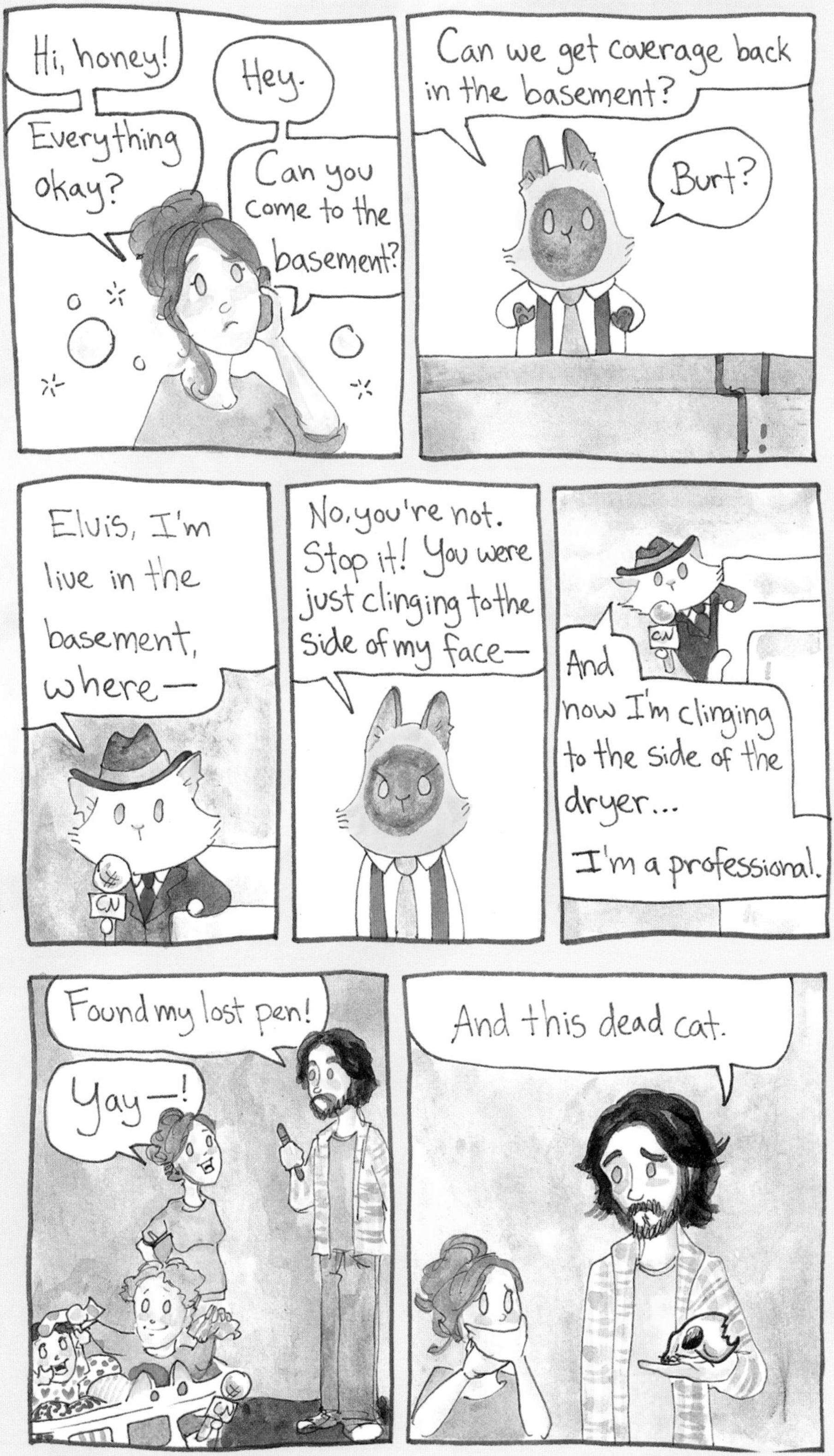
Hi, honey!
Everything okay?
Hey.
Can you come to the basement?
Can we get coverage back in the basement?
Burt?
Elvis, I'm live in the basement, where—
No, you're not. Stop it! You were just clinging to the side of my face—
And now I'm clinging to the side of the dryer...
I'm a professional.
Found my lost pen!
Yay—!
And this dead cat.

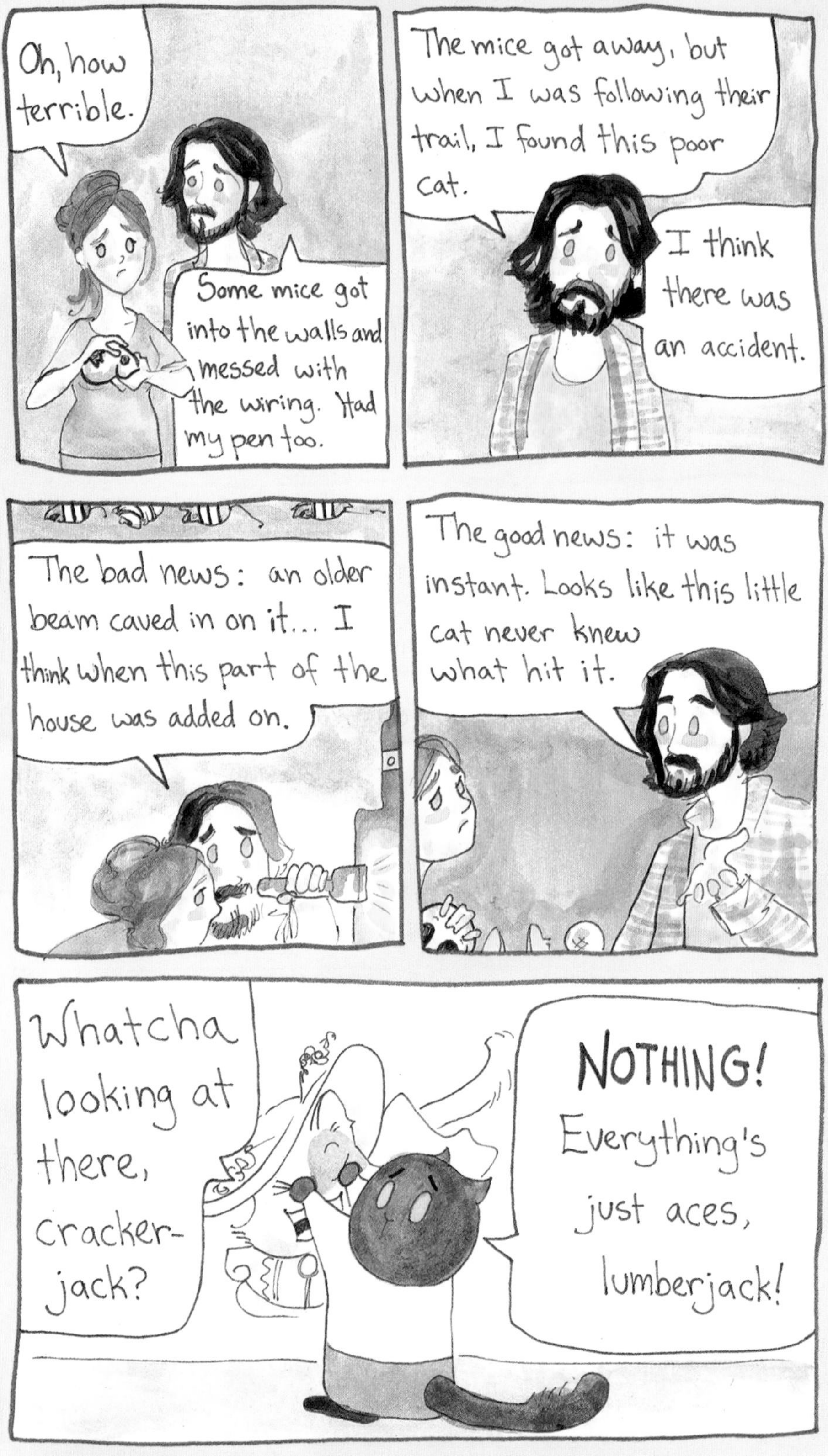
Oh, how terrible.
Some mice got into the walls and messed with the wiring. Had my pen too.
The mice got away, but when I was following their trail, I found this poor cat.
I think there was an accident.
The bad news: an older beam caved in on it... I think when this part of the house was added on.
The good news: it was instant. Looks like this little cat never knew what hit it.
Whatcha looking at there, cracker-jack?
NOTHING! Everything's just aces, lumberjack!

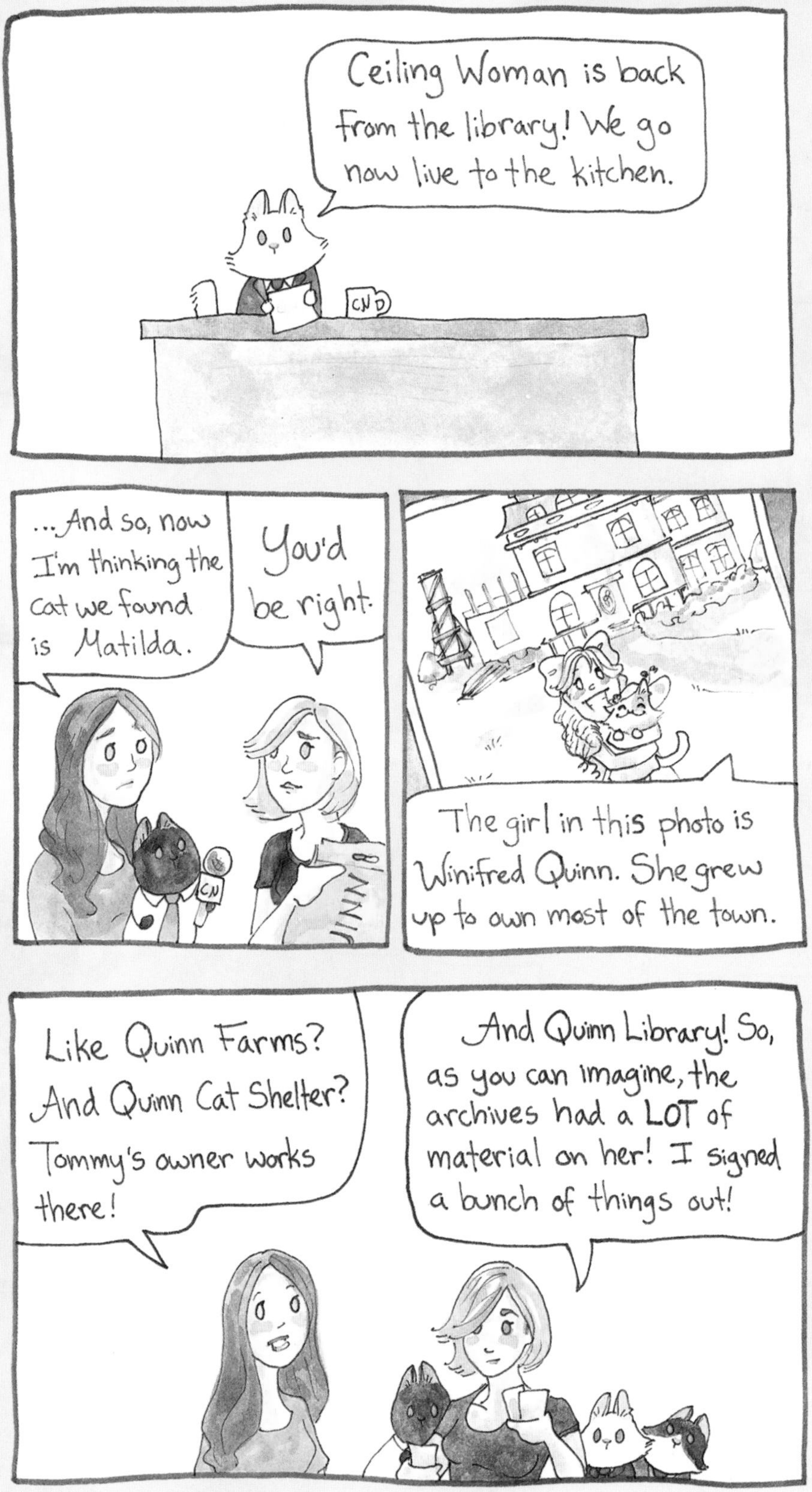
Ceiling Woman is back from the library! We go now live to the kitchen.
CN
...And so, now I'm thinking the cat we found is Matilda.
You'd be right.
CN
The girl in this photo is Winifred Quinn. She grew up to own most of the town.
Like Quinn Farms? And Quinn Cat Shelter? Tommy's owner works there!
And Quinn Library! So, as you can imagine, the archives had a LOT of material on her! I signed a bunch of things out!

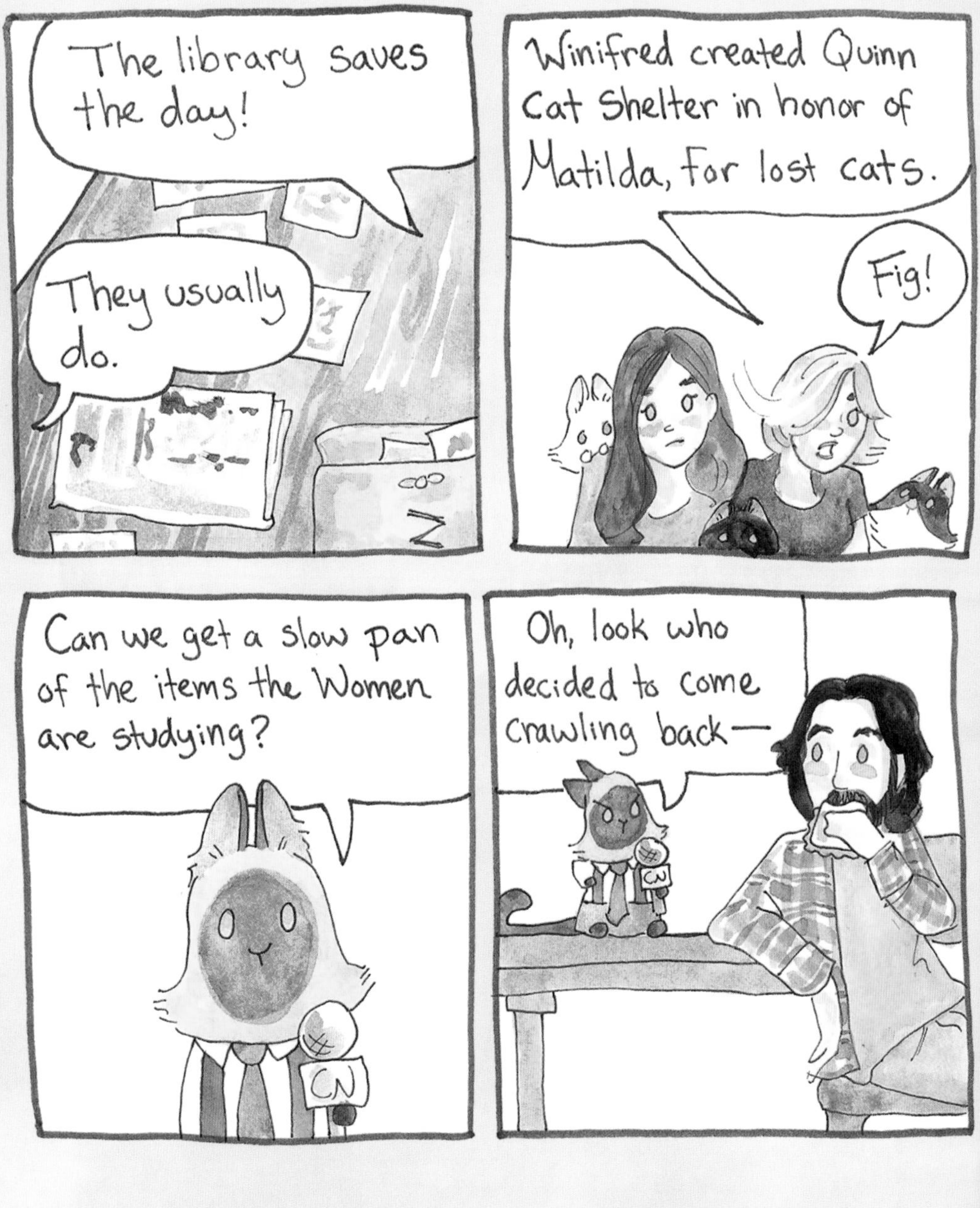
The library saves the day!
They usually do.
Winifred created Quinn Cat Shelter in honor of Matilda, for lost cats.
Fig!
Can we get a slow pan of the items the Women are studying?
Oh, look who decided to come crawling back—

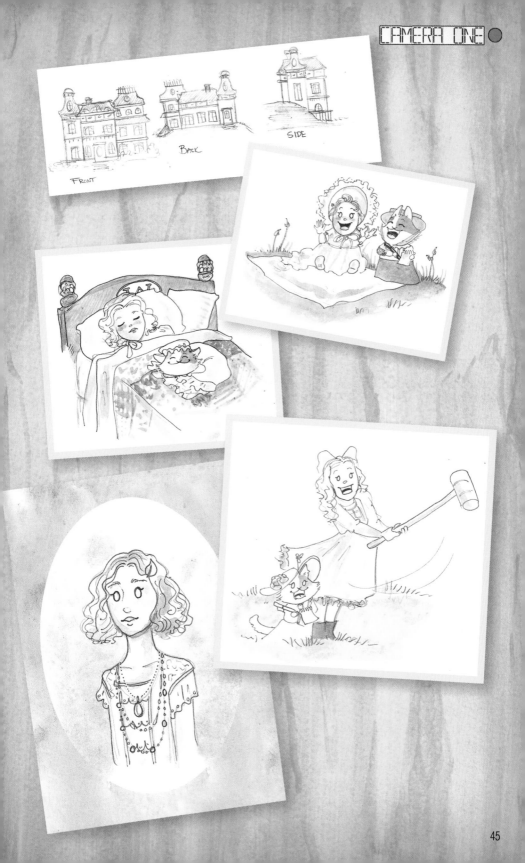

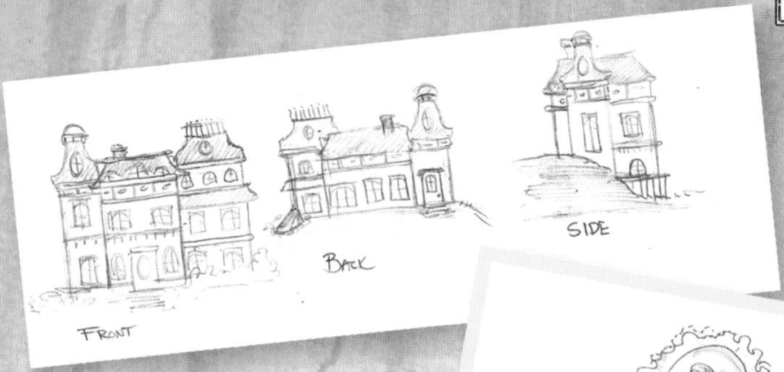
FRONT
BACK
SIDE

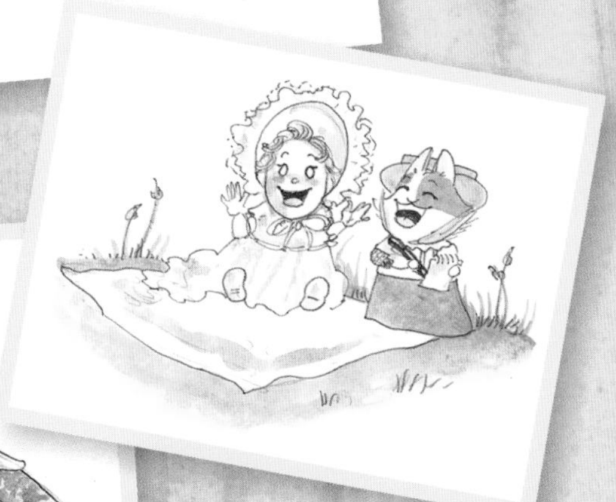

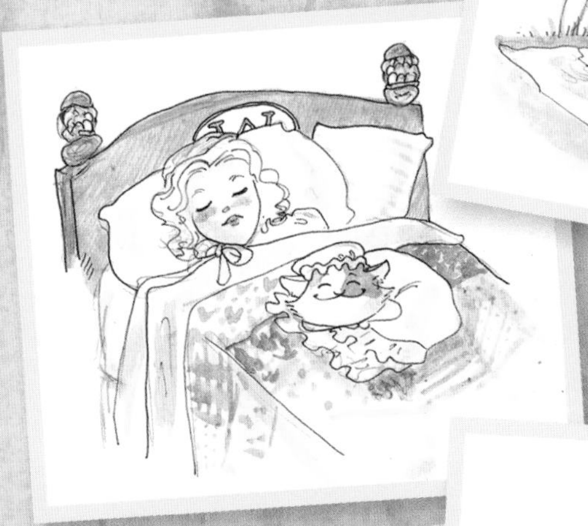

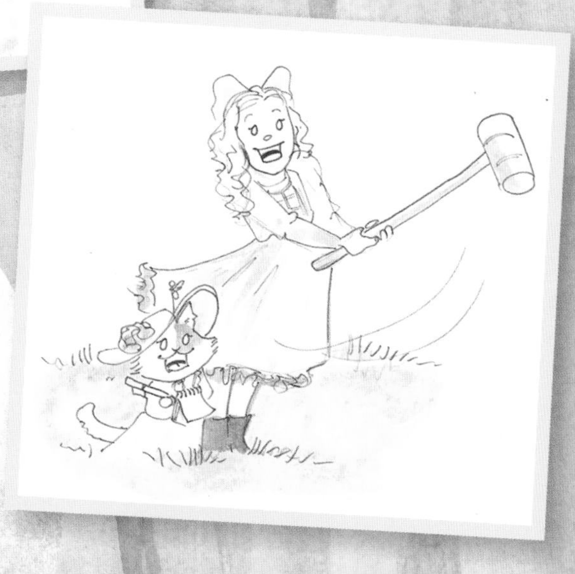

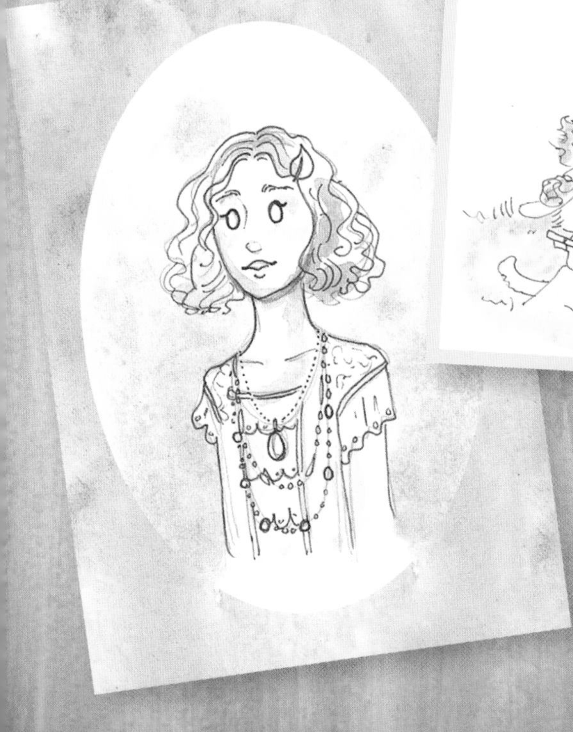

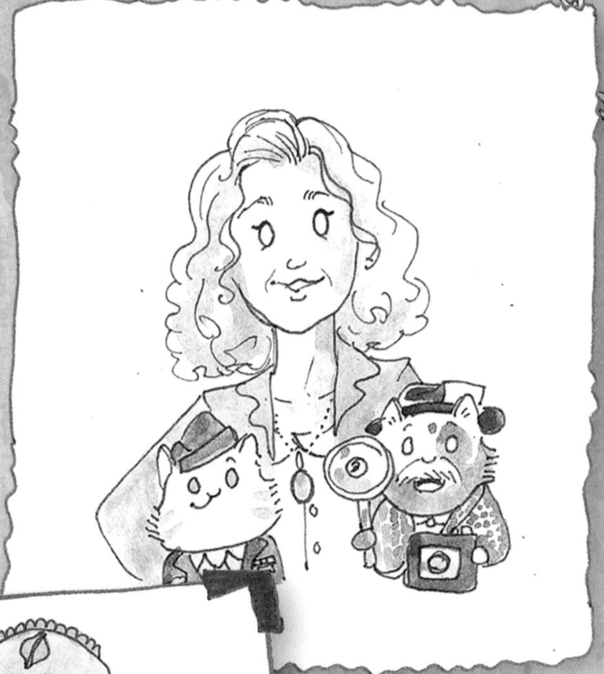

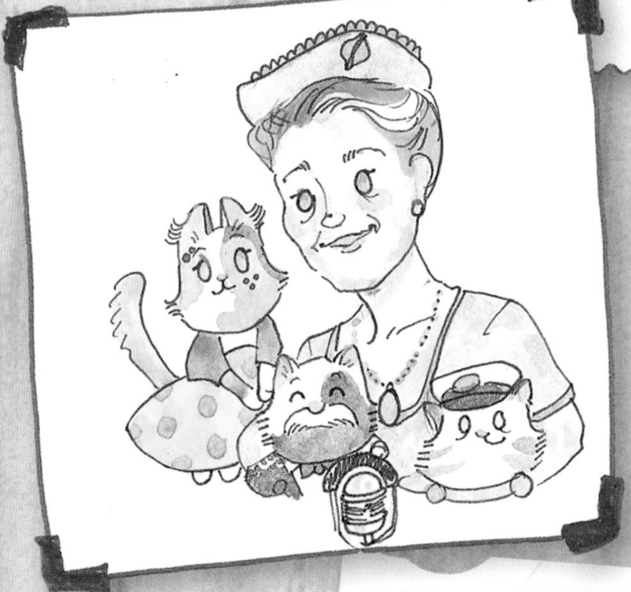

IF YOU FIND A CAT IN NEED, BRING IT TO THE QUINN HOUSE

Winifred Quinn is opening her doors to all local cats in need. "We'll take care of them until we can find them a home—and even if we can't."

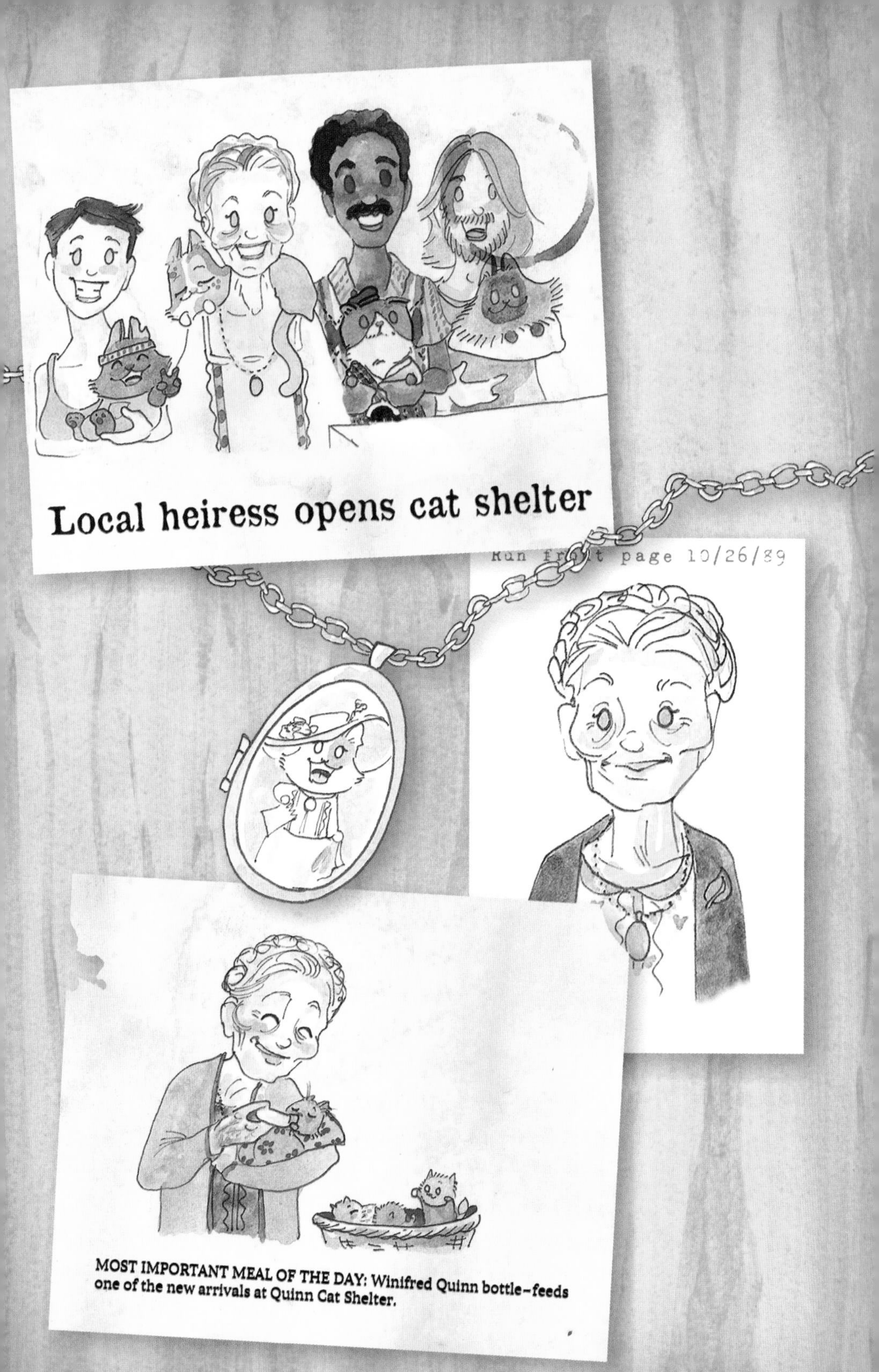
Local heiress opens cat shelter
Run front page 10/26/89
MOST IMPORTANT MEAL OF THE DAY: Winifred Quinn bottle-feeds one of the new arrivals at Quinn Cat Shelter.

October 26, 1989

THE MISSING CAT WHO STARTED IT ALL

WINIFRED QUINN LOOKS BACK

C. Greene

I had a chance recently to sit down with local cat benefactress Winifred Quinn. We began by talking about her childhood cat Matilda.

"Tillie–we called her Tillie–was a marvelous cat. A real spitfire, but gentle as anything. One of those cats who turns up everywhere and gets into everything. Curious, curious! As the story goes, she kept coming into the backyard to 'investigate the new baby' when I was first born. My parents became fond of her, even though I'm sure she was feral, and took her in. To hear them tell it, she had run of the house within days. A real rags to riches story," she says with a chuckle.

"We did everything together. We grew up together, really. And then one day she just disappeared. It was awful." Quinn toys with a locket at her neck and shakes her head. "We never did find her. My parents said she had probably returned to where she came from, but I never believed that. Tillie loved being a Quinn.

"I can't tell you how long I waited for her to return. There are times even now when I think I catch her out of the corner of my eye. Love has no expiration."

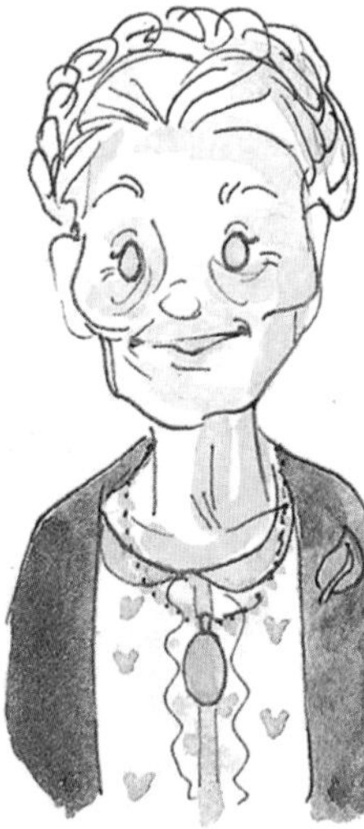

Winifred Quinn, local heiress to the Quinn Mill fortune.

Quinn would go on to become the sole heir to her family's fortune in her 20s, investing in local properties instead of the stock market and holding onto much of the family fortune through the depression and two wars. However, these days she prefers to focus on her investment in... You guessed it.

Cats.

"Ms. Quinn–" I begin.

"Please," she says with a warm smile. "Call me Freddie."

Continued on page B3

YEARS LATER, CATS STILL HAVE ONE WOMAN TO THANK

August 20, 2015

LOCAL SHELTER HONORS FOUNDER

A. Forbes

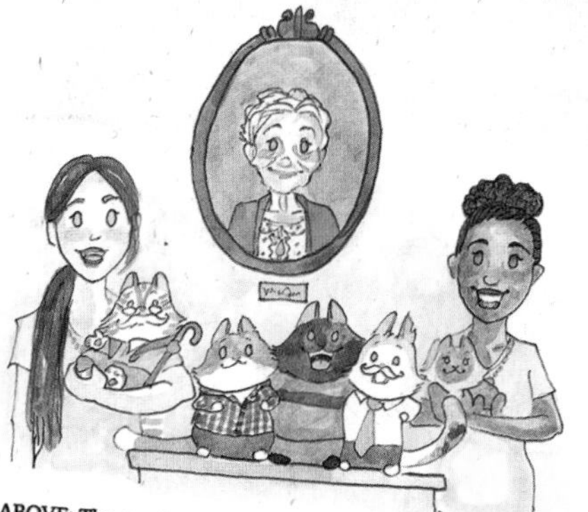

ABOVE: The employees of Quinn Cat Shelter pose with a few of the current residents. All are available for adoption!

ON WHAT WOULD have been Winifred Quinn's 111th birthday, employees of Quinn Cat Shelter placed a lit candle in the front window.

"She did this every year to remember her own lost cat, Tillie. So, now we do it to remember her," the manager explains.

Quinn opened the local shelter in 1968, converting the old stables on her estate into a fully functioning veterinary clinic and safe haven for local cats in need of a temporary home.

"This was her life's legacy," says the manager. Quinn, the sole heir to her family's vast mill fortune, devoted her life to rescue work. Even now, over 25 years after her passing, Quinn Cat Shelter still mostly operates through the support of a trust Quinn established to care for "her" cats. And her touches are felt today even by new employees.

"Each employee—everyone, technician, receptionist, female, male—receives a locket when they're hired. They're encouraged to keep a photo of the the cat who inspired them to go into rescue work inside." The manager adds, "My cat Thomas is in mine."

Personal touches connect today's worker with yesterday's founder.

"She put a lot of thought into

continued A13

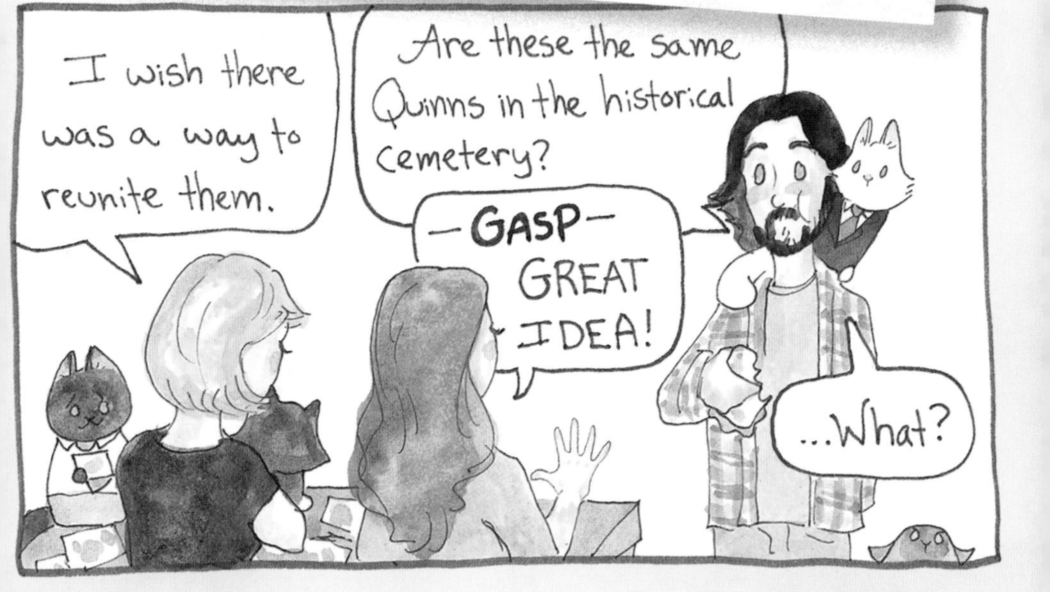
I wish there was a way to reunite them.
Are these the same Quinns in the historical cemetery?
—GASP— GREAT IDEA!
...What?

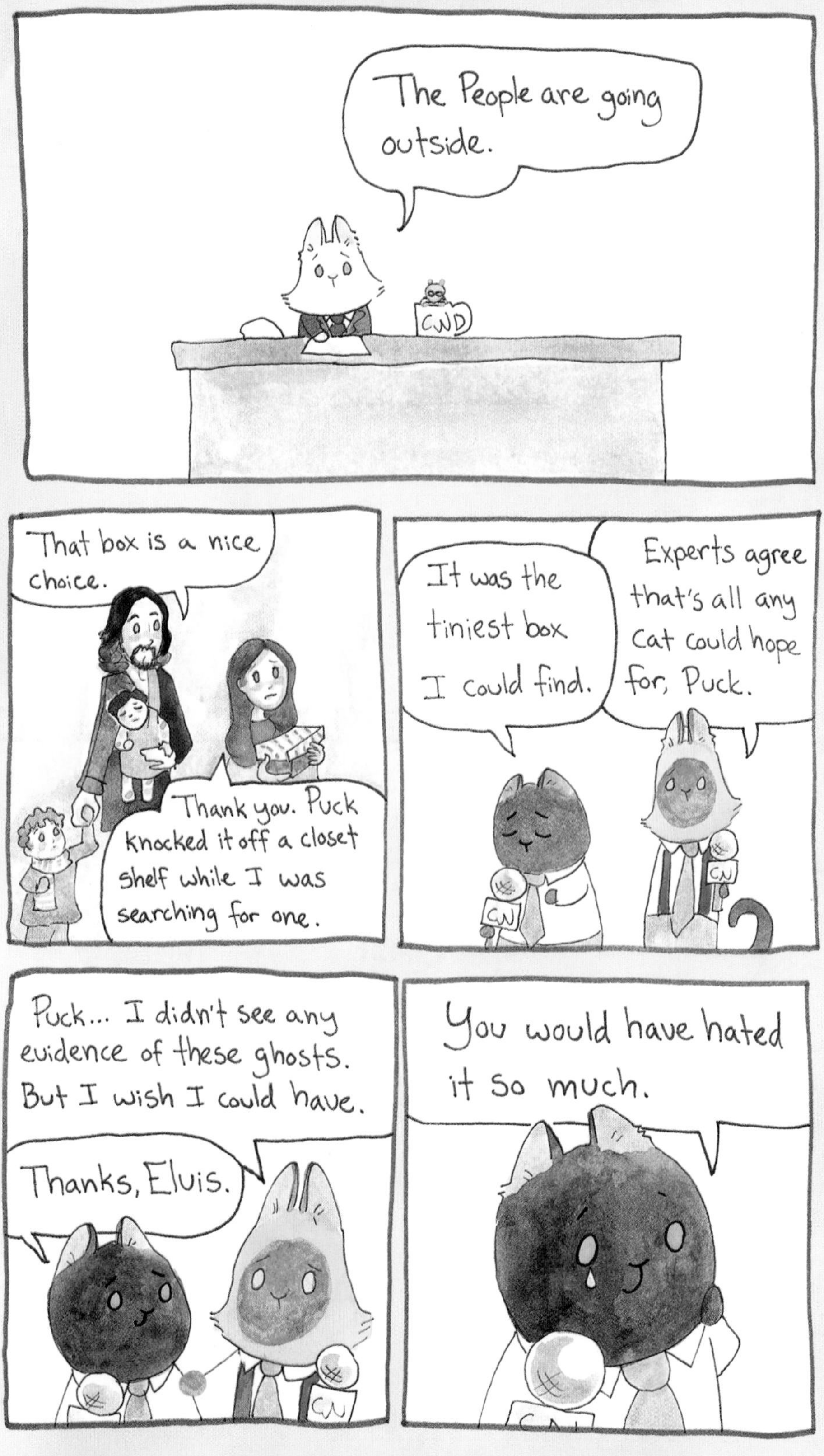
The People are going outside.
That box is a nice choice.
Thank you. Puck knocked it off a closet shelf while I was searching for one.
It was the tiniest box I could find.
Experts agree that's all any cat could hope for, Puck.
Puck... I didn't see any evidence of these ghosts. But I wish I could have.
Thanks, Elvis.
You would have hated it so much.

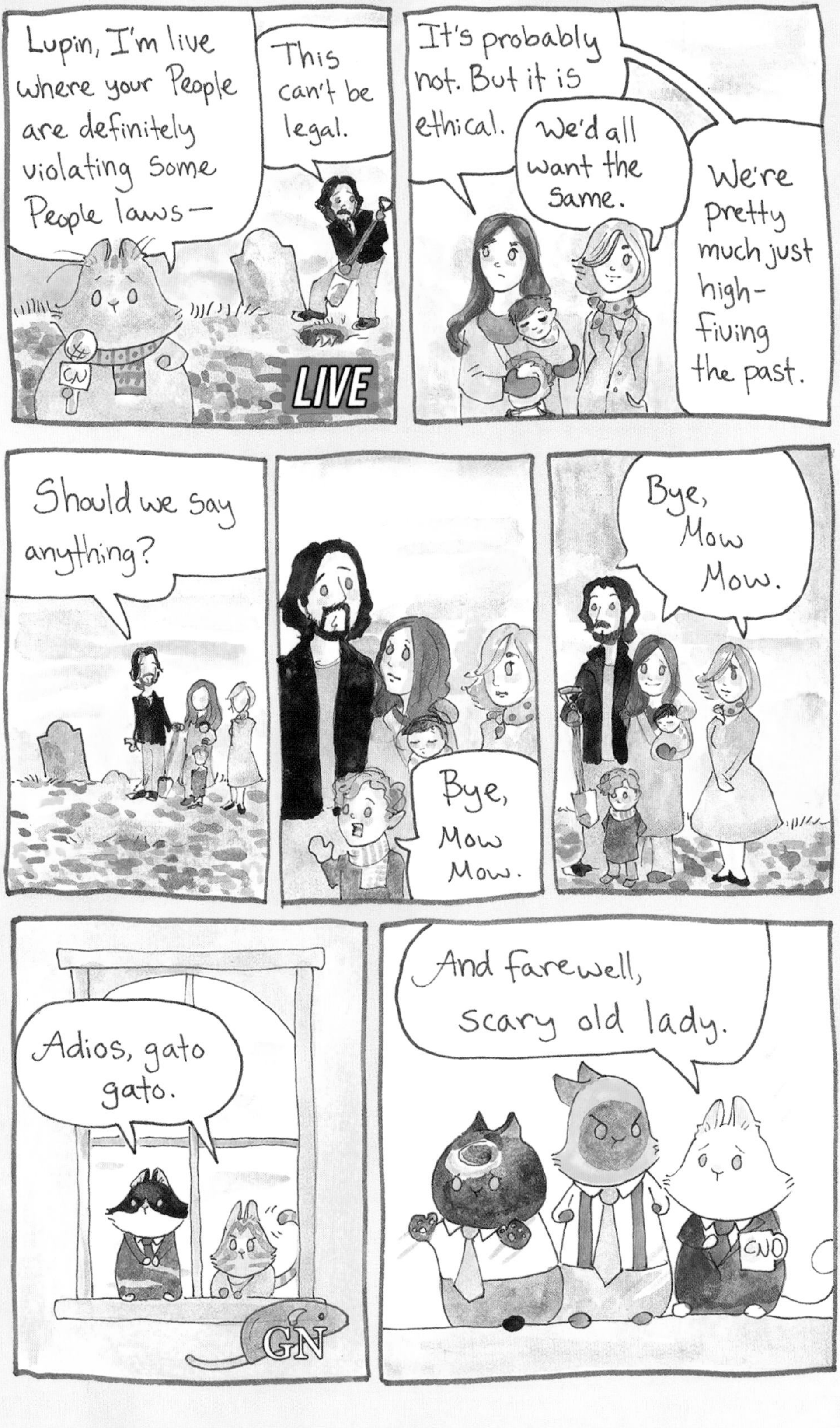
Lupin, I'm live where your People are definitely violating some People laws—
This can't be legal.
LIVE
CN
It's probably not. But it is ethical.
We'd all want the same.
We're pretty much just high-fiving the past.
Should we say anything?
Bye, Mow Mow.
Bye, Mow Mow.
Adios, gato gato.
GN
And farewell, scary old lady.
CNO

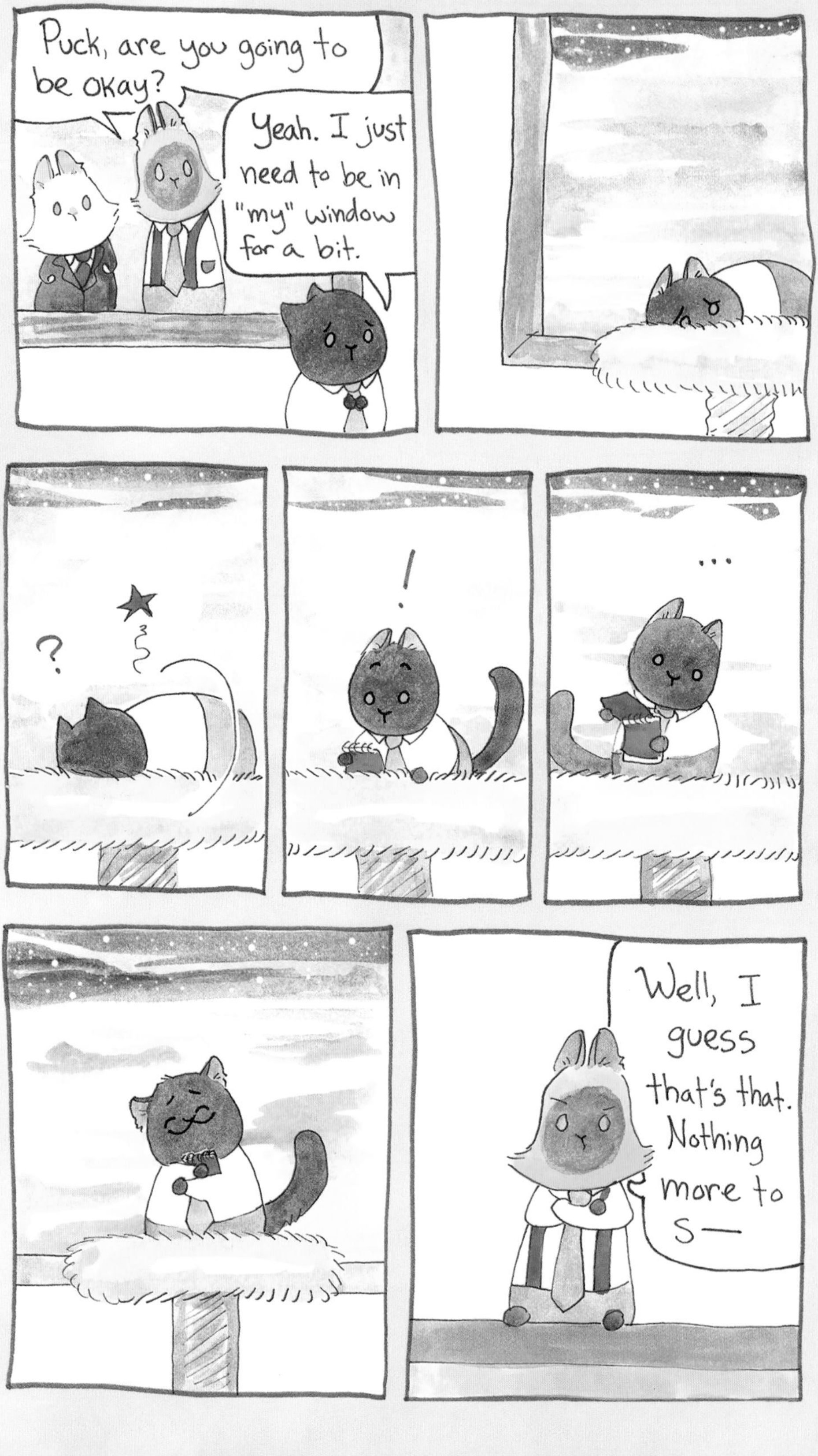

Puck, are you going to be okay?
Yeah. I just need to be in "my" window for a bit.
?
!
...
Well, I guess that's that. Nothing more to s—

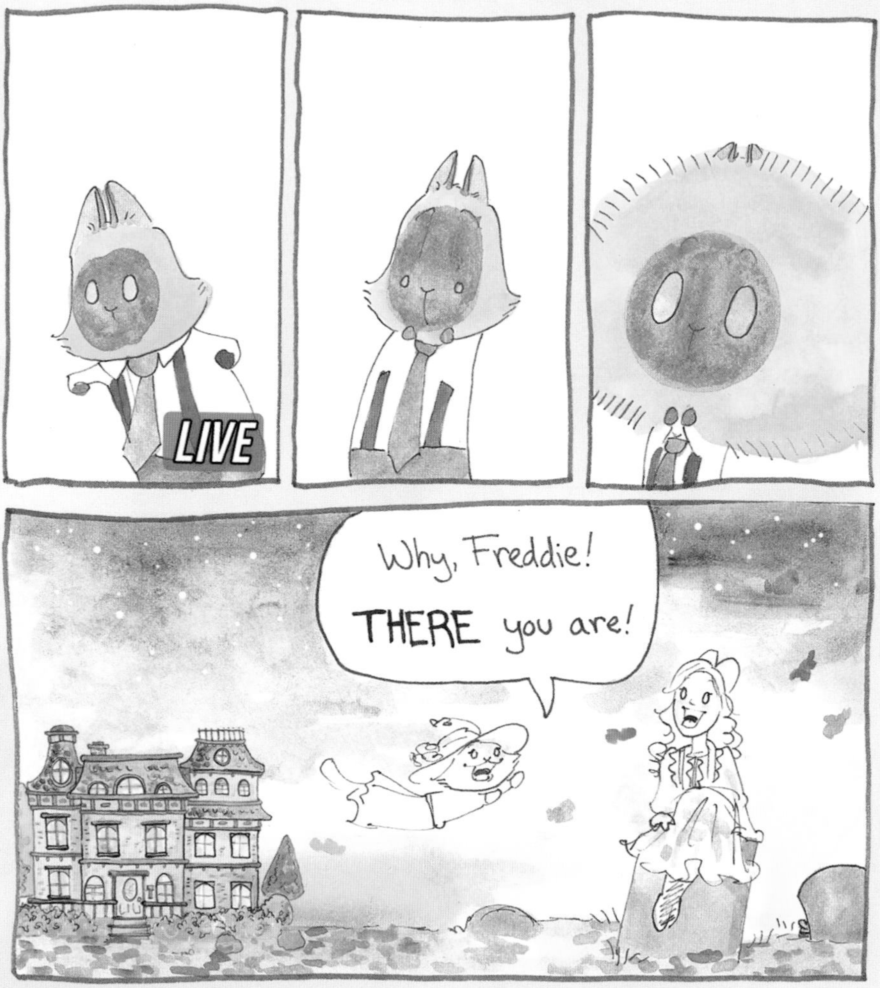
LIVE
Why, Freddie! THERE you are!

I've been waiting for you, old girl!

CAMERA ONE
Till we meet again, Crackerjack!

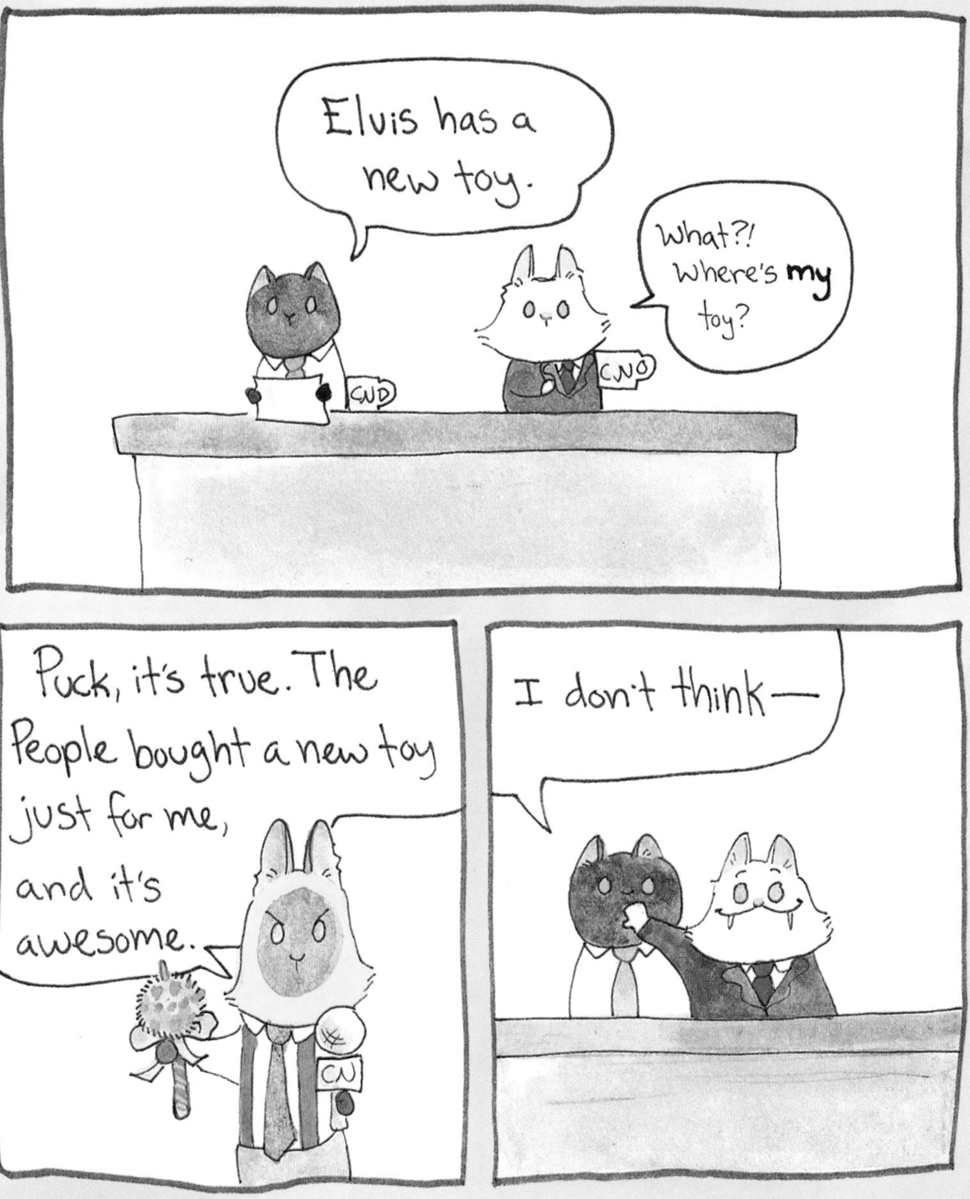
Elvis has a new toy.
What?! Where's **my** toy?
Puck, it's true. The People bought a new toy just for me, and it's awesome.
CN
I don't think—

Elvis, charts prove 9 times out of 10, the People get us toys in 3's.

USUALLY
THAT ONE TIME THE WOMAN STEPPED ON MY TAIL

Such a simple machine.

RATTLE
RATTLE

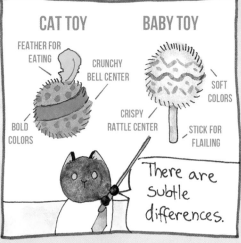

CAT TOY

FEATHER FOR EATING

CRUNCHY BELL CENTER

BOLD COLORS

BABY TOY

SOFT COLORS

CRISPY RATTLE CENTER

STICK FOR FLAILING

There are subtle differences.

The Woman and I have this cute game where she'll take the toy and put it in the Nursery and I have to sneak in and steal it back!

I KEEP WINNING!

Gimme that.

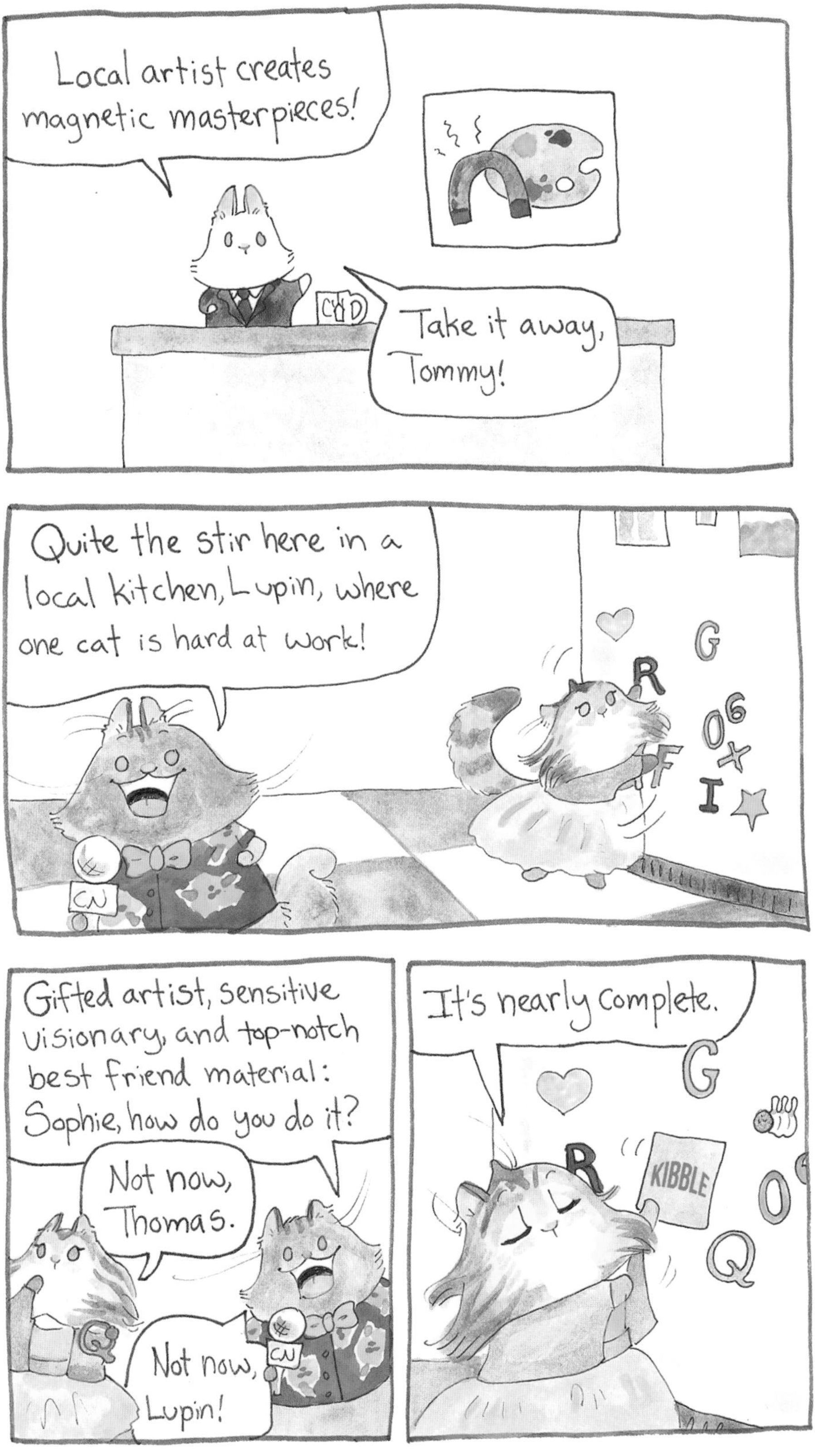
Local artist creates magnetic masterpieces!
Take it away, Tommy!
Quite the stir here in a local kitchen, Lupin, where one cat is hard at work!
Gifted artist, sensitive visionary, and top-notch best friend material: Sophie, how do you do it?
Not now, Thomas.
Not now, Lupin!
It's nearly complete.
KIBBLE

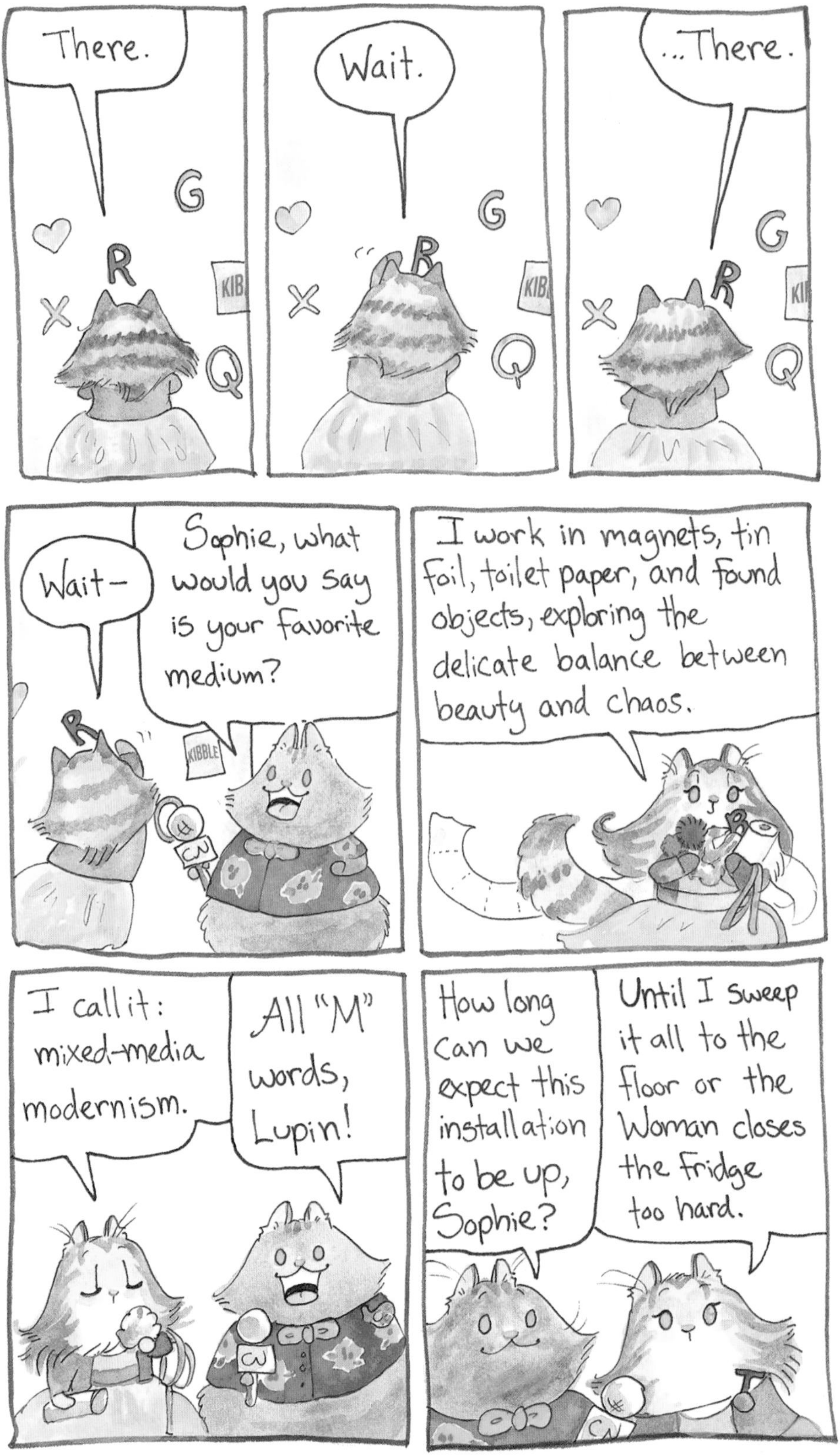
There.
G
R
KIB
Q
Wait.
G
R
KIBB
Q
...There.
G
R
KI
Q
Wait—
Sophie, what would you say is your favorite medium?
R
KIBBLE
CN
I work in magnets, tin foil, toilet paper, and found objects, exploring the delicate balance between beauty and chaos.
I call it: mixed-media modernism.
All "M" words, Lupin!
CN
How long can we expect this installation to be up, Sophie?
Until I sweep it all to the floor or the Woman closes the fridge too hard.
CN

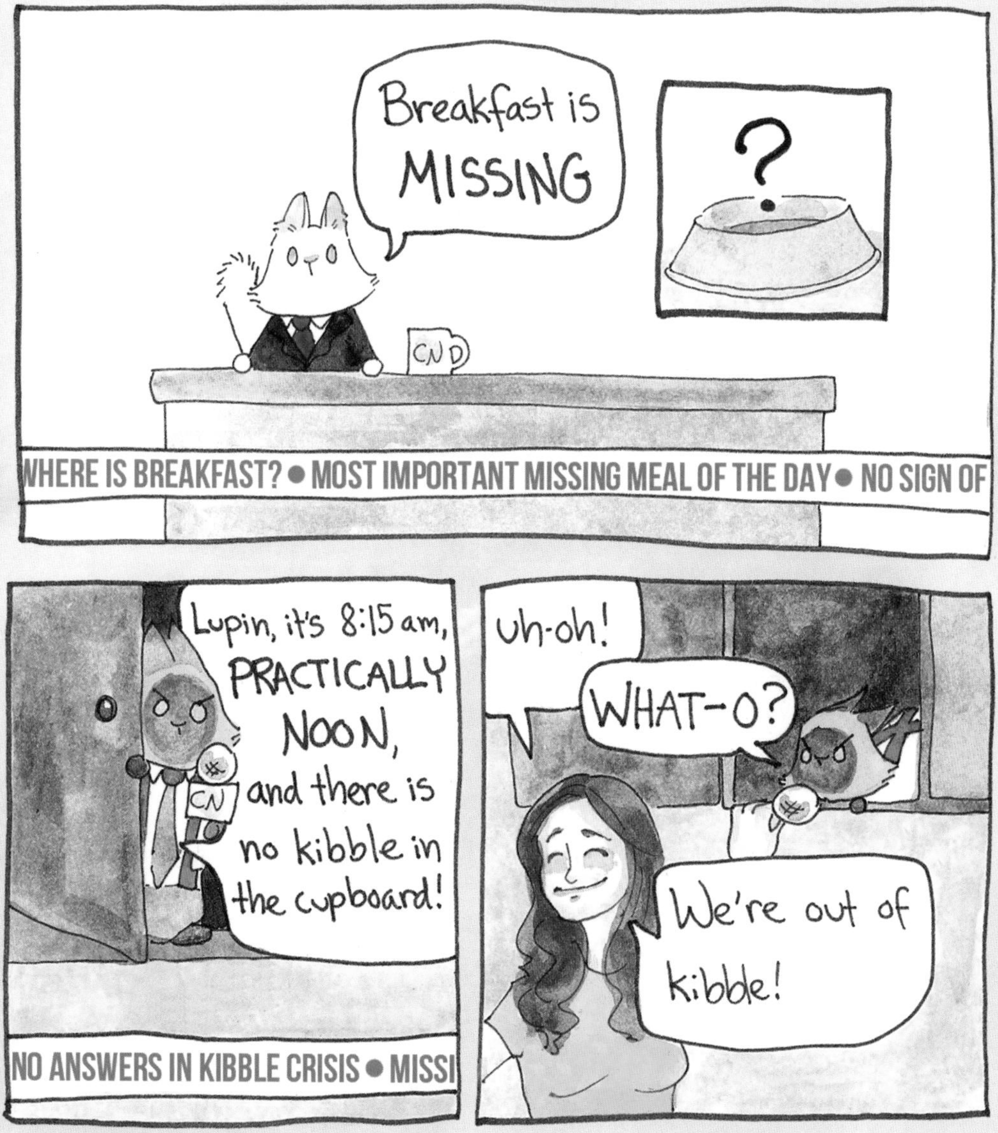
Breakfast is MISSING
?
WHERE IS BREAKFAST? ● MOST IMPORTANT MISSING MEAL OF THE DAY ● NO SIGN OF
Lupin, it's 8:15 am, PRACTICALLY NOON, and there is no kibble in the cupboard!
NO ANSWERS IN KIBBLE CRISIS ● MISSI
uh-oh!
WHAT-O?
We're out of kibble!

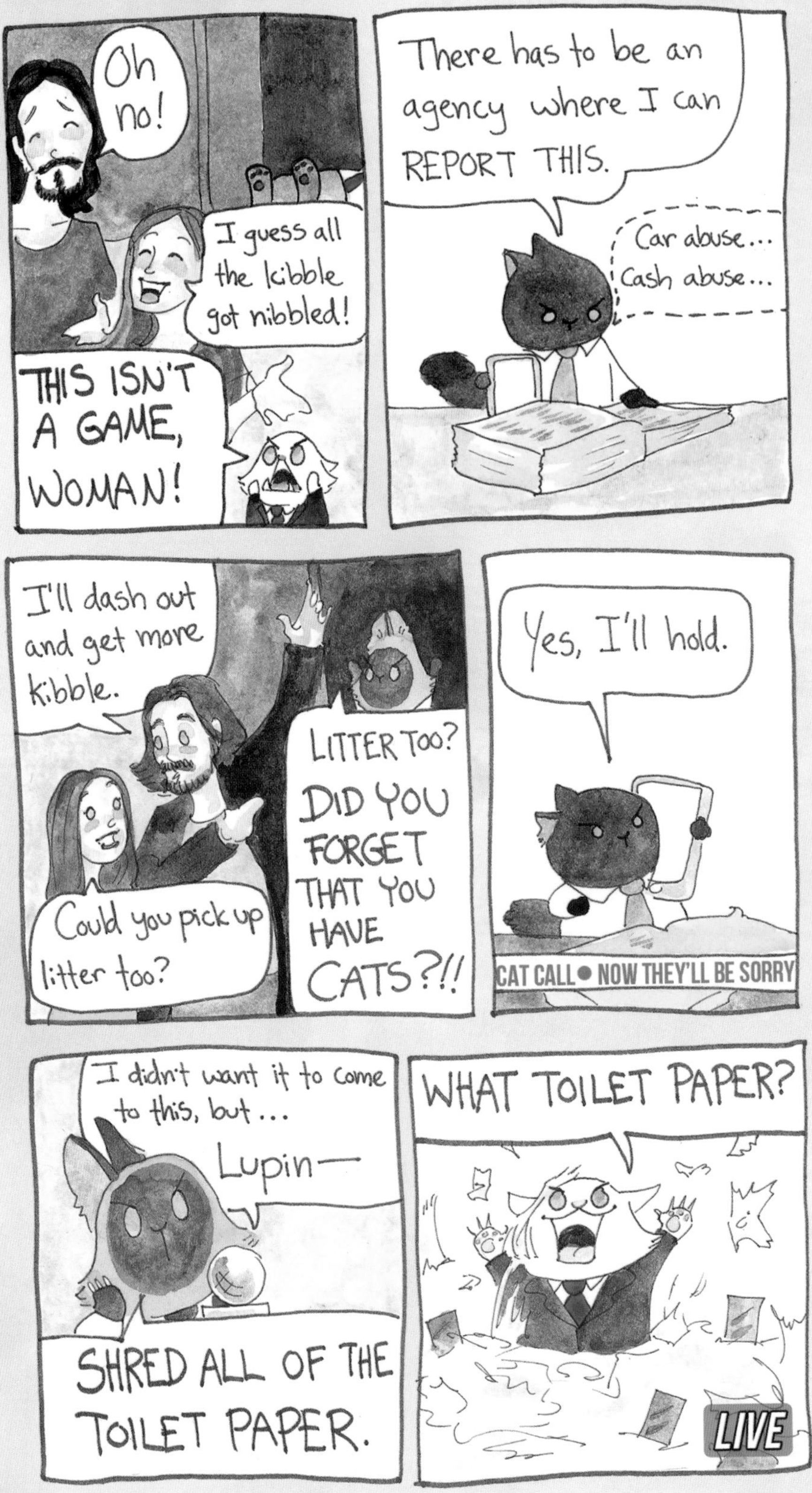
Oh no!
I guess all the kibble got nibbled!
THIS ISN'T A GAME, WOMAN!
There has to be an agency where I can REPORT THIS.
Car abuse... Cash abuse...
I'll dash out and get more kibble.
Could you pick up litter too?
LITTER TOO? DID YOU FORGET THAT YOU HAVE CATS?!!
Yes, I'll hold.
CAT CALL • NOW THEY'LL BE SORRY
I didn't want it to come to this, but...
Lupin—
SHRED ALL OF THE TOILET PAPER.
WHAT TOILET PAPER?
LIVE

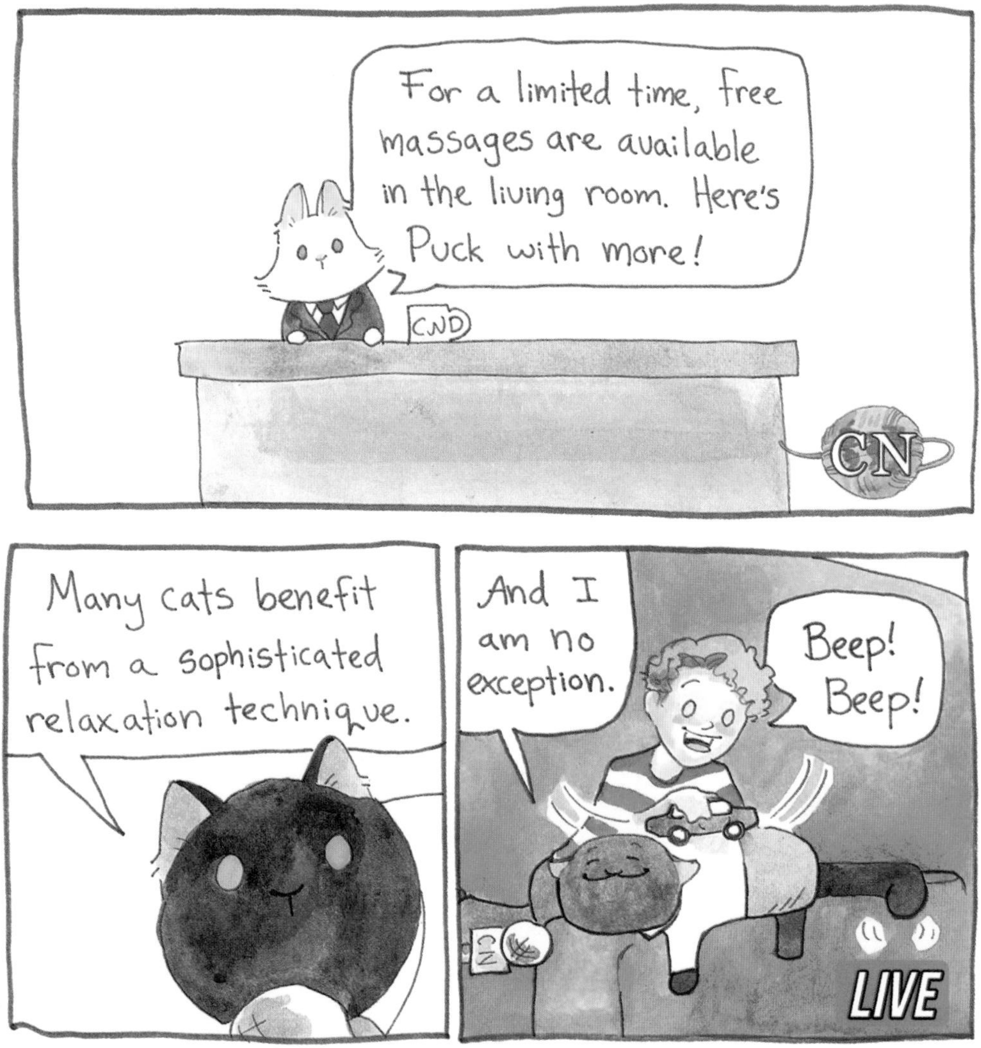
For a limited time, free massages are available in the living room. Here's Puck with more!
CND
CN
Many cats benefit from a sophisticated relaxation technique.
And I am no exception.
Beep! Beep!
CN
LIVE

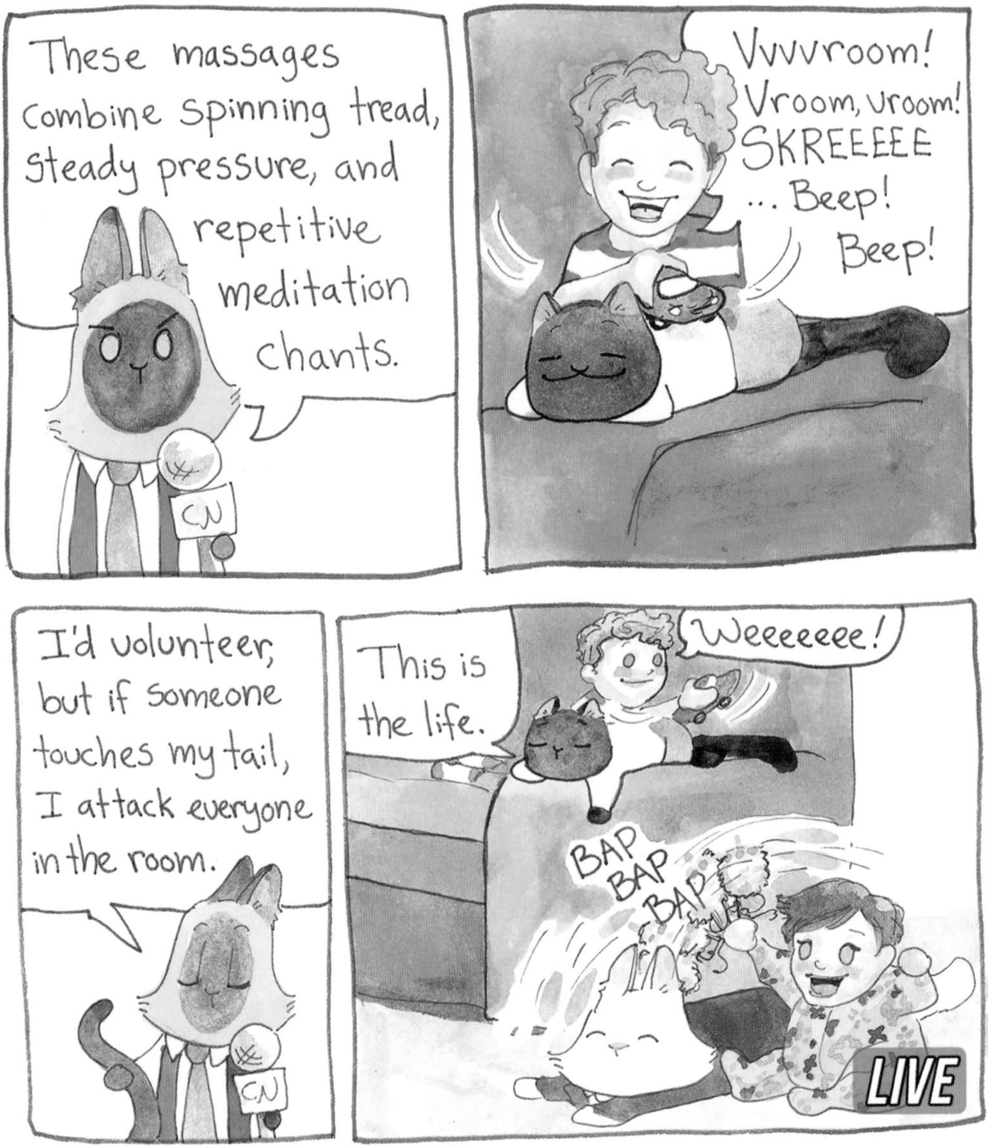
These massages combine spinning tread, steady pressure, and repetitive meditation chants.
CN
Vvvvroom! Vroom, vroom! SKREEEEE ... Beep! Beep!
I'd volunteer, but if someone touches my tail, I attack everyone in the room.
CN
This is the life.
Weeeeeee!
BAP BAP BAP
LIVE

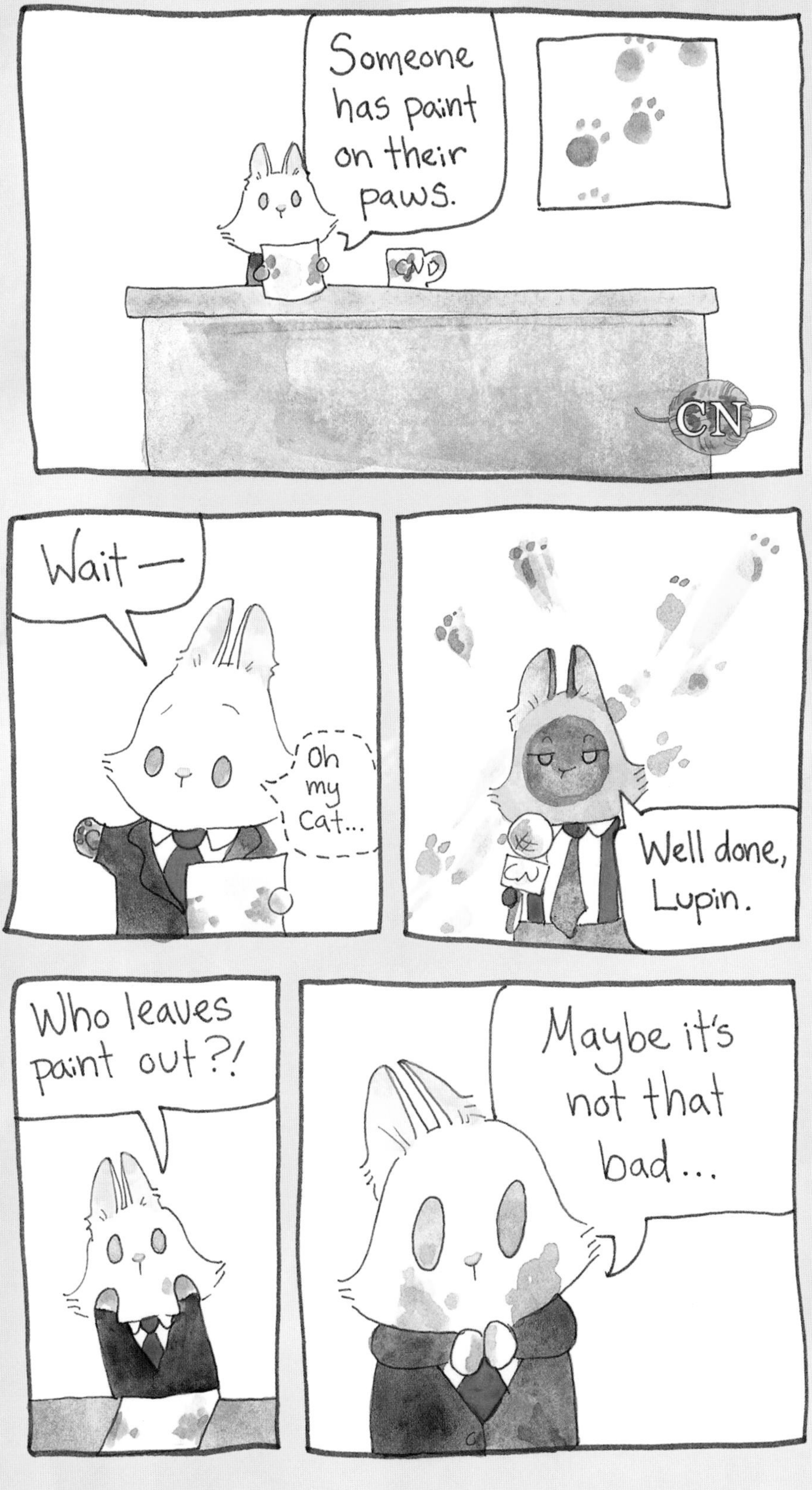
Someone has paint on their paws.
CND
CN
Wait—
Oh my cat...
Well done, Lupin.
CN
Who leaves paint out?!
Maybe it's not that bad...

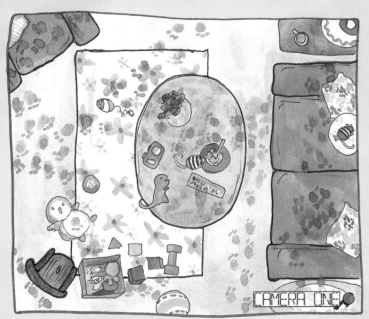

OH MY CAT!

Lupin, I'm live where it looks like maybe the bathroom is being repainted and... Um...

LIVE

Why did you have to race all over the apartment?!

I DON'T KNOW WHY I DO THIS STUFF!

Quick! Clean my paws!

I don't even like paint...

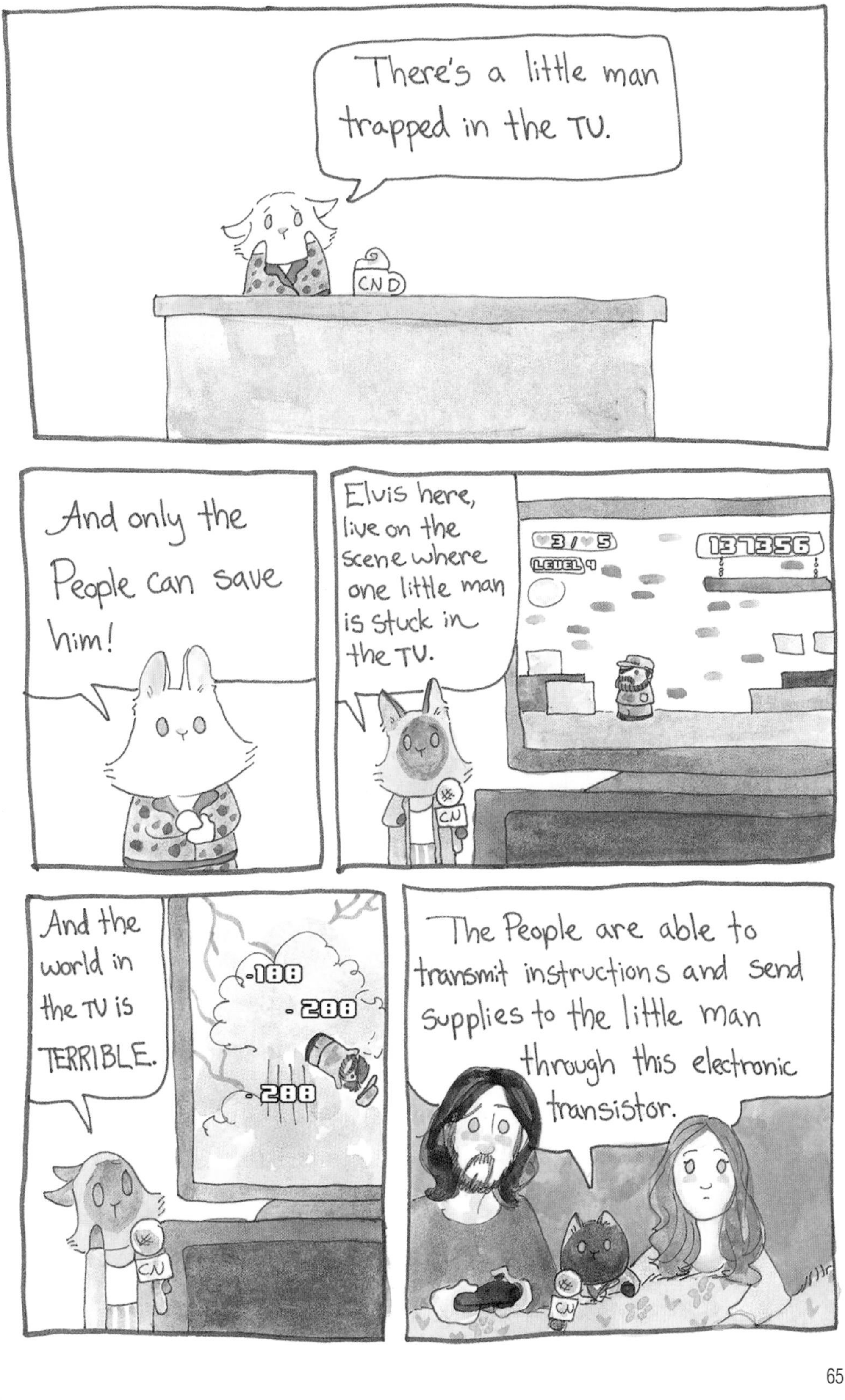
There's a little man trapped in the TV.
CND
And only the People can save him!
Elvis here, live on the scene where one little man is stuck in the TV.
3 / 5
LEVEL 4
137356
CN
And the world in the TV is TERRIBLE.
-100
-200
-200
CN
The People are able to transmit instructions and send supplies to the little man through this electronic transistor.
CN

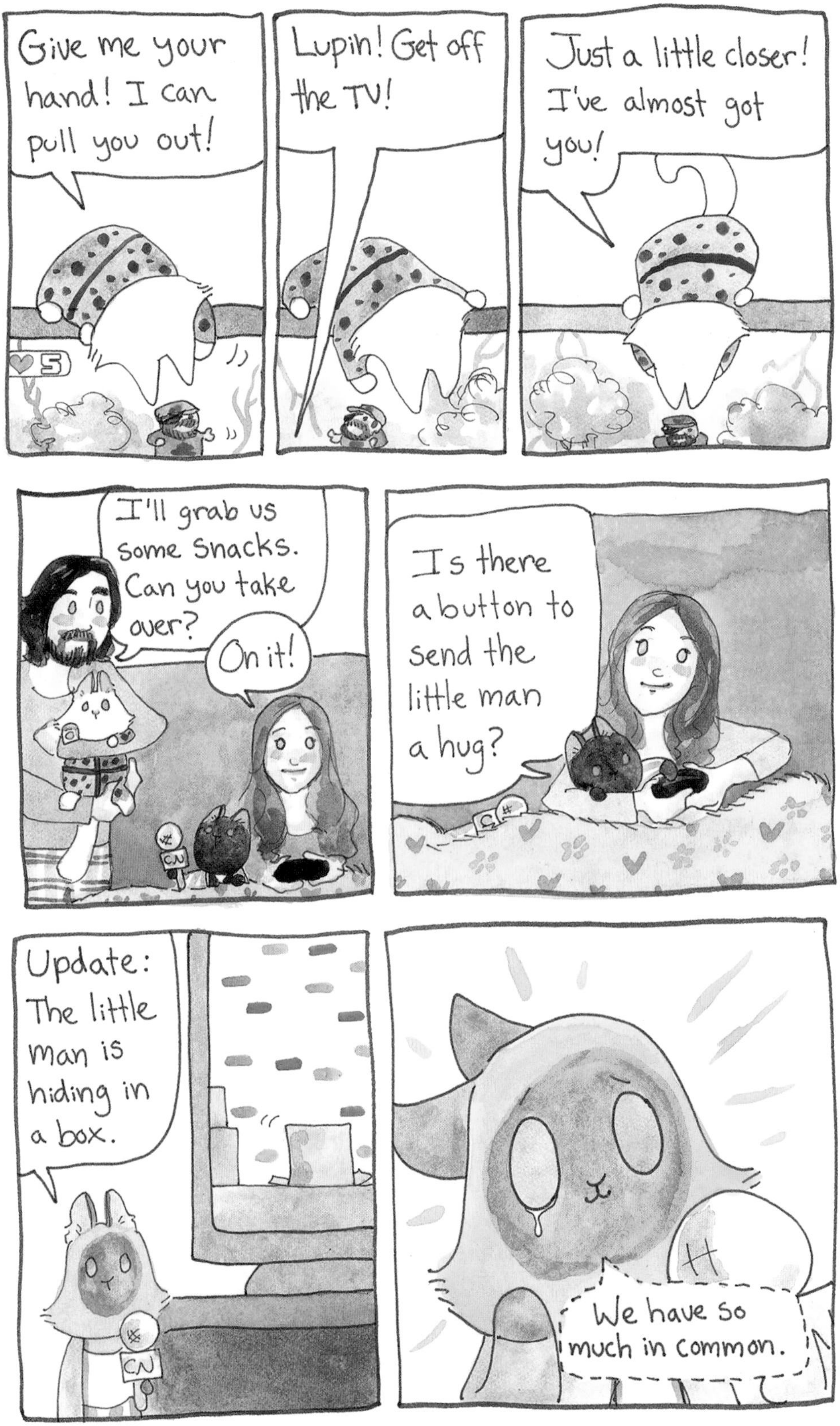
Give me your hand! I can pull you out!
5
Lupin! Get off the TV!
Just a little closer! I've almost got you!
I'll grab us some snacks. Can you take over?
On it!
CN
Is there a button to send the little man a hug?
Update: The little man is hiding in a box.
CN
We have so much in common.

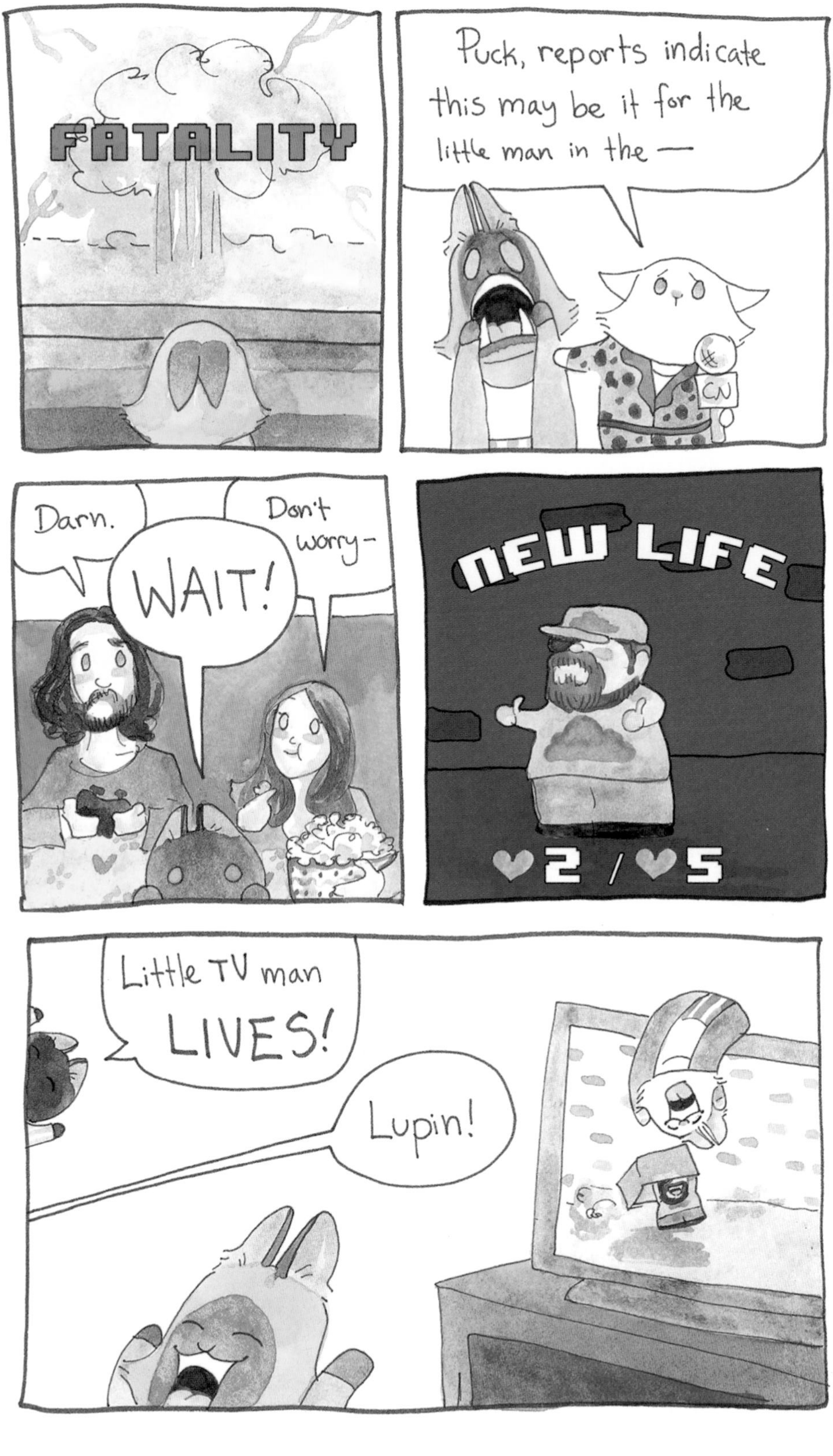
FATALITY
Puck, reports indicate this may be it for the little man in the —
CN
Darn.
WAIT!
Don't worry-
NEW LIFE
2 / 5
Little TV man LIVES!
Lupin!

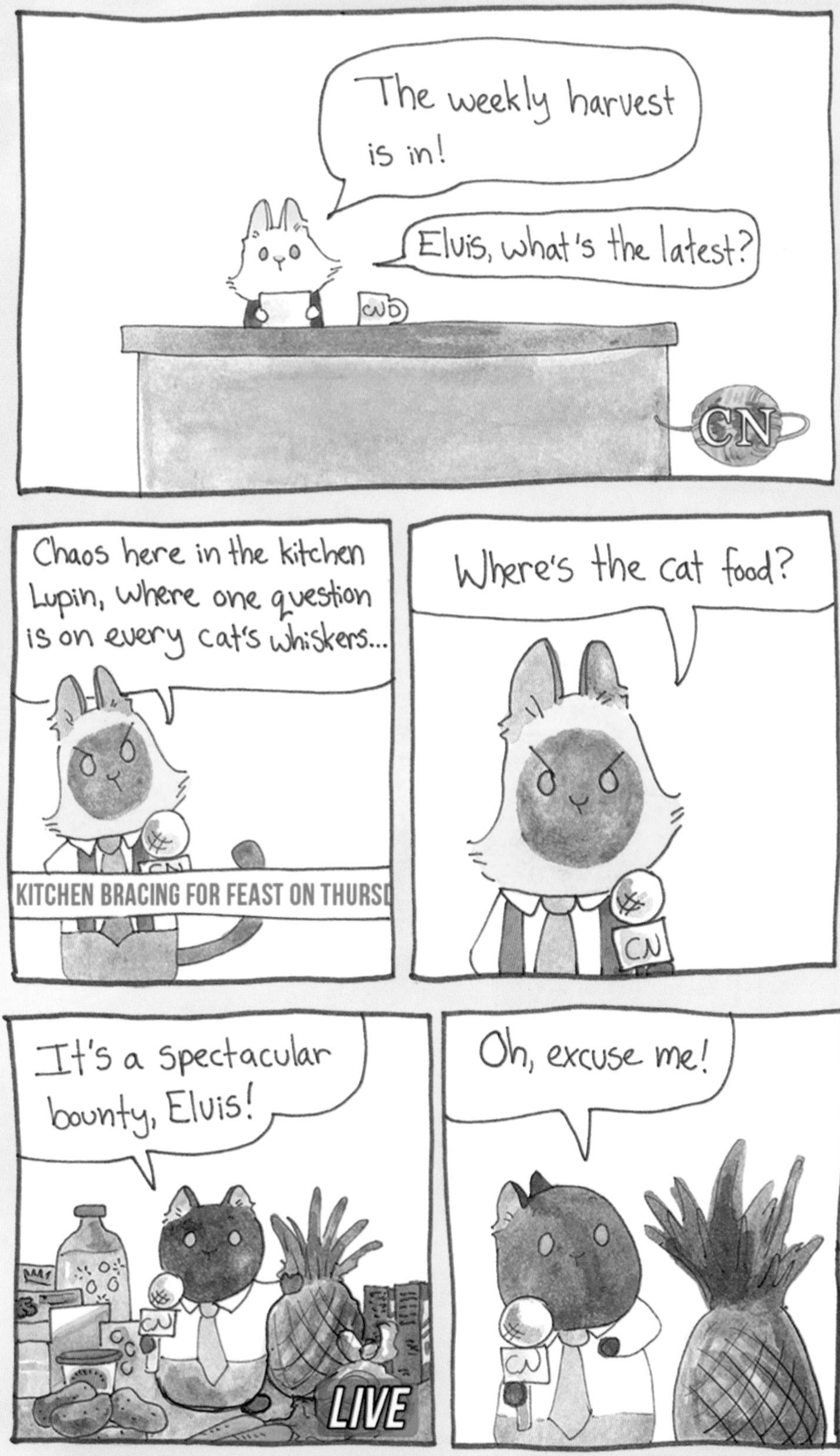

The weekly harvest is in!
Elvis, what's the latest?
CN
Chaos here in the kitchen Lupin, where one question is on every cat's whiskers...
KITCHEN BRACING FOR FEAST ON THURSD
Where's the cat food?
It's a spectacular bounty, Elvis!
LIVE
Oh, excuse me!

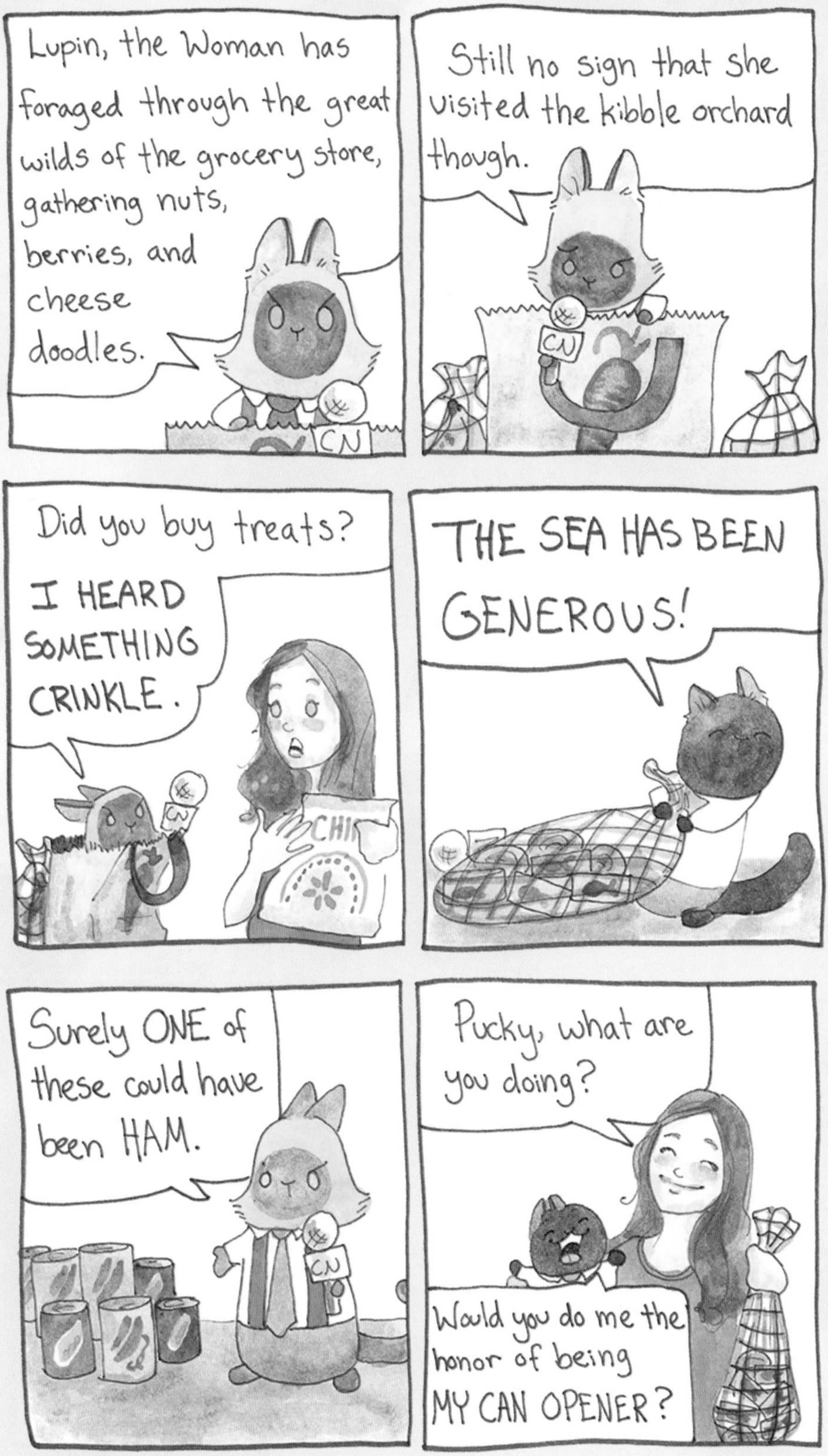
Lupin, the Woman has foraged through the great wilds of the grocery store, gathering nuts, berries, and cheese doodles.
CN
Still no sign that she visited the kibble orchard though.
CN
Did you buy treats?
I HEARD SOMETHING CRINKLE.
CN
CHI
THE SEA HAS BEEN GENEROUS!
Surely ONE of these could have been HAM.
CN
Pucky, what are you doing?
Would you do me the honor of being MY CAN OPENER?

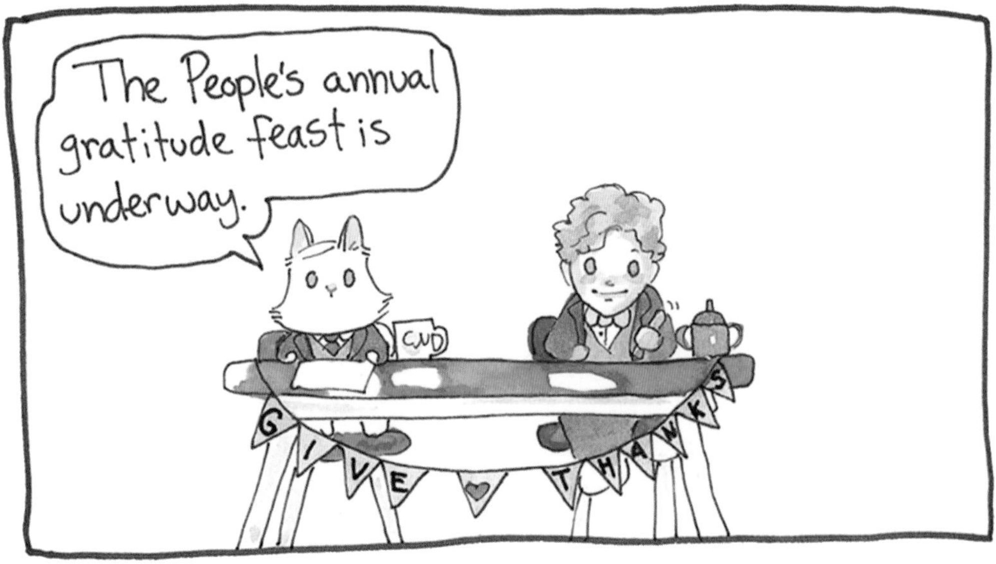
The People's annual gratitude feast is underway.
GIVE THANKS

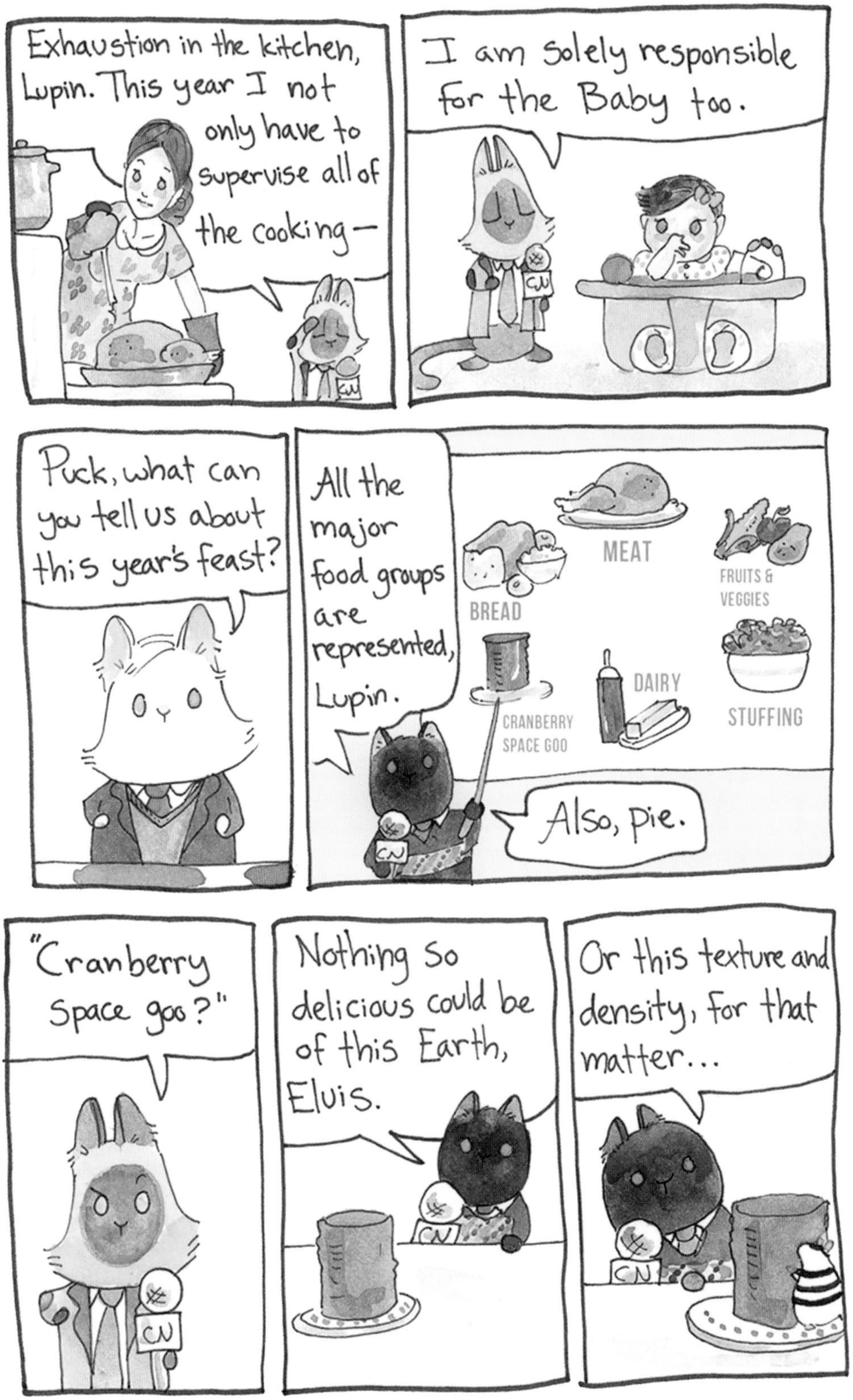
Exhaustion in the kitchen, Lupin. This year I not only have to supervise all of the cooking—
I am solely responsible for the Baby too.
Puck, what can you tell us about this year's feast?
All the major food groups are represented, Lupin.
MEAT
BREAD
FRUITS & VEGGIES
DAIRY
STUFFING
CRANBERRY SPACE GOO
Also, pie.
"Cranberry Space goo?"
Nothing so delicious could be of this Earth, Elvis.
Or this texture and density, for that matter...

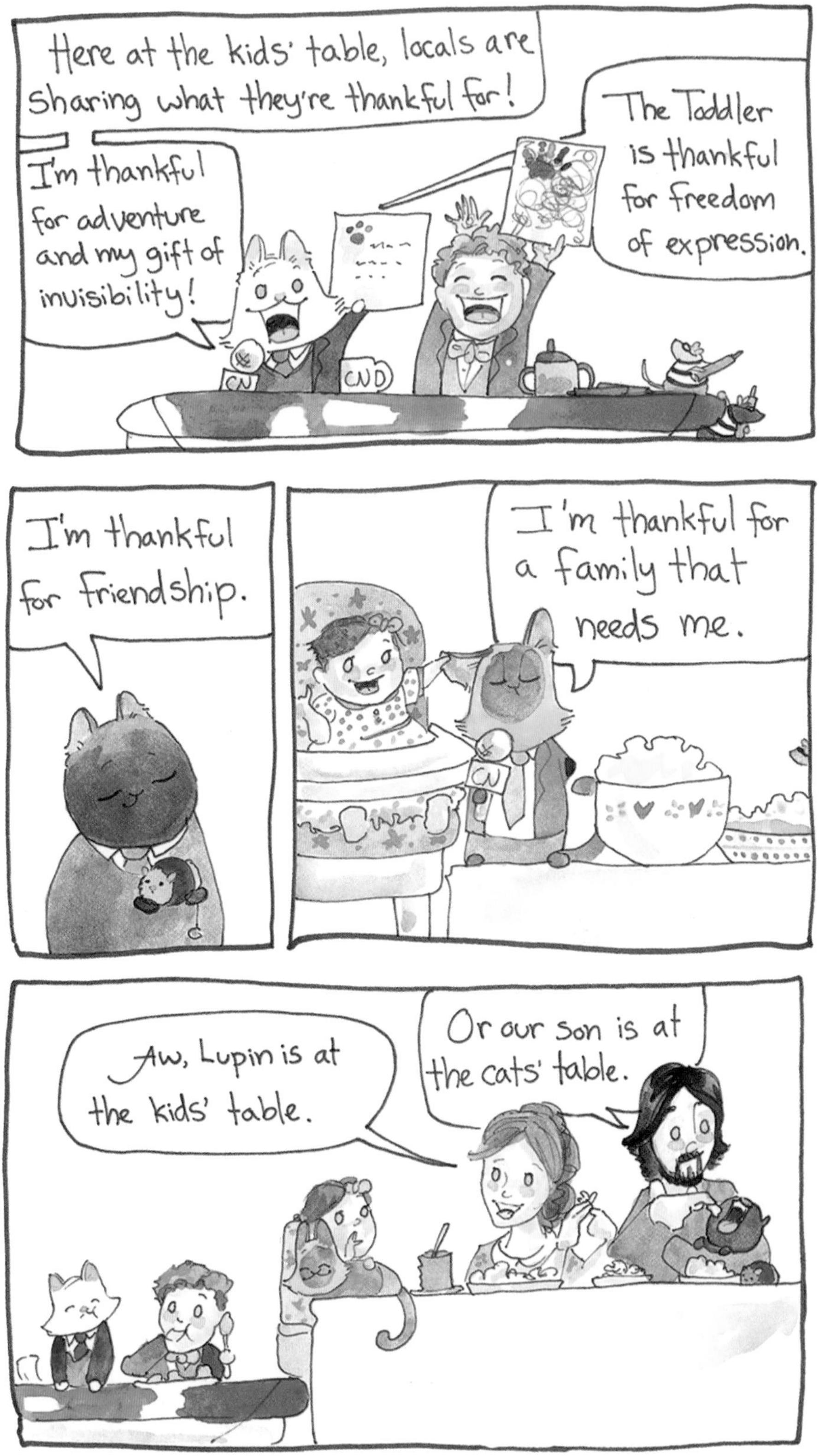
Here at the kids' table, locals are sharing what they're thankful for!
I'm thankful for adventure and my gift of invisibility!
The Toddler is thankful for freedom of expression.
CN
CND
I'm thankful for friendship.
I'm thankful for a family that needs me.
CN
Aw, Lupin is at the kids' table.
Or our son is at the cats' table.

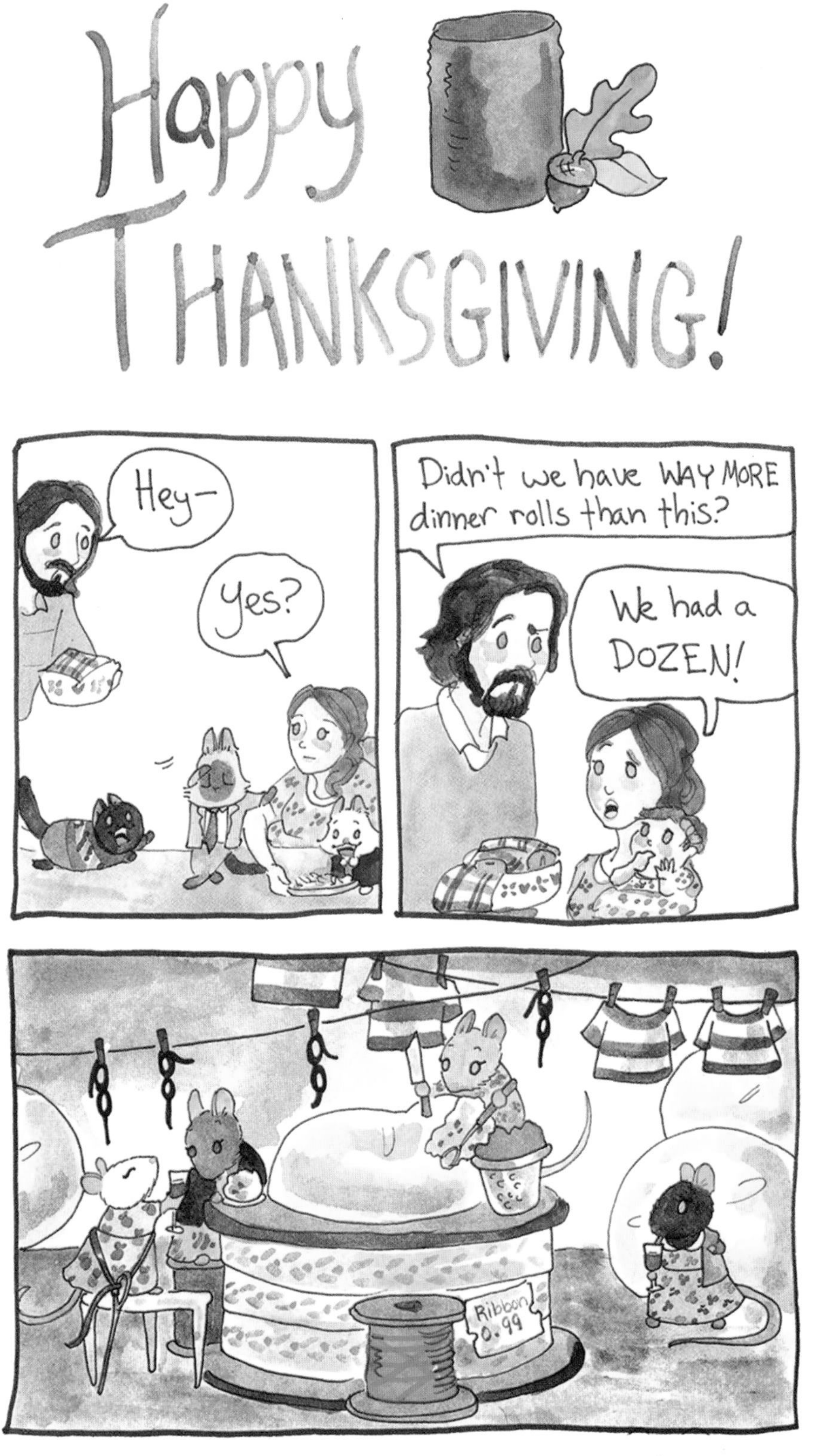
Happy
THANKSGIVING!
Hey–
Yes?
Didn't we have WAY MORE dinner rolls than this?
We had a DOZEN!
Ribbon
0.99

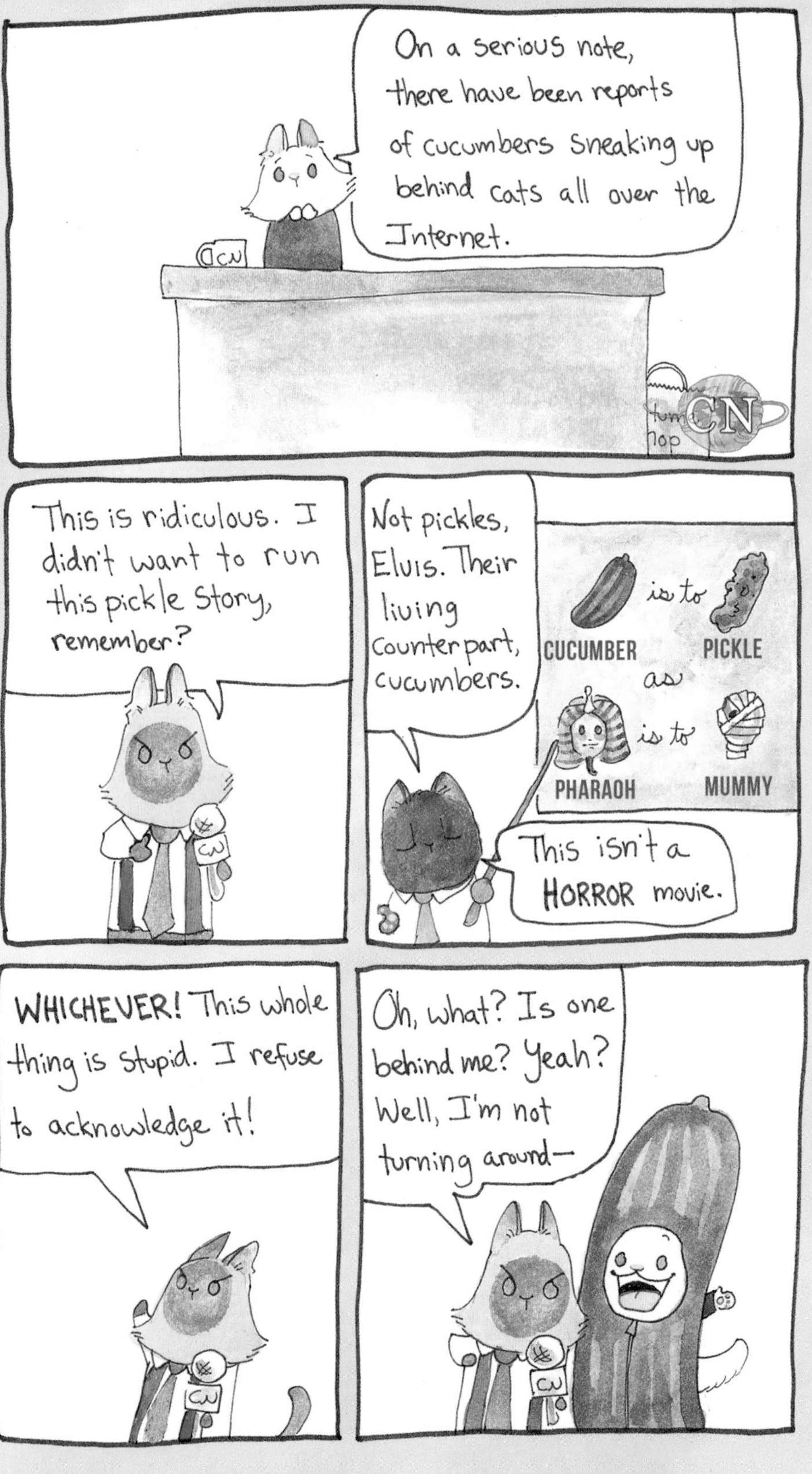
On a serious note, there have been reports of cucumbers sneaking up behind cats all over the Internet.
This is ridiculous. I didn't want to run this pickle story, remember?
Not pickles, Elvis. Their living counterpart, cucumbers.
CUCUMBER
is to
PICKLE
as
PHARAOH
is to
MUMMY
This isn't a HORROR movie.
WHICHEVER! This whole thing is stupid. I refuse to acknowledge it!
Oh, what? Is one behind me? Yeah? Well, I'm not turning around—

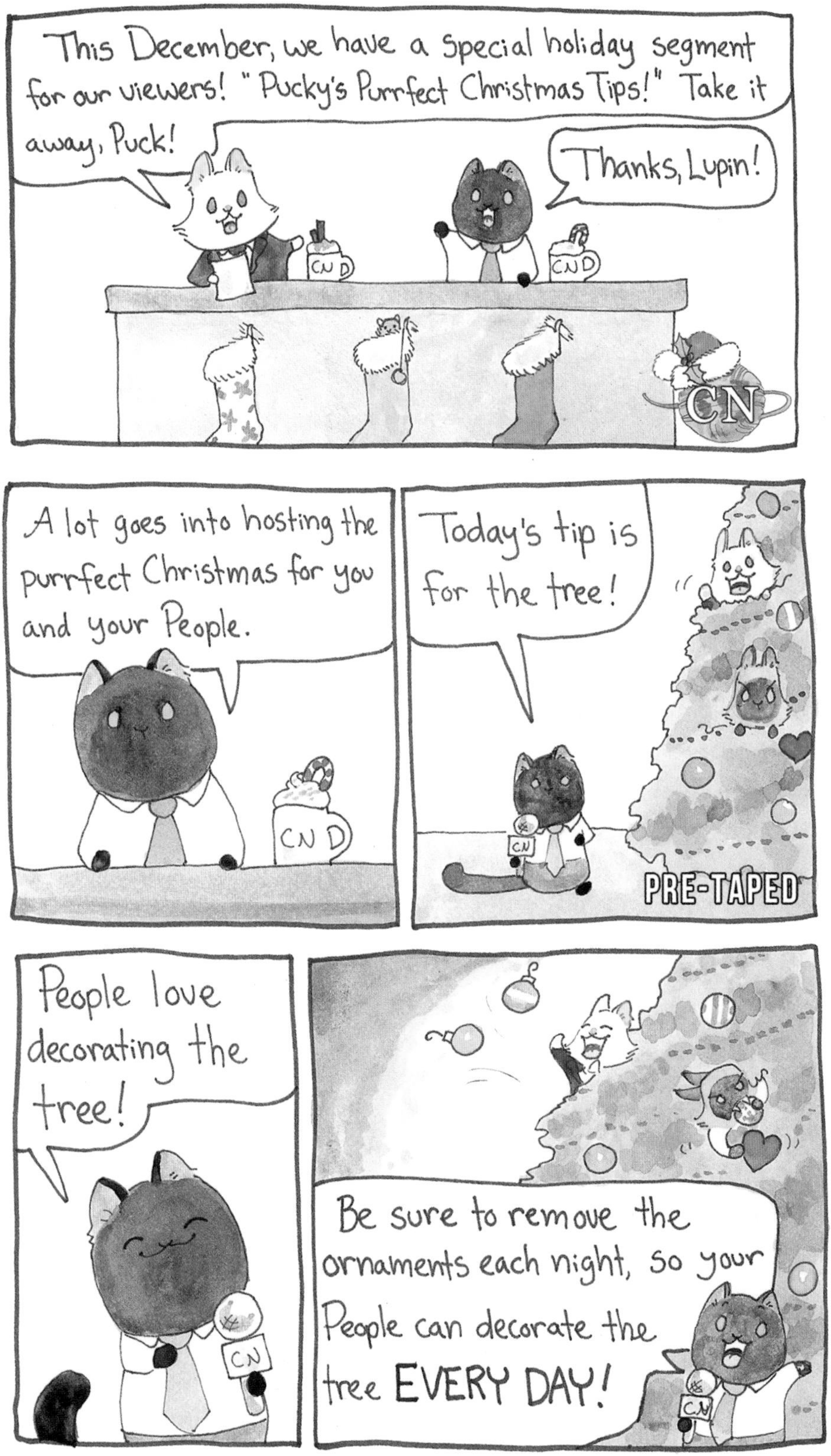
This December, we have a special holiday segment for our viewers! "Pucky's Purrfect Christmas Tips!" Take it away, Puck!
Thanks, Lupin!
CN
A lot goes into hosting the purrfect Christmas for you and your People.
Today's tip is for the tree!
PRE-TAPED
People love decorating the tree!
Be sure to remove the ornaments each night, so your People can decorate the tree EVERY DAY!

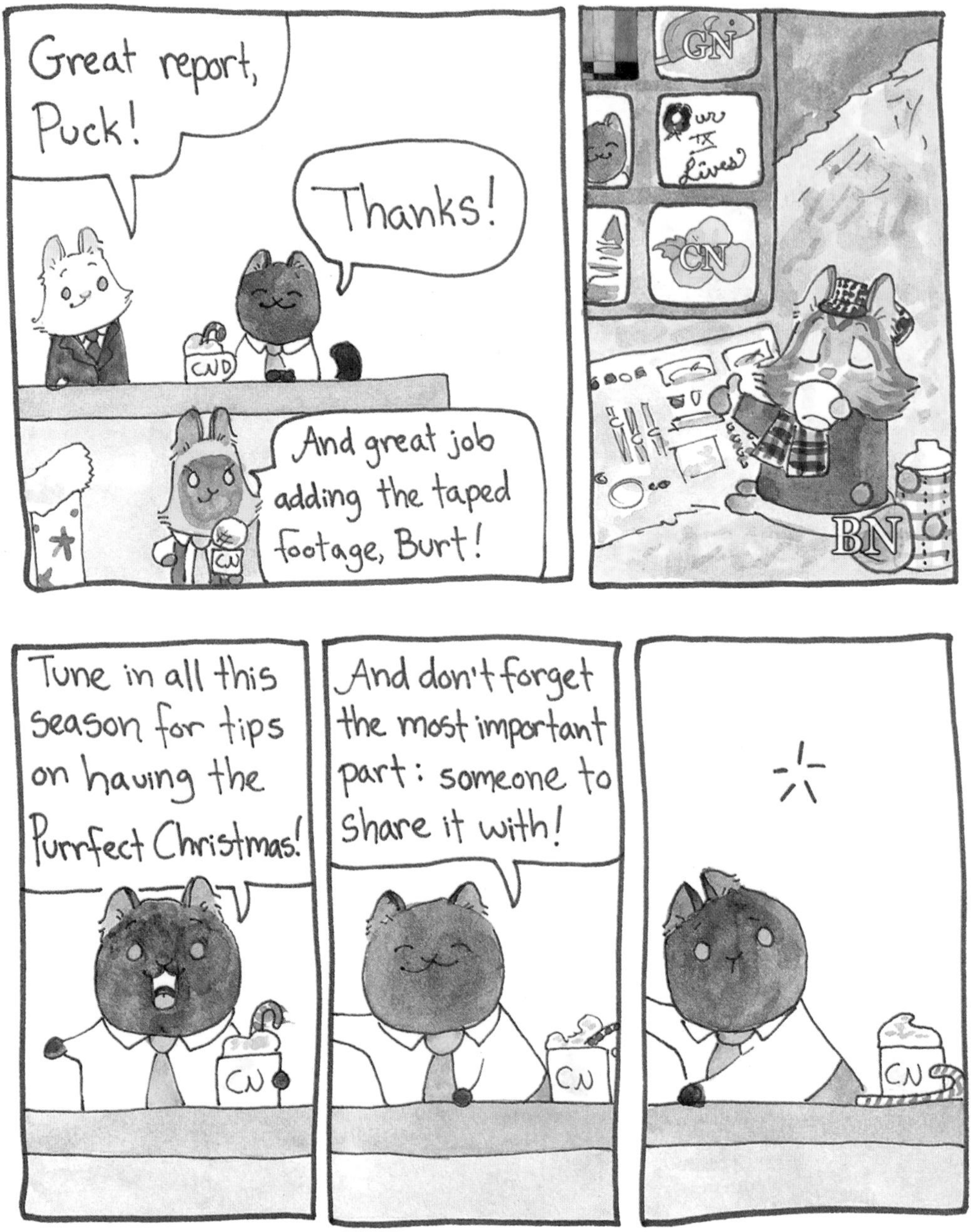
Great report, Puck!
Thanks!
And great job adding the taped footage, Burt!
GN
CN
BN
Tune in all this season for tips on having the Purrfect Christmas!
And don't forget the most important part: someone to share it with!

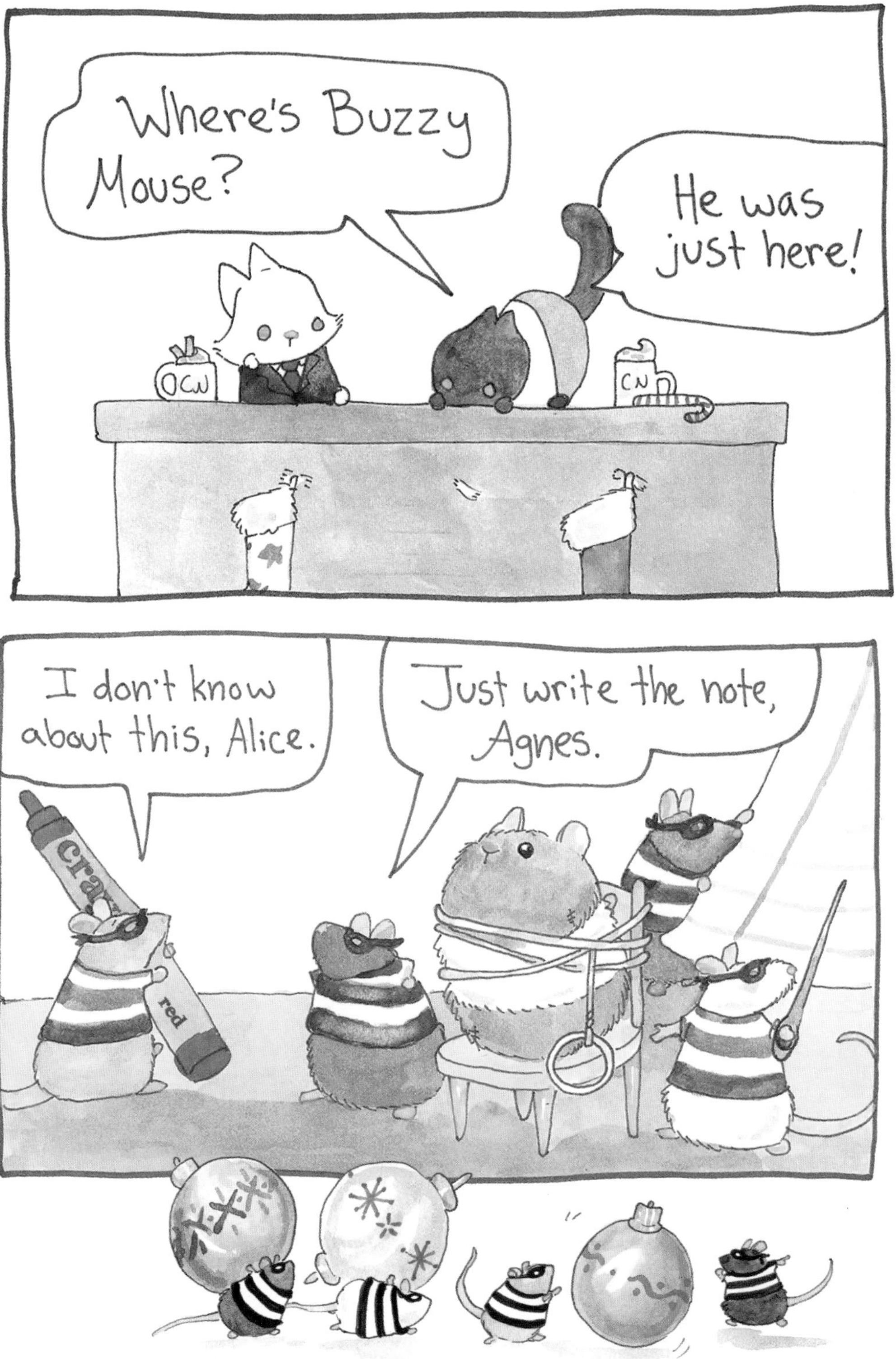
Where's Buzzy Mouse?
He was just here!
I don't know about this, Alice.
Just write the note, Agnes.
red

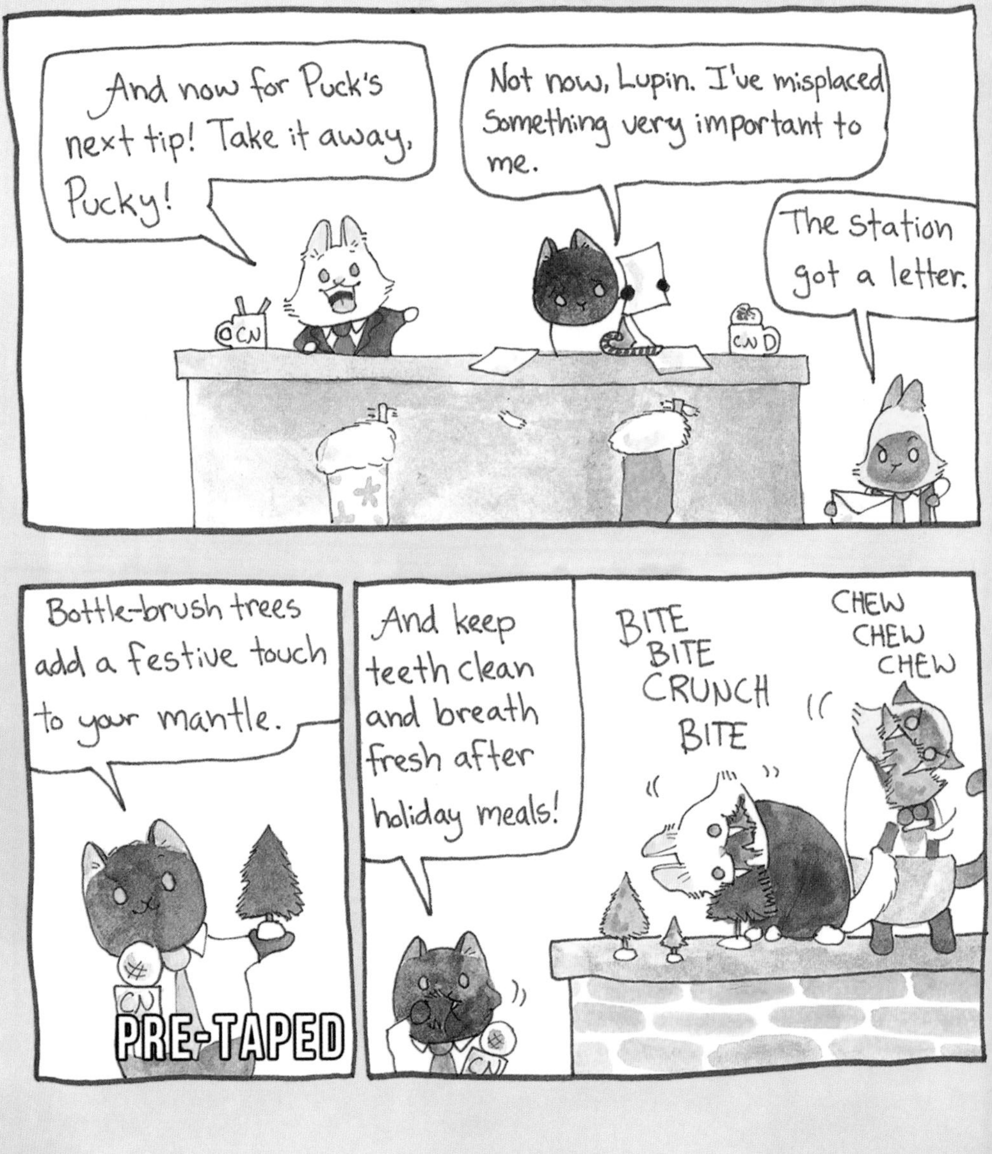

And now for Puck's next tip! Take it away, Pucky!
Not now, Lupin. I've misplaced Something very important to me.
The station got a letter.
CN
CN
Bottle-brush trees add a festive touch to your mantle.
CN
PRE-TAPED
And keep teeth clean and breath fresh after holiday meals!
CN
BITE
BITE
CRUNCH
BITE
CHEW
CHEW
CHEW

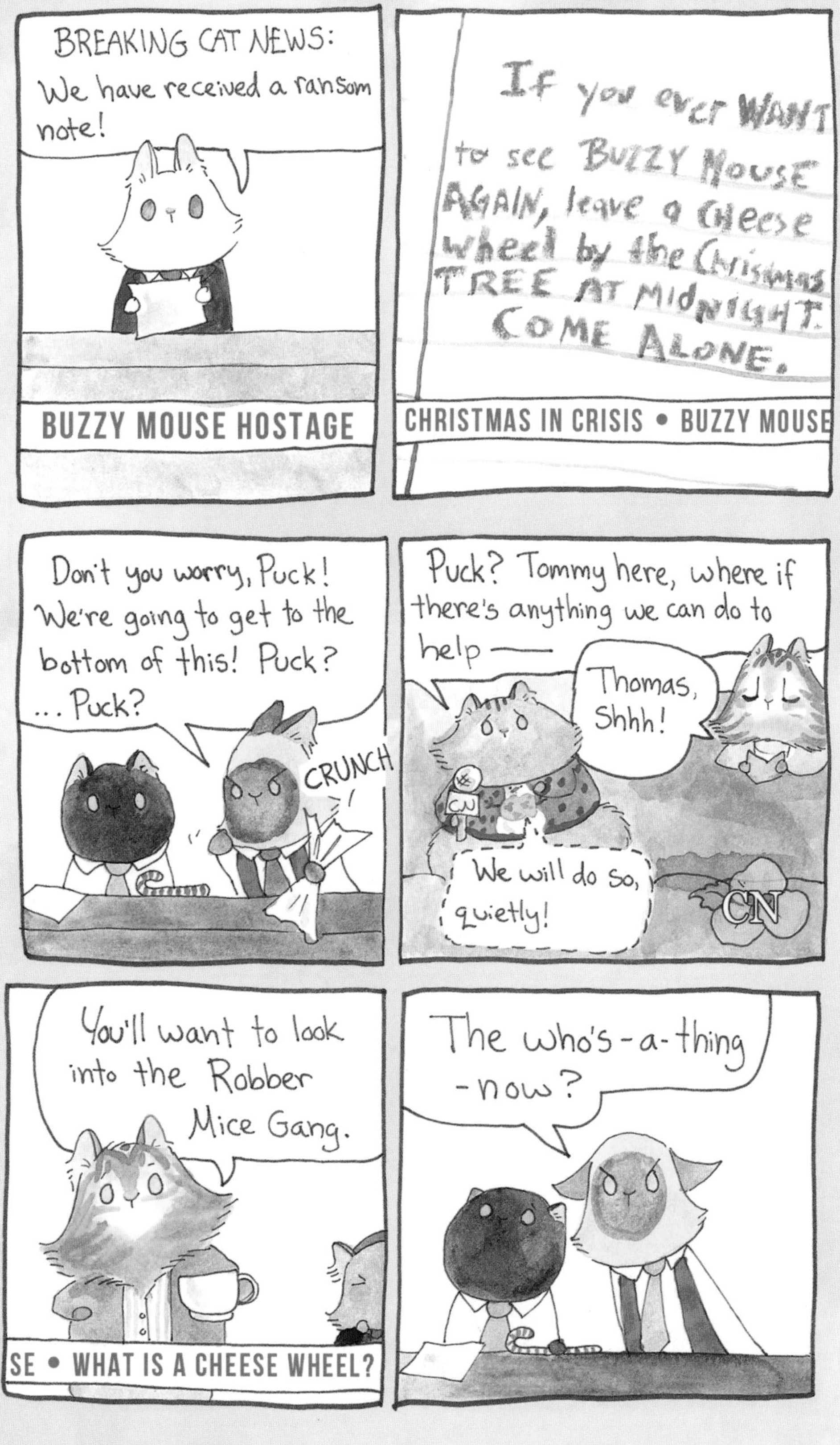

BREAKING CAT NEWS:
We have received a ransom note!
BUZZY MOUSE HOSTAGE
If you ever WANT to see BUZZY MOUSE AGAIN, leave a CHEESE wheel by the Christmas TREE AT MIDNIGHT. COME ALONE.
CHRISTMAS IN CRISIS • BUZZY MOUSE
Don't you worry, Puck! We're going to get to the bottom of this! Puck? ... Puck?
CRUNCH
Puck? Tommy here, where if there's anything we can do to help —
Thomas, Shhh!
We will do so, quietly!
CN
CN
You'll want to look into the Robber Mice Gang.
SE • WHAT IS A CHEESE WHEEL?
The who's-a-thing-now?

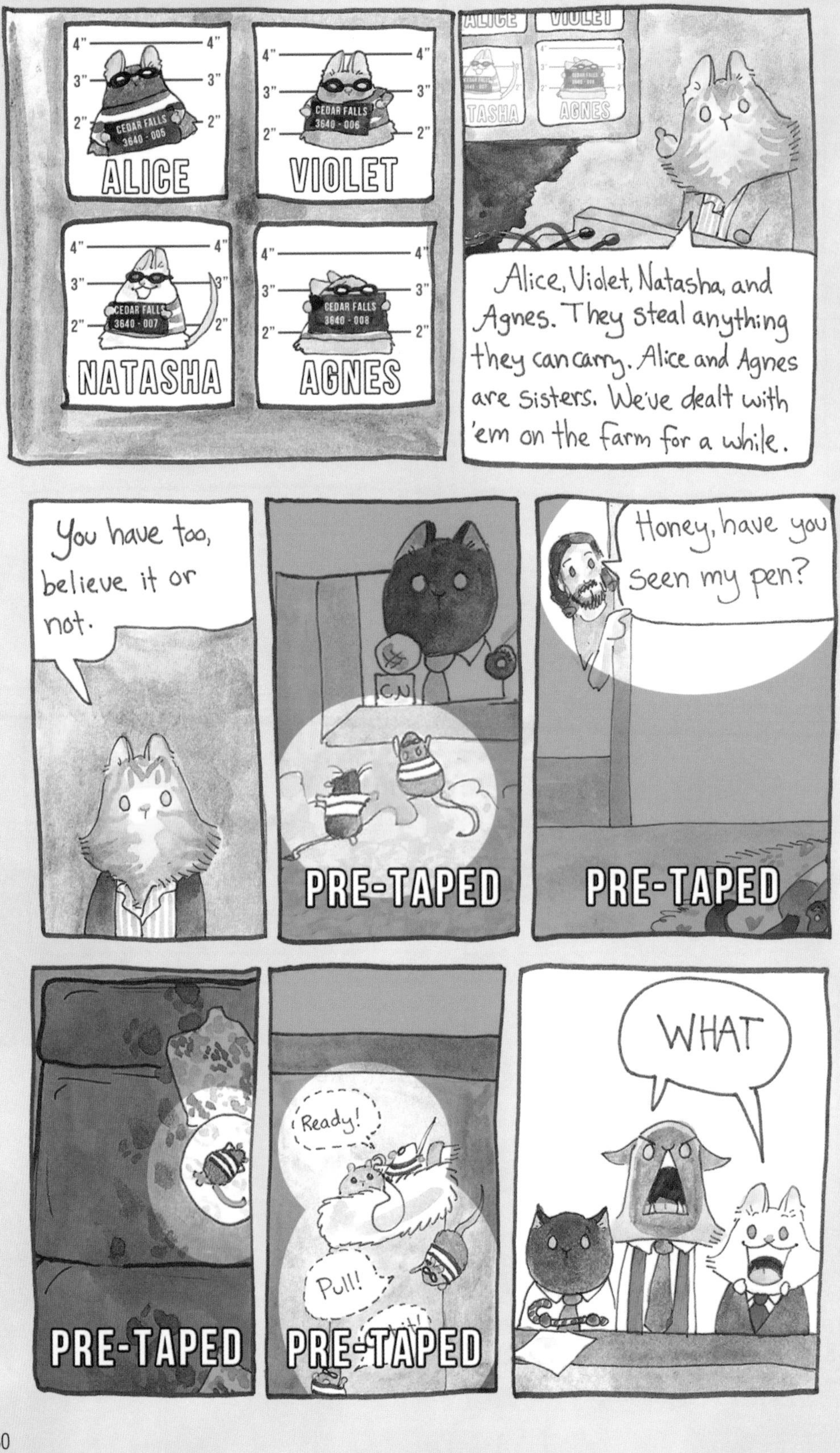
4"
3"
2"
CEDAR FALLS 3640 - 005
ALICE
CEDAR FALLS 3640 - 006
VIOLET
CEDAR FALLS 3640 - 007
NATASHA
CEDAR FALLS 3640 - 008
AGNES
Alice, Violet, Natasha, and Agnes. They steal anything they can carry. Alice and Agnes are sisters. We've dealt with 'em on the farm for a while.
You have too, believe it or not.
PRE-TAPED
Honey, have you seen my pen?
PRE-TAPED
PRE-TAPED
Ready!
Pull!
PRE-TAPED
WHAT

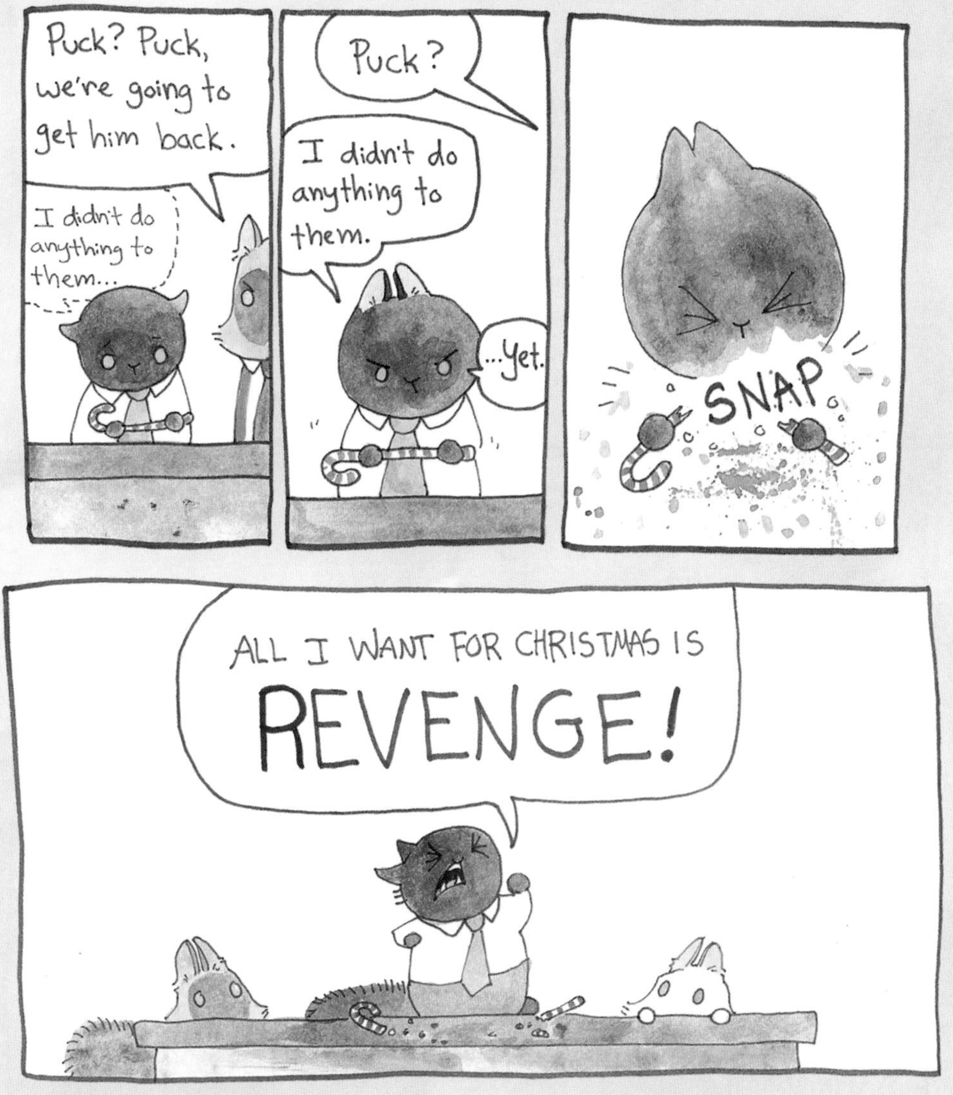
Puck? Puck, we're going to get him back.
I didn't do anything to them...
Puck?
I didn't do anything to them.
...Yet.
SNAP
ALL I WANT FOR CHRISTMAS IS REVENGE!

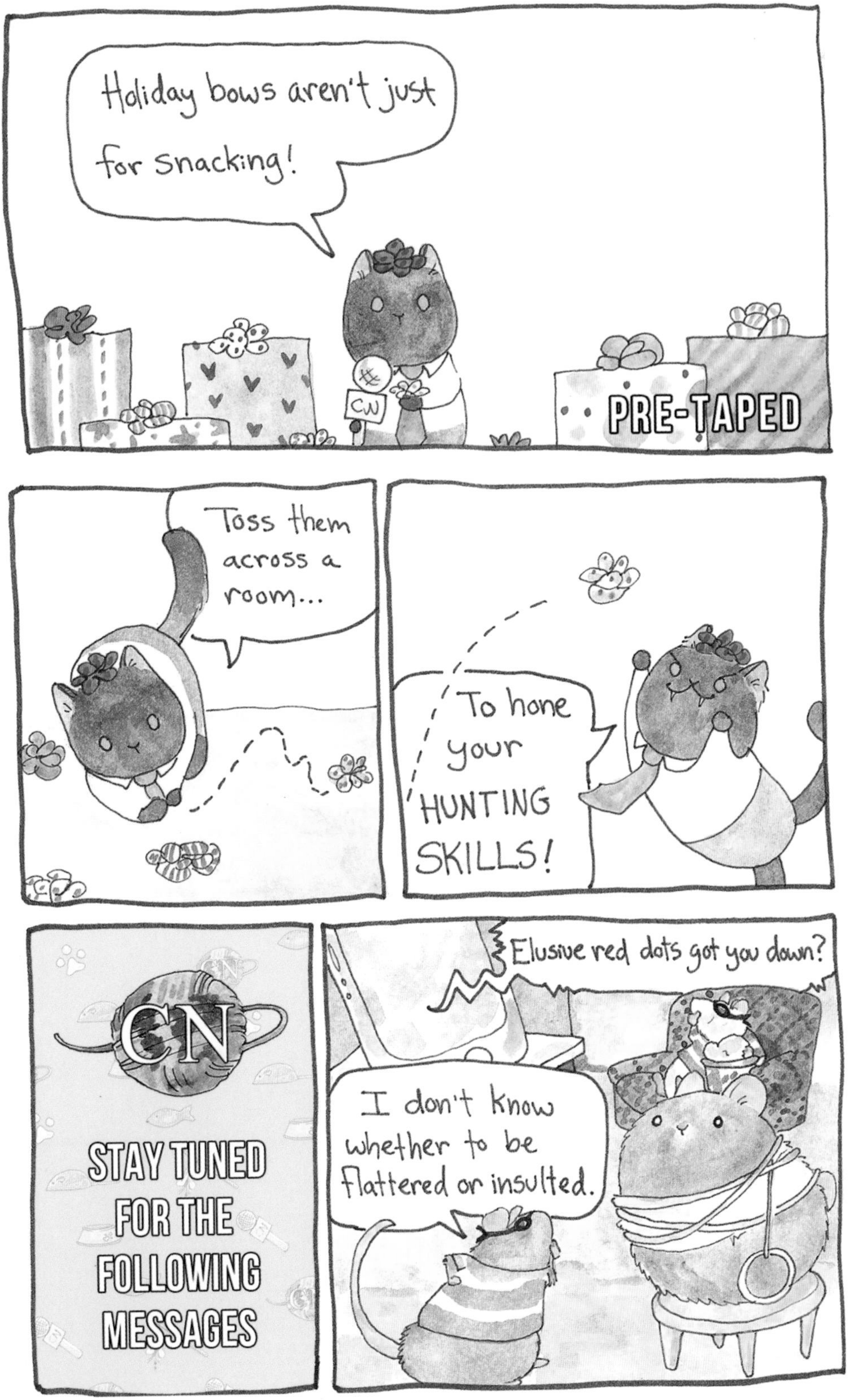
Holiday bows aren't just for snacking!
CN
PRE-TAPED
Toss them across a room...
To hone your HUNTING SKILLS!
CN
STAY TUNED FOR THE FOLLOWING MESSAGES
Elusive red dots got you down?
I don't know whether to be flattered or insulted.

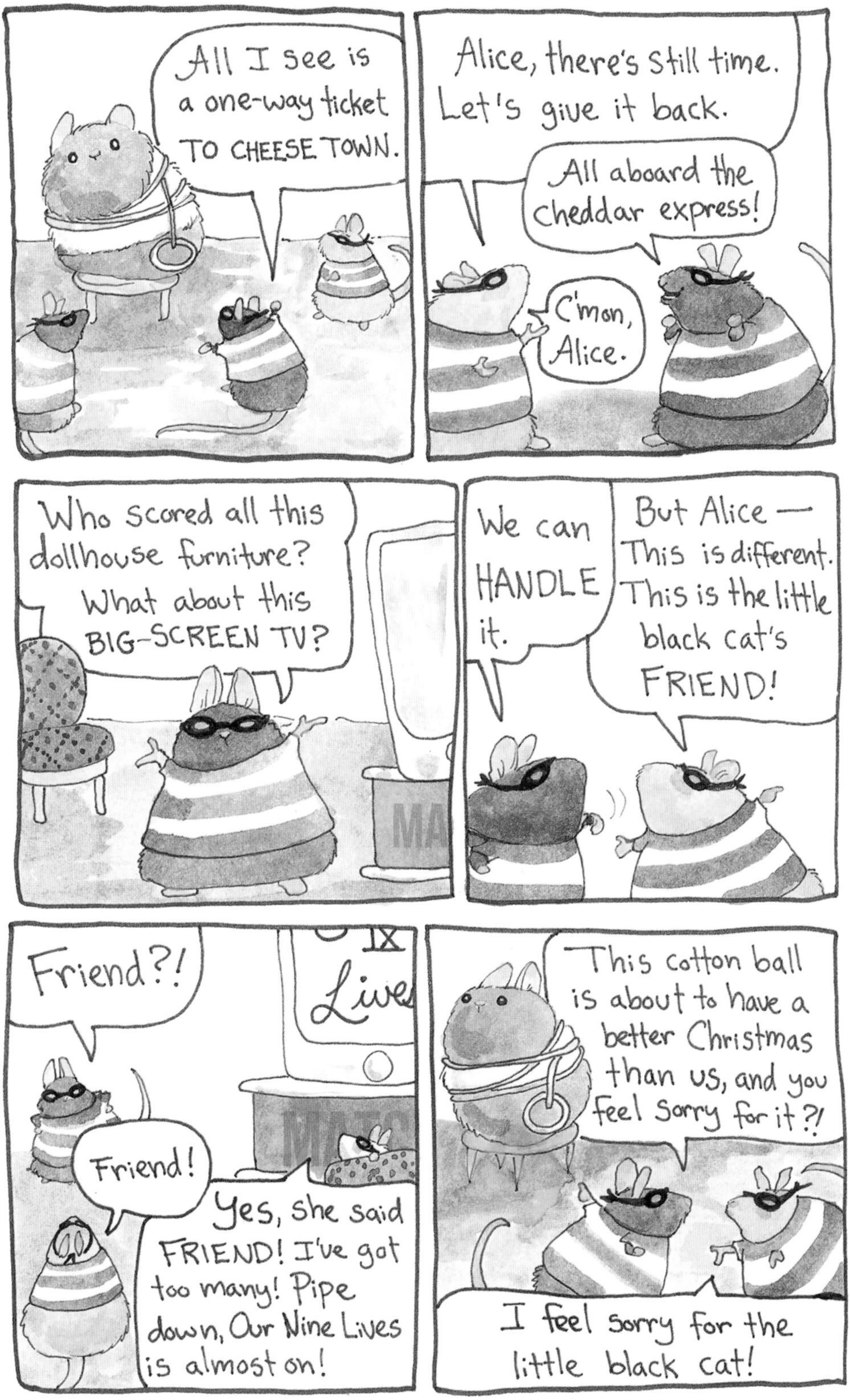
All I see is a one-way ticket TO CHEESE TOWN.
Alice, there's still time. Let's give it back.
All aboard the cheddar express!
C'mon, Alice.
Who scored all this dollhouse furniture? What about this BIG-SCREEN TV?
We can HANDLE it.
But Alice— This is different. This is the little black cat's FRIEND!
Friend?!
Friend!
Yes, she said FRIEND! I've got too many! Pipe down, Our Nine Lives is almost on!
This cotton ball is about to have a better Christmas than us, and you feel sorry for it?!
I feel sorry for the little black cat!

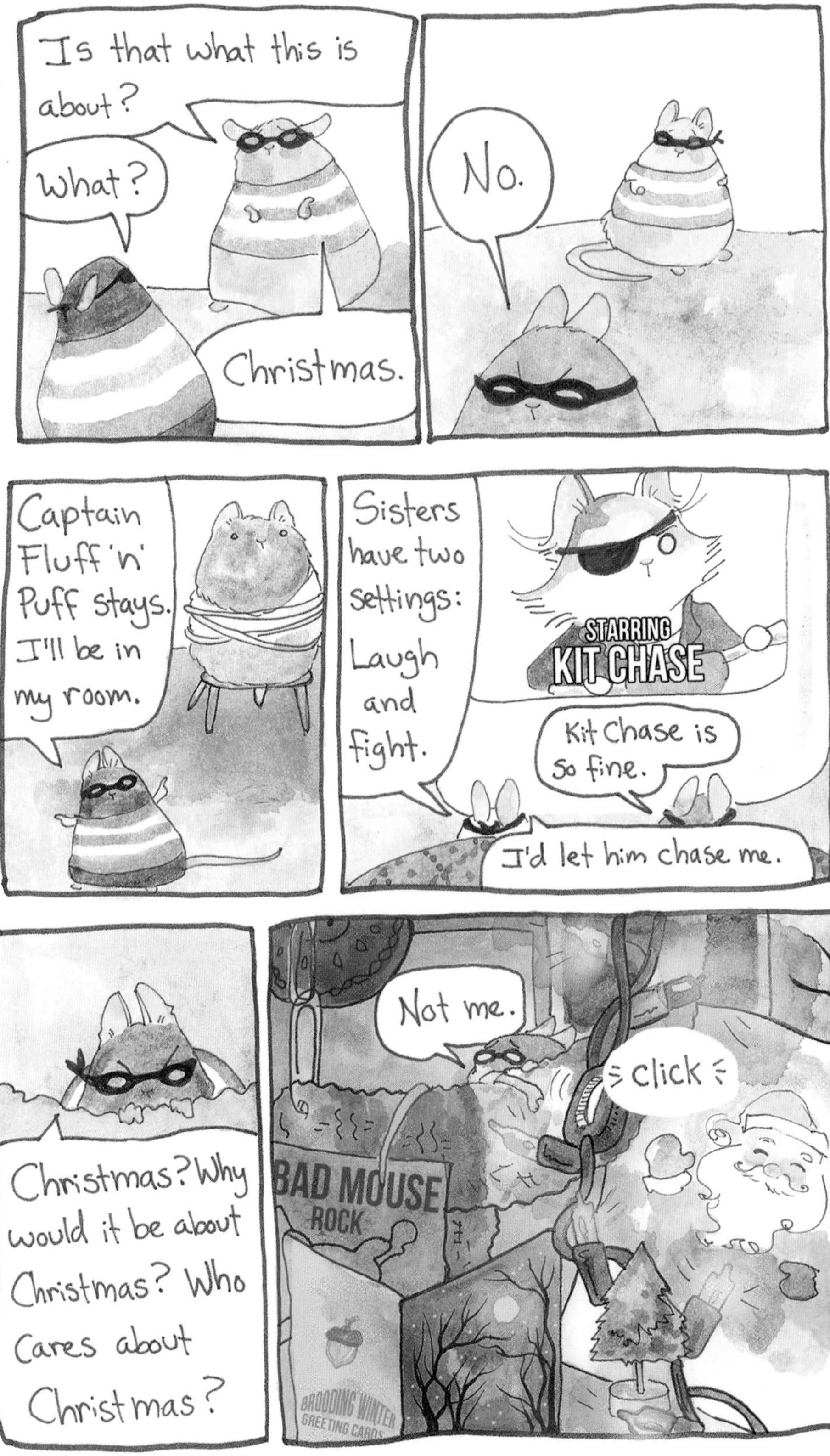
Is that what this is about?
What?
Christmas.
No.
Captain Fluff 'n' Puff stays. I'll be in my room.
Sisters have two settings: Laugh and fight.
STARRING
KIT CHASE
Kit Chase is so fine.
I'd let him chase me.
Christmas? Why would it be about Christmas? Who cares about Christmas?
Not me.
click
BAD MOUSE
ROCK
BROODING WINTER
GREETING CARDS

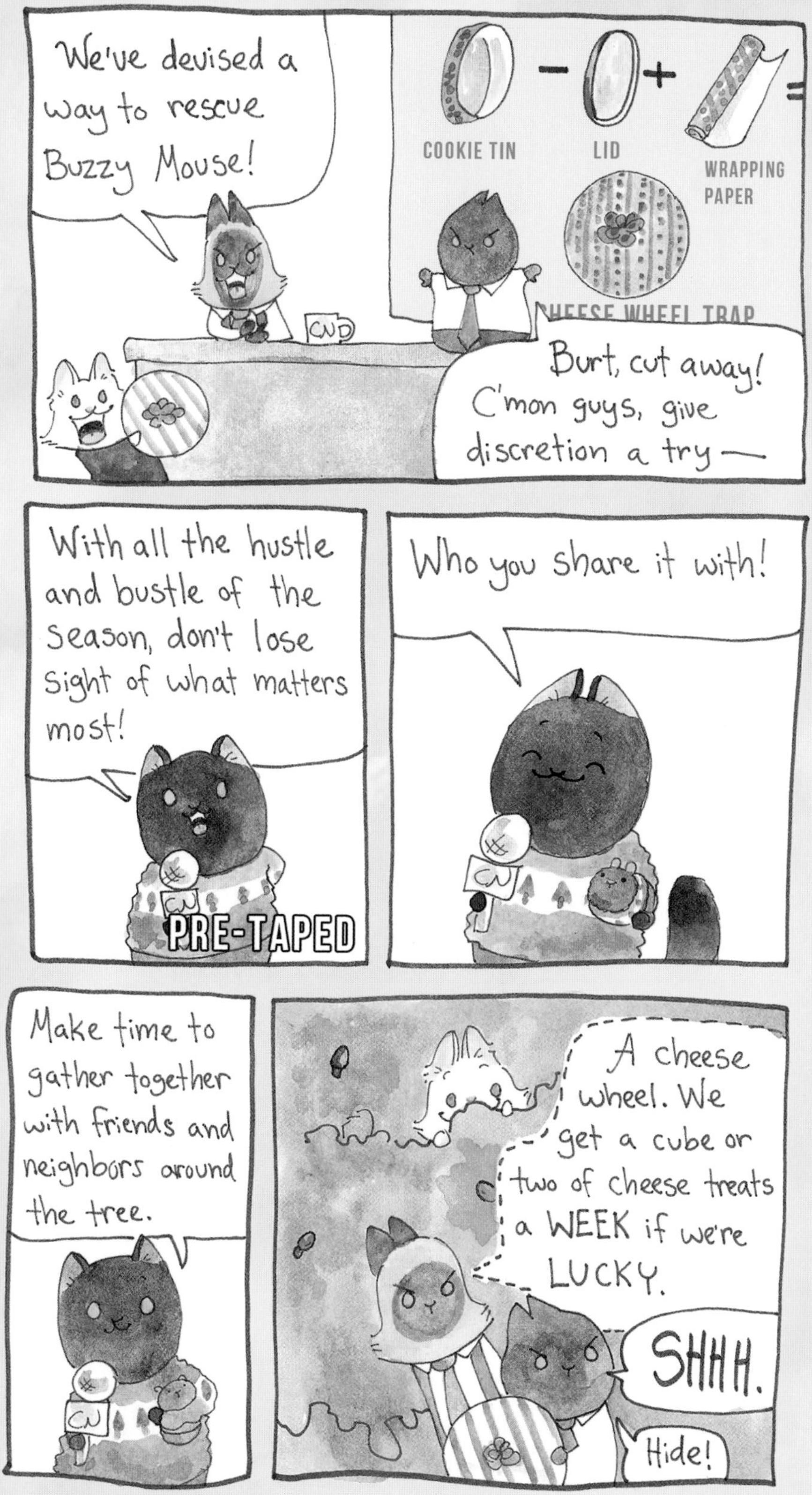
We've devised a way to rescue Buzzy Mouse!
COOKIE TIN
LID
WRAPPING PAPER
CHEESE WHEEL TRAP
Burt, cut away! C'mon guys, give discretion a try—
With all the hustle and bustle of the season, don't lose sight of what matters most!
PRE-TAPED
Who you share it with!
Make time to gather together with friends and neighbors around the tree.
A cheese wheel. We get a cube or two of cheese treats a WEEK if we're LUCKY.
SHHH.
Hide!

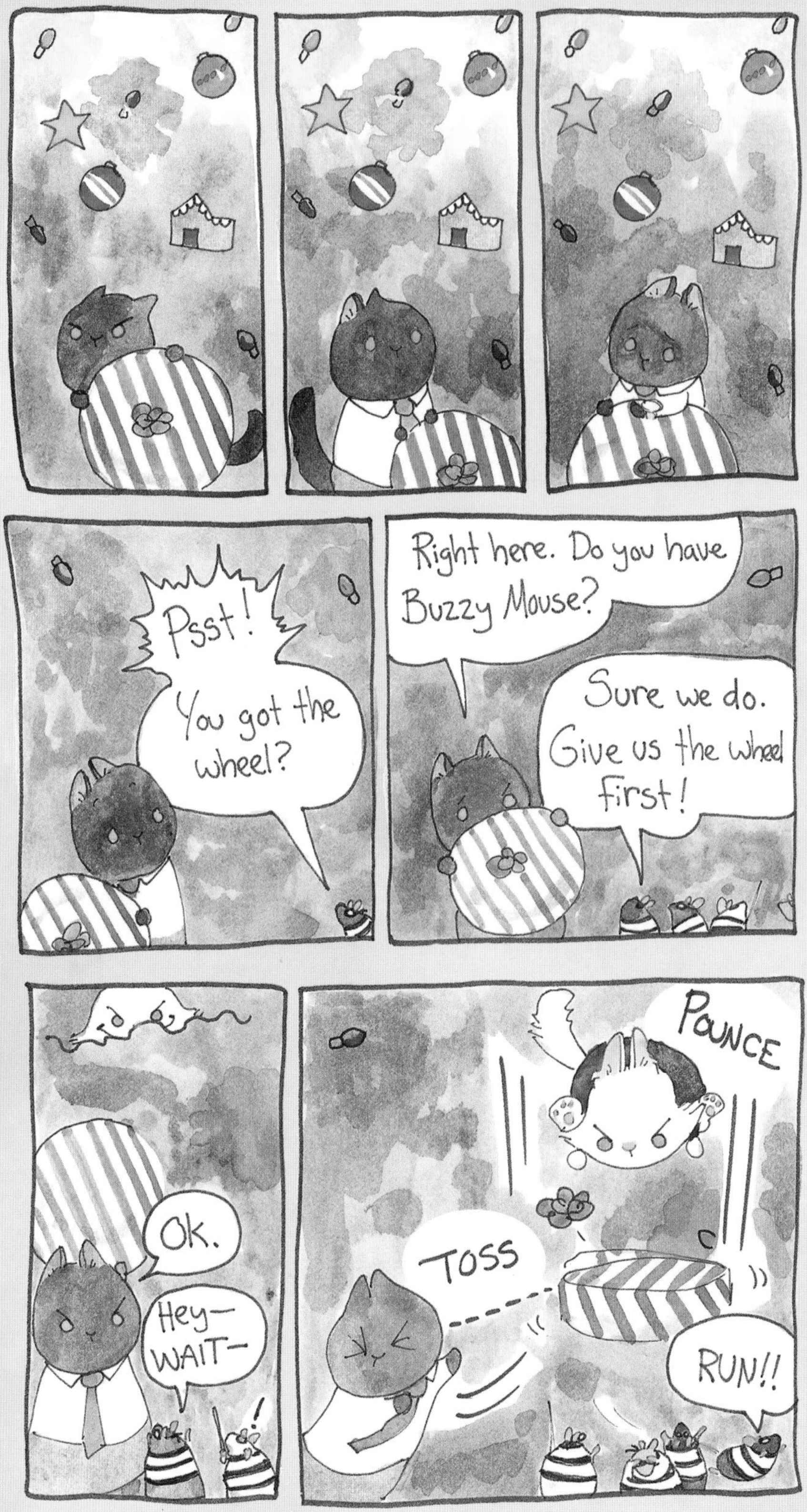
Psst!
You got the wheel?
Right here. Do you have Buzzy Mouse?
Sure we do. Give us the wheel first!
Ok.
Hey— WAIT—
POUNCE
TOSS
RUN!!

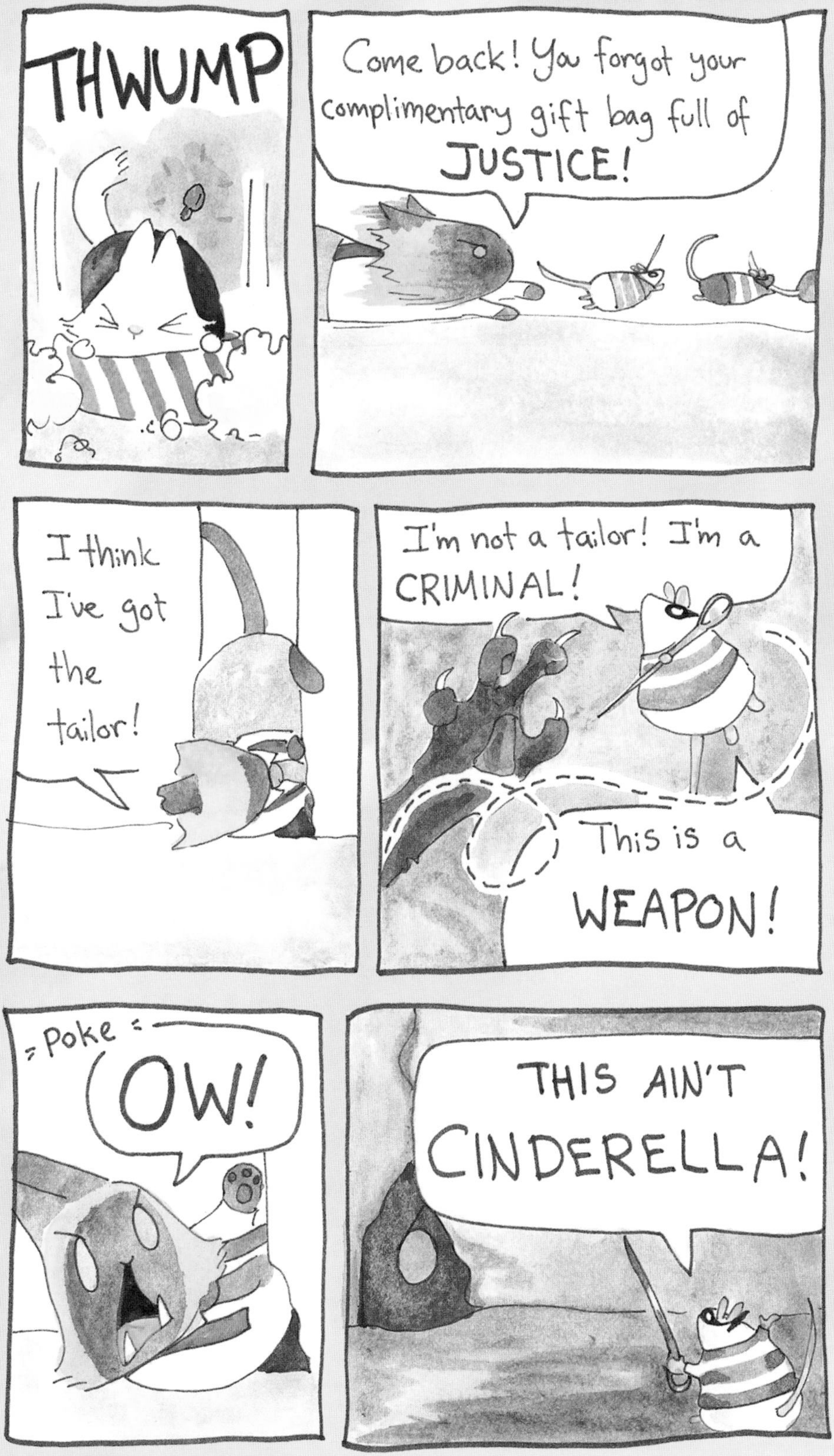
THWUMP
Come back! You forgot your complimentary gift bag full of JUSTICE!
I think I've got the tailor!
I'm not a tailor! I'm a CRIMINAL!
This is a WEAPON!
Poke
OW!
THIS AIN'T CINDERELLA!

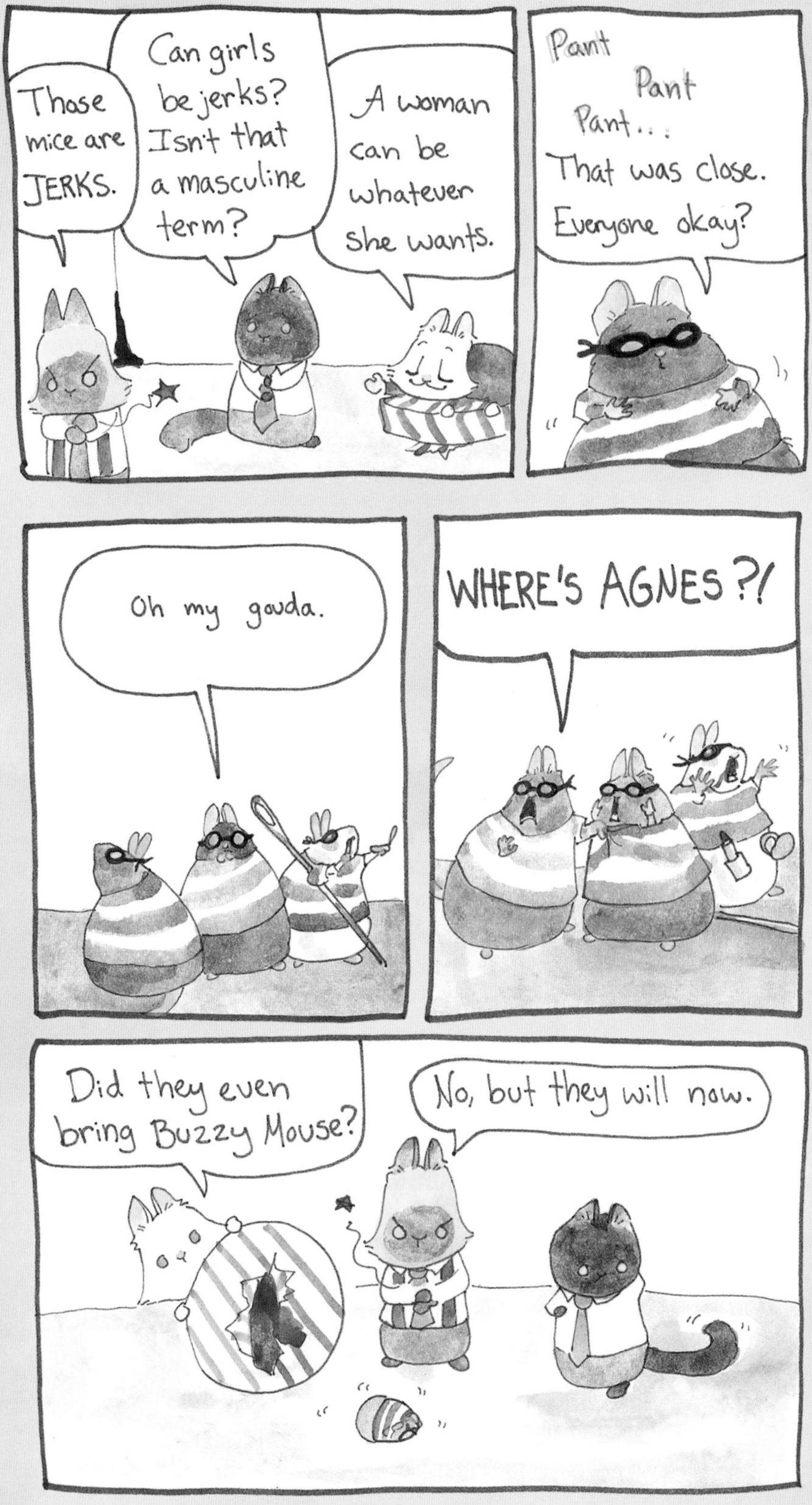
Those mice are JERKS.
Can girls be jerks? Isn't that a masculine term?
A woman can be whatever she wants.
Pant Pant Pant...
That was close. Everyone okay?
Oh my gouda.
WHERE'S AGNES?!
Did they even bring Buzzy Mouse?
No, but they will now.

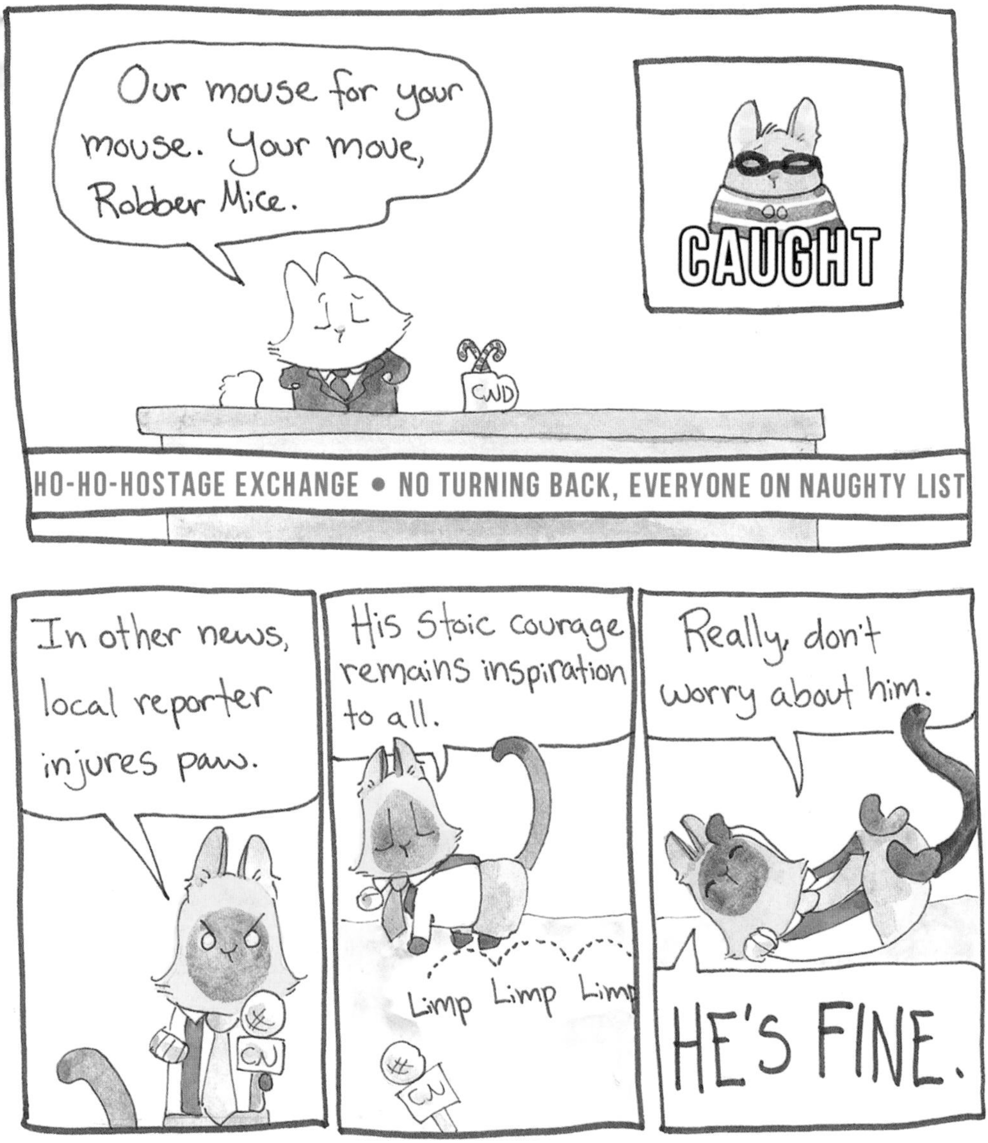
Our mouse for your mouse. Your move, Robber Mice.
CAUGHT
CND
HO-HO-HOSTAGE EXCHANGE • NO TURNING BACK, EVERYONE ON NAUGHTY LIST
In other news, local reporter injures paw.
CN
His Stoic courage remains inspiration to all.
Limp Limp Limp
CN
Really, don't worry about him.
HE'S FINE.

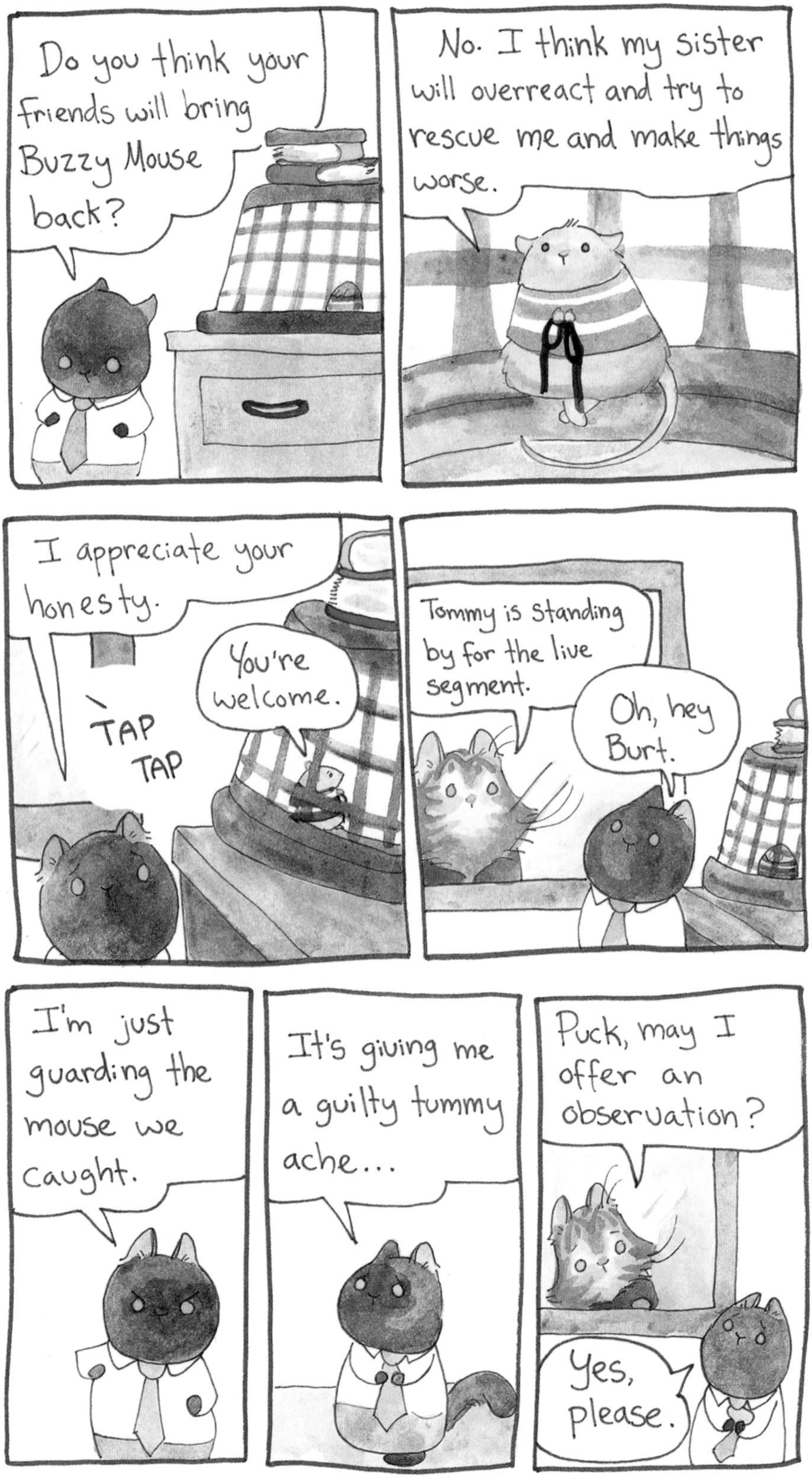
Do you think your friends will bring Buzzy Mouse back?
No. I think my sister will overreact and try to rescue me and make things worse.
I appreciate your honesty.
TAP
TAP
You're welcome.
Tommy is standing by for the live segment.
Oh, hey Burt.
I'm just guarding the mouse we caught.
It's giving me a guilty tummy ache...
Puck, may I offer an observation?
Yes, please.

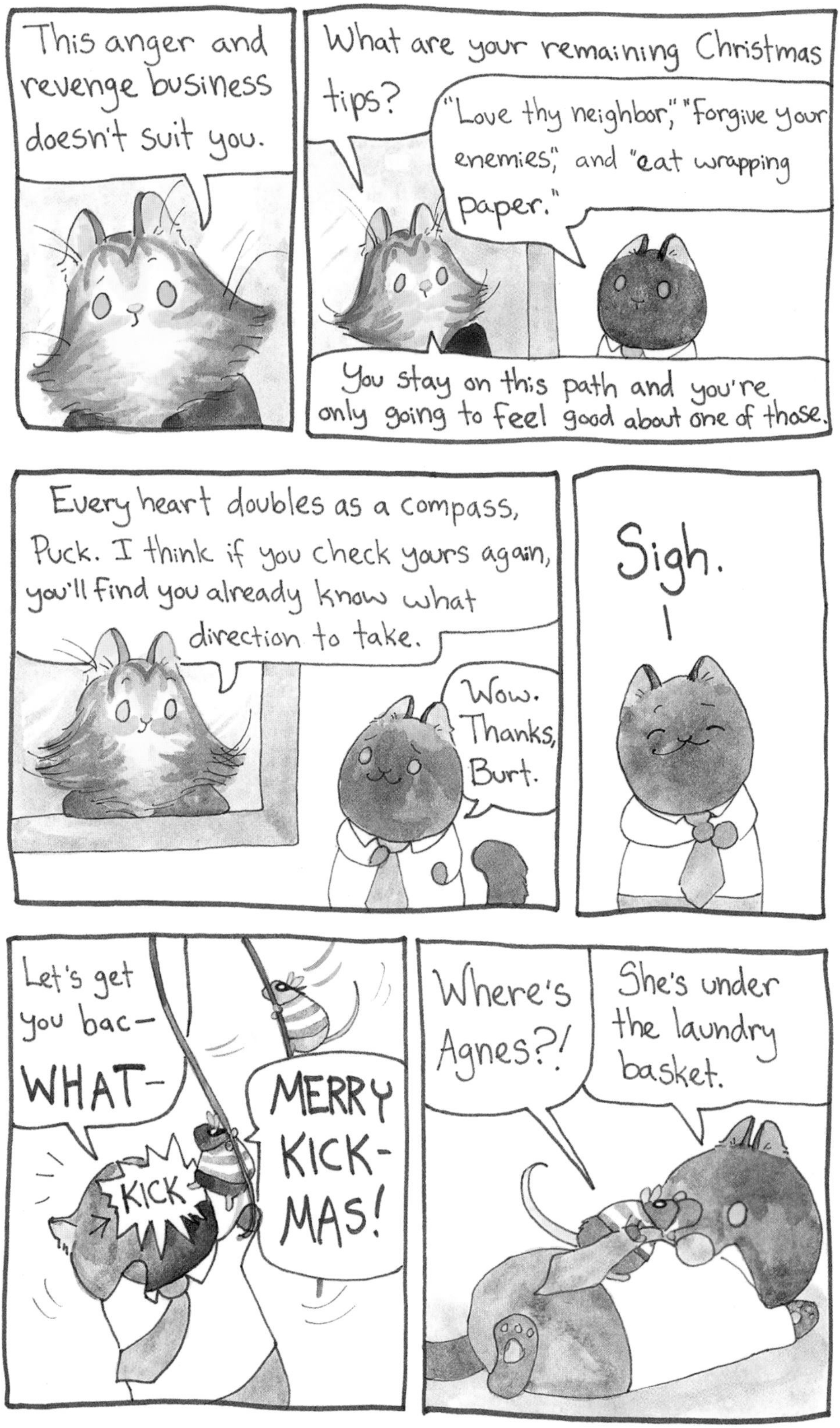
This anger and revenge business doesn't suit you.
What are your remaining Christmas tips?
"Love thy neighbor," "Forgive your enemies," and "eat wrapping paper."
You stay on this path and you're only going to feel good about one of those.
Every heart doubles as a compass, Puck. I think if you check yours again, you'll find you already know what direction to take.
Wow. Thanks, Burt.
Sigh.
Let's get you bac—
WHAT—
KICK
MERRY KICK-MAS!
Where's Agnes?!
She's under the laundry basket.

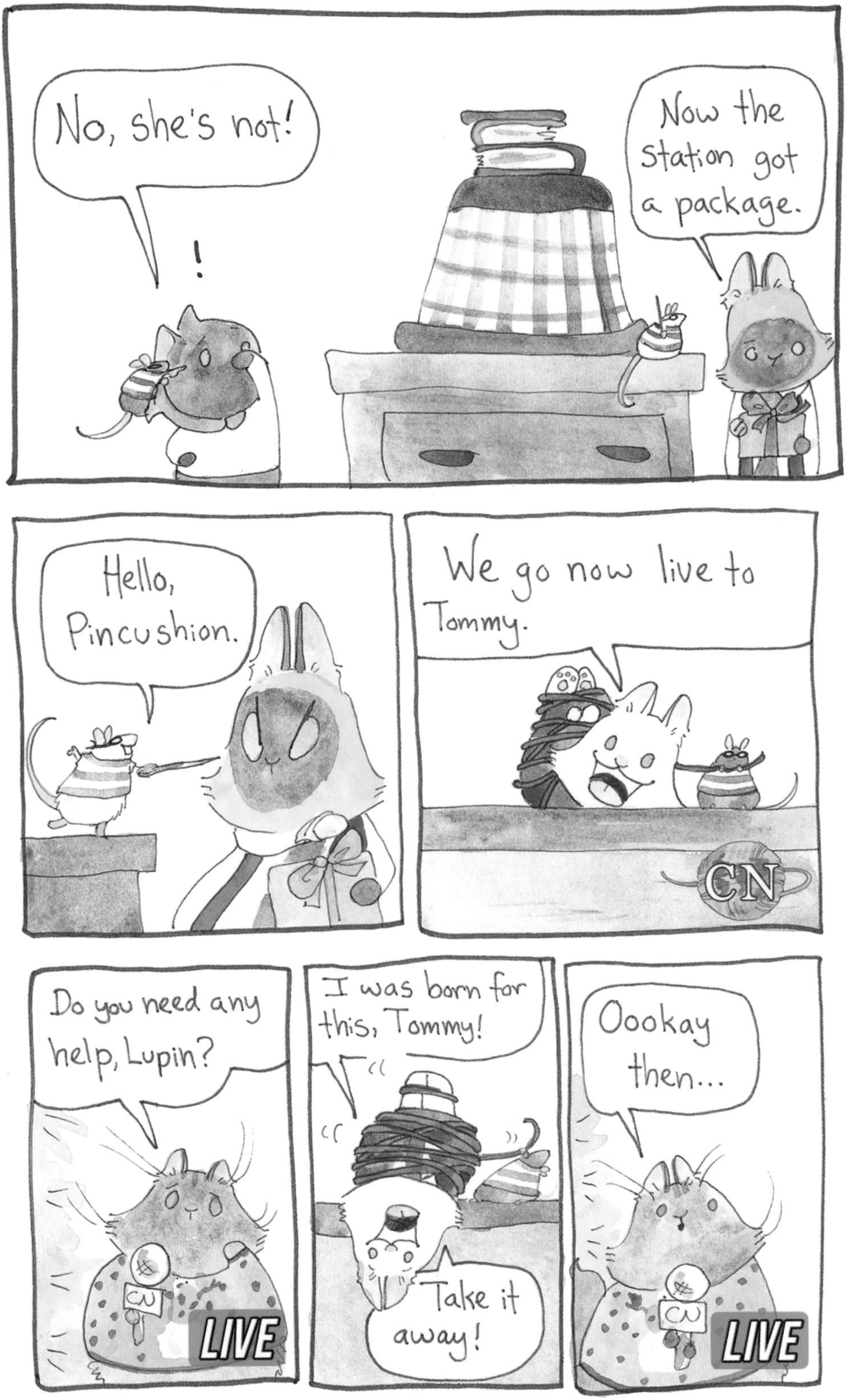
No, she's not!
!
Now the station got a package.
Hello, Pincushion.
We go now live to Tommy.
CN
Do you need any help, Lupin?
CN
LIVE
I was born for this, Tommy!
Take it away!
Oookay then...
CN
LIVE

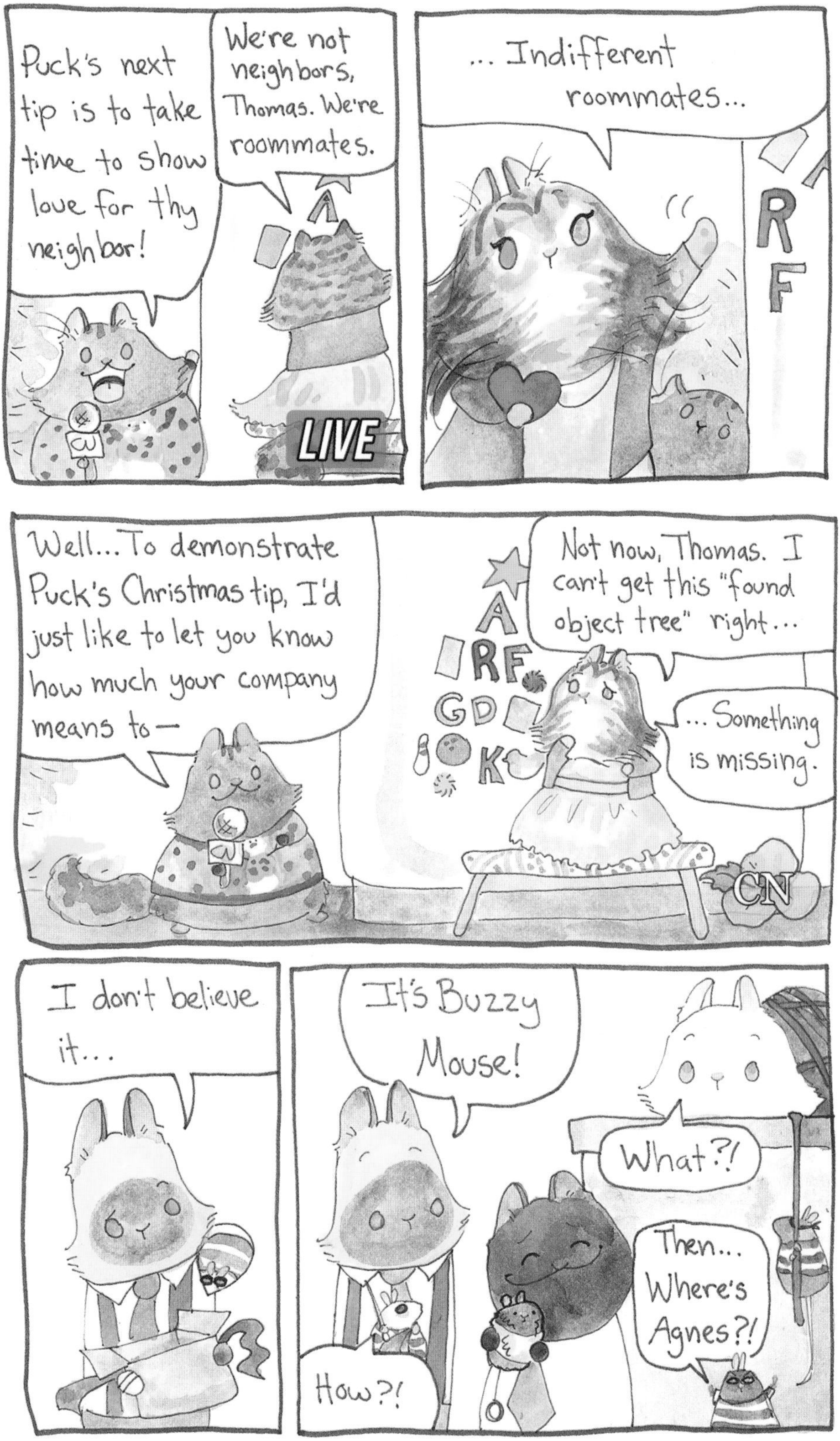
Puck's next tip is to take time to show love for thy neighbor!
We're not neighbors, Thomas. We're roommates.
LIVE
... Indifferent roommates...
R
F
Well... To demonstrate Puck's Christmas tip, I'd just like to let you know how much your company means to—
Not now, Thomas. I can't get this "found object tree" right...
... Something is missing.
A
RF
GD
K
CN
I don't believe it...
It's Buzzy Mouse!
How?!
What?!
Then... Where's Agnes?!

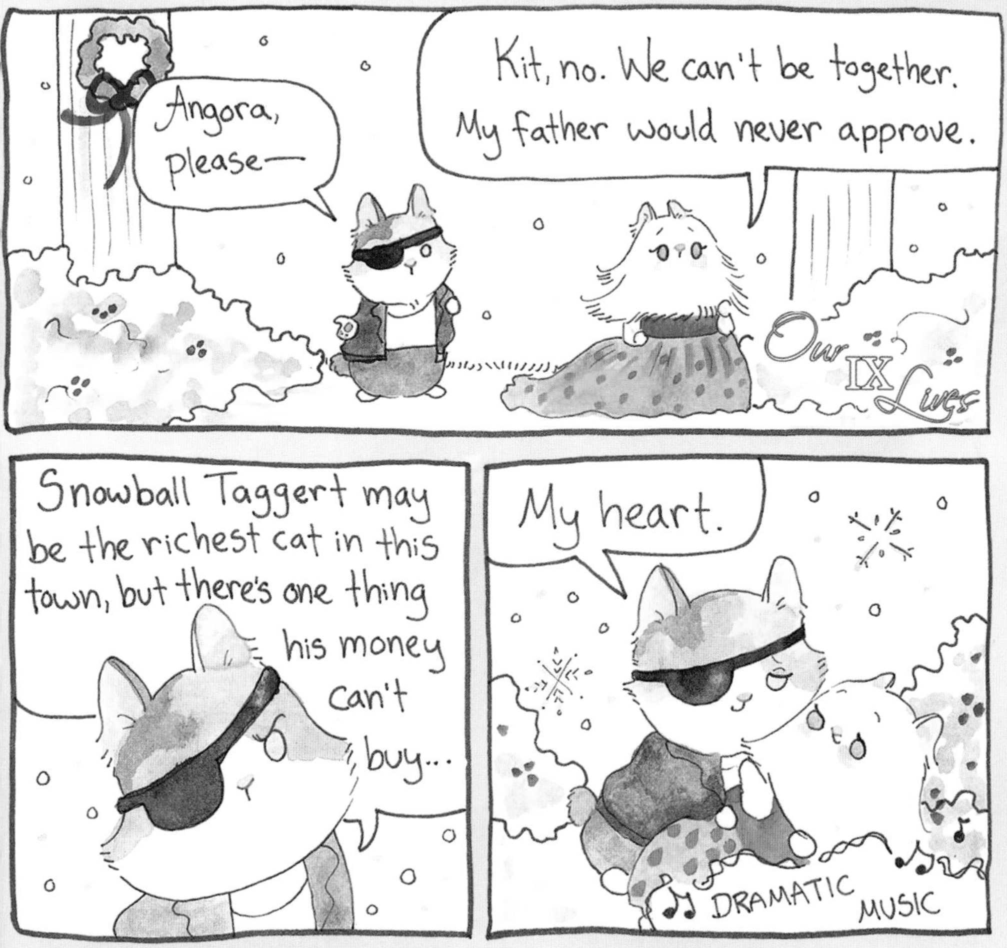
Angora, please—
Kit, no. We can't be together. My father would never approve.
Our IX Lives
Snowball Taggert may be the richest cat in this town, but there's one thing his money can't buy...
My heart.
DRAMATIC MUSIC

Oh, wow—

NEXT TIME ON

Our

Agnes! How did—

Oh.

Why—

I set things right.

They're not bad cats. And you're not bad mice. Just misguided...

Usually by Alice.

Hrmph.

I couldn't watch both sides hurting each other and making things worse any more.

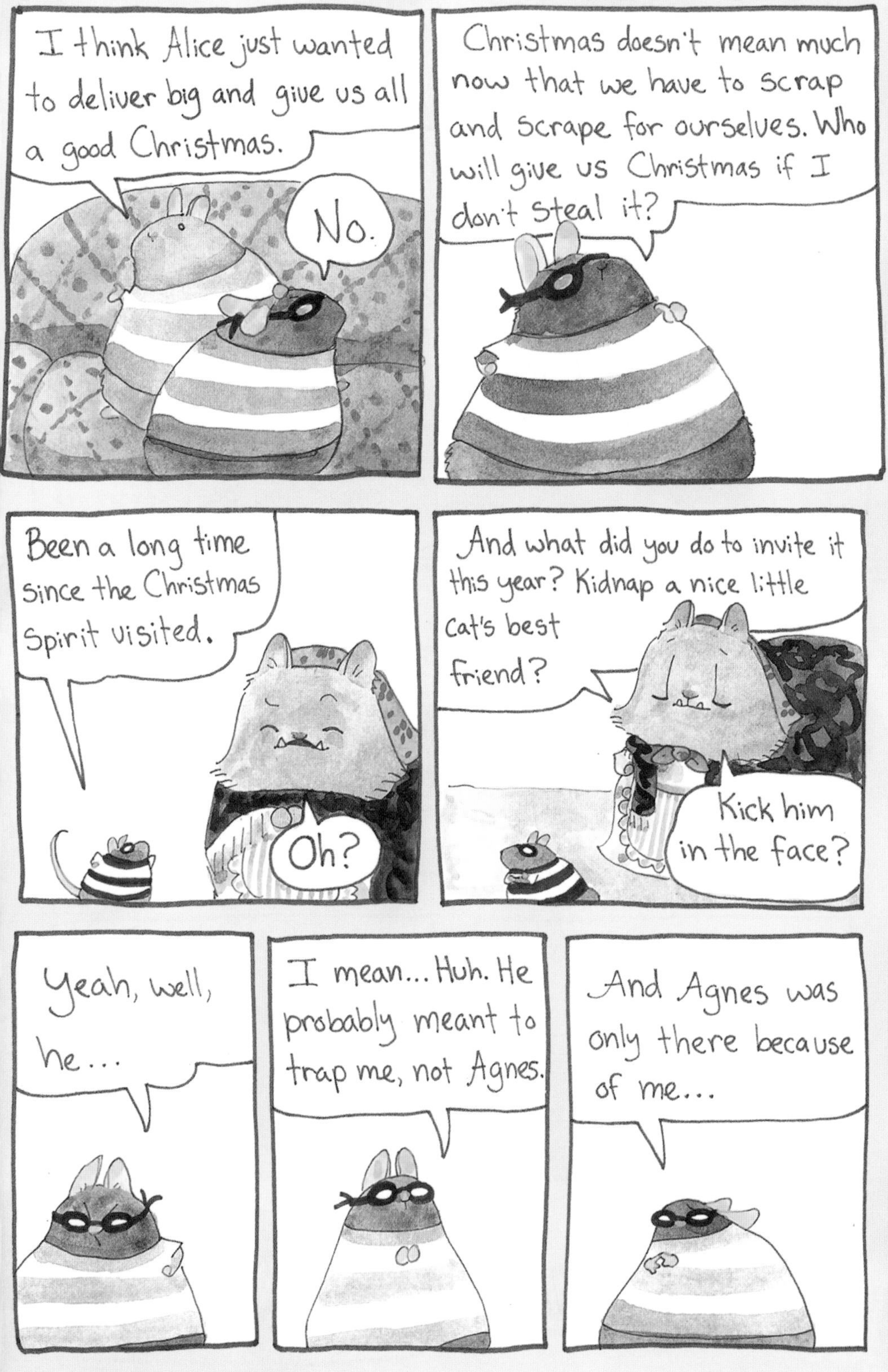
I think Alice just wanted to deliver big and give us all a good Christmas.
No.
Christmas doesn't mean much now that we have to scrap and scrape for ourselves. Who will give us Christmas if I don't steal it?
Been a long time since the Christmas Spirit visited.
Oh?
And what did you do to invite it this year? Kidnap a nice little cat's best friend?
Kick him in the face?
Yeah, well, he...
I mean... Huh. He probably meant to trap me, not Agnes.
And Agnes was only there because of me...

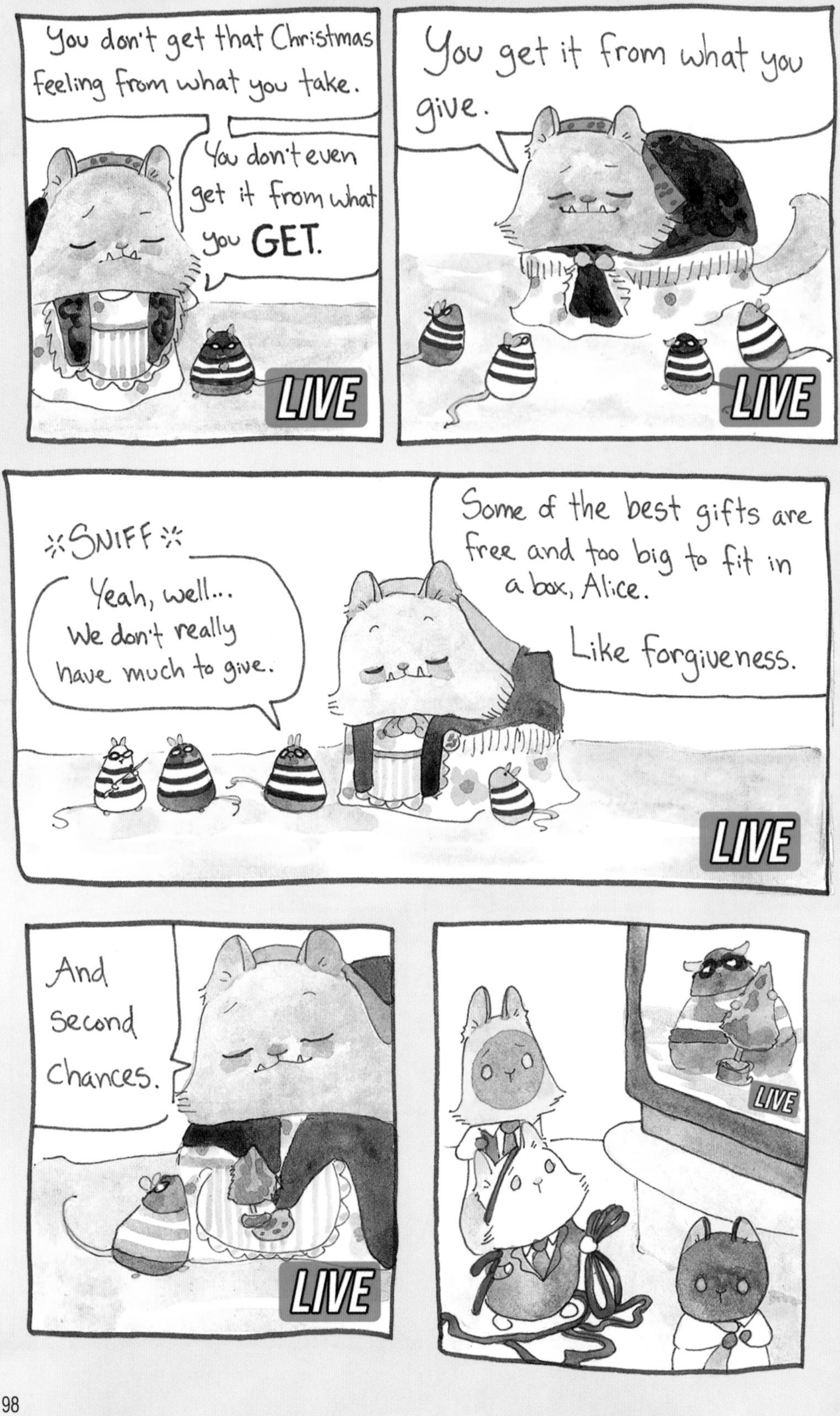
You don't get that Christmas feeling from what you take.
You don't even get it from what you GET.
LIVE
You get it from what you give.
LIVE
Some of the best gifts are free and too big to fit in a box, Alice.
Like forgiveness.
SNIFF
Yeah, well... We don't really have much to give.
LIVE
And second chances.
LIVE
LIVE

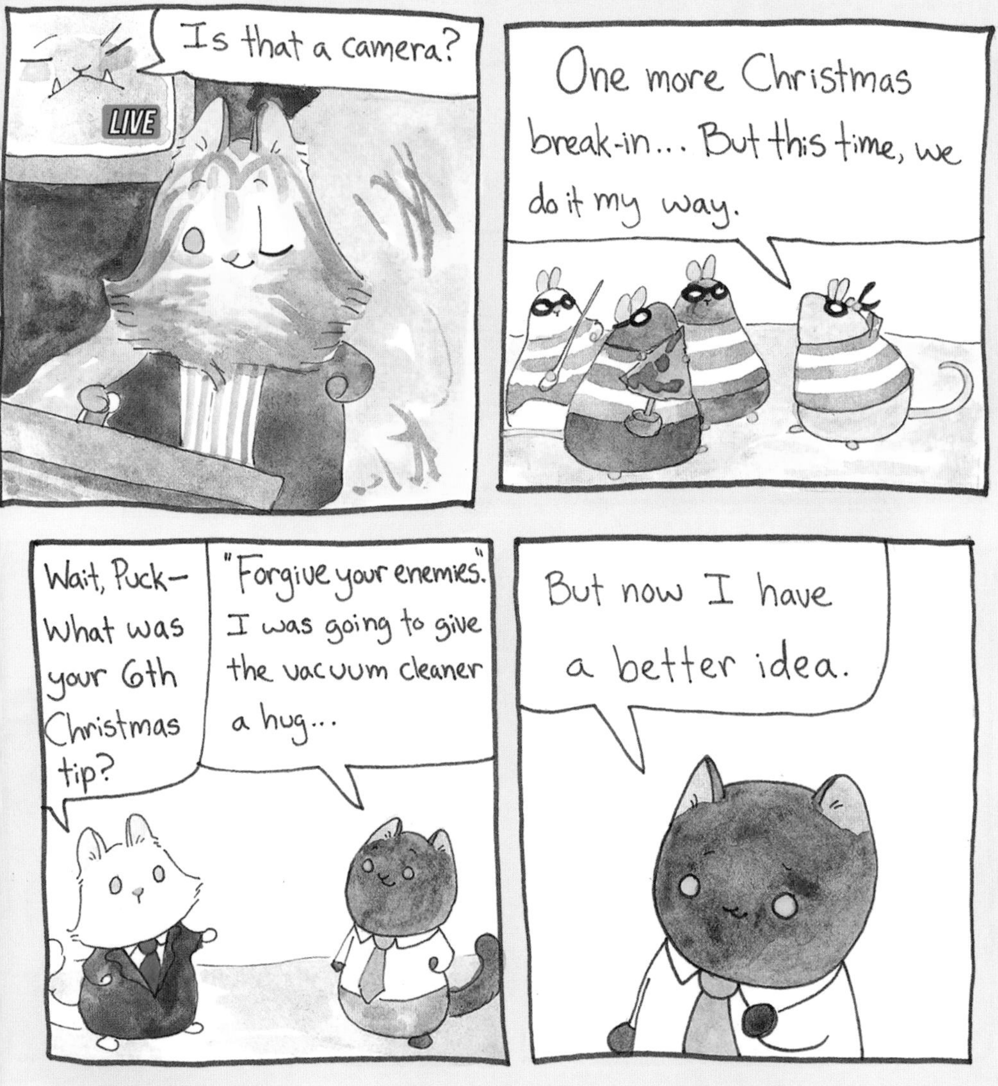
LIVE
Is that a camera?
One more Christmas break-in... But this time, we do it my way.
Wait, Puck— What was your 6th Christmas tip?
"Forgive your enemies." I was going to give the vacuum cleaner a hug...
But now I have a better idea.

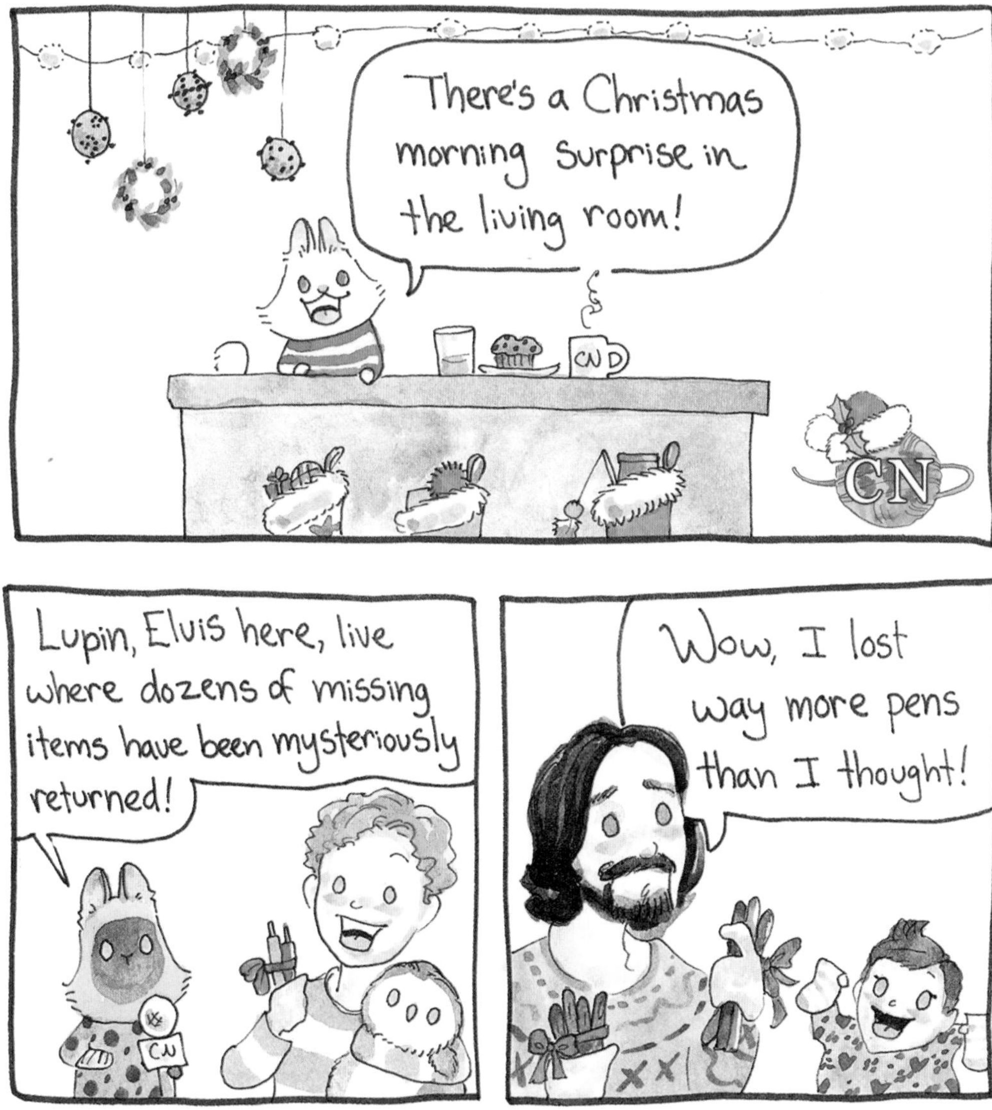
There's a Christmas morning surprise in the living room!
CN
Lupin, Elvis here, live where dozens of missing items have been mysteriously returned!
Wow, I lost way more pens than I thought!

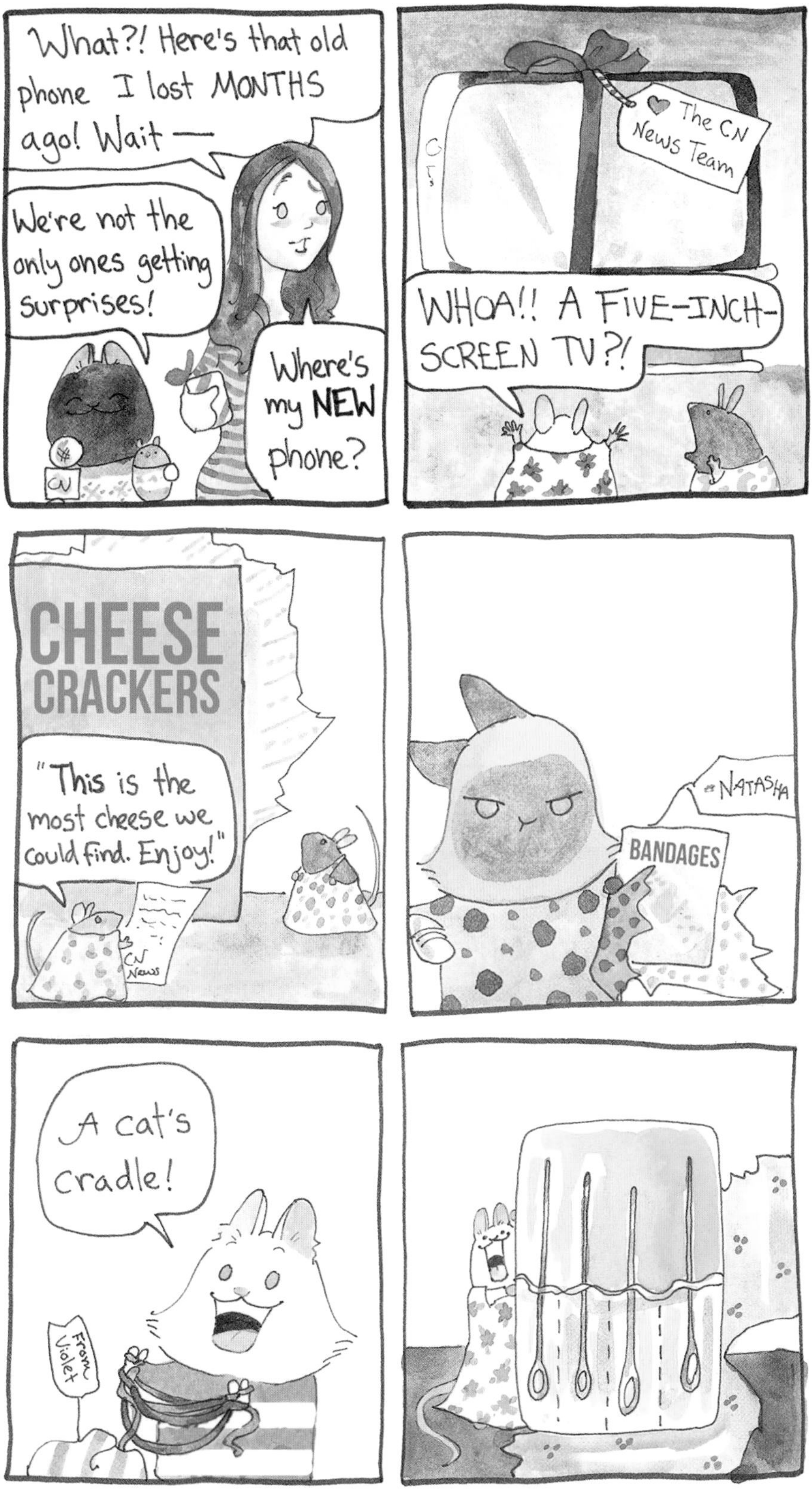

What?! Here's that old phone I lost MONTHS ago! Wait —
We're not the only ones getting surprises!
CN
Where's my **NEW** phone?
♥ The CN News Team
WHOA!! A FIVE-INCH-SCREEN TV?!
CHEESE CRACKERS
"This is the most cheese we could find. Enjoy!"
CN News
♥ NATASHA
BANDAGES
A cat's cradle!
From Violet

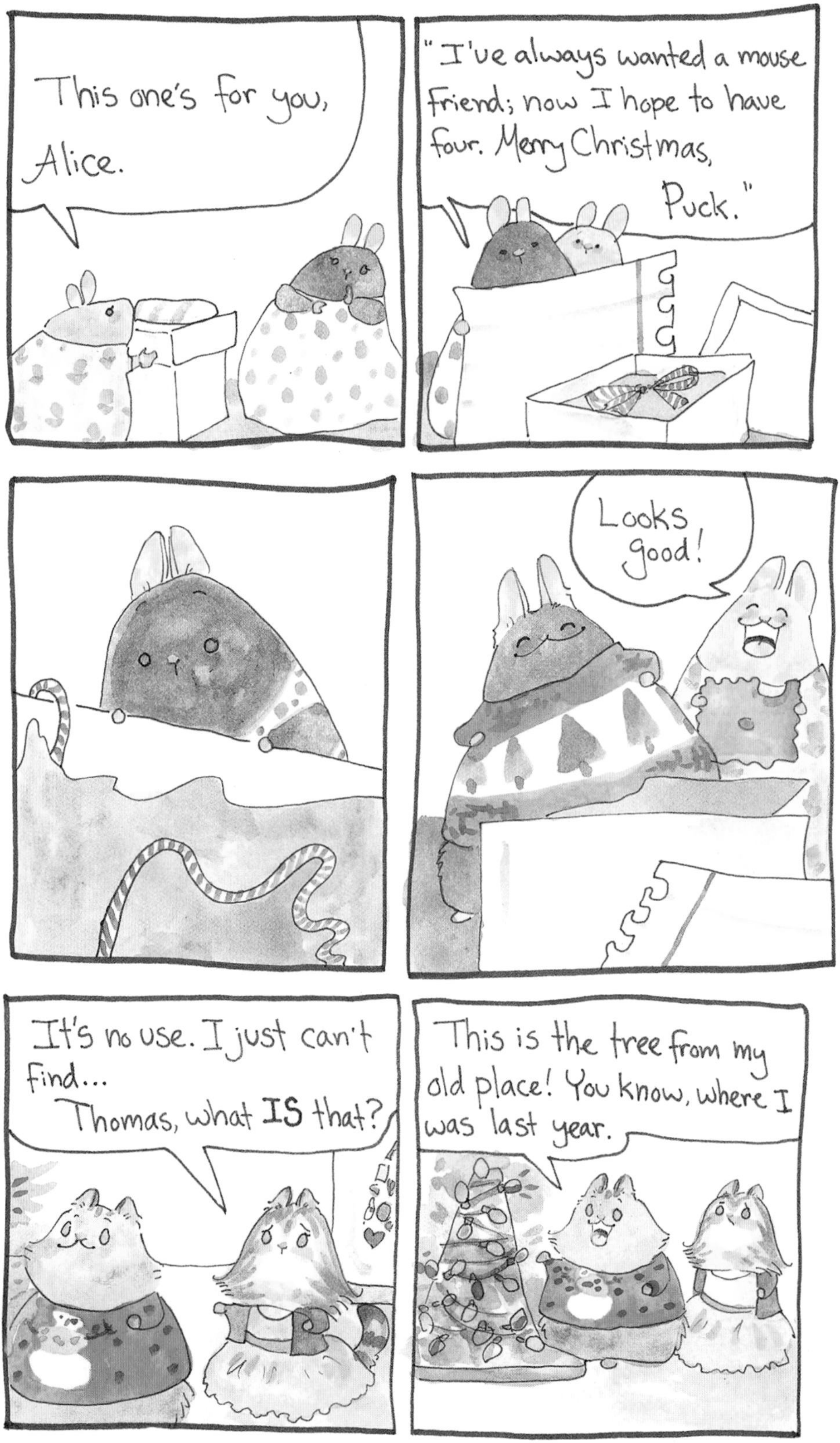
This one's for you, Alice.
"I've always wanted a mouse friend; now I hope to have four. Merry Christmas, Puck."
Looks good!
It's no use. I just can't find...
Thomas, what IS that?
This is the tree from my old place! You know, where I was last year.

Believe it or not, she's not a real tree.

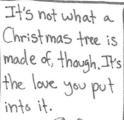

It's not what a Christmas tree is made of, though. It's the love you put into it.

Thomas—

This is kinda... MAGNIFICENT!

I'm glad you're home this year.

Me too.

LIVE

CN

BUMP

A package just arrived!

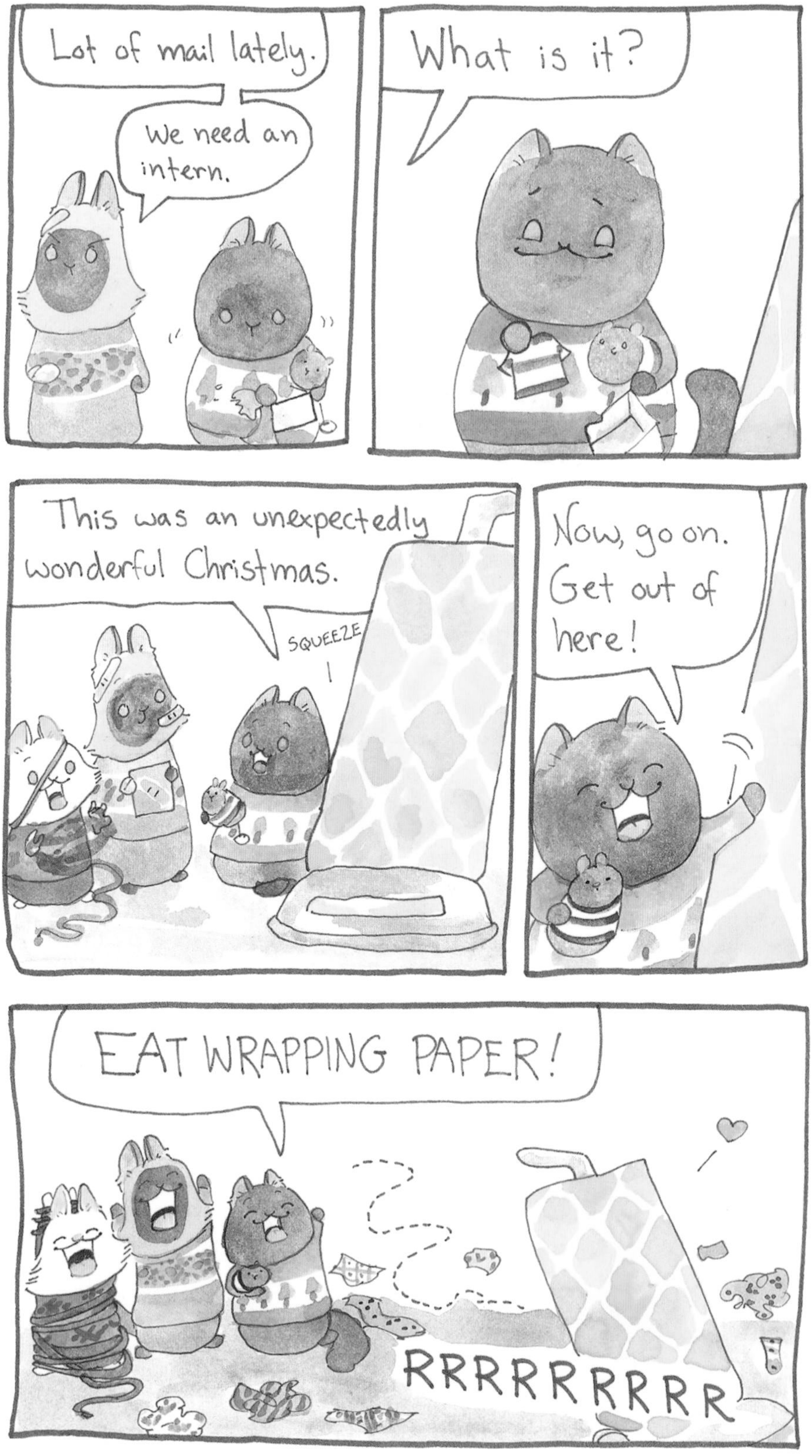
Lot of mail lately.
We need an intern.
What is it?
This was an unexpectedly wonderful Christmas.
SQUEEZE
Now, go on. Get out of here!
EAT WRAPPING PAPER!
RRRRRRRRRR

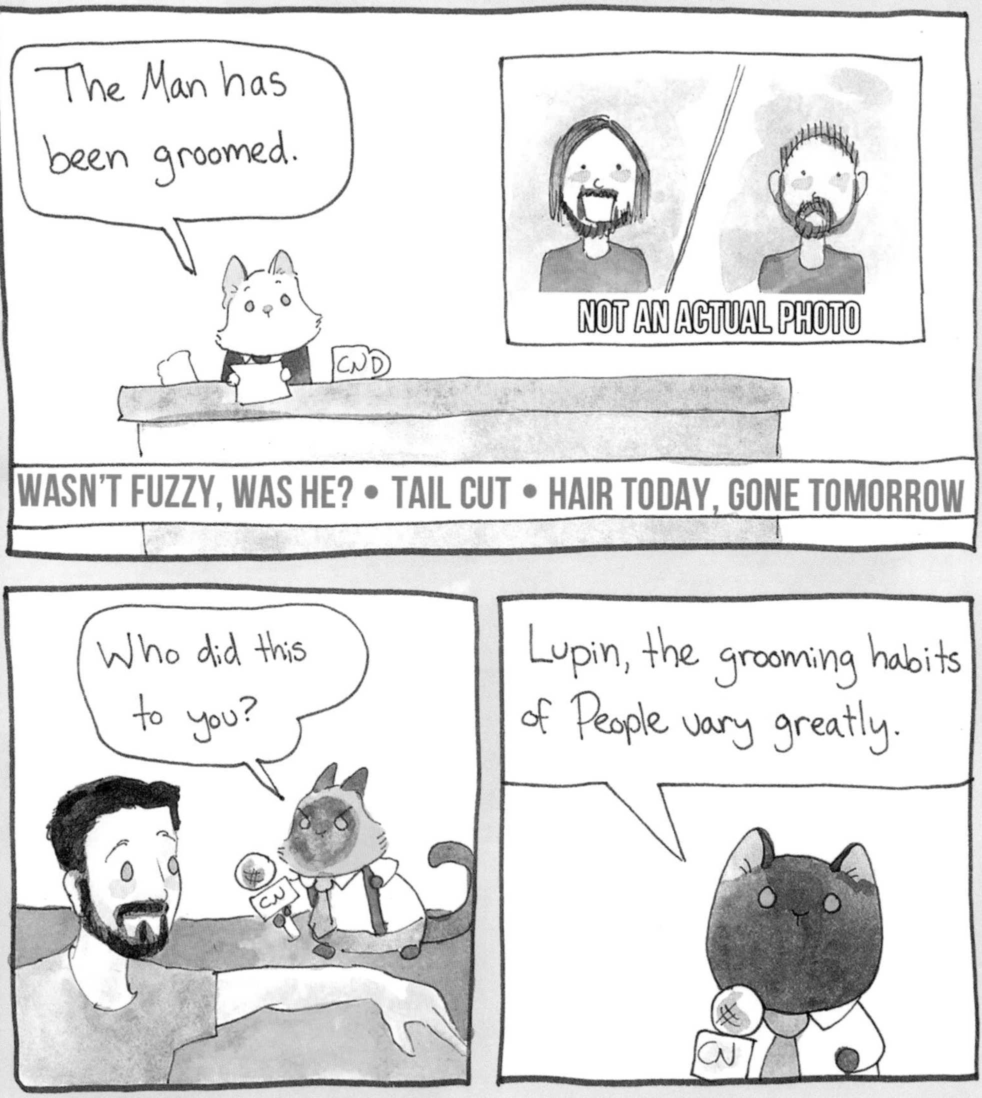
The Man has been groomed.
NOT AN ACTUAL PHOTO
CND
WASN'T FUZZY, WAS HE? • TAIL CUT • HAIR TODAY, GONE TOMORROW
Who did this to you?
CN
Lupin, the grooming habits of People vary greatly.
CN

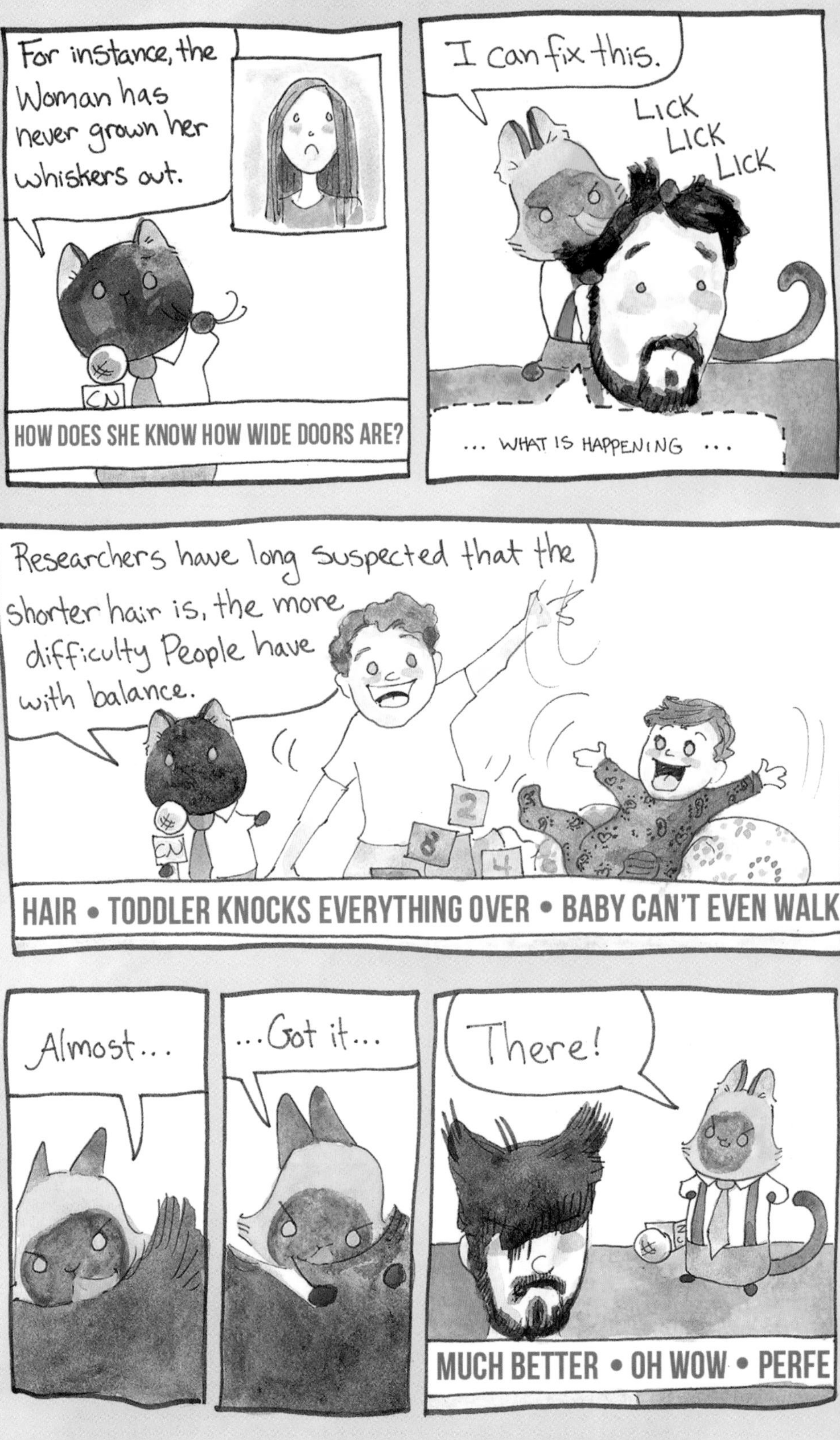
For instance, the Woman has never grown her whiskers out.
CN
HOW DOES SHE KNOW HOW WIDE DOORS ARE?
I can fix this.
LICK LICK LICK
... WHAT IS HAPPENING ...
Researchers have long suspected that the shorter hair is, the more difficulty People have with balance.
CN
HAIR • TODDLER KNOCKS EVERYTHING OVER • BABY CAN'T EVEN WALK
Almost...
...Got it...
There!
MUCH BETTER • OH WOW • PERFE

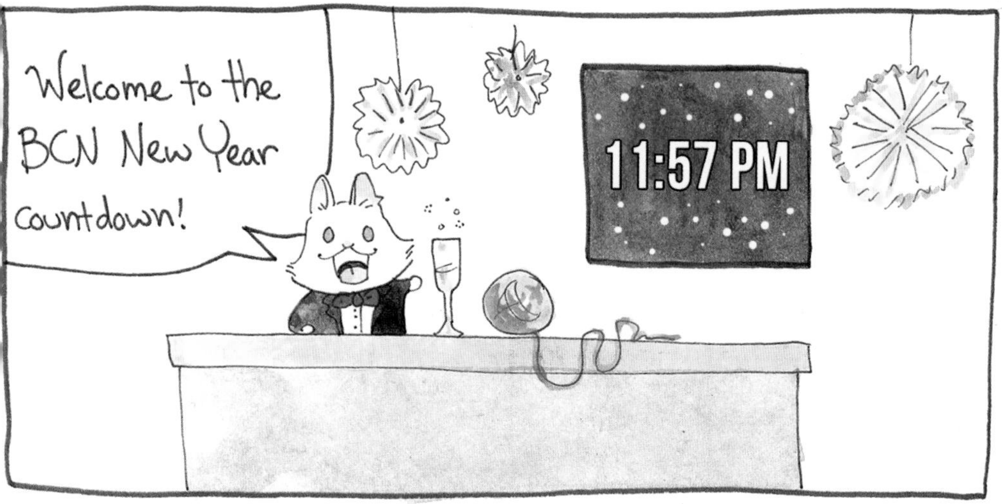
Welcome to the BCN New Year countdown!
11:57 PM

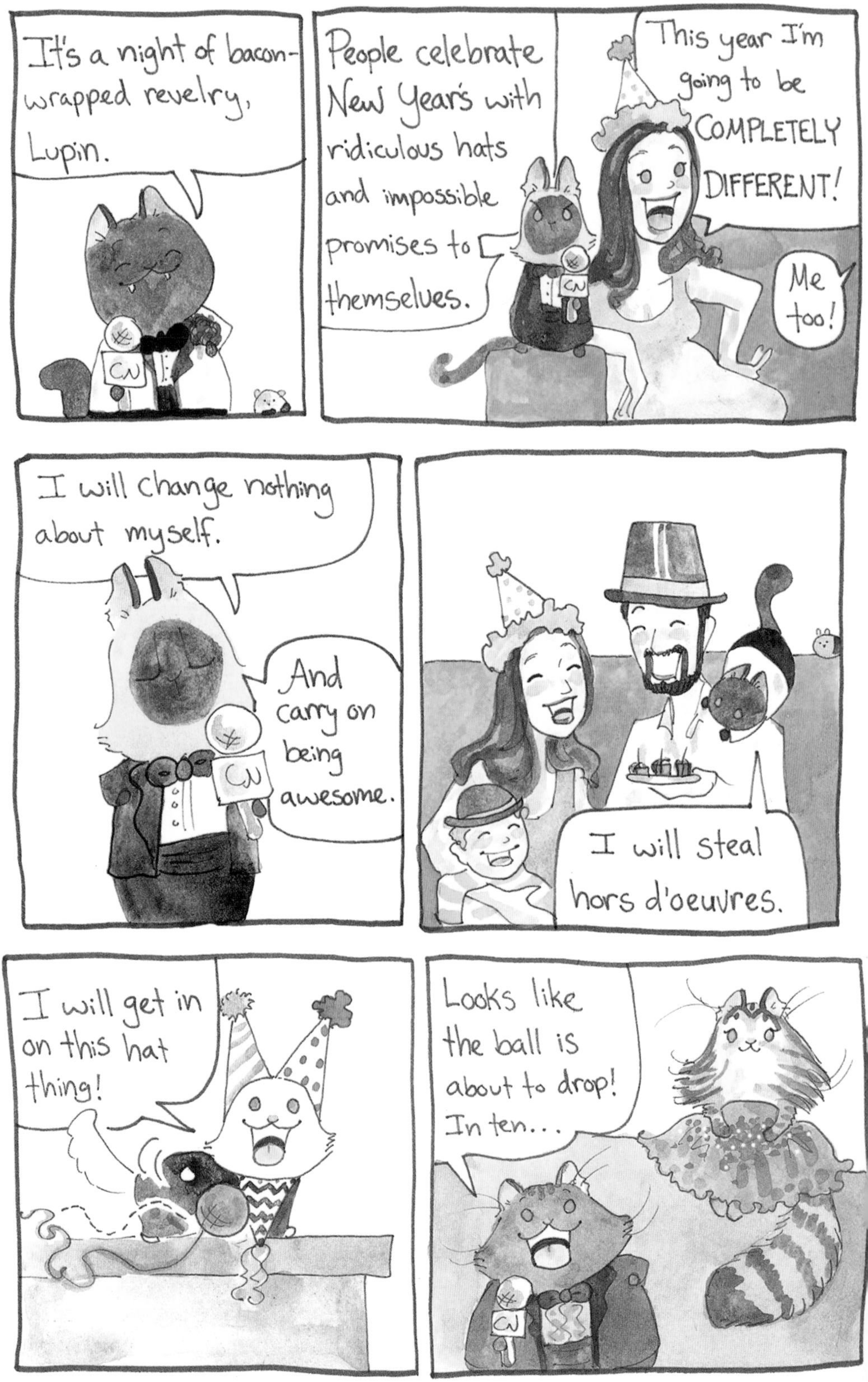
It's a night of bacon-wrapped revelry, Lupin.
People celebrate New Years with ridiculous hats and impossible promises to themselves.
This year I'm going to be COMPLETELY DIFFERENT!
Me too!
CN
I will change nothing about myself.
And carry on being awesome.
CN
I will steal hors d'oeuvres.
I will get in on this hat thing!
Looks like the ball is about to drop! In ten...
CN

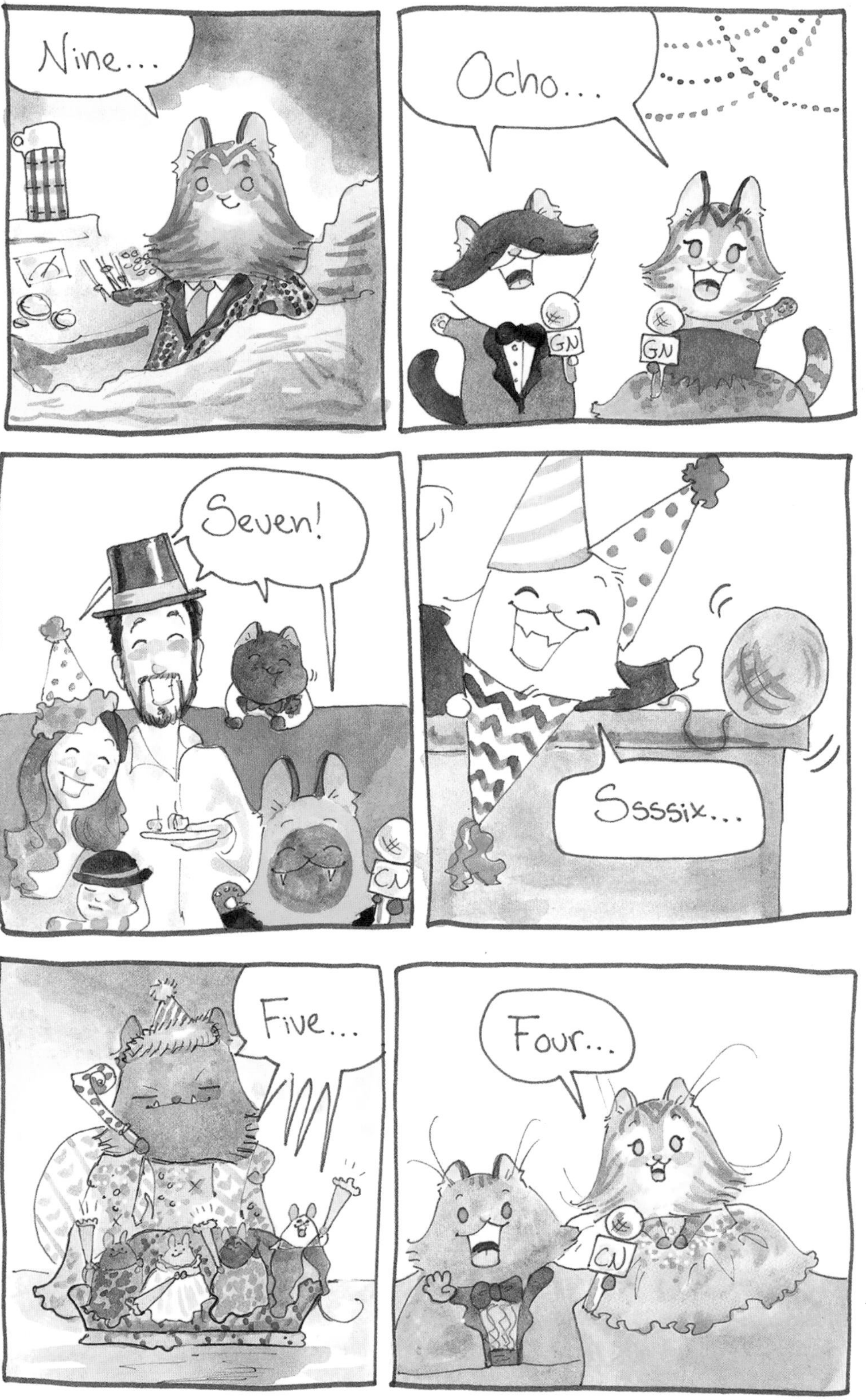
Nine...
Ocho...
GN
GN
Seven!
CN
Sssix...
Five...
Four...
CN

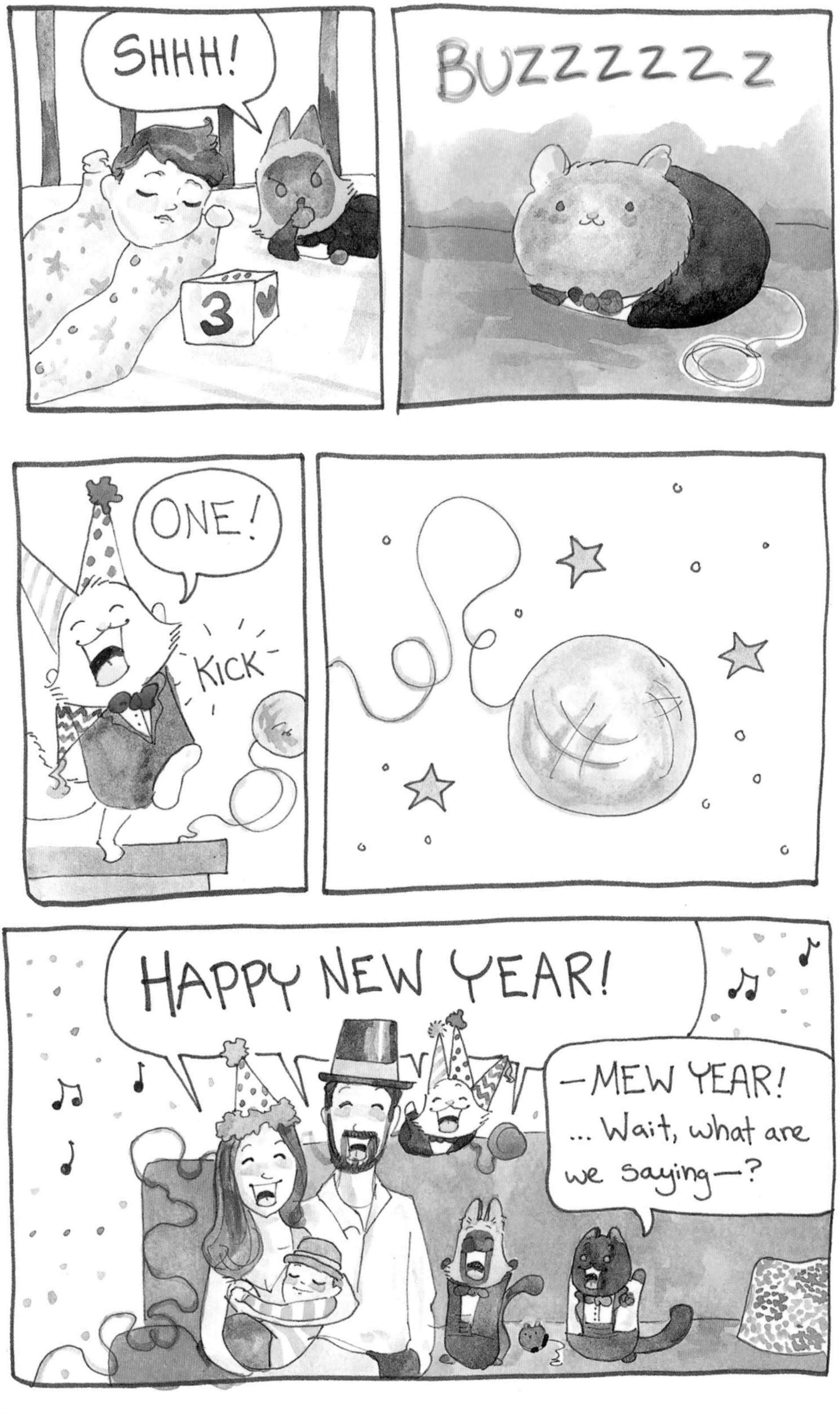
SHHH!
BUZZZZZZZ
3
ONE!
KICK
HAPPY NEW YEAR!
—MEW YEAR!
... Wait, what are we saying—?

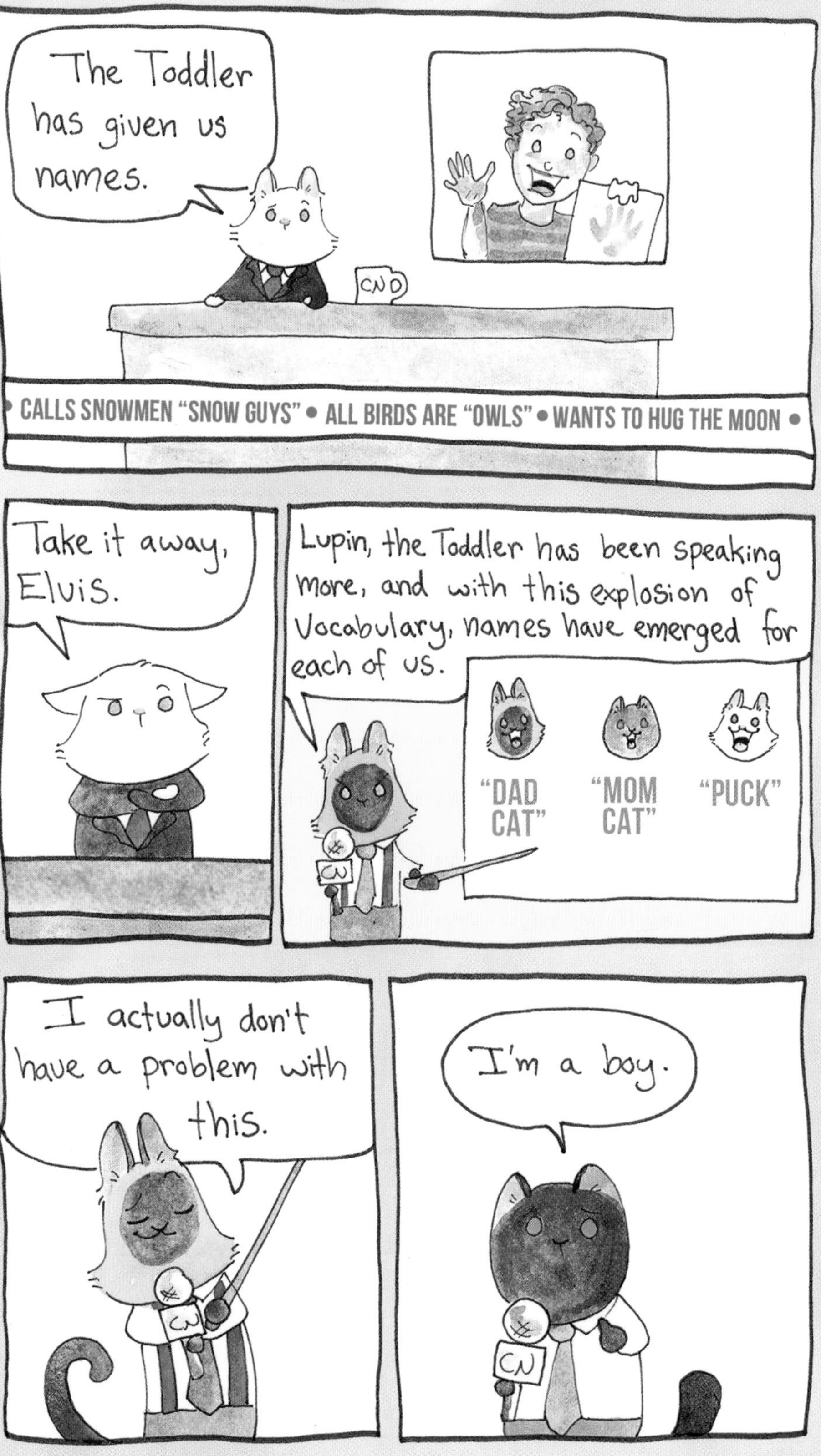
The Toddler has given us names.
CND
• CALLS SNOWMEN "SNOW GUYS" • ALL BIRDS ARE "OWLS" • WANTS TO HUG THE MOON •
Take it away, Elvis.
Lupin, the Toddler has been speaking more, and with this explosion of Vocabulary, names have emerged for each of us.
"DAD CAT"
"MOM CAT"
"PUCK"
CN
I actually don't have a problem with this.
CN
I'm a boy.
CN

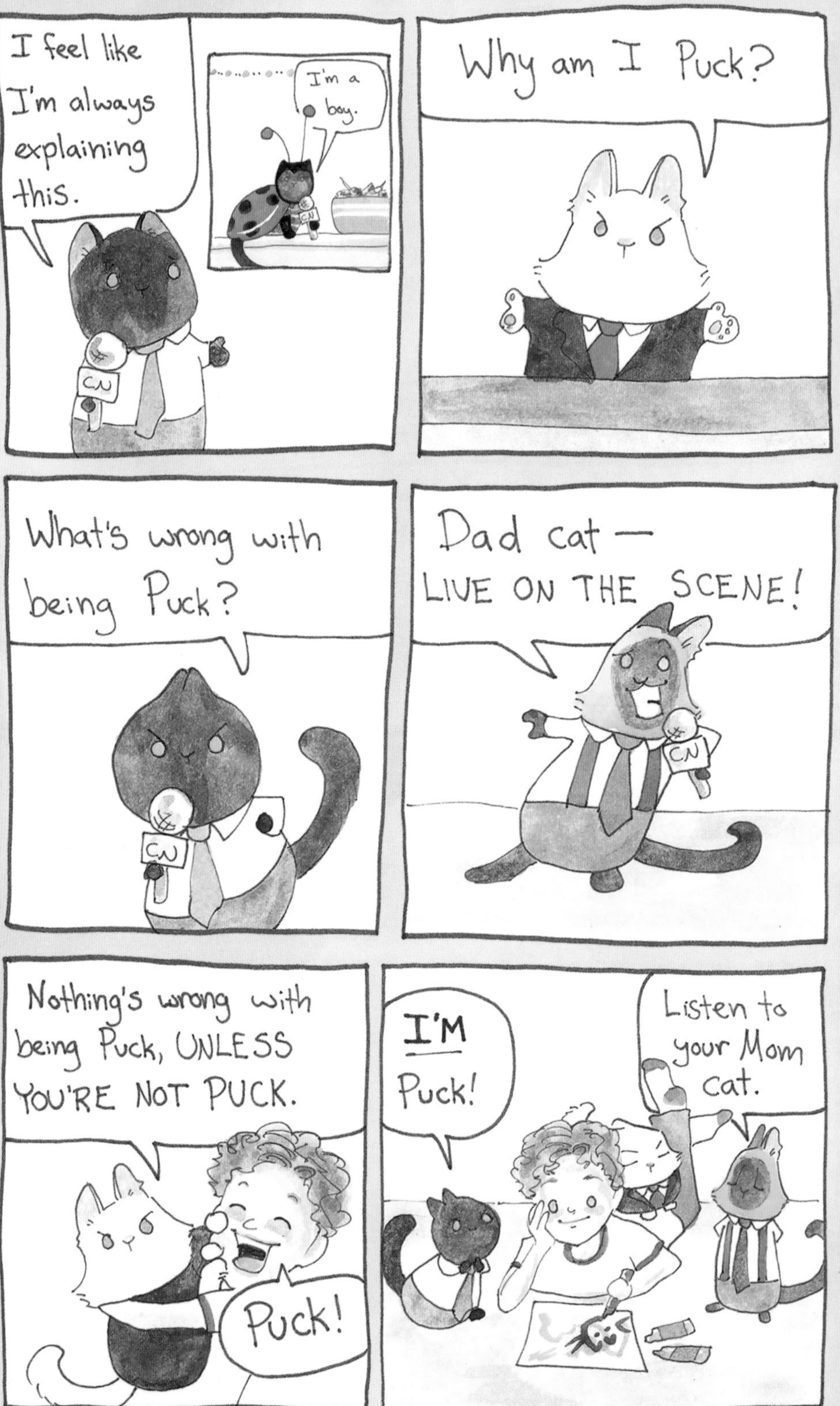

I feel like I'm always explaining this.
I'm a boy.
Why am I Puck?
What's wrong with being Puck?
Dad cat — LIVE ON THE SCENE!
Nothing's wrong with being Puck, UNLESS YOU'RE NOT PUCK.
Puck!
I'M Puck!
Listen to your Mom cat.

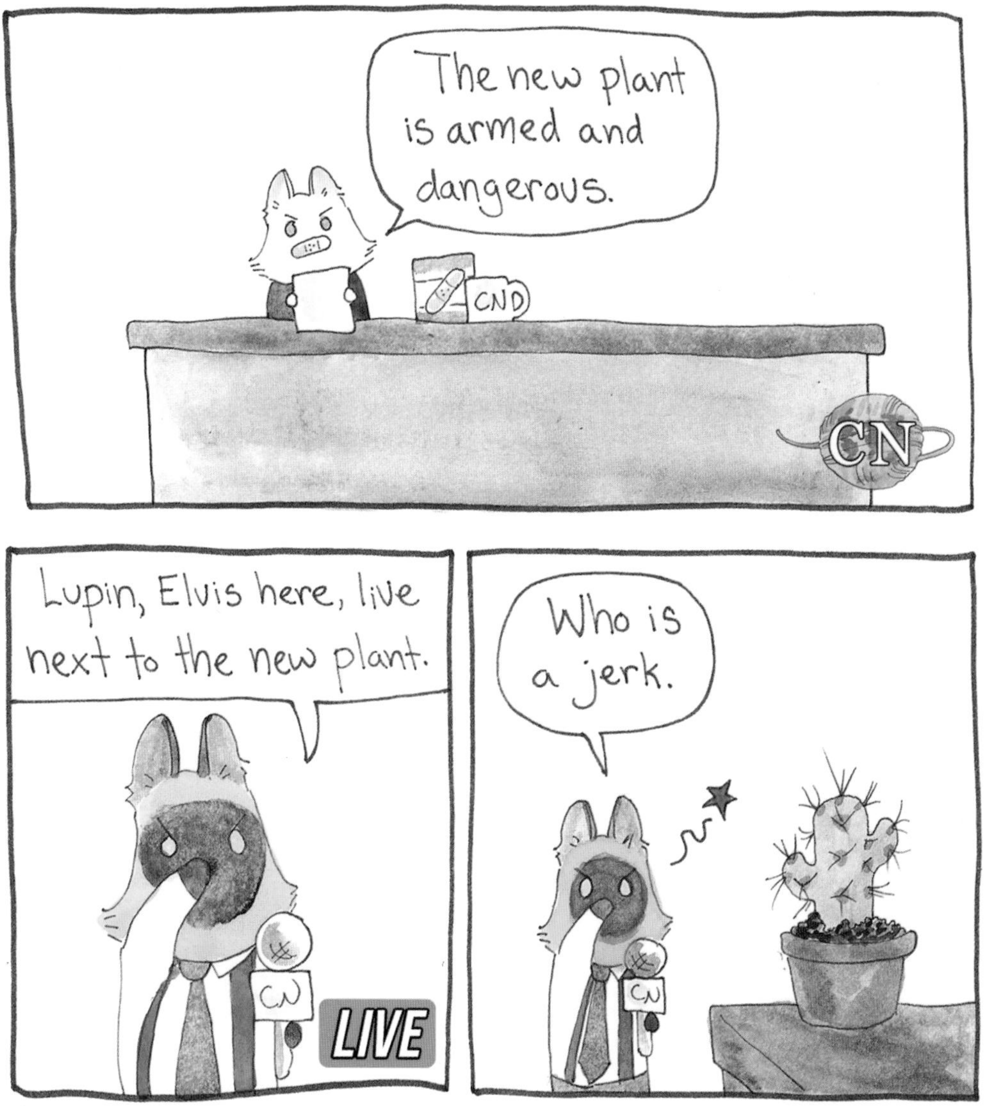
The new plant is armed and dangerous.
CND
CN
Lupin, Elvis here, live next to the new plant.
CN
LIVE
Who is a jerk.
CN

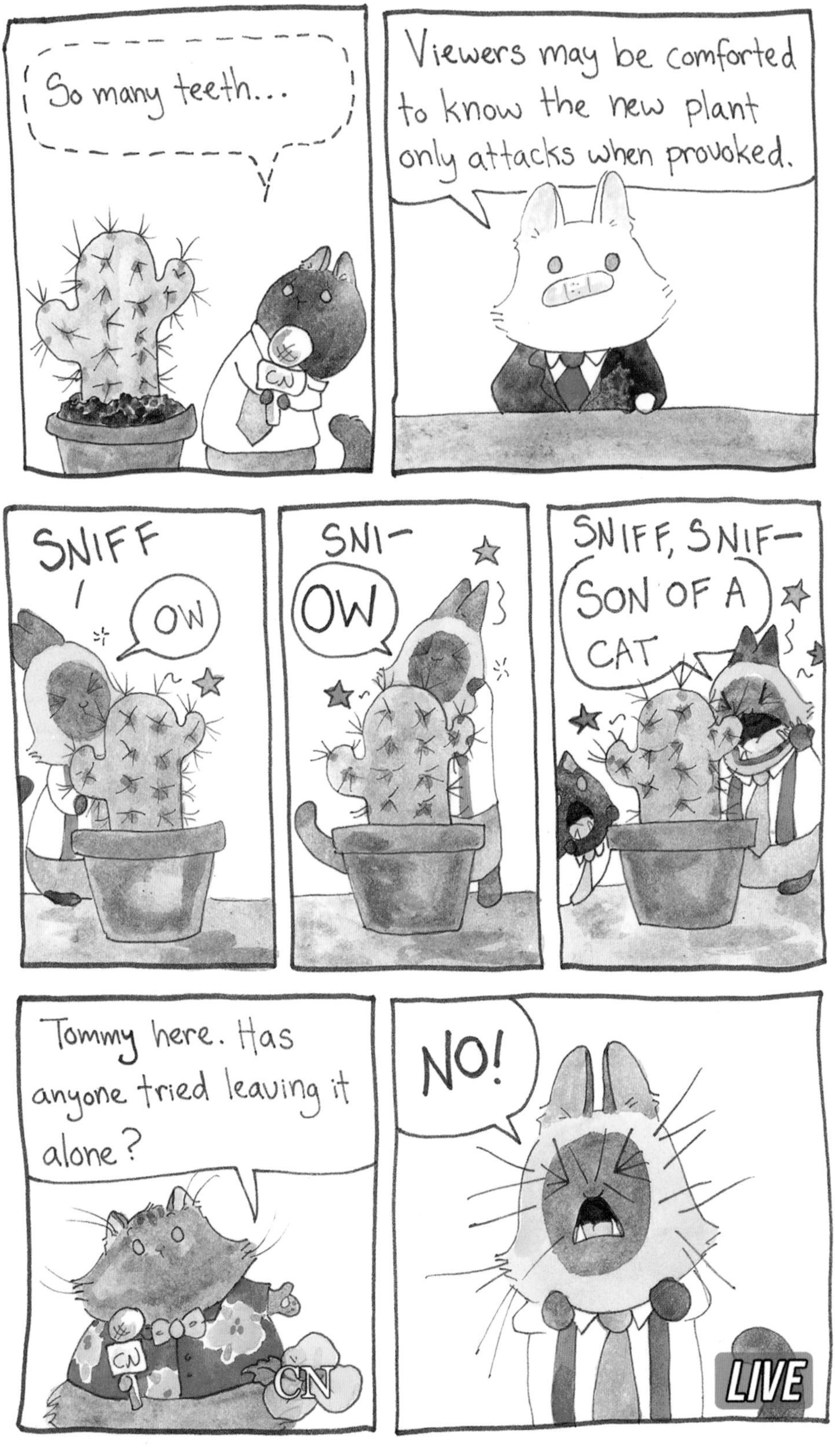

So many teeth...
Viewers may be comforted to know the new plant only attacks when provoked.
CN
SNIFF
OW
SNI-
OW
SNIFF, SNIF-
SON OF A CAT
Tommy here. Has anyone tried leaving it alone?
CN
CN
NO!
LIVE

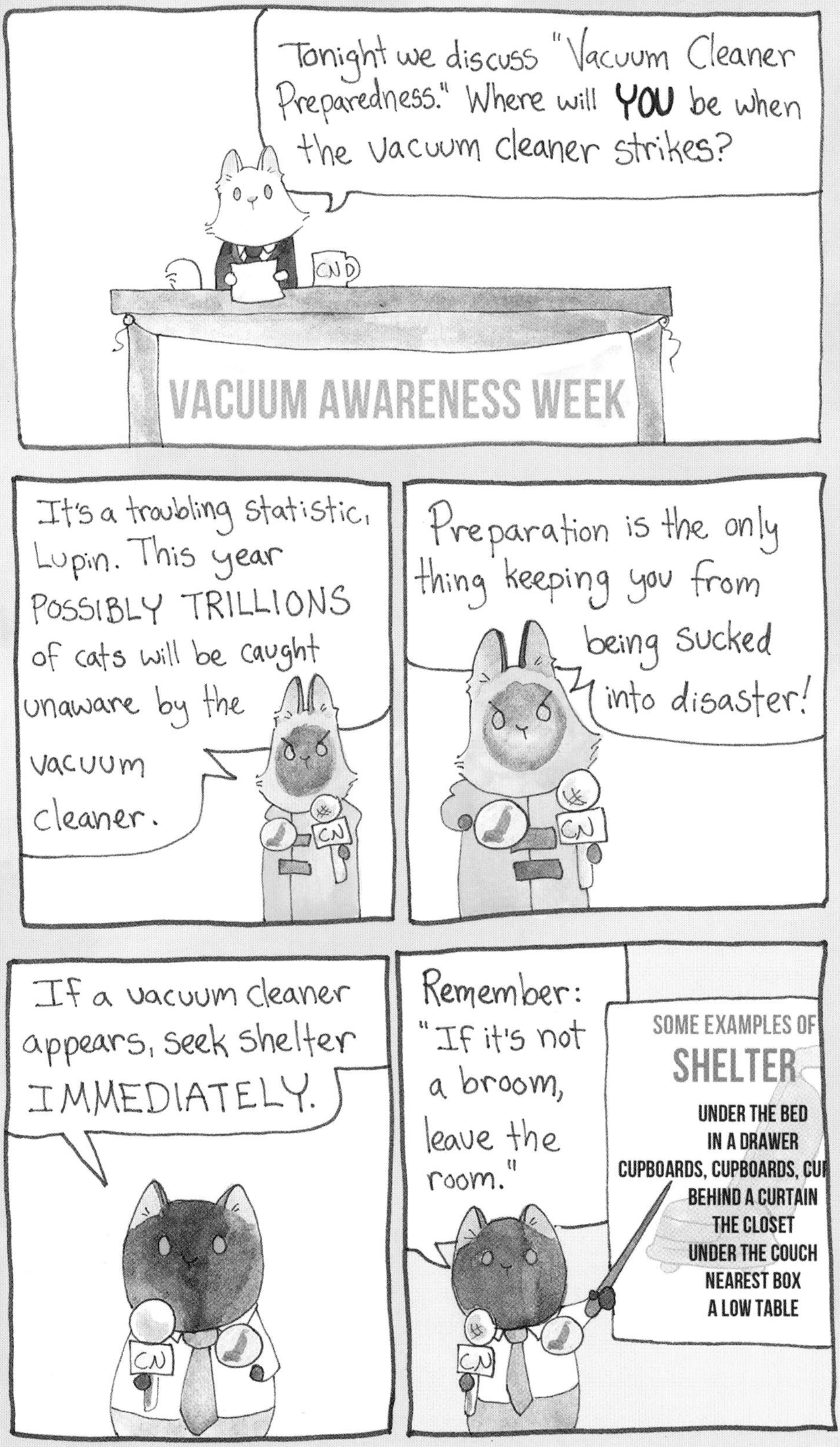
Tonight we discuss "Vacuum Cleaner Preparedness." Where will YOU be when the vacuum cleaner strikes?
CND
VACUUM AWARENESS WEEK
It's a troubling statistic, Lupin. This year POSSIBLY TRILLIONS of cats will be caught unaware by the vacuum cleaner.
CN
Preparation is the only thing keeping you from being sucked into disaster!
CN
If a vacuum cleaner appears, seek shelter IMMEDIATELY.
CN
Remember: "If it's not a broom, leave the room."
SOME EXAMPLES OF
SHELTER
UNDER THE BED
IN A DRAWER
CUPBOARDS, CUPBOARDS, CU
BEHIND A CURTAIN
THE CLOSET
UNDER THE COUCH
NEAREST BOX
A LOW TABLE
CN

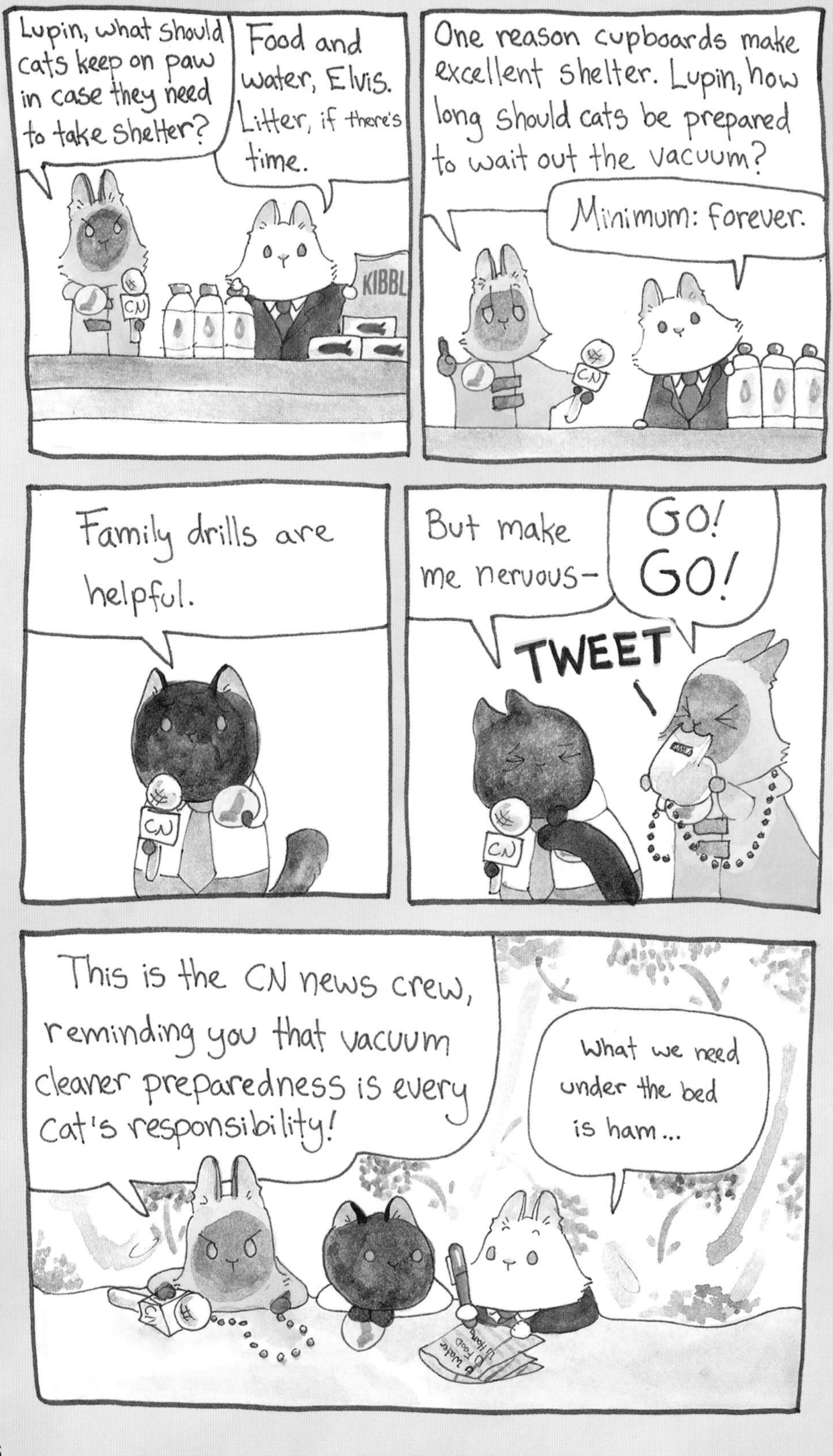
Lupin, what should cats keep on paw in case they need to take shelter?
Food and water, Elvis. Litter, if there's time.
KIBBL
CN
One reason cupboards make excellent shelter. Lupin, how long should cats be prepared to wait out the vacuum?
Minimum: forever.
CN
Family drills are helpful.
CN
But make me nervous—
GO! GO!
TWEET
CN
This is the CN news crew, reminding you that vacuum cleaner preparedness is every cat's responsibility!
What we need under the bed is ham...
Water
Food
Ham

And now for today's episode of
Our IX Lives
Angora-
I don't want you seeing that Kit Chase scoundrel.
It's bad enough Princess had to run off with that Sailor's cat... Only to have him LOST AT SEA—
!
SLAM

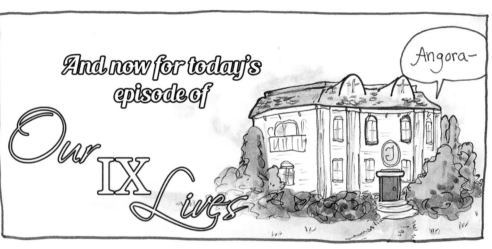

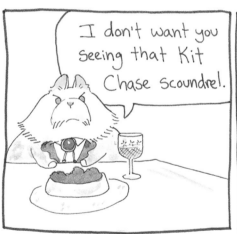

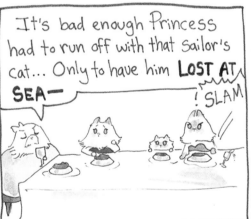

Captain Nimble and I were in **love.** You'd understand if you ever took the time to know him!

Mama—

This arguing is bad for my heart. Where are my pills...

Father!

Relax Angora, FATHER HAS NO HEART—

Took **you** back in, didn't I? Show up on my doorstep wrapped in a fishing net, with a **kitten**... Now, please. I need my rest.

Father—

Grandpoppy—

UGH

Thank goodness for my pills...

Cheese ball
YUMMY NOM NOM
KITTY TREATS

♫ DRAMATIC ♪ MUSIC ♪

WINK

Cheese ball
KITTY TREATS

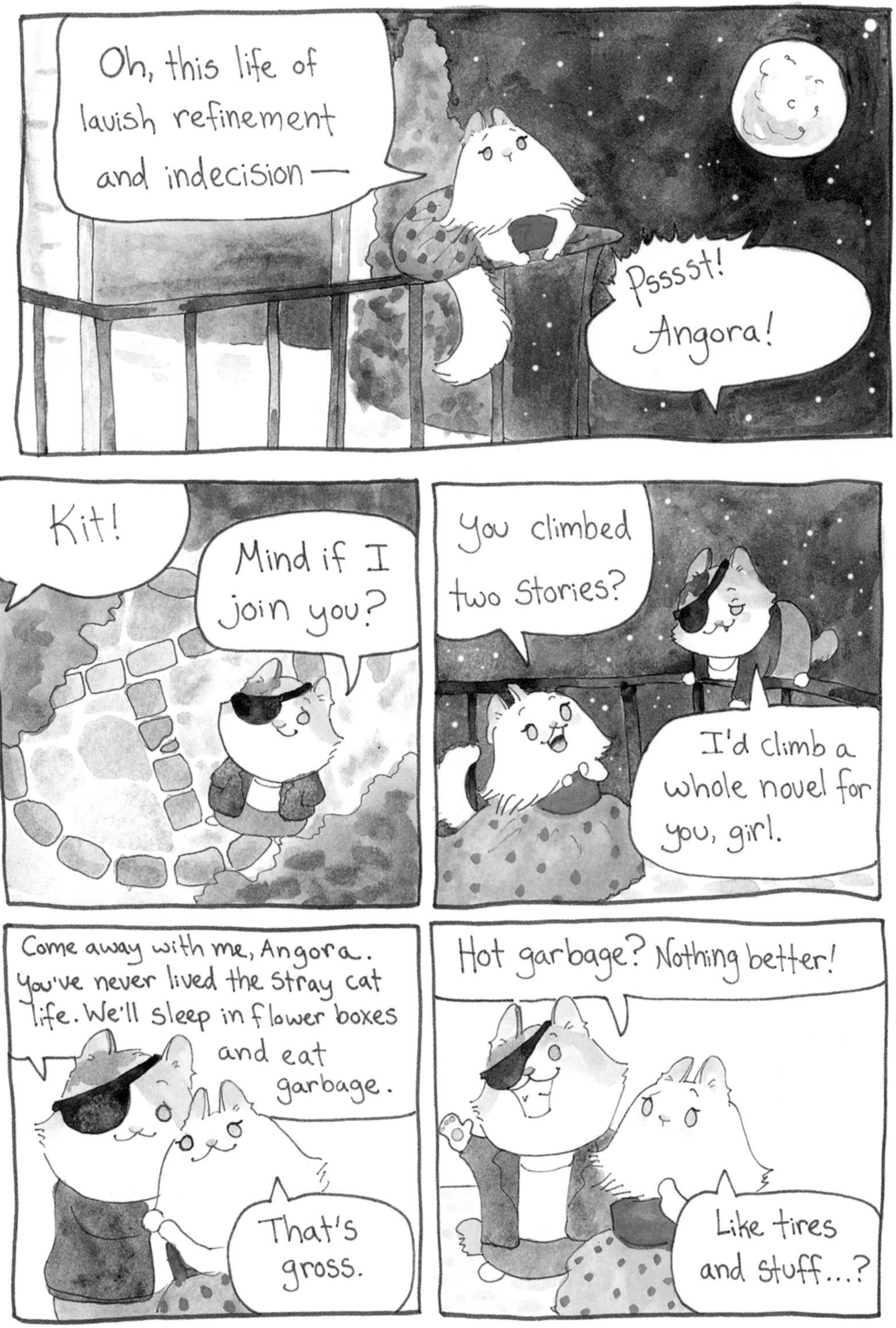
Oh, this life of lavish refinement and indecision—
Psssst! Angora!
Kit!
Mind if I join you?
You climbed two stories?
I'd climb a whole novel for you, girl.
Come away with me, Angora. You've never lived the stray cat life. We'll sleep in flower boxes and eat garbage.
That's gross.
Hot garbage? Nothing better!
Like tires and stuff...?

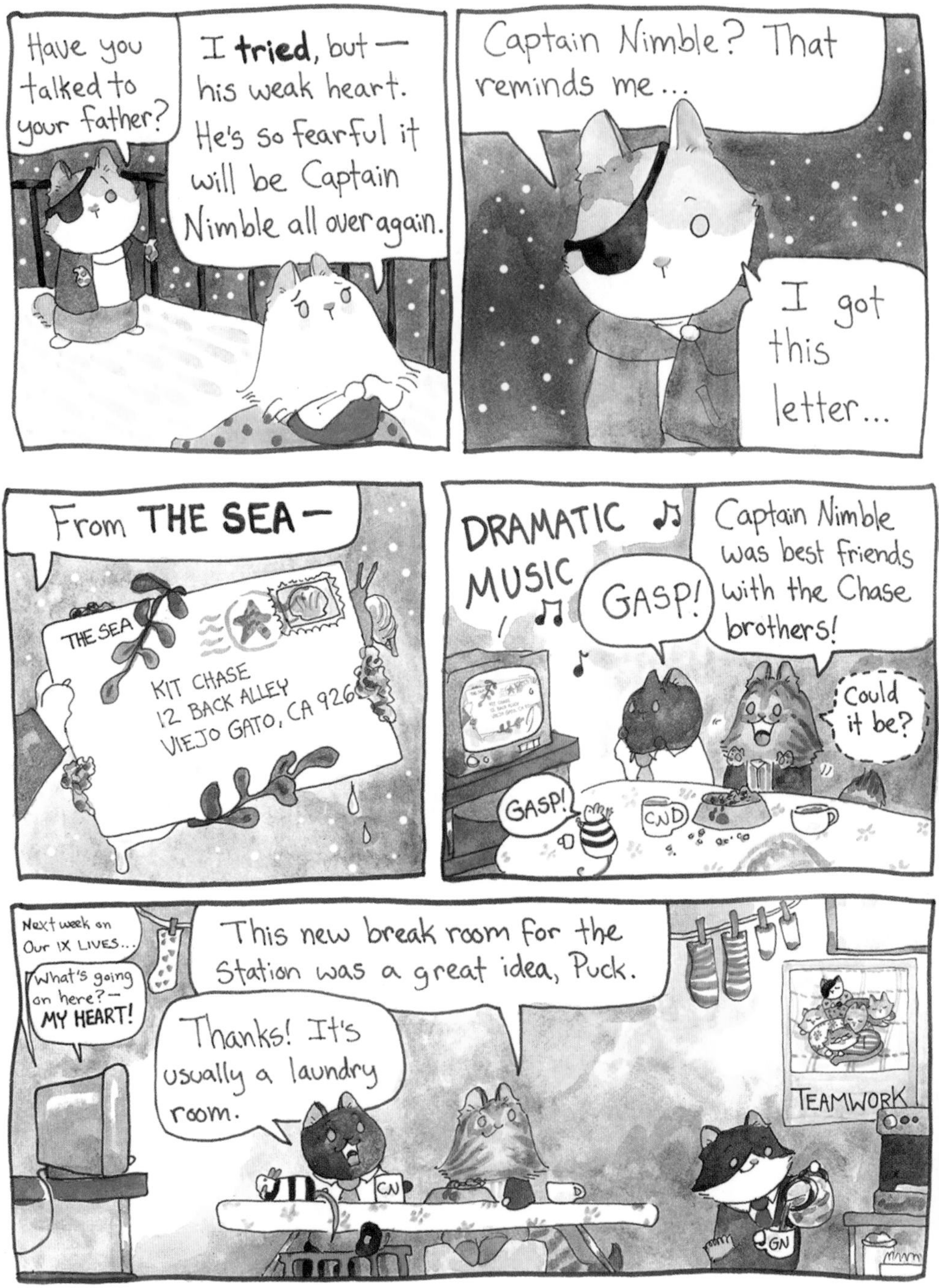
Have you talked to your father?
I **tried**, but— his weak heart. He's so fearful it will be Captain Nimble all over again.
Captain Nimble? That reminds me...
I got this letter...
From **THE SEA**—
THE SEA
KIT CHASE
12 BACK ALLEY
VIEJO GATO, CA 926
DRAMATIC MUSIC
GASP!
Captain Nimble was best friends with the Chase brothers!
Could it be?
GASP!
CND
Next week on Our IX LIVES...
What's going on here?— **MY HEART!**
This new break room for the Station was a great idea, Puck.
Thanks! It's usually a laundry room.
CN
TEAMWORK
GN

Elvis got into the butter.
CND
Lupin, Puck here on the scene where the Woman turned her back on the butter.
CN
And Elvis hopped the train...
Right to Buttertown.
CN

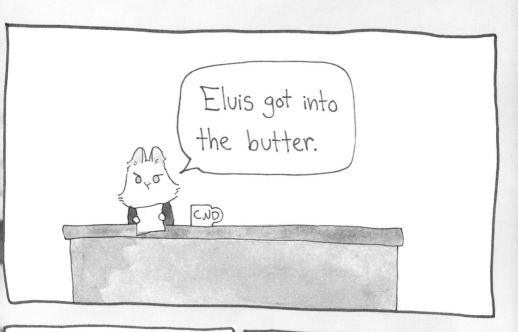

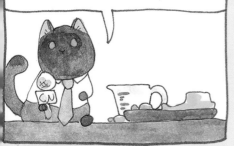

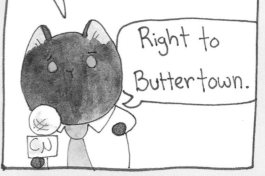

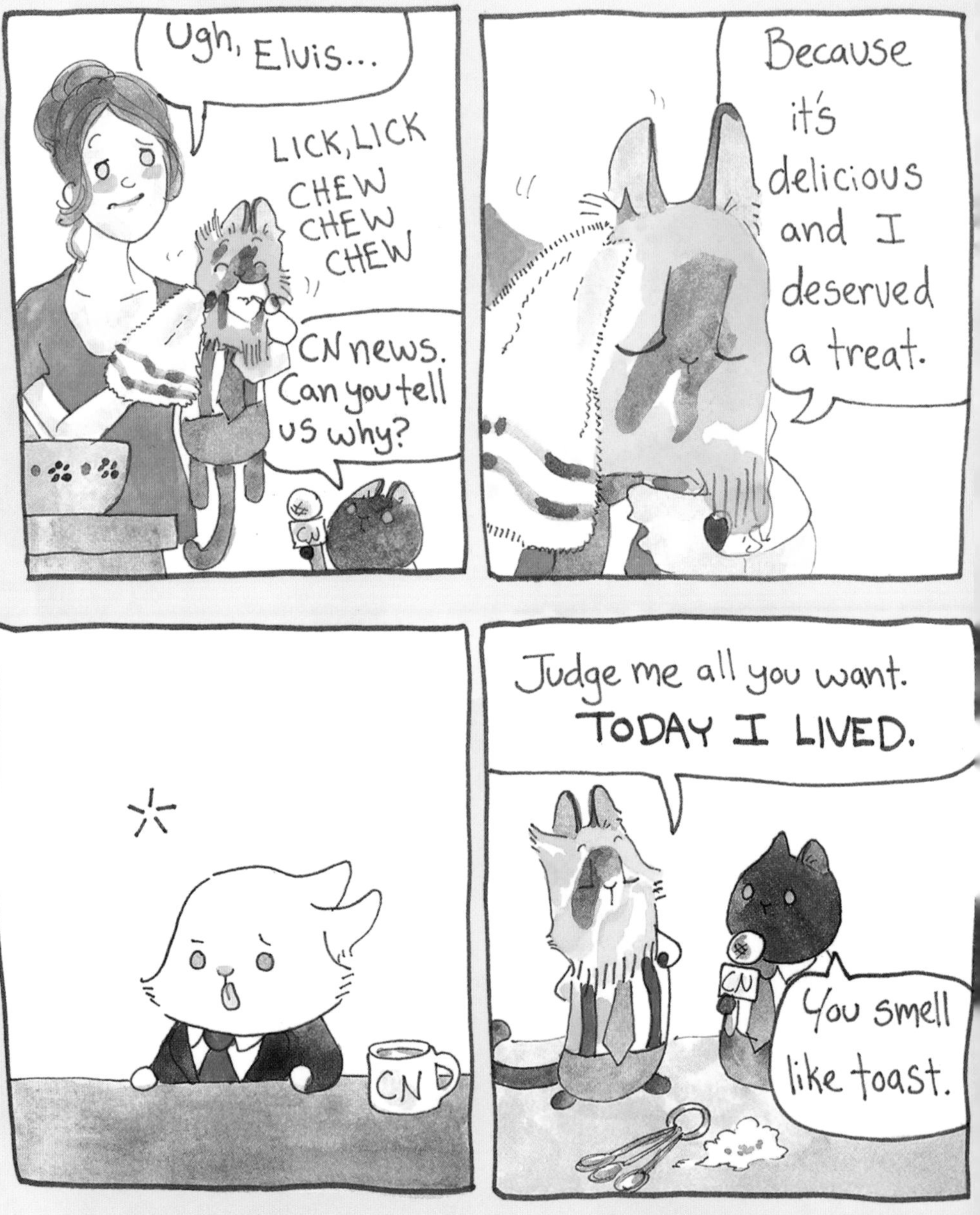
Ugh, Elvis...
LICK, LICK
CHEW
CHEW
CHEW
CN news. Can you tell us why?
CN
Because it's delicious and I deserved a treat.
CN
Judge me all you want.
TODAY I LIVED.
CN
You smell like toast.

MORE TO EXPLORE! Featuring cool activities and fun facts!

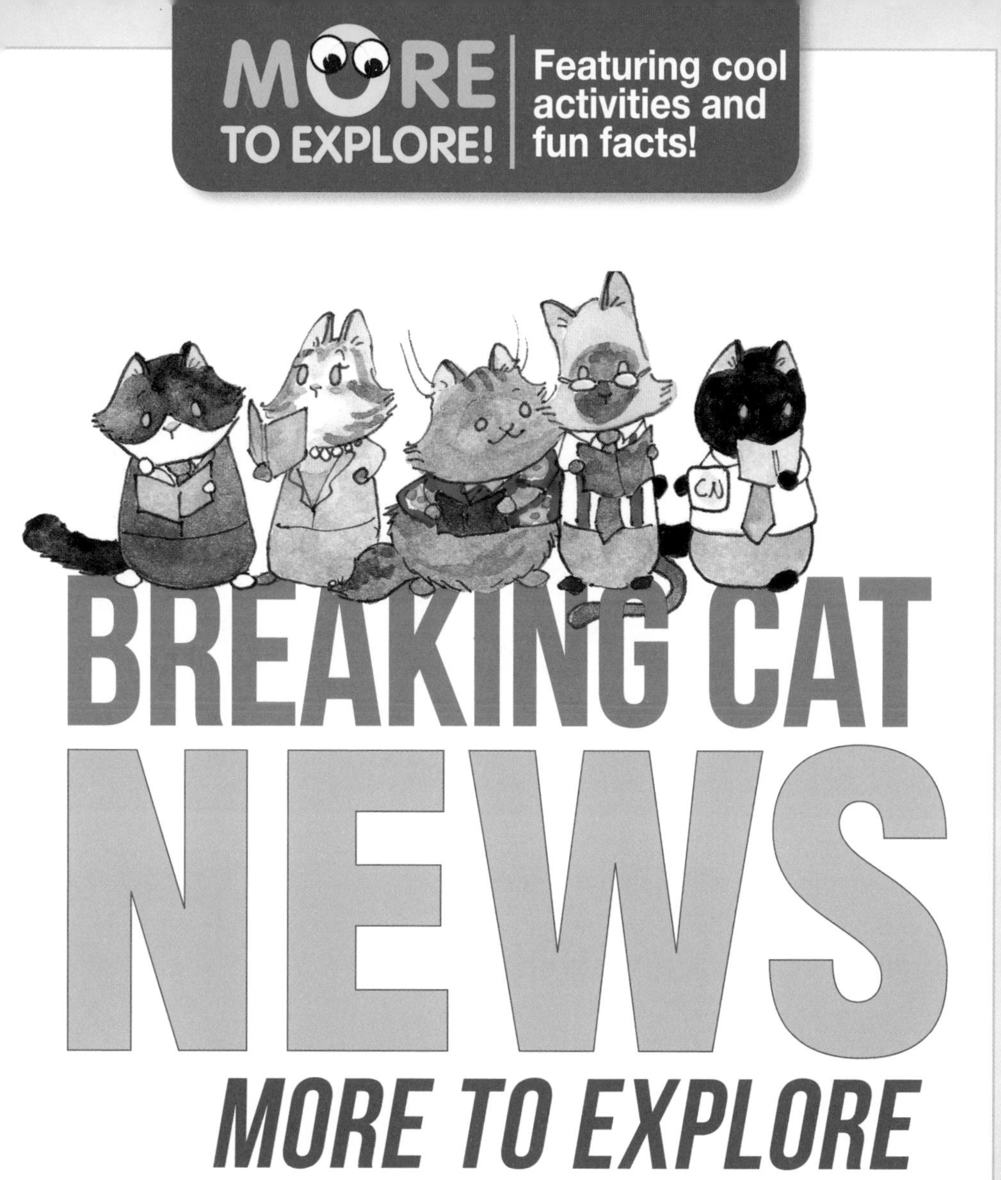
CN

BREAKING CAT NEWS

MORE TO EXPLORE

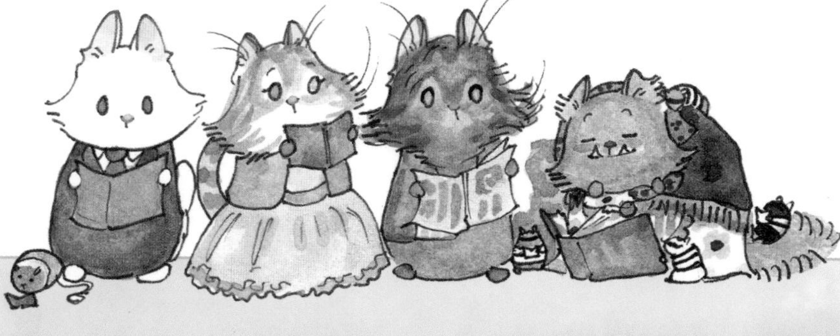

PET ROCK REPORTERS!

This fun art project is for everyone with allergies who would love a pet but can't have one. Or maybe you'd just like to have 15 cats without spending a fortune on kibble! Pet rocks are great listeners and fit right in your pocket. They're always ready for an adventure, and they love to report on the news too!

YOU WILL NEED:

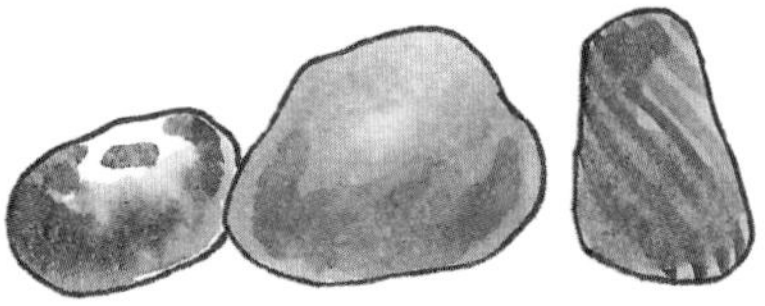

Rocks: Try to find smooth, flat rocks. These make great little canvases for painting. Don't be afraid of some weird, bumpy rocks though! It can be really fun to use a rock's unique shape in your design.

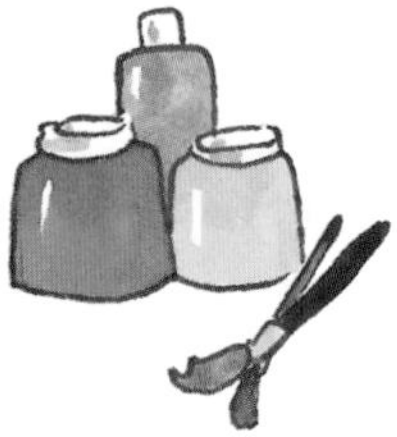

Paint and paintbrushes: I've found that water-based acrylics work best on stone.

PAINT YOUR ROCKS ONE SOLID COLOR

Wash your rocks, dry them, and paint them one solid color. White will allow for a lot of details. Light orange is great for a tabby. Black is perfect for black kitties!

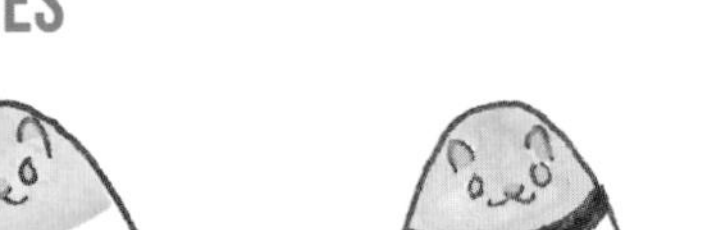

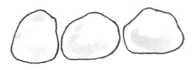

ADD FUR, FACES, AND CLOTHES

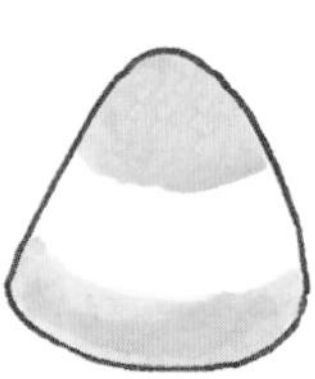

Start from the fur up!

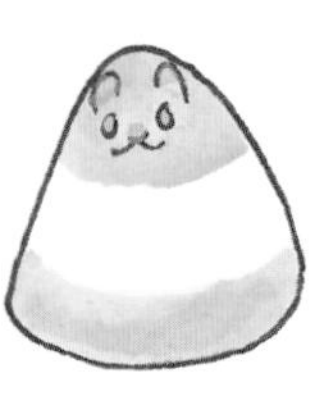

Add two eyes, ears, a nose, and a mouth.

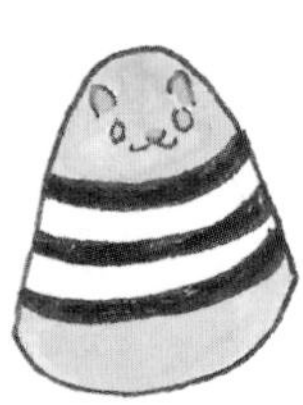

You're ready to paint the clothes!

Before you paint your rock, take a moment to study its shape. Where do you see a face? Where would you put your pet rock's shirt? Would a gown work on your pet rock?

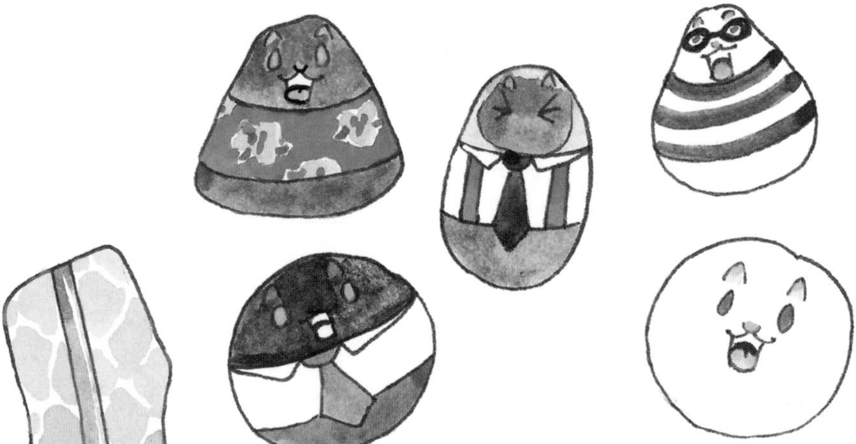

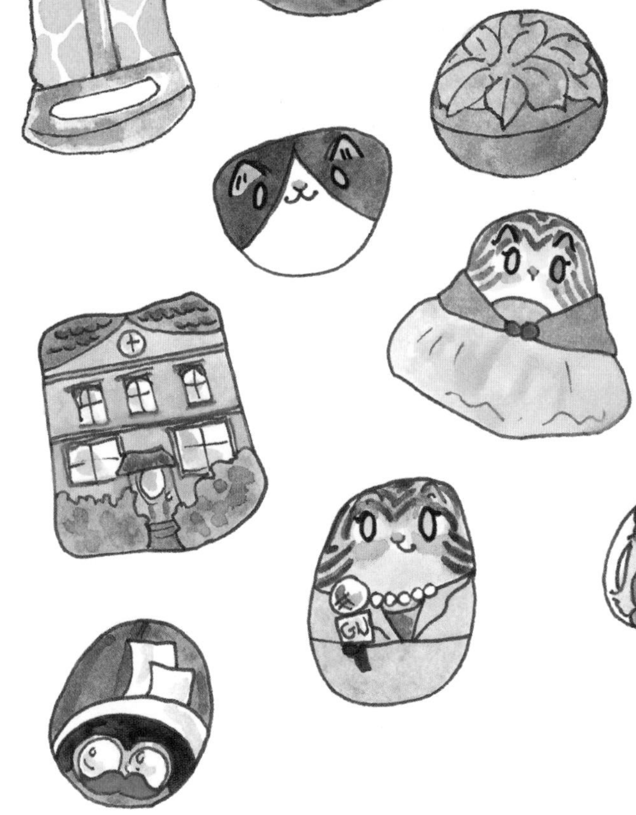
GN

Rocks are free and come in countless shapes and sizes! You'll never run out of rocks for your ideas!

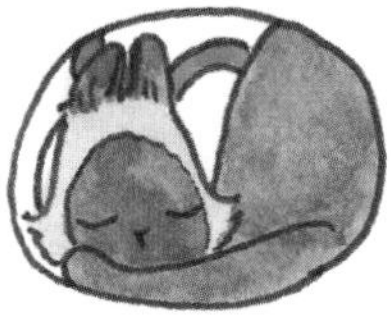

THE BIG PINK HOUSE

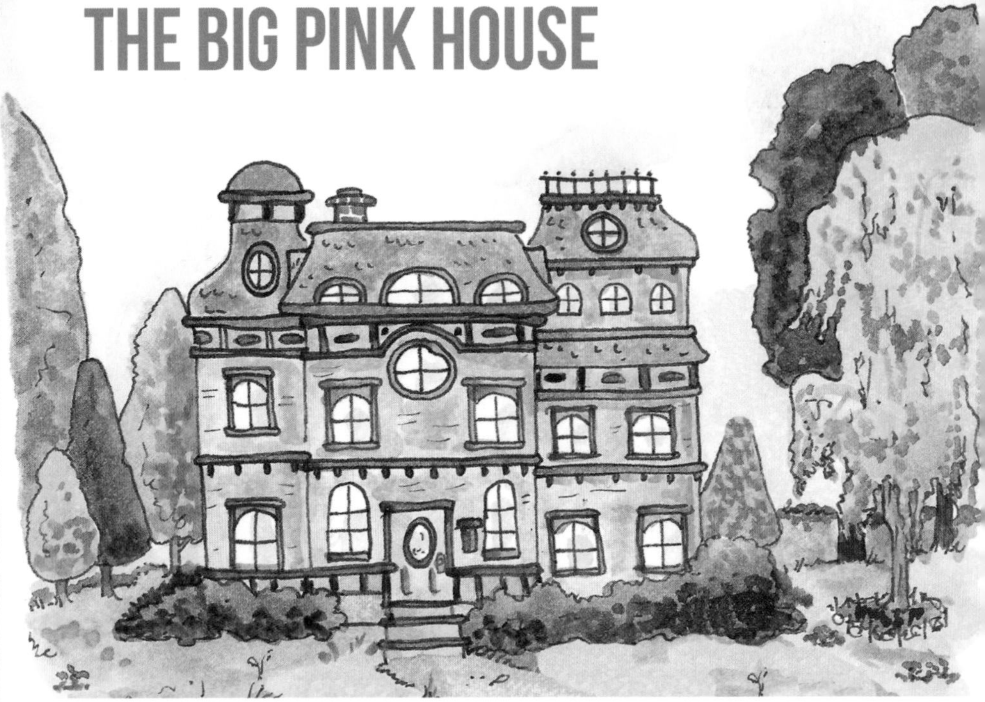

Most of the action in "Breaking Cat News" takes place in the Big Pink House, the apartment building where Elvis, Puck, and Lupin live with the People. Tabitha and Sir Figaro live upstairs. (Reporters do not know anything about the downstairs apartment at this time.)

The Big Pink House used to belong to the Quinn family, before it was sold and split into apartments. It still shares an attic, a basement, and several common hallways. It is built on a hill, so whenever Tommy or Burt are seen outside a window, viewers can assume they are in the backyard.

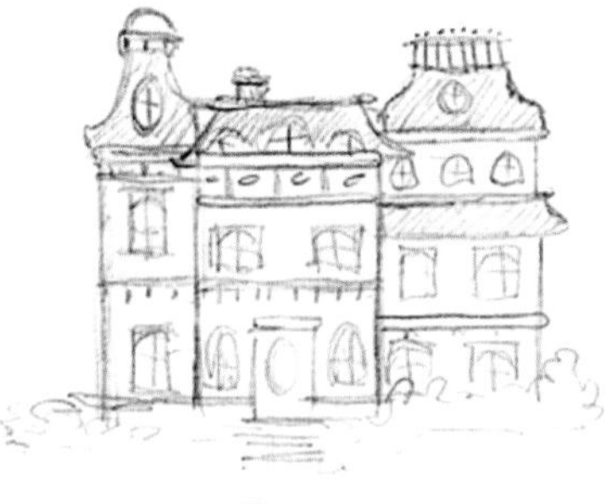

Front

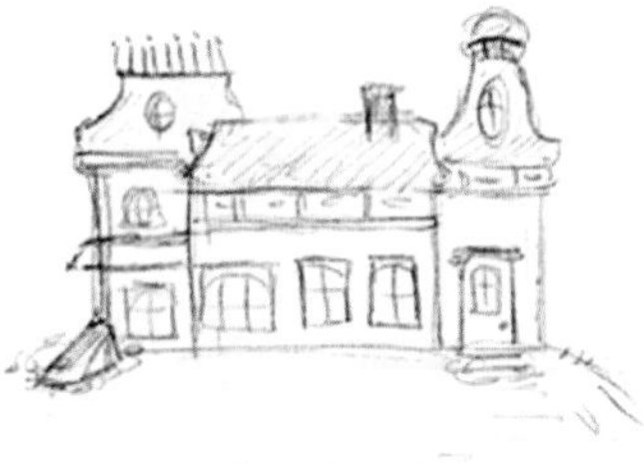

Back

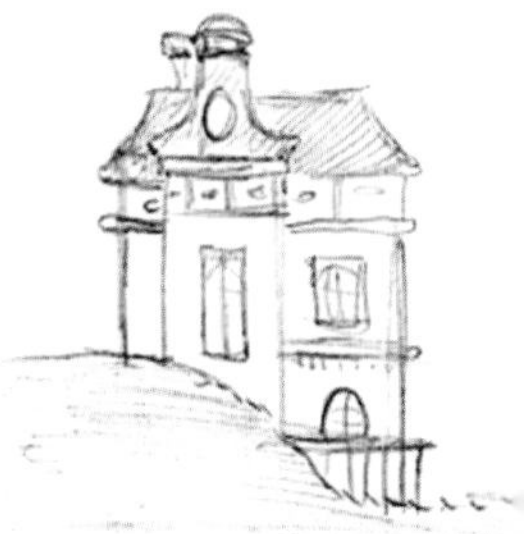

Side

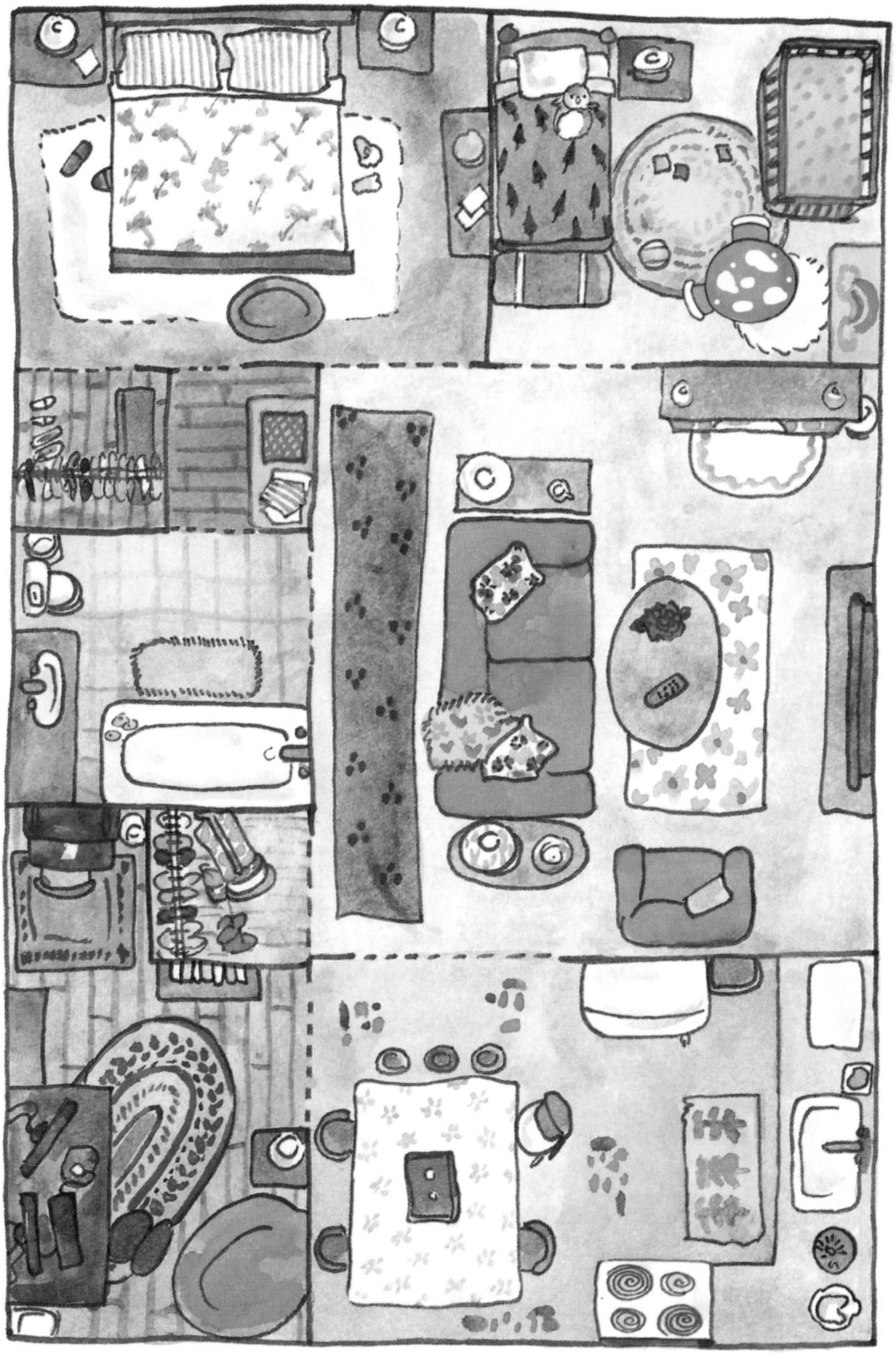

THE APARTMENT

TIPS FOR PAPER DOLLS!

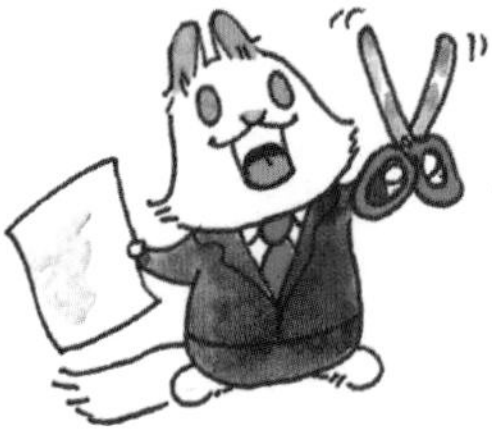

Scissors:
Safety first!
Be careful,
take your time.

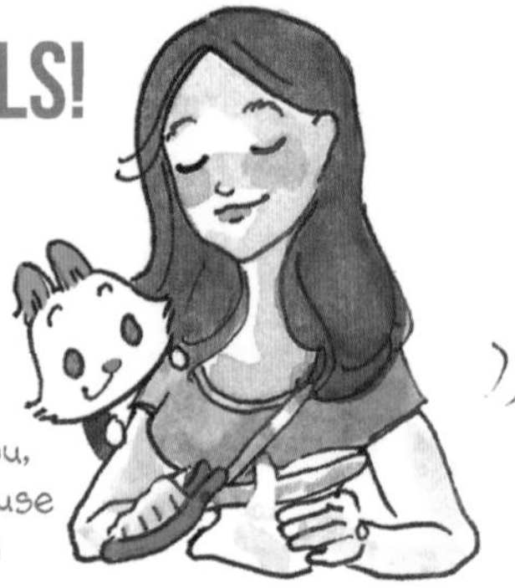

Ask someone to help you, if you're not allowed to use scissors. (...Like Lupin)

Make your own clothes:
Flip a patterned piece of paper over and trace an outfit face down. Cut it out and you've got pajamas or a fancy new suit! (Or draw and color an outfit on the tracing!)

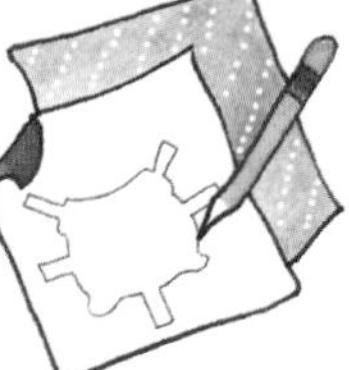

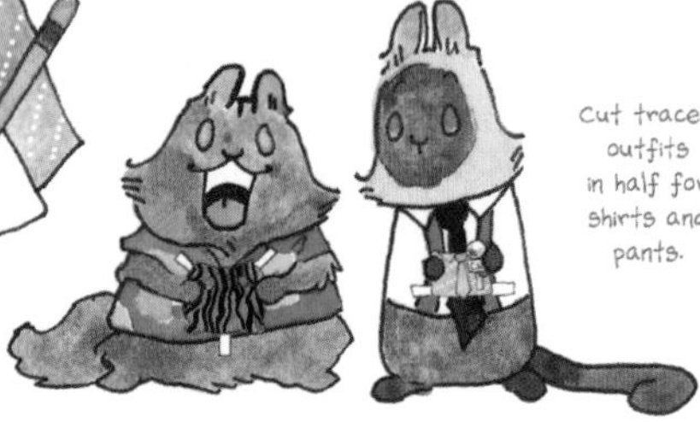

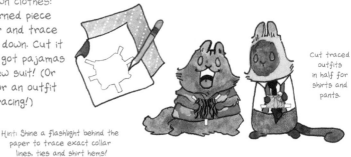

Cut traced outfits in half for shirts and pants.

Hint: Shine a flashlight behind the paper to trace exact collar lines, ties and shirt hems!

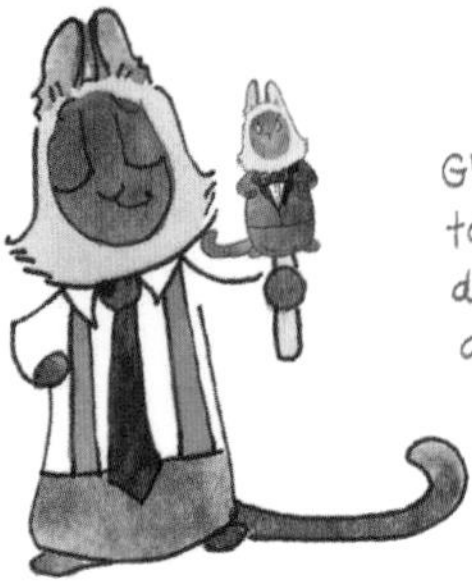

Puppets:
Glue a popsicle stick to the back of each doll, and you've got a little puppet to move around and voice!

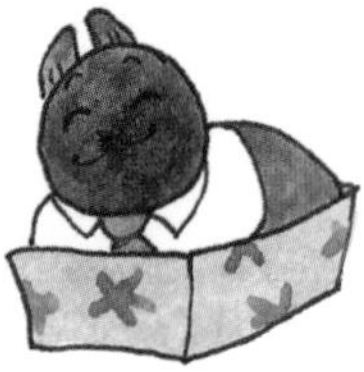

Boxes:
They're not just for naps anymore!
Turn any box into a puppet theater.

Puppet Theaters: By cutting a window into a box, you can create a puppet theater! You can even make your own cardboard television and act out broadcasts inside! Delivery boxes, shoe boxes, and oatmeal containers all make great little theaters.

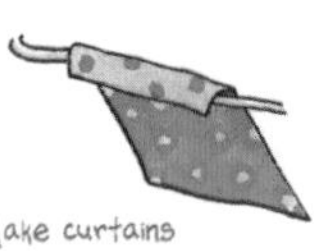

Make curtains for your theater by looping fabric over string and fastening it with glue, thread, or safety pins.

Decorate your theater with paint, crayons, craft paper, scraps of fabric, stickers—anything you have!

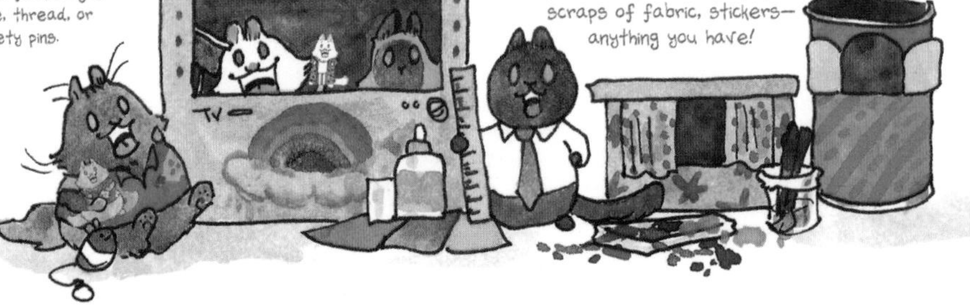
TV

BREAKING CAT NEWS PAPER DOLLS

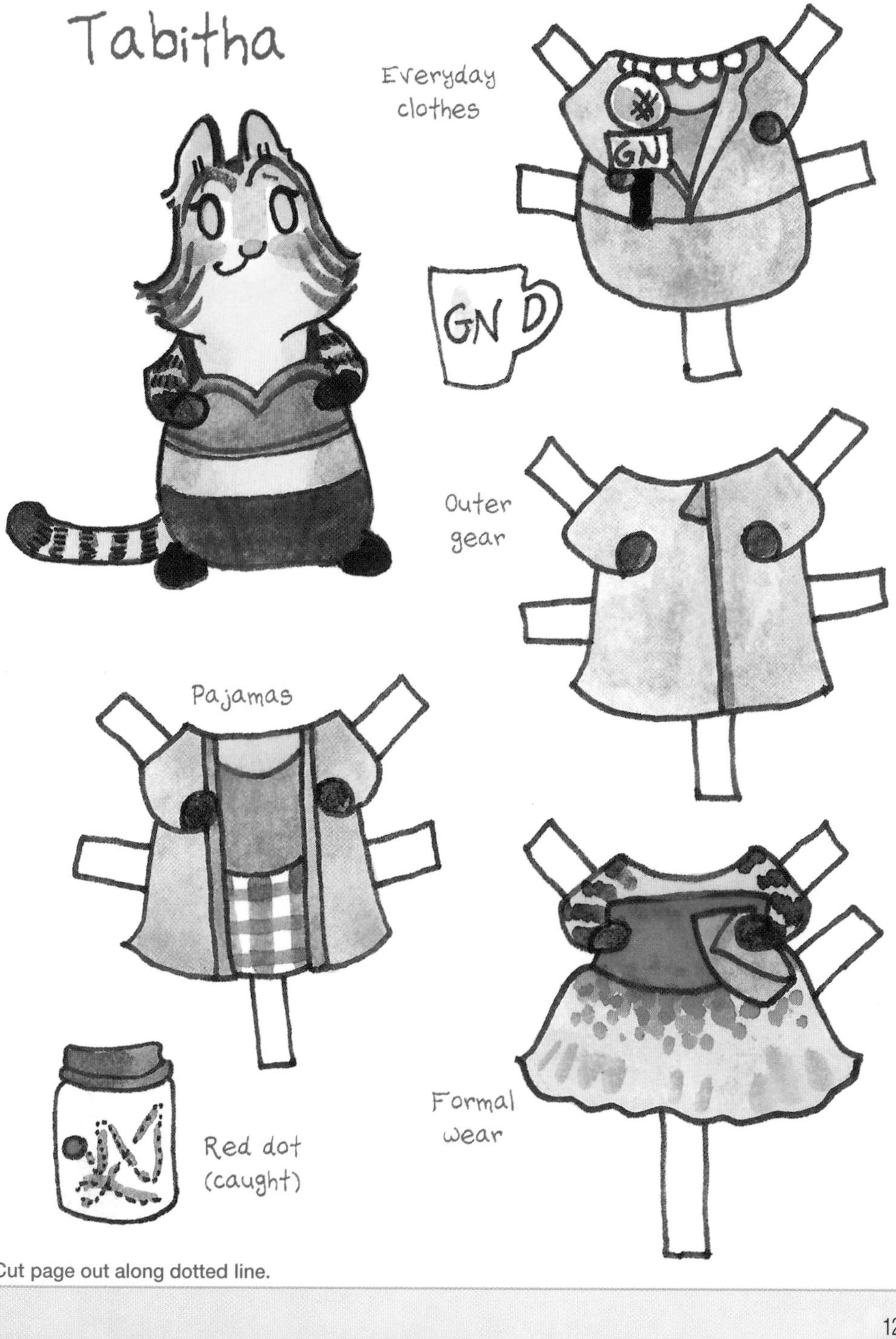
Tabitha
Everyday clothes
GN
GN
Outer gear
Pajamas
Formal wear
Red dot (caught)

Cut page out along dotted line.

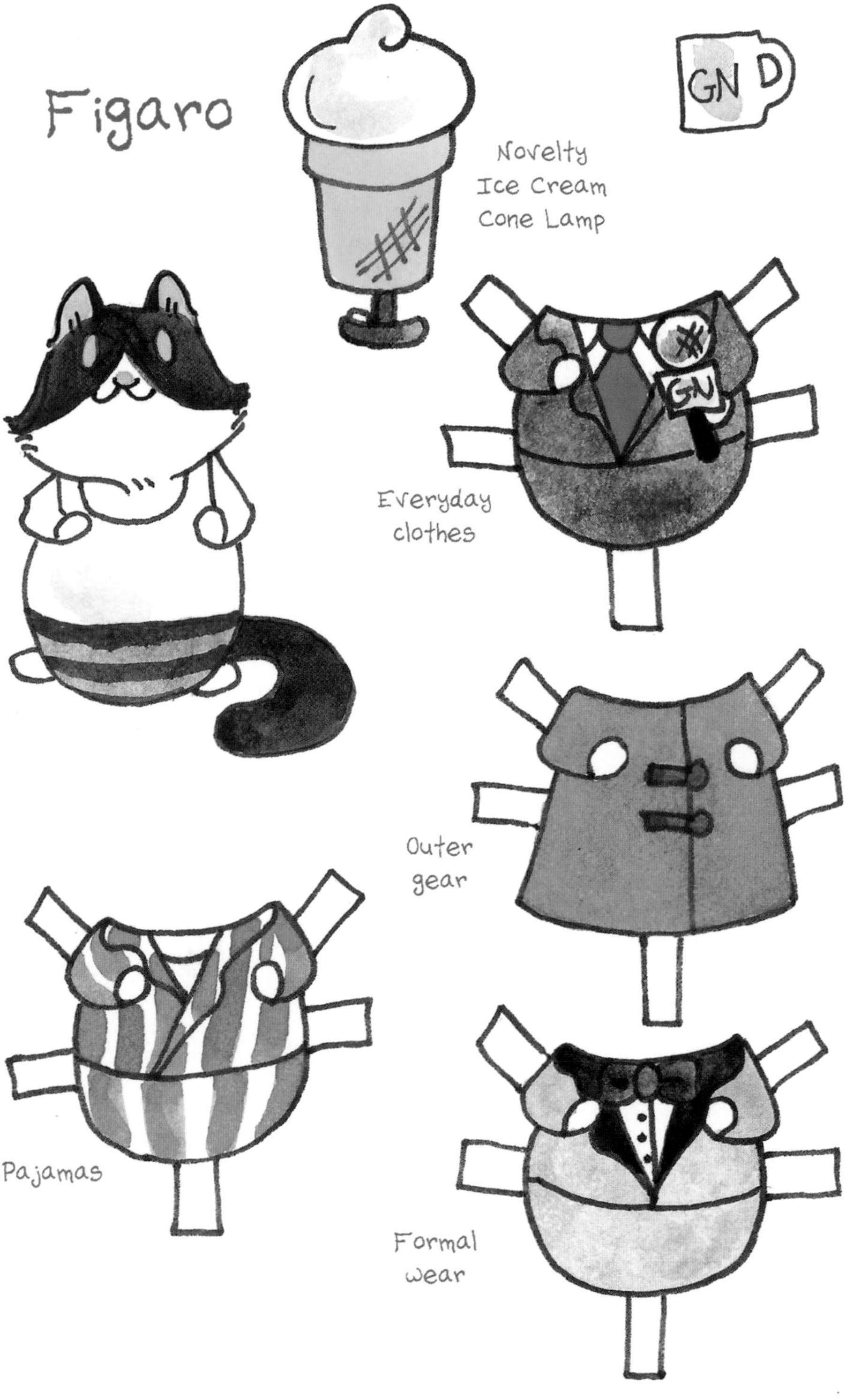
Figaro
GN D
Novelty
Ice Cream
Cone Lamp
GN
Everyday
clothes
Outer
gear
Pajamas
Formal
wear

Cut page out along dotted line.

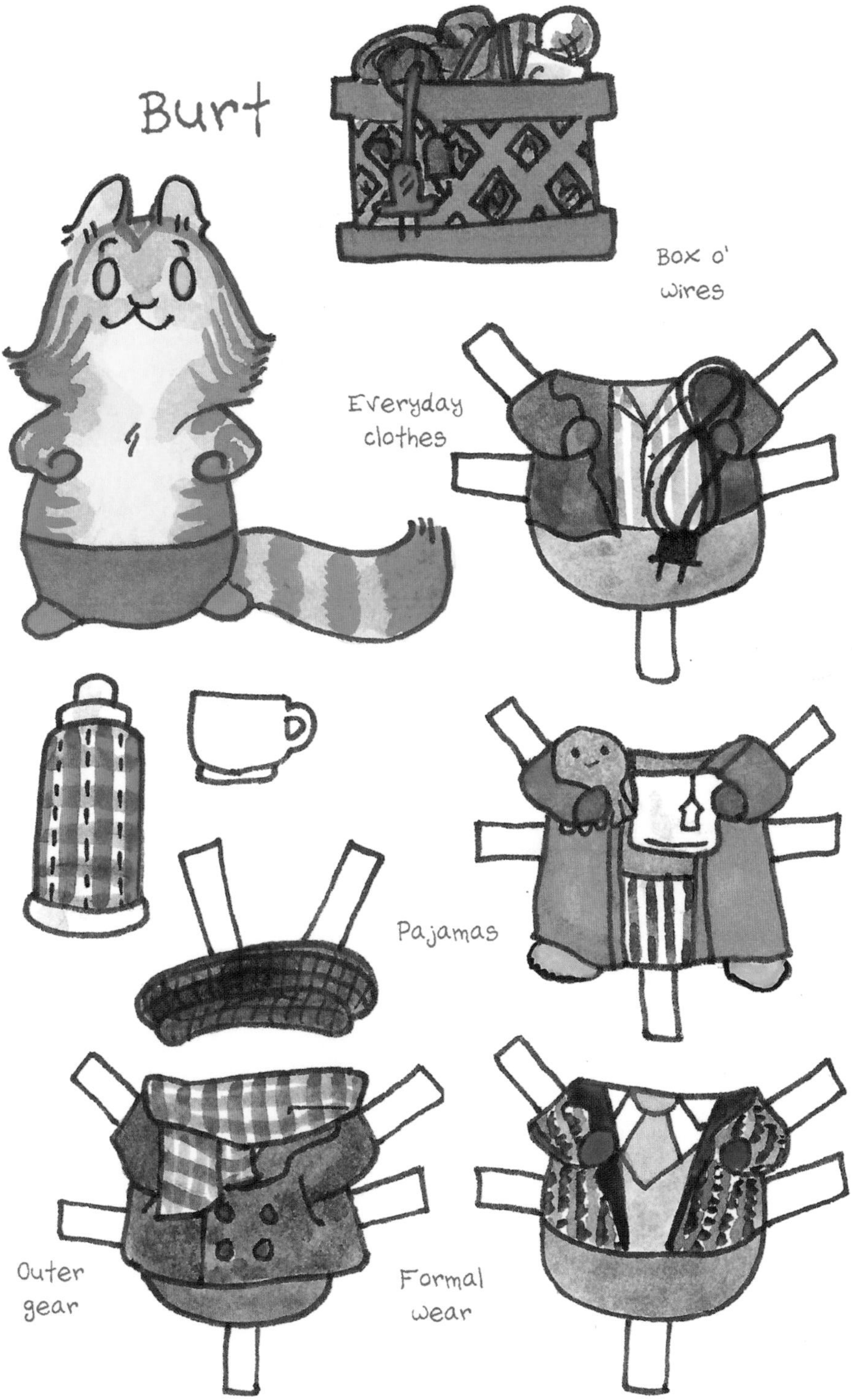
Burt
Box o' wires
Everyday clothes
Pajamas
Outer gear
Formal wear

Cut page out along dotted line.

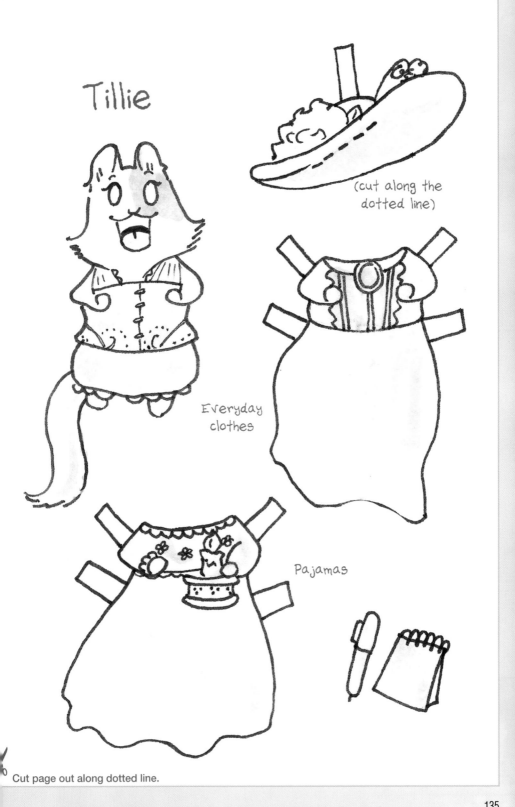

Tillie

(cut along the dotted line)

Everyday clothes

Pajamas

Cut page out along dotted line.

Tillie's clothes

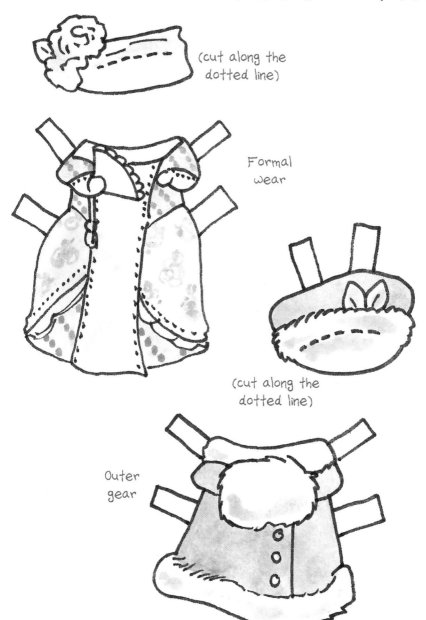

(cut along the
dotted line)

Formal
wear

(cut along the
dotted line)

Outer
gear

Cut page out along dotted line.

Andrews McMeel Publishing
a division of Andrews McMeel Universal
1130 Walnut Street, Kansas City, Missouri 64106

www.andrewsmcmeel.com
www.breakingcatnews.com

20 21 22 23 24 SDB 10 9 8 7 6 5 4 3 2 1

ISBN: 978-1-5248-5818-6

Library of Congress Control Number: 2019955035

Published under license from Andrews McMeel Syndication
www.gocomics.com

Made by:
King Yip (Dongguan) Printing & Packaging Factory Ltd.
Address and location of manufacturer:
Daning Administrative District, Humen Town
Dongguan Guangdong, China 523930
1st Printing—1/6/20

Background image pages 45-49 © iStock

ATTENTION: SCHOOLS AND BUSINESSES
Andrews McMeel books are available at quantity discounts with bulk purchase for educational, business, or sales promotional use. For information, please e-mail the Andrews McMeel Publishing Special Sales Department: specialsales@amuniversal.com.

Check out these and other books from Andrews McMeel Publishing

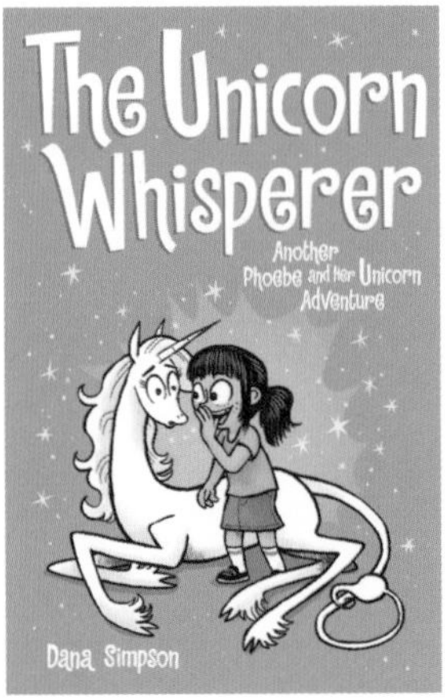
The Unicorn Whisperer
Another Phoebe and Her Unicorn Adventure
Dana Simpson

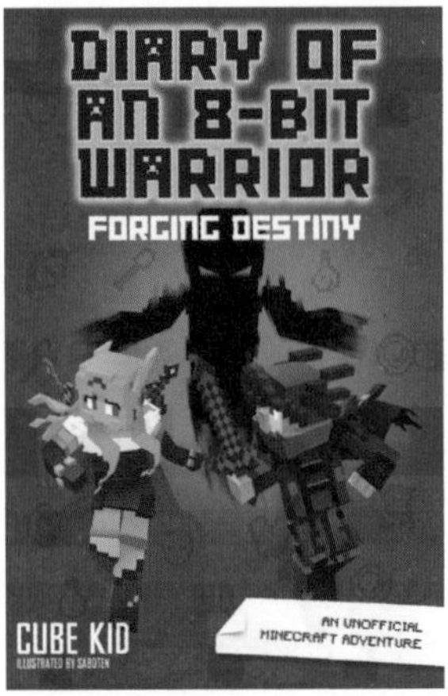
DIARY OF AN 8-BIT WARRIOR
FORGING DESTINY
CUBE KID
AN UNOFFICIAL MINECRAFT ADVENTURE

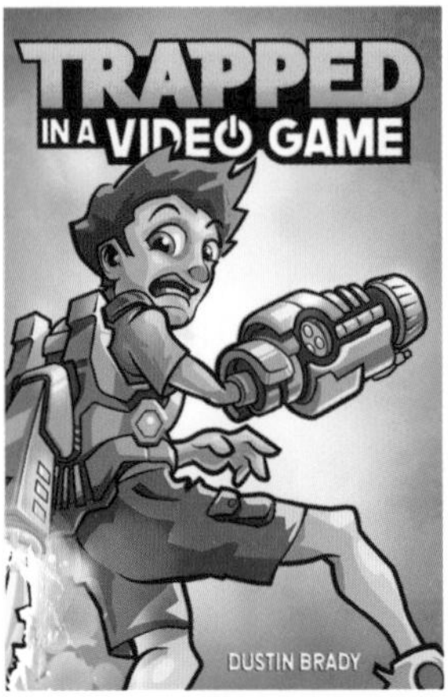
TRAPPED IN A VIDEO GAME
DUSTIN BRADY

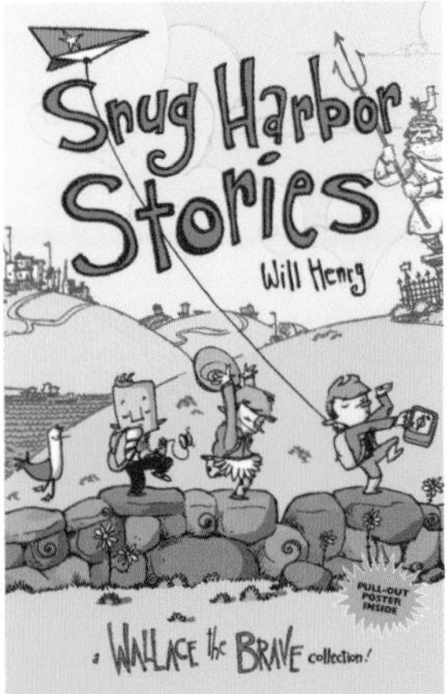
Snug Harbor Stories
Will Henry
PULL-OUT POSTER INSIDE
a WALLACE the BRAVE collection!

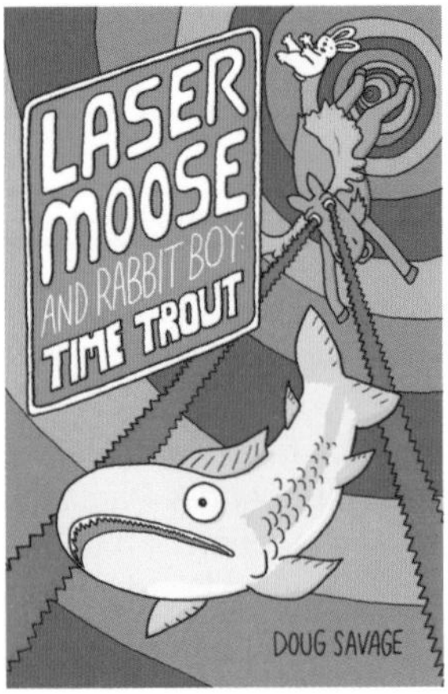
LASER MOOSE AND RABBIT BOY: TIME TROUT
DOUG SAVAGE

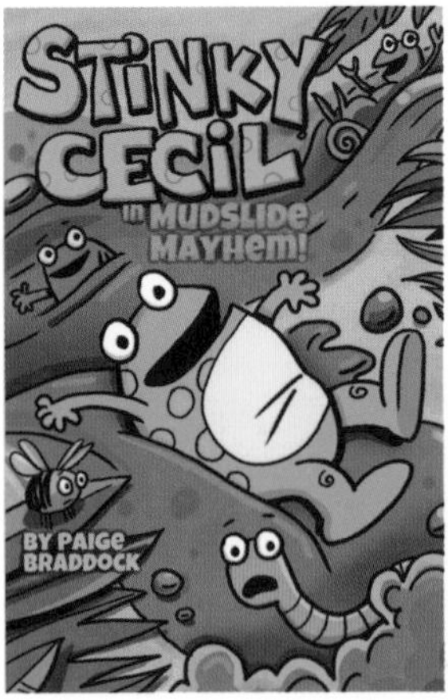
STINKY CECIL in MUDSLIDE MAYHEM!
BY PAIGE BRADDOCK

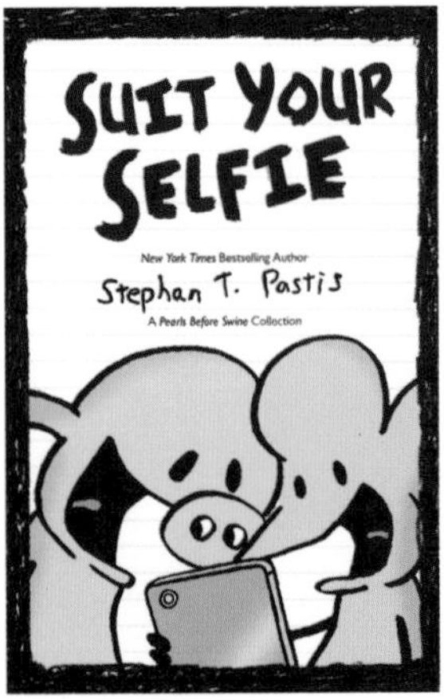
SUIT YOUR SELFIE
New York Times Bestselling Author
Stephan T. Pastis
A Pearls Before Swine Collection

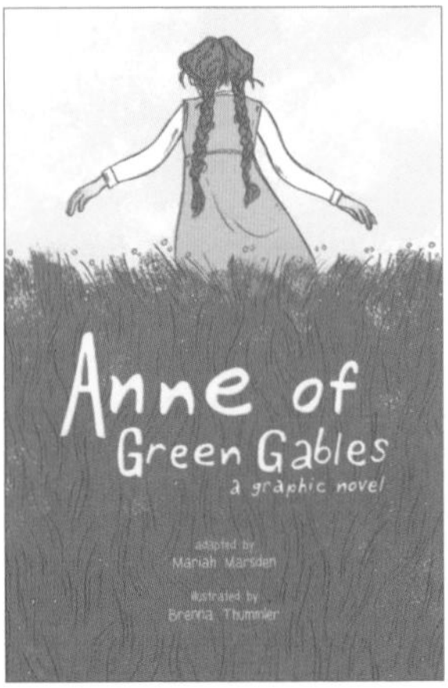
Anne of Green Gables
a graphic novel
adapted by
Mariah Marsden
illustrated by
Brenna Thummler

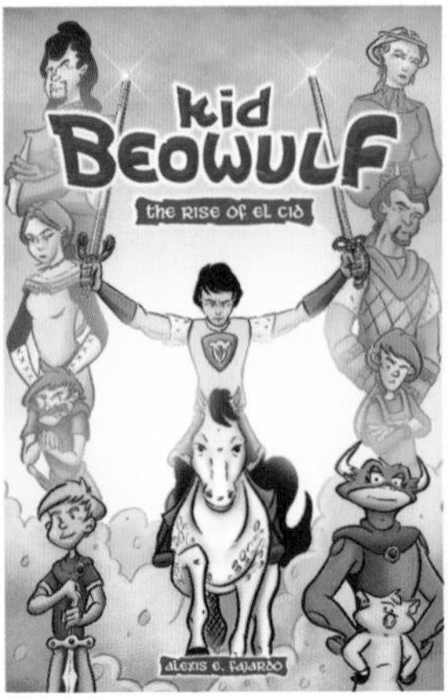
kid BEOWULF
the RISE OF EL CID
alexis e. fajardo